HAVOC

Published by Leith Holtzman
Copyright Leith Holtzman 2025
Cover Surf Photo by Russell Ord
Cover Motocross Photo by Leith Holtzman

Paperback ISBN: 978-1-7638850-0-4

leithholtzman.com
Facebook: Leith Holtzman Creative
Instagram: @leithholtzman
TikTok: @leith.holtzman

To Mum, whose unwavering support through my many questionable creative ventures led me to this point.

HAVOC

LEITH HOLTZMAN

A Dirth Spidder Chronicles Novel

Havoc - Confusion and lack of order, especially causing damage or trouble.

Prologue
THE BIRTHDAY PRESENT

Picker didn't notice the body until he almost tripped over it. His mind had been elsewhere while he struggled to maintain his half-drunken barefoot shuffle along the plastic strewn shoreline of the otherwise beautiful tropical black sand beach. The first rays of the morning sun were creating a typically spectacular Balinese dawn lightshow and despite the early hour it was already warm and humid, which was doing nothing to slow the onset of the mean hangover that Picker could feel coming.

He'd lost his shoes somehow, but thankfully he was still wearing most of the clothes he'd worn the night before. He'd awoken naked and hungover in random places with little memory of the previous evening many times in his life and they had rarely been good experiences. At least this time a quick check of his clothing revealed that while he'd also lost his wallet, he still had his point and shoot camera that produced outstanding quality photos but was small enough to fit in his pocket. Picker never went anywhere without some sort of camera, he'd learnt that lesson a long time ago.

Regardless of the beginnings of what would no doubt be a monumental headache, it should have been a special day for Picker. After all it's not every day you turn 40 years old and despite a lifetime of hedonism, debauchery, drugs, alcohol, poor diet and questionable lifestyle choices, Picker had got there in one piece.

For most people, their 40th birthday is a milestone to be celebrated among loving friends and family with a no expense spared, once in a decade party. A recognition of hurdles overcome and a raised middle finger in defiance of the obstacles ahead. A nod from the universe that you are one of the warriors of the planet, a gladiator that has so far survived everything it can throw at you and armed with the lessons of the past, is determined to make the second half of their lives even better.

If he was at all romantic, Picker would have appreciated the breathtaking sky streaked with its incredible mix of oranges, reds and golds that only nature's colour palate could create. He would have looked inland at the coconut palms, lush vegetation and the still active volcano, Mount Agung, rising majestically in the background with a layer of cloud covering its peak and he would have smiled and thanked the universe for such a beautiful moment to celebrate his achievement.

But Picker didn't have a romantic bone in his body, unless you count his love for money and there would be no handshakes and backslaps from mates or family gatherings in his honour. Oh, there had been a party last night alright, and a big one at that, but not one Picker had been particularly welcome at.

"I must be losing my touch," he cursed to himself, index finger reaching deep into his left nostril to dig out a chunky mix of dried booger and cocaine residue. "There was a time when no one would have dared reject me that way!"

He cast his mind back over what he could remember of the previous evening, trying to work out where it had all gone wrong. Earlier that day legendary American surfer Jimmy Slide had won an end of season top five shootout at the Keramas surf break and had been crowned the Global Surf Association (GSA) world champion for a record number of times. Picker had joined most of the world's best men's and women's surfers at the bar of the Komune Resort to celebrate. He hadn't told anyone it was his birthday, but he felt secure that they knew and were quietly planning at least a quick rendition of 'Happy Birthday' and a few free drinks at the bar in his honour.

Unfortunately, he was met with an indifference that had been becoming increasingly common in recent times. The stars of the GSA World Tour like Jimmy Slide, Taj Long, Gabriel Andre, Kalani Johnson and newly crowned women's world champ Stephanie Birch ignored him at best, or at worst favoured him with a look that said he wasn't welcome on the island let alone at the party. A lot of the other surfers who saw how the stars reacted to him followed their example.

Despite this there were plenty of sycophants, arse kissers and people downright scared of Picker's influence that meant he soon had a reasonable group hanging in his party circle while he held court. Once he'd deliberately let slip it was his birthday there was enough shouted drinks and fake love from those hoping to curry favour that things had begun to look up for the once legendary surf photographer.

As the night wore on, he'd gotten just shy of rotten drunk. Catching his eye was a young and impressionable rookie pro surfer who clearly was a little bit star struck and in need of that special kind of promotion only Picker could provide. Unfortunately, when Picker suggested they retire to his hotel room to go over the more 'intimate' details of what they could do for each other, the young pro expressed his disgust and ran away as fast as he could. A rejected Picker had then needed to search out and pay a creature of the night to satisfy his particular brand of twisted desires.

Picker was once one of the most famous surf photographers in the world. How he still remained in the industry was nothing short of amazing to those on the inside that knew his full story. To many he had been a guru. A man that, when in his prime, was almost mythical in his understanding of the surf industry, its players and how to make them famous.

That was of course well before the 'Pamela Affair' forever changed how surfing and surfers were seen by the rest of the world. The Pamela Affair turned previously relatively underground surf heroes into international tabloid media paparazzi gold mines almost overnight. With that came huge amounts of money and fame at the small cost of surfing's soul.

Surfing and the surfing industry had come a long way since Picker first picked up a camera. All those years ago he was just a fresh-faced kid working for the local newspaper with an innate ability and sense of timing to capture incredible images of fast-moving action sports. A weekend assignment to photograph a local kid who'd just won the state surfing titles was the lucky break he needed. The photos from that session were exceptional and that young surfer went on to be a star of the day. Picker quickly became the go to man for all the surf magazines during a period when pro surfing was just a brotherhood of friends united in trying to scratch a living out of the sport they loved with a passion.

As time went on though, Picker began to lose his Midas touch with the camera at about the same speed he was developing his more bizarre sexual habits. The problem was that Picker didn't surf. In fact, he was about as comfortable in the ocean as a camel and the new crop of surf photographers were all half decent surfers themselves.

It was the beginning of the end and he'd known it. How could an overweight, balding landlubber approaching middle age compete? These new photographers were all tanned and fit with perfect smiles that instantly made them friends with pro surfers, company magnates and magazine head honchos alike. Then came social media and suddenly these guys had tens of thousands of followers on Stalkbook and Instafamous as well. In fact, the surf magazines had begun treating the photographers themselves as some sort of hero to be worshipped. In Picker's eyes it was almost unethical!

It might have been the end for Picker and the increasingly seedy lifestyle his photography financed if it wasn't for a certain multiple world champion and his relationship with a big name and incredibly well-proportioned American movie actress.

Jimmy Slide was the clean-cut American kid who barnstormed onto the GSA World Tour and completely destroyed all challengers. Slide was the ultimate poster boy for surfing. Supremely fit with a shock of classic surfy blond, curly hair and bright blue eyes, Slide could have made a fortune as a male model. All around the planet people swooned over his image. Then he would open his mouth and speak so articulately and intelligently that anyone else who wasn't in love with him soon were.

Thousands of teenage girls had posters of Slide emerging from the surf clad only in a pair of board shorts with saltwater dripping from his immaculately tanned torso. Teenage boys had posters of him surfing all sorts of amazing waves in ways no one else could. Models desired him, milfs adored him, fathers wished their daughter would bring him home, LBGQTI magazines frequently ran photos wishing he was gay and more than a few perfectly straight men admitted they had a man crush on Slide. He was, to put it simply, a very hard man to dislike.

Slide quickly became the darling of the surf media. Then when he started winning world titles it was set in stone. Jimmy Slide was God. The Messiah who wasn't a naughty boy. Slide was the saviour of the surf industry and the figurehead of Quickbong, the biggest surf brand at the time and the man to take surfing from a fringe sport to a blue-ribbon Olympic event.

When he met and started dating Pamela Stack, the most famous female actress in the world with a string of Best Actress Oscar and Golden Globe awards to her name, the world went into a frenzy. Stack was a goddess, every part of her was something straight out of a teenage boys' ultimate fantasy - long golden legs, slim waist, full natural breasts, piercing green eyes and a shock of raven black hair almost reaching her waist. In just about every office in the world there were conversations around the water cooler as to who was the hottest female to ever live- Pamela Stack, Marilyn Monroe, Jayne Mansfield, Angelina Jolie or any number of other big screen goddesses.

Slide and Stack quickly became the biggest 'It' couple on the planet. Every single low down, dirty, no-morals tabloid magazine and website in existence had multiple cameramen dedicated purely to catching as much lewd filth as they could. Unfortunately for the gutter press, they were the squeaky cleanest of couples. There was less dirt to be found on them than under a manicurist's fingernails.

With no other choice they started to look elsewhere and fortunately with the hottest actress in fifty years dating a surfer it didn't take long for every actress, actor, model, CEO millionaire, billionaire megalomaniac, social media influencer and 90% of the rest of the planet to decide that dating a surfer was the ultimate thing to do.

Almost overnight surfing became an unrecognisable beast. Quickbong's shares that were trading at a few cents suddenly became worth hundreds of dollars, as did its main rivals GoMerch and Ricool. Right behind it came a whole host of surf companies that popped up overnight- Highlife, Voltan, Homegrown Maniacs, Rugged and many more. Suddenly if you were a surfer that had previously done alright in the local club contests and scrubbed up okay for the local ladies you were a good chance to have a seven-figure contract on your table, half a dozen lawyers competing for the right to make it bigger and way too many models and wannabe actresses offering sexual favours you didn't even think possible.

With a lazy million-dollar industry quickly turning into a crazy multi-billion dollar industry next came the filth, the dirty secrets, the twisted lusts and the depraved actions. Surfers had always been known as the ultimate hedonists due to their love of a good time, but they suddenly found that with access to millions of dollars and star power, their lusts and depravities could be expanded to a whole new level. Much to the paparazzi's delight, they soon found they didn't have to go far to find a river of muck so deep that they could fill every grotty tabloid website and magazine on the planet with low ball content for many years to come, and right at the forefront of all of that was Picker.

For Picker, the rise of surf tabloid journalism was a gift beyond all recognition. That photo of Taj Long doing some kind of amazing manoeuvre in perfect surf was worth maybe $1000 at best, perhaps a bit more if his sponsor GoMerch used it for an advertisement. However if you took a photo of Long, naked in the spa with Oscar nominated actress Cameron Dimary, like Picker managed to do from the bushes on one glorious night, then the gutter press would outbid each other well into the hundreds of thousands of dollars.

On that special night Picker had heard through his extensive list of underground surf gossip mongers that Long and Dimary might have something going on. Ignoring a solid swell pouring into the Margaret River surf contest in Western Australia, Picker had instead crawled through the dense karri forest behind Long's nearby home hoping to get the scoop. To be honest it wasn't that hard. He'd hidden in that same bush a few times before over the years for creepier reasons than this one and knew the perfect place to remain unseen, but with a clear view of any action that might go down.

Tucked in amongst that forest overgrowth with the very real threat of deadly snakes and red back spiders, Picker was as difficult to see as an elite soldier. From there he and his high-powered camera lens had the equivalent of a front row seat while he filmed straight into the luxury outdoor spa that was a big feature of Long's multi-million dollar residence. From there he captured one of the greatest illicit recordings ever, as Long and Dimary proceeded to emulate half a dozen scenes from the best pornographic videos ever made.

Picker burned every bit of camera memory card space he had in his possession that night. The first bids for his footage started at $50,000 and just kept going up. Tabloid magazine Womens Life bought the R rated photos for $650,000. For a while it looked like the X rated footage wouldn't see the light of day until GoMerch secretly paid Picker another million to release the raunchiest stuff viral on the net. Just like the classic home pornos of Karis Hitton and Lynne Ladashion the 'accidently' leaked sex tape turned the well-endowed and thus well named Taj Long into an internet sensation. GoMerch's stock price rose 25% overnight and once again Picker was a player in the surf industry.

Such were the many thoughts going through Picker's mind as he shuffled along the shore dodging fallen coconuts, bits of bamboo and scattered litter in that morning glow. Suddenly he became aware of someone just ahead laying on his back casually gazing up at the colourful sky. He looked familiar to Picker and as he took another step, he realised it was none other than Jimmy Slide himself.

It was of no surprise to Picker that Slide was here on the beach at dawn despite having just won a world title and been out celebrating the night before. Slide was always chasing the perfect uncrowded wave. He probably hadn't even got drunk!

"Typical," Picker thought. "Bloody hippy world champion! The sooner he retires to live out the rest of his days growing a beard and surfing his beloved waves the better. Maybe then a real champion like the wonderfully depraved Bunker Haze can win the world title!"

The idea brought an involuntary smile to his face for he knew that it would create a media shitstorm making hiding in the bushes worthwhile for many years to come.

"Beautiful morning," Picker called out with about as much conviction as a long-time junkie saying he was clean. "The swell is on the up!"

There was no response from Slide. Picker figured he was probably doing some kind of Zen, alternate meditation bullshit. For a moment he thought about leaving Slide alone but just in case there was some sort of juicy bit of gossip he could pry out of the world champ, Picker kept approaching.

As he took a step closer something felt off. That filthy, ghetto sixth sense Picker possessed when sniffing out the guts of a new dirty, half-truth tabloid story was screaming at him. He called out again and still there was still no response. Slide simply lay there continuing to stare at the sky. His eyes were open, but Picker suddenly realised they saw nothing and the soul that once inhabited this fine example of a human body had left for good.

Jimmy Slide, multiple world surf champion, the greatest person to ever stand on a surfboard, lover of the hottest woman on the planet and breaker of a million hearts, was dead.

Picker's heart pounded and his mind raced. A huge surge of adrenalin coursed through his body in a way that he had only felt once before on that fateful night when he caught Long and Dimary in the act. A small part of him wondered if he should try CPR and see if he could revive Slide.

"I should go to the authorities," he thought. "This is a crime scene and I shouldn't disturb it."

But then the rest of him realised in a happy kind of way that Slide was well past being resuscitated and there was no need for false guilt and a token effort to revive him. No, instead Picker's mind whirled with the possibilities. Right here in front of him was a dead world champ and not just any dead world champ but the GOAT- the Greatest Of All Time - who just happened to be the boyfriend of the most famous actress on the planet!

Picker mercilessly stomped down any guilt that might have existed in a normal human being and pulled out his camera. This was the scoop to die for! Slide was dead and he wouldn't care if a bunch of photos were taken of him in his final resting pose, would he?

Then another thought came to him. Who said this had to be his final pose? Surely there was a better position that took advantage of the morning light and was sufficiently sleazy that every website or magazine in the world would write a blank cheque for the privilege of featuring the best photos?

Picker re-adjusted Slides last position into something more to his liking. Fortunately, rigor mortis hadn't set in. As he snapped away and covered all the angles with his camera, his hangover and bitterness miraculously disappeared, and elation took over. This was the exclusive that guaranteed him at least another ten years in the game!

A dead world champ, it was the best birthday present he'd ever been given…

Part One
THE QUIKBONG PRO
Gold Coast Queensland

Chapter 1 CAPE FEAR

As the horizon darkened, Dirth 'Havoc' Spidder knew he was about to enter a world of pain. There was a not unrealistic possibility that sometime in the next sixty seconds Havoc would be dead. Strangely that thought was almost comforting for the fit, good looking detective from Cronulla, New South Wales. Months of frustration working undercover trying to bust open a drug ring while associating with lowball dealers, meth heads and various other local deadbeat scum had taken its toll.

Although he almost preferred the dipshits he was forced to hang with on a day to day basis than one of the other constants in his working life - his boss, Senior Sergeant Bruce 'Smithy' Smith. A man whom Havoc firmly hoped Hell had a special place reserved for when his heart finally gave up pumping blood around that bloated body.

To make matters worse the surf had been flat for way too long and Havoc, like many surfers, saw his time in the ocean as the best cure for all the shit going on in his life. There had been the odd little wave here and there, but Havoc was an adrenalin junkie. Try as he might, small surf just didn't go far enough towards healing his soul from the darkness that came with pretending to be someone he wasn't, to impress people he really didn't like, in the hopes of putting some of them in jail.

The only thing keeping him sane recently had been his love for other extreme sports. The local skate bowl had been okay for a spare hour, but the best fun had been the few wind free days he'd been able to load up his Yamaha YZ250 dirt bike and hook up with a couple of his Cronulla mates - Shagga and Robbie Rockstar. The trio would then head up the coast to Morriset, just out of Newcastle where the Clowe brothers- Magic

Mike and Lightening Luke - had a freestyle motocross compound with a couple of 75-foot ramps that were sweet to do tricks off.

The rush from hanging off the back of a dirt bike, superman style, while sailing over a big jump was right up there for Havoc. Not to mention the extra satisfaction knowing the gigantic fit he knew his boss would have if he had any clue of the risks Havoc took to satisfy his adrenalin junkie nature. One slight mistake jumping over that distance and broken bones were almost guaranteed!

Despite the fun Havoc had been having on his dirt bike, it was big waves that really tweaked his nipples. His frustration at the lack of swell had reached boiling point when Havoc finally saw an angry purple blob on the local swell charts suggesting a big swell was due to hit the East Coast of Australia very soon. Unfortunately, it had two things going against it- the wind direction for the peak of the swell looked less than ideal and he was supposed to be working!

At 23 Havoc hadn't even reached his prime but he was still an imposing figure. He had short, dark hair, clear blue eyes, strong chin and a very athletic build. He'd been a cop since he was legally allowed to join just after his 18th birthday. Growing up it hadn't been even remotely one of his dreams to be a policeman let alone an undercover detective. No, he'd wanted to be a fireman like his dad, Philip Spidder, but when his old man had passed away on the job fighting a huge bushfire threatening the lives of residents up on the north coast of New South Wales, the idea of being a fireman had immediately lost its appeal.

Havoc was just 15 years old when it happened and losing his dad had sent him into a downward spiral. If it wasn't for Philip's good friend, Glen 'Patto' Patinsen, himself a Detective Sergeant with the NSW Undercover Branch, who knows where Havoc might have ended up? Certainly there was a time when there was a much better chance Havoc could have been thrown behind bars himself, instead of helping to put people there.

It had been the patience of DS Patinsen, who perhaps got some measure of comfort for the loss of his best mate by mentoring his son, plus Havoc's love for surfing, mixed martial arts and extreme sports, that eventually saved him from going down the wrong path. He was a very good surfer in just about all surfing conditions, but at 186cms he was perhaps a bit too tall and muscular for small waves. However, he made up for it with a quickness and lightness on his feet that had surprised several low life thugs who thought they could outrun him over the local neighbourhood fences when he was back in his Probationary Constable days.

When he was young his dad had enrolled Havoc in self-defence classes and over the years he had trained in several different disciplines. He'd even won the odd amateur boxing and MMA fight. Despite the training Havoc was a pretty laid-back guy. He didn't really have a short temper, but if you prod a bear enough times that he snaps and goes nuts on you, then don't complain when that angry bear tears you apart. It was why Havoc enjoyed the odd fight in the ring. It allowed him to let the bear off the leash.

Many thought that was how Havoc got his nickname. Others thought it was from his love of extreme sports and his fearlessness in big, crazy waves. A number of surfing magazines had featured photos of his mad antics and he was well respected in underground surfing circles. The truth is that it was from neither, but something much darker from his lost years after his dad died that gave Havoc his moniker. He preferred not to think about those days but kept the nickname to remind him of a past he didn't want to return to.

As that first wall of death approached it appeared as though Havoc wouldn't have to worry about his past for much longer, or his future for that matter. To be perfectly frank, this was a downright stupid situation to be in, even by his standards.

Havoc was sitting on his own in a late afternoon angry, messed up ocean only a few metres from an incredibly shallow rock ledge off the entrance to Botany Bay, where over 200 years ago Captain Cook sailed past and laid claim to the continent of Australia. Waves impossible to ride surged onto that ledge in an explosion of white water almost as high as the cliffs above, then sucked back out to sea propelling huge chunks of wash to smash back into the incoming waves making them twice as big and turning the whole zone into a place no sane person should be.

Cape Fear the locals called it. At this moment never a truer name had been used to describe a surf spot. It was a start to finish death trap where if you messed up, huge rocks were just metres away ready and waiting to turn you into crab food. On a sunny day when the wind and swell is absolutely perfect, it's almost rideable and the few remaining genuine surfing magazines left after the Pamela Affair send their photographers to capture real surfing for an increasingly shrinking core audience.

When the swell is a bit bigger or not quite so perfect, jet skis are often used to give the surfers a chance to even the odds a little. By using the jet ski to tow the surfer in, they gain some extra time and speed to catch the wave. Hopefully that allows them a chance to outrun it into the safety of the channel and away from the ever-present barnacle encrusted rocks that have destroyed so many bones and egos since it was first surfed not long ago.

Then there are the days when it's just too big, the wind is wrong and the swell direction makes it almost impossible to escape the wave into the channel. The days when any sane human being would be somewhere else or coming up with excuses to tell their mates to cover their fear of being anywhere near the ocean when it's so freaking out of control!

It was one of those days that Havoc found himself out at Cape Fear wondering why he was so determined to have such a short existence on the planet. He could only put it down to sheer stupidity and a need to quit the system he was caught up in.

The setting sun had disappeared behind a bank of clouds making it even darker and Havoc still hadn't caught a wave. Some big sets had come through previously but even though Havoc was fearless and more than a little bit crazy, there's still a difference between crazy and downright suicidal and those waves simply weren't makeable.

Havoc had been starting to regret not having a go at one of those impossible waves. His ego was clashing with his sense of self preservation, and his ego was starting to win.

"I'm not going in without catching a wave," he thought determinedly. "This is my set. I'm going one of these waves no matter what!".

The first wave of the set looked the safest option to Havoc. Or was it? It was the smallest and with the barnacle covered rocks of what is affectionately known as the Surgeons Table only metres away, each subsequent wave, already larger than the first one, would collide with the backwash from the previous wave making it bigger and meaner.

But if Havoc fell on the first wave of the set, then he was nothing but shredded meat for the Surgeons Table when the next waves hit. To make matters worse there was nobody on the headland watching him to perhaps call an ambulance if things went wrong, he hadn't told anyone he was coming out here, not even his mum! If he disappeared the only indication of what happened would be his abandoned car.

"Fuck it!" thought Havoc. "If I'm going down, I'm going down in style!"

With the decision made he let the first wave of the set explode on the rocks and paddled out further in anticipation of the bigger waves behind it. This set was from a slightly better angle than the previous ones, perhaps giving him just a tiny extra chance of surviving. The second wave was big but clearly the third wave was by far the biggest as he could see it already feathering out the back, ready to unleash its full fury.

Havoc scratched over the top of the second wave and the monster behind it revealed itself in its entirety. It was bloody big, but there was a thickness to it as well. The sheer volume of water in this wave was nothing like anything that had come before.

"This is the one," Havoc thought, psyching himself up. "No time for being a pussy. No second thoughts. Don't worry about the backwash. Just put your head down, paddle fucken hard and go!"

With that Havoc's mind calmed and his thoughts cleared. These were the moments he thrived on and all the other bullshit going on in his life became background noise only, in fact it didn't even exist. Just one man, a wave and his desire to take it on and emerge unscathed.

As the black monstrosity approached Havoc spun his board and started to paddle as hard as he could. Ahead of him was a nightmare of huge rocks and swirling white water, enough to turn any man's bowels to liquid. While the natural instinct for a surfer is to paddle towards the safety of the channel, Havoc knew better. His one chance to make this wave was to paddle even closer to the rocks and perhaps get a lucky speed line right through the guts of the wave.

Havoc continued to paddle furiously as the sun came out from behind the clouds for a few moments of magic light. Somewhere under him he knew was a specific rock that created a slingshot into the wave giving him a better chance of surviving the take-off.

Suddenly it appeared just as the wave lurched to its full height. He had misjudged the location of the rock by a metre or so but there was no turning back now and as the wave heaved, he jumped to his feet and leaned forward as hard as possible, trying to get his momentum down the wave face.

He dropped down the near vertical wall holding on with only the tips of his toes just as the backwash from the previous wave hit. The wave jacked to twice its size and Havoc found himself airborne in complete freefall with his arms above his head and his feet completely detached from the board. Death or serious injury was now certain!

In years to come Havoc would often replay those couple of seconds back in his mind and at no stage will he ever understand how he could still be breathing let alone walking. He remembered the moment the backwash hit, throwing him off balance. He remembered the roar of the wave behind him and the clash of water on rocks just metres ahead. Some small part of his brain had recognised that he'd finally bitten off more than he could chew, and he was about to pay the ultimate price.

But somehow as Havoc landed at the bottom of the wave, he found his surfboard was still under his feet. He stumbled, then corrected himself and held on as what seemed like the entire ocean heaved over the top of him in a monstrous barrel so dark and round that had anyone been watching from the shore he would have completely disappeared from view.

It was like a scene from a movie theatre, not something real. Havoc's entire world became nothing more than an overloaded vortex of noise, adrenalin and swirling water. Now that he was on his feet with his board under him there was a chance. He was enveloped in a huge tube while in the distance he could see the golden light of the setting sun showing him the way out.

Time stood still and seconds felt like a lifetime as that image was burnt into his memory forever. He made some subtle adjustments and drove his board towards the rapidly closing exit. It felt like he wasn't going to make it, but then at the last possible second there was a loud hiss as the wave compressed, forcing a huge rush of air and water out of the tube and propelling one very relieved surfer safely into the channel.

For a few minutes Havoc sat alone, head in his hands, emotions firing in all directions as he tried to process and comprehend what had just happened. Part of him wanted to scream out loud and throw his arms in the air, but he found he couldn't muster the energy. Surviving that moment had taken everything he had. It was the wave of a lifetime.

As he clambered up the rocks in the darkness, he looked up at the big headland above and a small part of him wished there had been someone there to witness such an incredible moment. That way he could share the story and perhaps be reassured that the moment was as death defying and life altering as it felt. 'If no one saw it- then it didn't happen' was a term that Havoc and his mates often used when teasing each other about stories of bravado they told when no one was there to provide witness to the truth of the tale.

"Well I guess it didn't happen!" he chuckled to himself as he stripped down out of his wetsuit in the empty carpark a little while later.

What he hadn't seen was the photographer that had left in his car moments earlier who had captured the entire wave in all its glory.

Chapter 2 THE GLOBAL SURF ASSOCIATION

There was plenty of action in the office of the Global Surf Association's CEO - Peter Hirt. The GSA's world headquarters was an opulent, eight storey building overlooking the surf at Burleigh Heads in southern Queensland. Hirt's office occupied the penthouse suite on the top floor with a prime view of the surf, but more importantly had an adjacent suite that doubled as Hirt's living quarters. If asked why the GSA was funding such lavishly expensive living quarters for their CEO, Hirt would reply that it was so he could work day and night on keeping the GSA running and did not need to waste precious time stuck in traffic each day.

Hirt did indeed work very hard to keep his beloved GSA running smoothly, so while this was a valid reason, it was actually only partly true. The real reason Hirt enjoyed the privilege of such a glorious penthouse was that it provided a readily available Casting Couch for any young, sexy up and coming female surfer eager to push her case for being awarded a wildcard into the next big surfing competition.

It was almost too easy for Hirt. He'd invite them to his office and they would be star struck right from the start. The furniture was incredibly expensive, signed photos of world champions adorned the walls and the big glass windows looked almost straight into the barrel at the Burleigh Heads surf break. They would discuss how this was a huge opportunity to launch her career and that lots of girls were eagerly applying for that coveted spot in the competition. Hirt would drop a few hints suggesting a 'you scratch my back and I will scratch yours' type situation, see if the young lady was bright enough to take the hint and then whether she was desperate enough to follow through.

If she was either not street smart enough to read between the lines, or more likely, had enough self-respect to say, "thanks but no thanks", then Hirt would shake her hand and wish her the best of luck while advising that there were a lot of worthy candidates for the spot and he would call her with his decision in due course. Only on very rare occasions would the call be then made in her favour. This was usually when the candidate was simply too good a surfer to be overlooked, especially if the event was at her home beach. Like when the squeaky-clean current women's world champion, Stephanie Birch, first came on the scene a few years ago asking for the wildcard into the Quikbong Pro at her home break, Snapper Rocks.

Birch was a country girl at heart and just didn't pick up on what Hirt was putting down. She had no clue what the hints Hirt was dropping meant and she'd left the office on cloud nine thinking she had impressed him and was a good chance of being awarded the wildcard. Hirt on the other hand was left frustrated and determined not to give Birch the shot, despite the uproar it would have caused both locally and nationally, as all the true surf magazines had dubbed her the next big thing.

Two hours later the incredibly sexy Dyanna "Dream" Fream was in his office pitching why she should get the wildcard. Fream immediately picked up on Hirt's subtle hints and within a short time he was inviting her next door to his private suite, where she entertained Hirt with a series of extremely flexible and dynamic sexual positions that had sown up the wildcard spot in record time.

Later Hirt was working on the press release that would try to justify why Fream, a very promising up and coming surfer herself, was getting the wildcard instead of the local star in the making. He was struggling for reasons when he got a call advising that Hawaiian World Champ Karissa Kai was injured and had withdrawn from the event. With another spot open, Hirt was saved and both girls got a wildcard into the competition. Despite being a wildcard, Stephanie Birch went on to win her first ever world championship event, knocking out her extremely well performed fellow wildcard Dyanna Fream in the semifinals on her path to the win. Hirt had come out of it looking like a genius.

Images of Fream naked from that casting couch session replayed in Hirt's mind as he sat in his office looking out the window at the never-ending parade of bikini beauties walking up and down the footpath following the edge of the beach. She had probably been the best he'd had and to his mind a more than willing participant on the day. Much to his disappointment, she had never given him a second go. She'd taken her chance and made it count and was now firmly established on the world tour. By all accounts plenty of others had been treated to the delights of Dream Fream to the point she was also known quietly as 'Dirty Dy' behind the scenes.

Hirt dragged his mind away from sexual conquests and back to the job on hand. He was preparing for the second event of the new year – The Quickbong Pro. Which was not an easy task after the chaotic finish to last year's World Title showdown at Keramas in Bali and the equally challenging events since.

The death of the greatest and most significant surfer of all time, Jimmy Slide, within hours of being crowned a world champion for a record number of times, had provided a monumental challenge for the GSA and especially for Hirt, but it was one he had relished and thrived with. There was no doubt that the massively popular Slide was almost solely responsible for surfing becoming the monumental cash cow it now was, but in a way, Slide had been too clean, too nice and too much the pure surfer.

The world had started to get bored with the complete lack of gossip and smut from what had become a long-term relationship with Pamela Stack. Even Stack had started to shun the limelight and had become more like a devoted housewife than an international sex siren. Just prior to Slides death, Hirt had begun to notice a worrying trend in the worldwide surf market. Almost all the stock prices of the big surf brands had seen their value drop for the first time since Slide joined the tour. Even the GSA's significant revenue stream had slowed down and some of its more extreme spending, such as renting the entire luxury office block Hirt was now sitting in, had started to be questioned.

All that had changed with Slide's death. The paparazzi, mainstream media and gutter tabloids had gone into overdrive and wallowed gleefully in the pig trough of Slide's demise. Even now the momentum created from that publicity wasn't showing any signs of slowing down at all.

With the death occurring in a relatively quiet part of Bali, the easily corruptible and poorly trained local police force available when it happened suddenly found themselves in a situation way out of their league. Unfortunately, it didn't help that at the time of discovery, no one realised this wasn't just a drug addicted tourist they had found in a bizarre sexual position on the beach, but one of the most famous athletes in the world. So their response and preservation of the crime scene had left a lot to be desired.

Keramas is halfway up the east coast of Bali, an hour's ride from the far more chaotic tourist areas of the west coast like Kuta, Legian and Seminyak. The police were usually only called on to book the odd foreigner for not wearing a helmet on a scooter or occasionally make a minor drug bust that was easily forgotten with the exchange of a few rupiah. Serious crime such as murder was rare and usually solved within minutes when the very remorseful partner of the deceased confessed after half the community had intervened to solve the crime.

But the possible murder of Slide had been completely different. For one thing, the list of suspects for the local police to sift through extended far beyond a couple of close friends and relatives. Instead, there was the entire professional surfing tour- it's athletes, judges, organisers, sponsors, coaches, friends, partners, family, general hands, groupies and hangers on plus locals and copious random tourists as well. None of which the understaffed local police struggling with English as their second language had any real chance of properly interrogating. By the time the USA had sent some experts over to help find out what happened to their beloved hero athlete, circumstances had spiralled out of control, and it was too late.

Given Slide's supreme fitness and aversion to alcohol and drugs it was unlikely his death was from natural causes or accidental overdose. So there was a chance he had been murdered, but in a monumental cockup by the local authorities, Slide's body was mis-handled before the experts arrived and he was accidently cremated, destroying any chance of testing the body further.

And so, with almost no hope of the true culprit being found the media was at its most creative, especially with the aid of the epic photos of Slide's final resting pose that a mystery photographer had sold to the tabloids for a record price. According to any number of experts and inside sources, Slide's death was a result of anything from drug deals gone wrong to old favourites, like the spurned lover theory where anyone from the local prostitutes to international celebrities to possible gay lovers were trucked out and given their time in the spotlight as a potential culprit.

It was like some kind of bizarre comedy. Each week the paparazzi would uncover a person or theory that claimed to have solved the riddle of the death of the popular world champ.

"I had Slide's Illegitimate Baby so Pamela Stack had him Killed!" trumped one headline.

"Murdered Surfer Involved in Mexican Drug Cartel" screamed another or such pearlers as

"World Champ Surfer Murdered After Being Caught in Bed with Ladyboy Lover!" and the best yet

"International Cover Up as Alien Anal Probe Discovered as real reason for Champion Surfer's Death!"

Unsurprisingly, Slide's mysterious death had still yet to be solved and the way things were looking it may never be. But his death was the gift that kept on giving for Hirt and the GSA. It was as if Slide had one last contribution left to pro surfing and he'd made it count in the best possible way. Once again share prices of all the big-name surf brands were skyrocketing and the GSA's revenue stream was spectacular.

The GSA owned surf schools all around the world, plus dozens of wave pools, surf shops and, through a number of dummy corporations, even had significant stocks in some of the major surf merchandise companies. With Slide passing away the GSA was cashing in bigtime. Already they had made tens of millions out of the memorial merchandise like the 'Slide Lives On' T-Shirts. Best of all for Hirt was that he received a percentage of the royalties from Slide's final photos after he had secretly helped broker the deal for their sale for the gloriously depraved Picker.

Hirt didn't really like Picker, hell no one did, but he had to admit that his brand of gutter surf journalism was worth millions to the GSA. Hirt knew that Picker had disturbed Slides body, he just didn't care. Like musicians who write great songs and can live off the royalties forever, Slides death would be pumping money into Hirt's and the GSA's overseas bank accounts for many years to come.

Going into the first event of the new year, the prestigious Pipeline Masters in Hawaii, there had been lots of excitement within the old school surf media about who would take over the mantel from Slide. The main frontrunners were thought to be the hugely popular Hawaiian Kalani Johnson, Brazilian Gabriel Andre and emerging Aussie superstars Matt Wilson and Jake Roberts. Many believed these young surfers represented the future of world surfing. All were amazing surfers and just as importantly they all had massive followings on social media. Johnson and Andre had both already won their first world titles and most felt it was only a matter of time before Wilson and Roberts joined them.

Wilson was your typical Aussie ratbag surfer who had really made the most of his fame. At almost every surf competition he had a new super model under his arm. As such the paparazzi loved him and he loved them back. It was the perfect symbiotic relationship. Wilson used his time in the spotlight and elite Instafamous ratings to get some of the world's hottest ladies into his bedroom. He made sure there was always a curtain at least half opened in that bedroom and a sneaky text to a couple of his favourite paparazzi took care of the rest. The next issue of Womens Life would feature Wilson and the super model on the cover, both their Instafamous accounts would go ballistic, the paparazzi would collect their cheques and everyone was happy.

Gabriel Andre was the leader of the Brazilian charge. Born in the dirt poor favellas of Rio de Janeiro he was a super hungry surf contest machine. Nicknamed 'The Terminator' for his ability to totally destroy opponents and lack of emotion when he did, Andre was nevertheless one of the most popular athletes in Brazil, rivalled only by one or two soccer players. Andre also had a love for super models, although in his case it was usually at least two at a time, making him another paparazzi and GSA favourite.

Hawaiian Kalani Johnson was the opposite. He was the surf prodigy destined for greatness from a very young age and despite his shyness and shunning of the media, his sheer talent and good looks had helped cultivate a huge social media following. His image was squeaky clean and he regularly called his mum to say he loved her. Something that really pissed off the surf paparazzi.

Hirt had to agree with them. It had been bad enough with Jimmy Slide being so loveable but when Johnson came into the mix it was almost too much. Last year the two fought out a final in epic eight to ten foot Teahupo in Tahiti with Slide just getting the nod with a near perfect heat score of 19.90 out of 20 to Johnson's 19.50. The whole thing was an almost sickening straight out surf-bro hippy lovefest with everyone carrying on about how surfing was the winner. The core surf media had loved it. The worldwide paparazzi smut machine barely gave it a mention. Hirt had wanted to vomit.

So Hirt wasn't particularly upset when the second great tragedy struck the GSA. Kalani Johnson had drowned while surfing big waves at his beloved Banzai Pipeline in Hawaii just days before the Pipeline Masters was due to start. The stories were vague, but it seemed Johnson may have been overheard saying something about not feeling well and that he would catch the next wave in. A monster set appeared, he caught it but wiped out and then disappeared underwater for several minutes. Eventually his lifeless body was found with significant head injuries from hitting the reef and despite repeated attempts to resuscitate him, Johnson was pronounced dead on arrival at hospital.

Hirt was on the island at the time and had immediately rolled up his sleeves and gone into power CEO mode. This was the stuff he thrived on! It was why he got paid the big bucks and had been given the leeway for his penthouse suite and casting couch habits by the GSA Board of Directors.

He'd called a press conference and announced that out of respect to Johnson and his family, the Pipeline Masters would be cancelled for this year. It was a move met with approval from the surfers and core surf media. They had been concerned that the GSA's continuous grab for money and lack of morals would lead to a 'Show Must Go On!' mentality. The word around the athletes was that maybe with the loss of two of the world's best, the GSA had pulled its head in and started to take the feelings and wishes of the surfers into account.

Unfortunately, the reality was completely different. Running surf contests is an expensive exercise and they are really only created as a publicity machine to provide the framework for many of the GSA's other sometimes dubious income generating activities. Hirt had gleefully cancelled Pipeline and hopped straight on a plane home, knowing that he'd saved the GSA millions in running costs and believing the publicity generated by Johnson's death on the back of Slide's would more than make up for any perceived loss from the event not going ahead.

It had so far proven to have been a masterstroke by Hirt. Surf company stock prices were back to record levels and sales of Johnson's memorial merchandise was rivalling Slide's. Meanwhile the worldwide media had gobbled up the misery of the two surf superstar deaths like a truffle pig on heat and the anticipation coming into the Gold Coast surf contest was at an all-time high.

Hirt's mobile phone chirped and he checked to see who was calling him. It was Luke Perrot, former pro surfer, the current President of the Professional Surfers Union and a real pain in the arse. The PSU had been on Hirt's case big time lately. They felt that not enough had been done to find out what happened to Slide and if indeed he had been murdered.

Hirt mentally prepared himself for whatever lies he would need to tell and reluctantly answered the call.

"Hello Luke how's things?"

"Gday Pete, yeah not bad except for this shitshow that's been going down. Any updates on what happened to Slide?" Perrot asked in his typical Aussie drawl.

"No news at all mate. They've hit a brick wall. We're still trying to find out who took the photos of Slide on the beach to see where that leads but Women's Life aren't saying shit. They're claiming they were sent them anonymously but that's hard to believe."

"Yeah, I'm hearing you. Have they talked to that guttershit Picker? I'd bet my house that worm's involved there somehow. He was lurking around the presentations that night being the typical sleezy fucker he is."

"No idea," Hirt lied smiling to himself. "I haven't seen or talked to Picker since last year. He's been seen hiding around the usual night spots here on the Goldy with his camera now that all the surfers are in town and as far as I know he's still got the same car. Usually when he has a big score, he buys himself a new sportscar and disappears underground to whatever sleaze club he favours for a few months. So, I'm guessing it's not him." Hirt had specifically told Picker not to do anything out of the normal and miraculously he'd listened. They both knew if it got out who had taken the photos and who had profited from their sale, there would be a lot of trouble for all involved.

"Yeah, I heard that too," said Perrot somewhat disappointed. "The surfers are concerned about their safety at the Quikbong Pro. They think there won't be enough security. They're a bit nervous after the news about Kalani Johnson."

"What news is that?" asked Hirt genuinely interested.

"Didn't you hear? Word is Johnson might have been poisoned or drugged. Had he not hit his head and drowned he might have been dead anyway!"

"Shit no I didn't hear that!" Hirt was caught off guard.

"Yep, I was in a Surfers Union meeting with all the crew last night when I got the call from Johnson's mum. That's why they're all worried. I think they're waiting on a few more toxicology tests. She's going to let me know when they find out for sure.

Hirt's mind immediately went into overdrive. He wasn't sure if this was good or bad news. Mostly he was just pissed off that he hadn't heard about it first.

"So, what are you going to do about security at the Quikbong?" Perrot continued.

"Geez mate I don't know," Hirt replied. "I mean you suddenly tell me that surfers are worried about their personal safety. Not that long ago they were arguing that security was too strict, and they couldn't get enough groupies into the VIP section for their pre-heat blow jobs!"

"Steady on Pete that's a bit rough!" Perrot was clearly put off by the truth in Hirt's comment. "Even if that's true it's now possible one of those groupies could be a killer. Surely it's not going to cost you too much more to hire a few more security guards?"

"I suppose it can be done," Hirt conceded. "But I don't want to hear a peep out of your boys if security kicks out the wrong fluffer!"

"No worries. Thanks Pete. They're all a bit shell shocked anyway, so I'm not sure too many of them will be going overboard with the extracurricular activities. We've had two of our best gone forever in a short period of time. That shit scares you!"

"Is that everything Luke?" replied Hirt, keen to end their conversation quickly.

"Yeah that's all for now Pete. At least the surf will be good from Monday onwards. Have you seen that cyclone brewing out to sea?"

"Yes I did," Hirt lied. He wasn't going to admit he couldn't give a shit what the surf was like. "Monday you reckon?"

"Yep. Winds look good too. The weekend will be pretty small, but Monday looks epic!"

"Well, we will be running Saturday and Sunday no matter what. The sponsors have insisted they want the weekend crowds," Hirt lied again. The GSA secretly owned a significant chunk of Quikbong, so there was no pressure one way or another. Hirt just loved having competition days on weekends on the Gold Coast. There were ten times the number of bikinis on the beach and the parties were insane! "I guess we will just run the women's heats and the blokes can surf on Monday."

"Mate the ladies aren't going to be happy with that!" Perrot was now flustered. He represented all the surfers and while the males were generally satisfied with their lot, the women were always whinging about something. "Cooper's going to be pissed for sure. Guaranteed you can expect a heated phone call from her. The rest will be wanting an explanation too and nothing you can say is going to satisfy them. Surely you can wait until Monday? You've got the time haven't you?"

"Like I said Luke, the sponsors have spoken and my hands are tied. We start this weekend with the women's heats. Unless you want me to run the men's instead?" Hirt knew the answer he would get.

"No that will have to do," interjected Perrot quickly. They both knew the male surfers would crucify him if they had to surf rubbish when there was a chance to surf one of the most notoriously crowded waves in the world at its best with only one other surfer in the water.

Obviously the girls wouldn't be happy either, but if it had to be one or the other then it was a simple decision. There were more voting male surfers in the PSU than females who decided whether Perrot kept his job and who didn't like seeing Dyanna Fream, Belle Silva, Claire Cooper, Stephanie Birch or Tiffany Totthil in a bikini?

They said their goodbyes and Hirt hung up. The phone call had left him with a lot to ponder. The situation with Kalani Johnson was out of his hands. In due course no doubt the Hawaiian police or Johnson's family would release a statement about whether he had been poisoned or drugged before his head was plastered across the reef. When they did, he could just cut and paste the GSA's previous statements regarding Slides death, make a few changes and release them with Johnson's name attached. That part was easy.

The main job at hand was putting the finishing touches to the many details required to run a successful surf competition. Hirt had a good team that were well drilled in getting everything done but it was mostly left to him to take care of the ugly bits, like the greasing of local politicians and VIP's palms, keeping the surfers happy and making sure there were the appropriate drugs and ladies available for anyone who wanted to partake.

Security was run by an old friend from Hirt's childhood days- Trent 'Murder' Mercer- who happened to be president of a prominent bikie gang- The Cadaver Brothers. He was also Hirt's go to guy for the drugs and the ladies. The two of them supplied a huge quantity of narcotics and hookers every year and made a tidy side profit whenever the Quikbong Pro was on.

Before Perrot's phone call, Hirt had been casually wondering what to do in regard to the running order of the competition. Now the solution had become simple, but it would come at a price. Sure as hell that jumped up whinging cow, Claire Cooper, would complain once again about the women's heats being held in bad waves while the event waited for the surf to get good to run the men's. Surely she could see the bigger picture here? The men surfed better and the women looked better. It's just the way it was!

Why couldn't Cooper be more like world champ Stephanie Birch? She would be angry too, but at least she'd smile, don a bikini and go out there and wiggle that hot arse in the tiny surf as best she could. Even Fream knew how to play the game, and she was one of the best female surfers in big waves there was. Did she complain when it was small? No! Any excuse to put on the latest Quikbong micro G-string was a good one in her mind.

Then there was that smoking hot little sexpot, Tiffany Totthil. She had recently joined the GSA tour, and her surfing was only just good enough but no one seemed to care. The sight of her strutting around the competition area in a bikini not much bigger than a postage stamp with perfect surgically enhanced breasts and long blonde hair cascading down to a tiny backside made life worth living!

Thanks to her poorly kept secret affair with head judge Renae Parry, Totthil had done very well in the last few competitions but that really had to stop. If that little minx was going to fuck anyone behind the scenes to get places on the GSA Tour, it would be Peter Hirt that bent her over the couch, not an easily replaceable surf judge.

So, the contest would begin on Saturday. If Hirt ignored the whinging surfers everything else seemed to be in place for a smooth start. Thanks to all that beautiful new revenue from the deaths of Slide and Johnson, the Quikbong Pro was now offering the biggest prize purse for a surf event ever.

All those thoughts of money and bikinis triggered a familiar bulge in Hirt's pants. He smiled to himself, pulled out his mobile phone and searched Tiffany Totthil's number.

It was time that strumpet earnt her place on the GSA World Tour.

Chapter 3 SOMETHING NEEDS TO BE DONE

Claire Cooper was furious! The first day of the Quikbong Pro had just finished and once again another women's surf contest had been held in garbage waves when it didn't need to be. To make matters worse she'd been knocked out by that skanky piece of no talent fluff, Tiffany Totthil!

If she was honest with herself, Cooper had to admit that the whole scenario wasn't a surprise, and she should have been better prepared for the disappointment. These days the majority of the women's surf industry was a farce run by misogynistic assholes. The guys always seemed to have their heats when the surf was at its biggest and best. Then when the surf went to crap, they'd roll out the women's heats and try and get as much of that out the way before the waves got good again. Even better if it's on a weekend and the sun is shining so the competitors can all wear their favourite skimpy bikini.

Cooper was at her best in real waves that required skill and courage to ride. This year the forecast predicted small waves for the first few days before a bomb swell kicked in Monday and Tuesday and stayed solid for the rest of the ten-day waiting period. In her mind the decision was simple. Wait to the swell hits, run the men's event in the biggest surf (although she'd love to be out there herself), then finish with the women's event as the swell groomed itself into perfection later in the week. It seemed like a win/win situation for all involved.

Instead, the GSA run by that self-righteous wanker Peter Hirt decided to hold the women's event in tiny surf over the opening weekend. Their reasoning was that they wanted the men's final to be the pinnacle of the event and not detract from that by having the women's heats in the days following.

Cooper hated that women's surfing had become nothing more than a glorified catwalk. It was a shame as there were some amazing female surfers on tour. Current World Champ Stephanie Birch could surf incredible in any sized waves. Others like Sally Lord, Karissa Kai, Molly Perkins and Dyanna Fream regularly blew minds, especially in real waves that had heavy consequences if you messed up. Unfortunately, their opportunities to showcase this talent seemed restricted entirely to their own Stalkbook and Instafamous pages and never to a GSA event.

Then there was the 'fairy floss' girls as Cooper liked to think of them. Girls that made their way onto the world tour with minimal talent but a love for wearing bikinis not much bigger than a piece of dental floss and a penchant for sleeping with the odd judge or two.

It was one of those little fairy floss girls, Tiffany Totthil, that really ground her gears. All fake tits, tiny backside and fluffy bleached blonde hair, she acted dumb but Cooper knew that was just playing into the role she had cast for herself. "Look at me," her image screamed. "I'm just a bimbo that looks hot and likes to pretend I'm a surfer because that's what people think is cool. But really I'm only doing this to fulfil every man's fantasy that I'm ready to drop my miniscule panties and let them have me!"

"That little bitch is way smarter than she pretends to be!" Cooper said out loud to herself. As much as she hated to admit it, Tiffany Totthil could surf okay. She might not be much when the surf got serious, but it seemed the way the GSA was structured these days, that meant nothing.

Totthil represented everything about the modern GSA female surfer that Cooper hated. She could wiggle that butt with the best of them to get through heats and she was the darling of all the gutter tabloid magazines. She also maintained a huge online following on Stalkbook and Instafamous. Totthil's web presence was such that she could post a photo of a dog poo she had stepped in and get 100,000 likes. To make matters worse, Cooper had a strong suspicion she was rooting head judge Renae Parry on the sly.

Cooper believed women's surfing had been the loser today. So far, the biggest headline to come out of the event hadn't been who was still in the running to win it, but instead the massive publicity around the new 'Sea Thru Bikini' that Brazilian World Number 16 Belle Silva had worn during her round one loss to Cooper herself.

What hurt the most was that Silva was now the new focus of the surf media universe. She was already being paid five times the money by her sponsor GoMerch than Cooper was getting from her sponsor Homegrown Maniacs - which was one of the few true core extreme sport brands left but had a lot less money to spend on its athletes.

Hailing from Margaret River in the southwest of Western Australia, Cooper herself was a very attractive Latin/Australian girl with shoulder length auburn hair and an extremely fit, femininely muscular body that both men and women found very attractive. She also didn't mind wearing a sexy yet practical swimsuit either and always looked good when she went out socially.

So, it wasn't as if Cooper didn't appreciate a woman's body, but when she'd seen Silva walking down through the crowd for her heat, Cooper's genuine first impression was that she had completely forgotten to put on her bikini! Such was the clear view she had of Silva's breasts and perfectly manicured vagina through the tiny piece of transparent cloth she'd chosen to wear.

Unsurprisingly the surf paparazzi had gone crazy, and the rest of the world had followed. The internet had lit up with just about every news website on the planet running photos of Silva in her near naked glory. Any photos that didn't feature Silva were almost exclusively of Totthil in her skanky G-string.

Only the very odd news service that pretended to take themselves seriously mentioned the results. Even those didn't bother to feature any actual good surfing footage but instead focussed on the girls running down to the water's edge in their bikini with their surfboards, or maybe the ever-classy duck dive shot that would see the surfer stick her backside in the air as she pushed her board under a wave.

As soon as she had heard from Luke Perrot that the girls were being made to surf on the weekend, Cooper had got straight on the phone to

Peter Hirt and given him a mouthful. That went about as well as expected, which basically meant she may as well of picked up a banana, pretended it was a phone and yelled at that for 15 minutes. Hirt was at his typical political Teflon best and refused to be swayed in any way with Coopers pleads for the women's event to be delayed until the surf was better.

Cooper's anger was interrupted by the ringing of her phone. She looked to see who it was and felt some of the rage dissipating as she answered the call.

"Hey babe what's up?" asked Dyanna 'Dream' Fream brightly. "Sorry you lost to that little bitch today. I'm sure she was over scored."

"Yeah the mole!" Cooper replied, her anger rising again. "I saw that last wave she got from the beach and thought I had it in the bag. I couldn't believe they gave her the score she needed. I tried to go and have a talk with Renae Perry about it but some fat biker looking dude with a security shirt on wouldn't let me near the judges. Since when does that happen?"

"I know! Security is out of control this year. There's a meathead in every corner of the event site, all of them chewing on their bottom lip like they are four lines deep into a bender," Fream laughed. "But you've got to know how to deal with them babe. Just smile and flash a bit of cleavage and they'll do anything you want!"

"That might work if I had enough cleavage to flash!" Cooper was already starting to feel better. Fream's brash sexuality and love for life had that effect on her.

"Nonsense babe you're smoking hot and don't forget it. Maybe you need to use a bit of that sex appeal and bang one of the judges like Totthil. Or go straight to the top and fuck our esteemed CEO. I'm sure that sleezoid would like a crack at you. Small dicked prick that he is."

"Oh my god!" Cooper exclaimed passionately. "Do you really think Totthil is rooting a judge? I've always suspected her and Parry had something going on!"

"Got it in one babe. I walked in on the two of them going at it like rabbits behind the judges' scaffolding one time. They didn't see me, but I took a couple of shots of them with my phone. I couldn't give a damn who either of them screw, but I figured that if I ever came up against Totthil in a heat and Parry was judging I'd show the photos and make sure he took himself off the panel. I should have done it for you today but didn't think he would be so blatant with his favouritism. Sorry babe."

Cooper ended the call in a worse mood than when it started. Having it confirmed that she had indeed lost thanks to her opponent cheating was the final straw. Since the celebration on the night after the previous year's Top 5 shootout in Bali her life had changed immensely. On that crazy evening she'd met someone special who had convinced her that playing too nice would never allow her to achieve her goals. Despite that, deep down she was a warm-hearted girl, and she'd resisted the notion as best she could in the following months, but with this new revelation Cooper could feel the final shackles of resistance peel away.

If she was ever going to achieve her dreams, then she needed to get dirty and crawl right down into the sewer where these scumbags existed on a daily basis. Fortunately, she knew just the person to help her.

Chapter 4 THE DREAM

Dyanna 'Dream' Fream was feeling good as she returned to her hotel room from her latest conquest.

"Ahh yes! Always nice to break in another young, up and coming surfer," she thought grinning to herself.

She'd spotted the evening's entertainment the day before. He'd been hanging around the competitor's area at the Quikbong Pro when she collected her contest rash vest before her first heat. Apparently he was the next big thing to come out of the Gold Coast and he'd been granted a wild card into the men's event due to start tomorrow. Normally most of the men wouldn't bother to be at the contest site when the women's event was on, but he was probably just happy to be allowed into the VIP section and was making the most of it.

Fream didn't care one bit about his potential, although if she really thought about it, she would probably have conceded it added to his appeal. No, all she saw was a sexy young man with broad shoulders and a six pack for a stomach who hopefully could do the horizontal tango all night.

As soon as Fream had decided he was her next target she'd gone straight up to him, introduced herself and started flirting outrageously. The young stud was clearly smitten, but he missed all his cues to ask for her number until she'd thrown any sense of subtlety out the window and asked for his details. It was only then he begun to understand what was going on and then he couldn't give her his number fast enough, almost shaking as he typed into her phone. It's just as well he did as she couldn't remember his name.

Her thoughts drifted to the previous day's phone call to Claire Cooper. Cooper just didn't know how sexy she was, and Fream had been wanting to run her hands and mouth all over that bronzed, rock hard body ever since she first saw her at a Pro Junior surf event when they were both in their late teens. Back then they were from opposite sides of the country and on the few times Fream saw Cooper at events since, she was always with her long-term boyfriend.

That had all changed at the GSA Awards ceremony held late last year in Bali on the night the world champions had been decided at Keramas. A newly single Cooper had turned up solo wearing a little black dress that had turned everybody's heads. Not that Cooper was aware of course. She just didn't know how hot she was!

On land she was a polite, quietly spoken person, but that all changed if she got riled up about something she was passionate about, like the state of women's surfing. Get on the wrong side of her on that topic and you best stay out of her way! It was also how she behaved in the surf when the waves were dangerous - all fearless fire and passion.

Fream had rarely seen Cooper drink alcohol, but on that occasion in Bali she'd let her guard down and got talked into a few cocktails. As the night wore on, she became more than a bit tipsy and revealed a side of her that Fream had never seen before. With the courage supplied by the alcohol, Cooper had propositioned a very surprised Fream. Unfortunately, she already had bedroom plans for the night and had it been with almost anyone other than a certain record winning world champion who was supposedly devoted to his movie star girlfriend, she would have cancelled and gone home with Cooper.

Since then, Fream had dropped a number of subtle hints that they could get it on anytime Cooper felt the need but while the answer was never a flat no, it had also never been a yes. Fream didn't like to think too deeply about that. She had a sneaking suspicion she had been friend-zoned, and her ego refused to believe that anyone would do that to her.

Standing at just under six feet tall with long honey blonde hair and a fit, tanned body to die for, Dyanna 'Dream' Fream was a real-life Amazon surf goddess. Also occasionally known as 'Dirty Dy' she might have looked like some kind of oversized barbie doll surf chick, but she was also a straight up hell woman with no fear in big scary waves and a good surfer in small waves too. She'd grown up in Wollongong on the south coast of New South Wales and discovered her love for big waves on the many heavy reefs that the area is known for.

These days few people called her Dirty Dy and most of those were the people she had rejected. Fream was a sexual dynamo that blew the minds of men and women alike. Her sublime bedroom activities were a surprisingly well-kept underground secret, especially in the day and age of the world's paparazzi so focused on surfing, its stars and what smut they get up to.

It was a pretty simple concept really. Fream was straight up the most amazing woman in bed that any of her partners had ever had. The passion she dedicated to chasing the most extreme waves on the planet also manifested itself sexually.

A night with 'The Dream' was the equivalent to winning lotto. The only thing better than a night with The Dream was two nights and that secret was fiercely protected. Open your mouth and brag about sleeping with The Dream or call her Dirty Dy and you can guarantee that not only is it the last time you will ever experience such pleasure, but you can also count on being crucified by her many lovers which included surfers, journalists, judges, paparazzi, industry CEO's and so on.

Fream had fucked them all and more. She was like a secret perfect wave, a hidden waterfall, a can't miss fishing spot or the sweetest fruit imaginable - something to be cherished, savoured and protected for all time.

Over the years some had tried to mess with her. While on a surf trip to the Mentawai Islands in Indonesia with the Quikbong junior team, Fream had gone along to help inspire the next generation of surfers. Quikbong had hired a luxury yacht complete with helicopters and jet skis for the two week cruise through the wave rich archipelago. Also along for the ride were some old school legendary photographers and journalists that still worked for the last core surf mags in the world – Surfing World and Tracks. They'd been blessed with epic Indonesian conditions all trip, and everyone had gone home happy having made some new friends and scored some incredible social media edits.

When they returned, rumours surfaced that Fream had slept with a few of the people on the boat at varying stages during the trip, including possibly taking the virginity of several of the junior surfers. A few of the parents got wind of the rumours and they thought it would be a good chance to sue Fream and Quikbong for a lot of money.

What the parents and their high-priced lawyers didn't count on however, is that not one of the young surfers involved agreed to testify. In fact, every single one of them went on record to deny anything untoward ever happened whatsoever. After all, when a blonde amazon sex goddess takes your virginity and absolutely blows your mind why would you risk the chance of it happening again by bragging about it? Not to mention how much your mates would vilify you.

Had any of the young surfers on that boat opened their mouths then it would have been a fair bet that at least 70% of the males and 40% of the females associated with the GSA Tour would never have forgiven them. Their career as a pro surfer would be over and one of selling wax at the local surf store would have begun.

Fream grabbed a vodka out of the mini bar in her hotel room and sat back to ponder her next move. Thoughts of Claire Cooper had got her horny again. It was still early and while the young surfer that had been her evenings sexual distraction was enthusiastic, he was sadly lacking on the experience side. That didn't bother Fream as inexperience could be very appealing, but she was a true insatiable nymphomaniac and the sexual itch rarely felt fully scratched. As she picked up her phone she decided that the time for subtlety with Cooper was over, she would not be friend zoned.

"Hey sexy what's up?" Fream cooed down the line when she heard Cooper's voice.

"Hi Dreamy. Just chilling in my hotel room," replied a sleepy Cooper. "Hey congratulations on the semifinal finish, that's not a bad effort in those tiny waves and Stephanie was ripping in your heat."

"Thanks babe," Fream loved the way Cooper called her 'Dreamy'. It did things to her that she had trouble processing. "Yeah she pretty much smashed me, but at least I can say that I got beaten by the winner and the prizemoney wasn't too bad either for a change.

"And you smoked that bitch Totthil," Cooper said with passion. She was more awake now. "I thought she was going to have a fit when the judges didn't give her the score on that last wave. I watched it online and she was mad as hell in the post heat interview. I have a feeling at least one judge isn't getting any nookie tonight. Did you end up showing those photos to Parry?"

"Sure did. There was no way I was going to let them pull the same shit on me as they did on you," said Fream gleefully. "I wish you were there to see it. Parry went white when I showed him. He didn't even try to deny it. The photos were too clear. He knew I could have ruined him right there and then, so he's bloody lucky all I asked for was him to take a break for that heat so I could beat Totthil fair and square."

"Oh I so would have loved to see his face," chuckled Cooper. "Hey listen I think some of the girls should get together and talk about what we can do to put an end to the rubbish that we have had to put up with lately. You know like having to always surf the worst conditions, judges sleeping with athletes and all the other misogynistic crap that's going on. What do you think?"

"What do I think?" purred Fream "I think you should stop worrying and come around here so my tongue and I can smooth away all that stress. A few orgasms will free your mind from any GSA bullshit, and I've got a couple of other toys handy I can introduce you to that will have you creaming your panties in minutes."

"Oh I wish Dreamy," Cooper replied with a disturbing lack of passion. "But I'm just about to call a taxi. I've got the red eye flight home tonight. My mum's not too well so I want to get back as soon as possible to make sure she's OK. But hey can we talk about what I said about getting the girls together soon please? It's really important to me."

"Sure babe. Give me a call when you're settled back at home and we can make a plan. All the best to your mum and safe travels sexy lady!" Fream said as she hung up. She knocked back half the vodka in one swallow and sat back to savour the buzz. She was a little puzzled by Cooper's attitude but there's no way she would be friend-zoned so it must be her worry for her mother. In any case The Dream was not one to give up easily. She reached for her phone again and this time called an Uber.

"What if someone killed both Jimmy and Kalani?" asked Aussie bad boy pro surfer Matt Wilson for what felt like the tenth time. "Who do you think the killer might be?"

Fream had bumped into Wilson a few hours earlier after catching her Uber to the Coolangatta Hotel. The Cooly was one of the best hang out locations when the Quikbong Pro was on and Fream's favourite spot to get herself a bit of hard, fast loving.

"Fuck I don't know Matt! Why ask me?" Fream replied, frustrated by a line of conversation that had been going on for too long. "Probably some weird freaktoid that follows the tour. There are thousands of them out there. You should know that better than most. You've got more Instafamous followers than anybody. I'm betting at least a few could be messed up enough to kill someone!"

Fream had been disappointed at the lack of talent on hand at The Cooly. There had been some cute surfer guys and the odd freestyle motocross boy with those full sleeve tattoos that got her wet, but none managed to get past the screening questions. Although a couple had come close.

Strike one was a tall, tanned, good looking young surfer type, the kind that are a dime a dozen on the Gold Coast of Queensland. She could tell he had a good body under the standard Quikbong shirt and long cargo shorts. He was toned from paddling against the strong rips of the coast's point breaks with strong shoulders and nice eyes. Fream wondered what he might be like when he was naked and pinned to the bed while she sat atop him and took her pleasure. So, when he sauntered up to Fream and bought her a drink, she began to think they both might get lucky, even though she had already fucked someone earlier that could have been this guy's twin.

Unfortunately, just as things were looking promising, he began to ramble on about how he had almost made it as a pro surfer, how good he still is, and can she maybe have a talk to her sponsors about giving him another shot? Then, if that wasn't bad enough, to her horror he began to profess his undying love and how he'd always had a feeling they were meant for each other.

She turned around and left him standing there without so much as another word. She wanted a fuck not a husband and nothing kills horniness like talk of a relationship with some random failed pro surf metrosexual she'd just met.

Next Fream had casually made a beeline for a tattooed moto dude that was the complete opposite of surfer boy. He had one arm with a full sleeve of tattoos and the other well on its way. His earlobes were stretched out by giant earrings, his nose and lip were pierced and completing the look was a belt with chains hanging off it and a pair of shorts slung so low you could see his underwear. He was well muscled from riding dirt bikes and had a confident bad boy attitude that was very appealing

After the limp wristed metro surfer, Mr Dirt Bike whispering in Fream's ear about what he was going to do when he got her naked had her ready to take him outside and fuck him in the carpark right there and then. And she would have had he not, in a ridiculous attempt to prove his manhood and alpha male status among his mates, drunk one too many tequila shots. Thereby transforming from bad boy sex god into a drunk slurring idiot and strike two.

Closing time was fast approaching and Fream was still as horny as hell thanks to the drunk idiot moto boy's dirty sex talk. There didn't seem to be much hope for satisfying that urge except with one of her favourite vibrators and some internet porn.

That's when that sexy stoner Bunker Haze and Matt Wilson had walked in with about a half dozen wannabe models. They immediately commandeered a VIP section and began throwing money and overpriced champagne around like it was tap water.

Fream and Bunker had got it on a few times previously. When he wasn't loaded on drugs, Bunker was almost a match for Fream at her sexual best. There had been one especially memorable night, with a couple of event promo girls and her complete travel pack of vibrators and dildos, that she still occasionally masturbated to while watching the home videos they'd filmed that evening.

Fream and Wilson had also dabbled in the occasional casual nights fling on tour when neither could find a better option. So, when Bunker had passed out in the VIP booth with an equally drugged out model under each arm, she'd settled for Wilson. Although with his incessant talk about the demise of Slide and Johnson, Fream was already beginning to wish she had settled for her favourite vibrator instead.

Fream had to admit Wilson was a good-looking rooster. You can't be a pro surfer and not have a good body. Add to that the typical surfy bleached straight blond hair, vibrant blue eyes, big white teeth and the whole naughty schoolboy image and you had the ingredients for a thousand dropped panties. Actually, it was probably more like a hundred thousand panties based on his phenomenal number of Instafamous followers.

In many ways, they were the pro tour's male and female equivalent of each other, in both looks and reputation. Recently there had been speculation in the tabloids of love affairs between the two but no photos had surfaced. That was something Fream was keen to avoid, unlike Wilson who seemed to enjoy seeing his pecker splashed double page across the latest trash mag. As such she'd been insistent that they be careful to leave The Cooly separately to avoid any unwanted suspicion

Now it appeared Wilson had his mind on things other than the goddess in front of him. Word had begun to filter through that the Hawaiian police had released a statement confirming that traces of Fentanyl had been found in Johnson's system when he died and were appealing for information. Johnson was considered a squeaky-clean athlete so foul play was suspected. With the mystery already surrounding Slide's death, the worldwide media immediately begun to speculate they might be linked.

"Yeah I suppose it could be some kind of crazy, pro surfer groupie stalker," Wilson pondered as he lounged half naked on the sofa. "But what if it's not? What if it's someone on the pro tour? What if it's one of us? I mean if they are linked then whoever it is has already taken out two of the best surfers on tour. Maybe they are trying to rid themselves of some competition? What if I'm next?" he asked working himself into an increasingly agitated state.

Fream had expected that last question for a while and forced a smile when she heard it.

"Well maybe you are," she said letting her frustration show. "Best fuck me now, just in case it's your last night on the planet!"

"I dunno Dy. I'm not really feeling it," replied Wilson. "This shit's got me worried ya know. I mean it's one thing to worry about hitting the reef or drowning or something, but someone out there might be killing pro surfer dudes. And everyone's saying that it must be someone we know to be able to get close enough to slip us drugs!"

"Oh for chrissakes Matt are you going to stick that pretty little head of yours between my legs and get to work or are you going to sit there all night and whinge like a little girl?" Fream exclaimed ready to chuck her drink at him.

"Fuck I'm sorry Dy," said Wilson confused. "It's not you it's me. My head's all over the place. Those guys might not have been my best friends, but they were still part of the crew ya know. Hell, I'm not sure I'd even be able to get it up anyway. I'm so messed up!"

Fream's frustration was rapidly turning to white hot rage. No one says no to Dream Fream when she's in the mood. That just didn't happen to her, let alone twice in one night! An idea that had been in the back of her mind since she first saw Wilson was rapidly gaining momentum. He'd been royally pissing her off and she'd had enough.

"Well, I suppose you have a heat tomorrow," Fream called over her shoulder as she got up to go to the kitchen. "So I can accept that, but let's have one more before I go." She made sure he couldn't see what she was doing and reached into her handbag, drawing out a couple of small packets of different coloured powders, and begun to mix them into Wilson's vodka.

"So, who are you up against anyway? Do you think you can take them?" she asked raising his glass to the light to make sure there was no sign of the extras in Wilsons drink.

"Ahh I dunno actually. A Brazilian I think. To be honest I've been that rattled I hadn't even bothered to check the draw."

"Well I'm sure you will smash them anyway. Your style suits the Gold Coast point breaks."

"Yeah, but those guys can win in any conditions these days." Wilson replied loudly. He sounded happier now they were on a subject that didn't involve the thought of him dying.

"Well, this will help ease your worries." Fream said as she sauntered back into the bedroom, smiling as she handed Wilson his glass of special vodka. There was no way Fream was going to have strike three. Matt Wilson should know better than that and now he was going to pay.

Chapter 5 BUNKER

Bunker took a long, deep inhalation on the bong and leaned back on his couch savouring the rush to his head of the tobacco and marijuana combination. He knew he shouldn't be sucking on a dirty bong as he had another heat later in the day, but as always Bunker couldn't help himself. He was, after all, 'The' Bunker Haze, and his reputation had to be preserved. Or at least that's how he tried to justify it to himself as he reached for the mull bowl to pack himself another cone.

Bunker was an anomaly. A one in a million freak. You can line up thousands of smokers, alcoholics, druggos, speed freaks and pill poppers and chart their course to destruction. Then there will be that one guy who has chain smoked since he was a kid but can hold his breath underwater for minutes and free dive to ridiculous depths. Or maybe a high functioning alcoholic who you can never tell if he is pissed or straight, or the guy that can pop ecstasy pills all night then wake up the next day happy and normal while everyone else was hating life. That was Bunker.

Bunker was a real-life Jeff Spicoli from the classic old movie 'Fast Times at Ridgemont High'. Actor Sean Penn had played Spicoli as the classic surf stoner and the first time Bunker and his best friend Matt Wilson had watched it, Wilson had burst out laughing as soon as Spicoli had started talking. At the time Bunker couldn't understand why, so he had asked.

"Mate that's you!" cackled Wilson hysterically. "You talk and sound just like him. Hell, you even look like him!"

And Wilson had been right. Bunker had the same stoner drawl that Spicoli had and the same long, dirty blonde hair almost going to dreadlocks. The only difference was Bunker wore newer clothes and owned half the world.

Like Spicoli, Bunker also loved his drugs. He mostly steered clear of what was in his mind the real evil ones like heroin, speed, crack and meth but the rest were fair game. He loved his weed the most. Cocaine and ecstasy were good so long as they were reasonably pure and not mixed with any number of dodgy chemicals. LSD was a blast so long as it was the old school 'real LSD' like his mum used to take back when she was young. Magic mushrooms could be fun so long as you didn't get a bad batch like Bunker had endured a couple of times. Once he'd spent several days hiding under his bed convinced he'd turned into a moth.

He was incredibly popular as a competitor on the GSA tour. Bunker just being Bunker on a normal day filled pages and pages of tabloid magazines, not to mention he probably had more internet websites, blogs, chat pages and podcasts devoted to him than any other surfer. He was a walking, talking headline with no filter in his brain that made him stop and think "should I say this" before he opened his mouth. Nope it all came out in a flood of swearing, soulful, intelligent, idiotic or profoundly insightful drivel. Like his surfing, a Bunker Haze interview could go anywhere.

A volatile and completely unpredictable talent, Bunker was probably close to the best surfer in the world when he was truly on song. In those rare moments he was untouchable, a genius. Think Hendrix, Prince or Slash on guitar, Hunter Thompson with a pen or Jim Morrison and Michael Hutchence on stage. His friends agreed drugs were the biggest problem. Only they couldn't agree as to whether it was better if he was straight or fucked up. Those flashes of brilliance seemed to come when they came and there was no rhyme or reason as to when Bunker switched on and destroyed his opponent or spent the heat communicating with dolphins. Probably even Bunker didn't know.

The previous year during a heat in awful onshore mush in Brazil, he simply started paddling up the coast without bothering to catch a wave. The commentators and crowd were left bemused as he disappeared around the next headland with his contest rash vest still on. Eventually he paddled ashore several miles from the contest venue, walked to the nearest road and hitched a ride back to his luxury beachside condo, where he remained hidden away and unavailable for comment for a week.

The GSA punished him of course. They had to at least be seen to do the right thing when one of their athletes was clearly off chops, but they'd done some internal research to get a gauge on what Bunker's presence on the tour was worth to the surf industry. The data was clear, with the media tsunami that he regularly created, the GSA World Surf Tour with Bunker as a full-time competitor was worth many millions more, than one without him. He was the all-time surf paparazzi favourite. A literal walking headline. If it had been a scandal free week on the GSA, the best option was to just go camp on Bunker's doorstep and wait for him to emerge. If he wasn't off his face on drugs, then he was parading his latest supermodel girlfriend or girlfriends.

Bunker also didn't know how to filter his mouth, nor it seemed did he know how to lie. So, if the paparazzi asked Bunker what he's been up to the past week and he'd just tied German supermodel Heidi Flum to his bedpost and flew in American pornstar Lisa Wild to get freaky while he filmed it, then that is exactly what he would tell the media.

The GSA issued Bunker with a record fine for his effort in Brazil but stopped short of suspending him from competing. With a net worth in the gazillions, it had no effect whatsoever on Bunker. There were some appropriate press releases from the GSA and Bunker's media team, then it was swept under the rug and Bunker was allowed to continue surfing and competing. It helped that for every fine the GSA gave Bunker, he donated fifty times that amount to a worthy local charity. Bunker may be rich as shit, but in many ways, he was the people's champion. Everybody loved him.

The only son to B grade actress, Playboy Bunny and American socialite Betty Herchel and aging Australian media billionaire Rupert Haze, Bunker had grown up with media attention all of his life and had somehow remained immune to its destructive influence. The marriage of the 22yr old Herchel to the 62yr old Haze was initially ridiculed by the press as the typical gold-digging bimbo meets ageing playboy rich man. But against the odds they'd conceived Bunker and had lived a happy life, until fourteen years later when Rupert Haze passed away from a heart attack with a bloodstream full of Viagra and a still very attractive, lingerie clad Betty Herchel on top of him. She inherited billions and Bunker got a trust fund equivalent to the combined income of a number of small countries.

With her finances secure enough for fifty lifetimes, Herchel retired to the family mansion overlooking Manly Beach in New South Wales to live her life with a variety of young lovers and quality LSD. Meanwhile Bunker discovered surfing and somewhere along the line, surfing discovered him.

It was natural that Bunker would become a surfer given that his first sight as he rolled out of bed in the morning was the beach. The surprising bit was that such a natural athlete could spring from the loins of a man widely regarded for his intelligence only and a mother whose entire athletic abilities were limited to the bedroom.

Growing up Bunker was a pretty normal kid considering he was heir to a biblical sized fortune. He was intelligent and well respected by his peers but didn't stand out in anything in particular, except the creative subjects like music and art. As surfing took hold of his life the rest suffered. Bunker spent less time worrying about his schoolwork and more time at the beach or on his guitar.

At an early age he was already paddling out into huge surf with the old warriors or mastering complicated riffs on his guitar. Bunker may have been born with a silver spoon in his mouth, but he was a loveable rogue who treated everyone the same way. That together with his creative genius stopped him from becoming a spoiled rich boy.

Still, when you have access to that much money without having to work for it, motivation can be hard to find and boredom easily kicks in. It was no surprise then, that Bunker eventually found drugs. He'd grown up watching his mum indulge and didn't particularly like how it affected her. But he got bored one day, raided her weed stash and the rest was history.

Bunker gave little thought to that first smoke of his mum's weed as he inhaled his fifth bong for the session. After that many bongs there wasn't really a lot on Bunker's mind at all. Just a comfortable, relaxed nothingness that allowed him to absorb the many beautiful intricacies of

The Doors song 'Riders on the Storm' that was playing on the stereo in the background of his luxury condo overlooking the beach at Kirra, just up the coast from the contest site.

Usually whenever there was a competition on, Bunker and Wilson would stay together in whatever accommodation Bunker purchased or rented. Rarely seen apart, the two of them were always getting up to mischief in one form or another. They'd been at it again last night at the Coolangatta Hotel, only Bunker still couldn't remember much of what had happened.

He'd already been pretty wasted when they'd left the condo and jumped in the limo for the ride to the pub. They both had heats the next day but that never stopped Bunker. In the limo Bunker had done some Black Sambuca shots and sucked down a big spliff. Wilson on the other hand was a little more serious about how much he consumed before surfing a heat the next day and had quietly sipped on a beer.

As soon as they'd got in the door, ladies flocked straight to the pair in droves. Bunker had ordered ten bottles of the most expensive champagne the venue had for the girls and a bottle of expensive vodka for himself. At some stage he'd passed out in the VIP section and when he'd woken up, he found himself nestled in between four hot gold coast specials and Wilson was nowhere to be seen.

When he got home Bunker and the girls had gone straight upstairs to jump into one of the spas the two-storey condo had. On the way up Bunker noticed the door to Wilson's room was shut so he figured his friend had come home early to prepare for his first heat the next day. He'd briefly thought about waking Wilson up and inviting him to join them, but there were only four girls so there wasn't really enough to go around.

With the girls keeping him busy doing the funky monkey most of the night and having to surf an early heat in the morning, Bunker hadn't even bothered to sleep. He'd had one last horizontal folk dance, done a couple of lines of coke, then they'd all jumped into the limo. They arrived at the contest area just in time for Bunker to grab his contest rashie, kiss the girls goodbye, paddle out behind the rocks at Snapper and in true Bunker style, straight into the best wave of the morning.

It was a solid six-foot backwash filled sand dredging tube that Bunker completely disappeared into and emerged well down the beach. The judges gave him a 9.3 for it. Minutes later he backed it up with an almost as good 8.8 and it was over for his opponent. Bunker didn't even bother to surf the rest of the heat. With ten minutes to go he paddled in, handed back his rashie and was back on the couch with a bong not long after.

He was just about to smash another cone when his phone beeped to say he'd got a text message. It was from Luke Perrot, the President of the Professional Surfers Union.

The text read: "Hey Bunker have you seen Matt? He's late for his heat. Everyone is running around like mad dogs trying to find him".

It was then that Bunker realized he hadn't seen Wilson at the competition at all throughout the morning. Admittedly he hadn't been there for long, but his good buddy nearly always came up to have a chat before or after the heat.

He got up off the couch and went to Wilson's room. Maybe he'd slept through his alarm or something?

"Hey Willo, are you awake?" Bunker called out banging on the door. "Your heats on soon mate you better hurry." There was no answer, so Bunker opened the door to see if he was OK. Inside there was no sign of Wilson and his bed was still made.

"Looks like Willow must have got lucky and stayed elsewhere," thought Bunker closing the door behind him. "I wonder why he's not at the contest though? It's not like him to miss a heat. She must have been a hell of a root!"

Bunker picked up his phone and tried to call him. It was ringing at the other end, so Bunker expected to hear a hungover voice answer any second. It went to message bank, so he tried again. This time he was just about to leave a message when he thought he heard a sound similar to Wilson's ring tone out on the balcony of the lower floor.

"Shit I hadn't even thought to look out there. He's probably fallen asleep in the spa again!" Bunker reflected as he pulled back the curtains and opened the screen door that led out to the downstairs spa that Wilson normally used.

Sure enough he could just see the top of Wilson's head above the spa as he relaxed looking out over the ocean.

"Oi sleepy head! Wake up ya drongo! You're gunna miss your heat! Geez she must have been an animal to wear you out this much!" Bunker called out over the sound of the spa bubbling away.

There was no response from Wilson as Bunker approached so he reached out and grabbed his friend by the shoulder and gently shook him. As he did Wilson's head fell sideways and it was then that Bunker saw his face. His eyes were kind of half open, but it was clear something was wrong. Whatever drug fog Bunker had been in cleared almost instantly.

"Willow! Hey dude wake up! C'mon man talk to me! Open your eyes mate. Willow it's me Bunker," he shouted as he shook Wilson and gave him a couple of hard slaps across the face. Still no response.

Bunker dragged Wilson out of the spa and laid him on the ground. He checked his pulse and listened to see if he was breathing. There was nothing. He immediately called an ambulance, checked his airway then got to work performing CPR, crying as he did so. Nothing in Bunkers super privileged life had ever prepared him for this moment, when he held a dead mate in his arms and tried to bring him back to life.

Deep down he knew it was over and his best friend was gone. He continued on for a few minutes more then gave up. With tears in his eyes, he leaned back against the spa and looked down at his wingman from so many epic nights.

"Geez dude I hope she was worth it," he said trying to laugh through the pain. "Because whoever it was, sure did fuck your brains out!"

Chapter 6 IS SOMEONE BUMPING THEM OFF?

The pro surf tour was in shock following the news of the death of another of their favourite sons, this time it was the loveable Aussie ratbag, Matt Wilson. There had been only mild concern when he hadn't turned up for his heat. After all he was a pro surfer and pro surfers in general were hardly the most reliable people at the best of times, let alone one that had been known to party hard on a regular basis. Most expected Wilson to turn up at some stage later in the day sporting a huge hangover and a crazy story based around a wild night spent with a couple of super models and a video camera. But he hadn't appeared, and it wasn't until late afternoon that word started to spread around the contest site that Wilson had been discovered dead at Bunker's condo.

Peter Hirt had been the one to take the call from the police that confirmed Wilson's body had been found. They weren't saying much else but the policeman in charge of the preliminary investigations, Sergeant John Borgio, had advised they suspected a drug overdose and were waiting on toxicology reports. He didn't say foul play might have played a part, but he didn't rule it out either. It had been Bunker who had found the body, and he was still with the police assisting them with their enquiries.

Sergeant Borgio had said that Bunker was visibly upset although he wasn't sure if it was because his friend was dead or that they had found small quantities of marijuana, cocaine and ecstasy when they had conducted a search of his condo. They'd charged him with possession but that was all at this stage.

"He got lucky Pete," said Sergeant Borgio relaying what he could to Peter Hirt. The two of them knew each other casually from a few VIP functions around town. He was a good cop, maybe just a little too honest for Hirt's liking. "He was blubbering something about being with a bunch of girls all night, but the poor drug fucked idiot couldn't remember any of their names. Fortunately, one of them had left her ID in his limo so we were able to track them down. The girls confirmed they were with him all night up until he got to the contest, so we don't think he's involved except maybe to supply the drugs that might have killed Wilson. That's about all I can tell you at the moment. This must be a hell of a headache for you on top of trying to run a competition."

"Yeah thanks John. It's a long way short of ideal that's for sure!" replied Hirt.

"Hey isn't that the third one of you lot that's gone down in the past few months? What's with that? Is someone bumping them off or something?" queried the Sergeant, suddenly making a connection Hirt was not all that happy about.

"Ahh don't know John, I doubt it. Jimmy Slide died back in October last year in Bali but who knows what happened there. The local police accidently cremated his body before they could do a proper examination. They can't even be sure how he died or if it was an accident or deliberate. There was about twenty theories including a suggestion the police might have even been involved. I suppose it's possible but even if it was some dodgy local cops, they wouldn't have had anything to do with Wilson's death here surely.

"As for the other guy," Hirt continued. "His name was Kalani Johnson and yeah, the Hawaiian police did find significant traces of Fentanyl in his system, but you know he also hit his head on the reef and that was actually what killed him. He was known to suffer from depression too. Maybe he was looking to put an end to it and took the Fentanyl himself and went for a last surf? So, no I don't think we are dealing with any sort of killer bumping off pro surfers. What would be the point?"

Hirt had felt bad about lying to the Sergeant with that last piece of information. As far as he was aware Johnson had been a normal happy surfer, albeit not as depraved as Hirt would prefer. Suicide would not have been on his radar at all, but Borgio wouldn't know that and the last thing Hirt needed was the police all over his event site spreading rumours that there was a killer out there with a taste for elite surfers. If they dug too deep who knows what they might uncover? Both Hirt and the GSA were not without its secrets and skeletons in the closet.

"Well with all due respect Pete I might just leave that one as a possibility for the time being. If there's just the slightest chance there's a surfing serial killer out there, we are going to have to look into it. I'll give you another call later with some more questions." Sergeant Borgio was a pro. He wasn't going to be put off that easily.

"Yeah no worries John. Call me anytime but do me a favour, can you not mention serial killers to the media. That's going to fuck with my contest bigtime. By the way, do you know what's going to happen with Bunker? He's still in the event." Hirt asked, ever the ruthless CEO.

"We'll let him out on bail tonight but I'm not sure he's in any state to continue in your contest. He's just lost his best friend after all. As for mentioning serial killers there's no way we need a bunch of panic merchants running around screaming at every shadow either. I'm not so sure about the media though. I'm willing to bet just about every news site out there is going to have their own serial nutjob theory as the number one headline tomorrow. Talk soon Pete, take care mate, don't be next!" Borgio laughed as he hung up.

Hirt had to concede that Sergeant Borgio was probably right. The media weren't going to let this one go any time soon. It was far too juicy and with two events left on the Australian leg of the tour after the Quikbong Pro, one at Margaret River in Western Australia and one at Bells Beach in Victoria, it was likely that at each stop there would be fresh media interest in any developments with the three deaths.

Hirt opened his desk and pulled out a cigar and lighter. He lit the cigar and sat back, he puffed away while trying to see the angles that he needed to bring into play next to get the best for the GSA. He was confident that, like the two previous deaths, the GSA would emerge stronger for Wilson's departure from the land of the living. This time however he wouldn't cancel the competition. If he did that would mean the first two events of the year didn't have winners and there was a danger people would lose interest in the race for the World Title.

Hirt decided he'd postpone tomorrow's heats for at least a couple of days, just so he had some time to make a plan and get the surfers onside. He'd probably start with a visit to Bunker to give his condolences and hopefully convince him to keep competing in memory of his good mate. Once he got Bunker onside the rest would probably agree with whatever he thought was best.

So, he had the makings of a decent contingency plan and quietly congratulated himself on the stellar performance he had put in over the past six months as he oversaw the biggest growth in the surf industry since the beginning of The Pamela Affair. His personal wealth had kept pace with the industry surge to the point he could probably buy his own island now and live on it comfortably with a few choice ladies on rotation to keep him company. But money was only a measurement of success and not the real reason he loved doing what he did. Like many rich arrogant pricks, Hirt loved power more than anything and every dollar he earnt granted him just that bit more.

That feeling of power created a sexual desire in Hirt to dominate. After a few seconds consideration he dialled Tiffany Totthil. A few days earlier he'd called Totthil into his office and confronted her about her affair with head judge Renae Parry. Hirt had laid it on thick, explaining that sleeping with judges was extremely frowned upon and that she faced immediate and permanent expulsion from the GSA tour. The reality was he didn't really give a fuck who she slept with as long as he was one of them, but Totthil bought it hook, line and sinker. She burst into tears and was suitably apologetic. In between bouts of crying and sniffling into a tissue, she prattled on about how pro surfing meant everything to her and she wanted to be the best and most famous surfer ever.

Hirt had let her stew in her misery for a while, making sure she understood the full seriousness of the situation she was in before he delivered her the lifeline. As soon as he suggested that maybe the two of them could work something out, Totthil's tears had dried up remarkably fast. When she battered her eyelids, stuck out her cleavage and said with her best duck lips pout that she would do anything to stay on tour, he knew that she understood the rules of the game. He hadn't even bothered to take her to his casting couch, instead he'd pushed her face down onto his office desk, lifted the tiny little skirt she had on and porked her right there and then, oblivious to anyone who might walk in.

It had been a very arousing experience indeed. Laid over the desk with her skirt hiked up and panties around her ankles, Totthil had looked as good as any porn star on the planet. Unfortunately for Hirt it was over far too quickly. The way she looked and how she felt when he was inside her sent him over the edge in record time. He wasn't sure if Totthil had enjoyed it herself, but whether she did or not meant little to him. He'd had fun and that was all that mattered.

When it was all over Hirt had told Totthil she could continue on with Parry if she wanted so long as she answered his calls. She'd agreed and got out of the office as quick as she could. Hirt had figured he had just said goodbye to the next female winner of the Quickbong Pro, so he was more than a little surprised when she had lost her quarter final heat to Dirty Dy. Judging from how pissed off Totthil was in her post heat interview, he thought he probably wasn't the only one that was surprised at her result.

He realised with all that was going on he probably didn't really have time for sex, so he almost hung up, but thinking about Totthil's sublime rig had got him as horny as fuck.

"Oh well," he thought as he heard Totthil's voice answer the phone. "I didn't last long last time anyway. Maybe I'll just go for a quick blowjob instead?"

Chapter 7 THE PICKER KINK CLUB

The sun was shining brightly in a cloudless sky and there were tanned, masculine, waxed chests on display everywhere as Picker strolled through the Quikbong Pro contest site as happy as a pig in shit. He paused to dig a bit of green magic out of his left nostril, admired his handywork stuck to the end of his finger and flicked it away where he watched it land in the bucket of hot chips an unsuspecting tourist was eating. Picker watched his bit of nose candy merge with some tomato sauce as the tourist disappeared into the crowd before he could see whether the poor guy ate it or not.

The event arena was packed despite the contest being called off for the second day in a row. A shrine to Matt Wilson had been created featuring a large portrait of his smiling face surrounded by flowers, condolence cards and more than a few ladies' panties. Groupies were everywhere hugging each other and crying uncontrollably. Others were there for simple voyeurism in the same way people liked to slow down at the scene of a car crash while striving for a glimpse of a mangled body in the twisted wreckage, just so they could have something to talk about at the pub later that night.

Anyone glancing at Picker would have thought he looked as sad as everyone else despite the fact he was smiling on the inside. It was true that the death of Wilson meant the GSA tour had lost a member that could always be counted on to perform some kind of debauchery that was worth a few dollars, but recently those photos had become repetitive and not very financially rewarding. These days there was always another cock-sure pro surfer on the way up who exhibited the right levels of ego driven narcissistic behaviour to replace Wilson, so that was no great loss.

The real value in his death lay in the most recent footage Picker had taken of a naked Wilson in a threesome with a famous model and equally famous porn star. Those photos and video were now caught in a bidding war and the price was already more than five times what he'd originally hoped to get. Even better, he'd also begun to take orders on his seediest old school Wilson back catalogue.

There was also the collective misery to cash in on. The police were everywhere, and Picker had his zoom lens in hyper drive as he captured every tear shed by pro surfer and groupie alike while they were interviewed in the search for clues. After all, it wasn't inconceivable that if there was a killer, then that person could be amongst this crowd. A shot of him or her looking even slightly guilty with the police talking to them could be worth a lot of money.

Picker's phone rang from a number he recognised as a being from a burner phone that Peter Hirt used when he didn't want it traced back to his role at the GSA. That meant he was probably ringing to provide an update on what price the Wilson photos had got to in the bidding war.

Picker originally marketed his product himself, and he was relatively happy with the prices he had been getting. That all changed when Hirt had got wind of the rumours of Picker's success in capturing the images of Taj Long and Cameron Dimary doing the dirty in the spa. Hirt had immediately called asking what price Picker would sell the whole package for. Picker had thought of his highest number then added some more to it just for the hell of it. He had been very surprised when Hirt claimed he could get more than double that price through his network of contacts. Picker didn't believe him for a second, but figured he had nothing to lose except the agreed 30% commission.

Initially it had sounded like a huge chunk of money that Hirt was claiming just to sell a product Picker could sell himself, but when the record cheque came back from Hirt it had surpassed all his expectations. He'd immediately signed a secret agreement that gave Hirt the exclusive rights to Picker's best work. It was a double win for Picker, as not only was he getting more money for his work, but he was also free to spend a lot more time doing the thing he loved most - hiding out in the bushes with a camera filming people's most private moments.

"Hello Peter. How's life on the Global Extinction Tour?" Picker said laughing at his own poor taste joke.

"Not funny Picker. Geez you're a twisted little bastard. You love this shit don't you!" Hirt snapped in reply.

"Oh and you don't Peter? Tell me the GSA isn't making millions out of all this! You got the Matt Wilson memorial T-Shirts out in record time. I'm at the event site now and every second person is wearing one."

Even by their standards Picker had been impressed at how quickly the GSA and Quikbong's publicity machine had gone to work. It hadn't been much more than 36 hours since Wilson's death before the merchandise was available. Even more impressive was the complete rebranding of the whole site now proclaiming the event as the 'Quikbong Pro – A Decadent Celebration of Matt Wilson'. How they had been able to print up so many banners so quickly amazed Picker. It was almost as if they knew that he was going to die!

"Fuck you Picker," countered Hirt only half seriously. "Do you want to know how those Wilson photos are going or not?"

"What's it at now? Is it still going up?" asked Picker hopefully.

"Sure is. Before he died what were you hoping to get for the package? Maybe ten or twenty thousand? They were hardly unique."

"Something like that yeah."

"Well once I leaked that the footage existed and it was the last of a kind, I got interest from everywhere. The price went up and up until slowly the bidders dropped off. The leading bid at the moment is from a GoPayMe page that a bunch of surfers have set up to try and stop it from being released and get this, it's so they can protect his legacy! Can you believe that?"

"What!" Picker was incredulous. "Do you mean to say there's a chance it won't ever see the light of day?"

"Haha come on Picker, you know me better than that. I've already talked to Gordon Green, the CEO at Quikbong. He said he will pay whatever they raise plus one dollar more if the photos do get released. He's already making a fortune out of the Matt Wilson memorial merchandise and those photos and videos will sell millions more."

"Thank god," breathed Picker with a sigh of relief. "So what's the GoPayMe page at now?"

"It's over two hundred grand and climbing at about ten thousand an hour.

"Fuck are you serious?" Picker exclaimed completely bewildered.

"Yep. How does it feel to make ten grand an hour without lifting a finger? I think I better put my commission up if this keeps going."

"That's good work Pete I'm impressed. When do you think I will get the money?"

"I think we should let it ride until the donations start to slow down. Maybe wait until the contest is over. There will be a point there somewhere where we will have to balance out waiting for a few extra dollars against losing good publicity if we wait too long. And we don't want to piss Gordon Green off either. He will want to see it in the media soon. Better to stay in his good books because we're always going to want to sell him more photos."

"OK that sounds good. I'll let you make the decision on that one. I'm already way ahead of where I thought I would be, so I trust you to make the right call."

"Well then you are smarter than I gave you credit for Picker. At least when this money comes through you can spend it how you want and not hide it like the money from the Slide photos. I'm glad you did the right thing there. I've had a lot of pressure from a lot of people trying to find out who took those."

"Yeah you don't have to tell me twice on that one. That shit has blown out big time. I don't envy your job right now Pete that's for sure. Thanks again mate and call me with the final figure." Picker ended the call. He was so excited he wanted to do a little dance but looking around at all the sad faces he didn't think it would go down too well.

Picker wasn't sure what he would do with the money once he got it, but he had a few ideas. Maybe he would buy himself another sports car? There were a couple of new models he had his eye on. Certainly, he would go and hole up at his favourite Kink Club and get his freak on for a couple of weeks. Hell, he had enough money now to buy the club outright if he wanted to.

"Now there's an idea," he thought happily. "Club Picker or maybe the Picker Kink Club? Yeah, the Picker Kink Club. That has a very nice ring to it!"

Chapter 8 THE NEW ASSIGNMENT

"I'll get straight to the point," said the fat old bastard. "I don't like you one little bit Spidder! You're a cock-sure, arrogant little prick! You think you know everything, you're god's gift to women and your shit smells like roses. You don't give a fuck about authority, you bend the rules and aren't a team player. You probably don't like me either but that means less than two farts in a brothel. I'm your boss and that's the way it's always going to be. In my perfect universe, you would be handing out parking tickets for the rest of your life in some dipshit meth town as far away from the ocean as I could find!"

The conversation certainly wasn't looking promising for Havoc. It was Thursday morning and he'd just been called into Senior Sergeant Bruce 'Smithy' Smith's office. They were in a fairly non-descript office building on a quiet street in the outer suburbs of Sydney. While the building didn't look much from the outside it's what went on inside that was a little more impressive.

The building was a base for the Undercover Branch of the New South Wales police force and technically Havoc's place of work although he rarely set foot in the office himself. When he did there was a protocol to be observed to avoid him being seen coming and going. The fact that Havoc had been called in today to face an irate Smithy suggested something important was happening. The only question was, how bad is it going to be?

Even on a good day the old wanker was never happy, but he seemed to take special pleasure in making Havoc's life hell whenever the opportunity arose. He figured it was probably jealousy because Smithy likely hadn't had a root for twenty years and he knew that a lot of women wouldn't mind Havoc parking his police boots under their beds and showing them his concealed weapon.

Today Smithy looked especially pissed off as he leant back on his poor, abused office chair, hands resting on his ample waistline. An ugly fucker at the best of times, Smithy was considerably overweight, balding and a long-term smoker as evidenced by his yellow, nicotine-stained teeth and the permanent cigarette butt size curl in his upper lip - a result of years of his life spent with a cigarette sitting in the exact same spot in his mouth.

It was hard to believe he was still alive and not dead of cancer or heart disease, let alone the fact that he'd managed to make it so far in the police ranks and not been turfed out for the dinosaur he clearly was. He had the red nose of a long-term alcoholic and a ruddy complexion that got redder and redder the angrier he got. Today that complexion was at about a nine out of ten on the angry fat man meter and threatening to go to Spinal Tap level.

Whatever it was, Havoc was betting he wasn't going to like it one bit.

"You know I can't even begin to believe I'm contemplating saying this to you," continued Smithy as he sat at his desk, clearly agitated beyond all normal levels now. "Someone must have slipped some whacky weed into my morning donut because what I'm about to tell you is probably going to give me nightmares for the rest of my life until Alzheimer's kicks in and I can finally forget that this day was the day my life truly dipped down into the lowest levels of sewer turd sludge imaginable."

"Sorry sir I don't get what you mean?" Havoc said standing there confused.

"I'm about to give you your dream job and it's more painful than anything I can even remotely imagine. I gave more than half of everything I ever earnt in my life to my bitch ex-wife and that felt like a long, soothing blow job compared to this. I mean, fuck, I might just end this conversation now and go and buy a hammer and some nails and pin my ball sack to the noticeboard outside. That would be more fun than what I'm about to do. Do you understand Spidder?"

"Umm, not really sir." Havoc replied but his interest was aroused now. Something was going down and if Smithy didn't like it, then perhaps he would.

"Sit down," Smithy sighed gesturing Havoc to a chair and throwing a stack of papers down in front of him to look at. Havoc did what he was told and a cursory glance at the papers immediately perked his interest further. Suddenly he had an inkling of what this was all about and it took all of his self-control to hide the excited smile from his face. While Havoc read a bit deeper Smithy got up and walked over to his office door. He opened it and called out.

"You can come in now Detective Sergeant!" Smithy held the door open and in walked a familiar face. This time Havoc couldn't hide his smile.

"Hello Dirth, how are you?" said a grinning Detective Sergeant Glen 'Patto' Patinsen. One of the few people who actually called Havoc by his first name.

"Patto! I mean sorry, Detective Sergeant Patinsen. It's good to see you sir," Havoc jumped out of his seat to eagerly shake his mentor's hand. While they both technically worked for the NSW Undercover Branch, DS Patinsen tended to work further afield than Havoc, so they rarely saw each other. "What brings you here sir?"

"This," replied DS Patinsen gesturing to the paperwork Havoc had been looking at. "I know you love your surfing, so you probably know some of what has been happening on their World Tour lately."

"A little bit sir. I know they have lost three of their best male surfers in the past six months. I don't think anyone knows what happened to Jimmy Slide in Bali, but I heard Kalani Johnson might have been poisoned in Hawaii, and I've seen a few news reports about Matt Wilson being found dead up on the Gold Coast a few days ago but that's about it sir."

"Yes, well unfortunately from as far as we can tell, what you just said about covers everything that anyone knows regarding this whole thing," added Smithy seeming to have calmed down a little. The presence of DS Patinsen had that effect on people. It was one of the reasons why Havoc loved him so much. "It's unbelievable to think that three people have kicked the bucket, all fit athletes at the top of their sport and always at or around a big event. Yet no one has a fucking clue! Maybe like me they figured a couple less surfers in the world isn't such a bad thing!"

"What we do know," interjected DS Patinsen scowling at his senior officer. "Is the result of the toxicology tests the Queensland Police performed on Matt Wilson's body. It seems he had quite the cocktail in him. They found traces of alcohol and cocaine, albeit none of them at dangerous levels. He'd also consumed a decent amount of Viagra but again nothing that should have adverse effects on a fit young man. What has sent everyone into panic mode though, is that they also found significant amounts of Fentanyl in his system. More than enough to kill him."

"Okay wow!" Havoc immediately grasped the significance of the information. "So, you think he might have been murdered and not an accidental overdose?"

"It looks that way," replied DS Patinsen. "Everyone the police interviewed described Wilson as a very happy person who loved drugs but rarely touched anything other than a few beers when there was a contest on. There's no indication he might have been upset in any way that might have led to him deliberately overdosing on fentanyl himself. I suppose it's possible, but it seems highly unlikely especially when you consider the Hawaiian police also found significant traces of fentanyl in Kalani Johnson's body. The traces were lower in Johnson's case but still probably enough to kill him if hitting his head on the rocks didn't take care of him first."

"And so based on that you think that Jimmy Slide might also have been killed?" Havoc wondered.

"It has to be a possibility Dirth," answered DS Patinsen. "But the truth is we may never know. I'm sure you are aware that Slide's body was accidently cremated before any tests were done. And then there's that weird, sexual position he was found in that doesn't fit with the other two, but there's enough similarities that we need to keep him in the investigation."

"So, there's a chance that we could have a serial killer knocking off pro surfers for fun," Smithy added delightedly. "And while personally I want to give him a medal, there's people higher up the food chain that want him caught. With the first two dead being much loved American citizens, the FBI has already contacted the Police Commissioner here. Apparently even their President has called our Prime Minister to express an interest in the proceedings if you can believe that! All of which means the poor Queensland police are now under the pump from all angles to solve the case. They've reached out to us for help and that's where you come in unfortunately."

"But how do I go undercover?" Havoc asked. "The surf industry is pretty tight and you can't just waltz in there and say, 'Hey I'm a pro surfer, can you point me to the guy who is going around killing you guys for fun'. They will smell an imposter from a mile away!"

"Yeah right!" Smithy snorted. "That lot of pencil dicks don't think about anything other than their next roll in the hay or where they can score a bag of weed. But even if they did, you leaking fart sack, your little stunt last month when you should have been working the meth lab case has given you a chance to sneak in through a side door if you play it right."

"I'm sorry sir I don't know what you mean?" Havoc lied. Technically he was supposed to be working when that last big swell had hit, but he'd only taken a few hours off and nobody had said anything in the weeks since, so he thought he'd got away with it. Perhaps he hadn't. "What stunt are you talking about?"

"Oh come on Spidder!" Smithy raged. "Do you really think I'm that stupid that what you get up to doesn't find its way back to me one way or another? You should know there's no secrets with the internet, I've seen the article 'The Mysterious Havoc Defies Death at Cape Fear'. I seem to recall the only storm that has hit this region in months is when you should have been undercover at Redfern finding that meth lab cooking the dodgy shit that sent those junkies to hospital. Not floating around the ocean seeking glory like some jumped up peacock!"

Havoc was surprised his Senior Sergeant even knew the internet existed, let alone use it to catch him in the act. The case had been going nowhere, taking a few hours off for a surf would have only meant a few extra bags of meth on the street at worst. Hardly anything to lose sleep over given the sheer volume available to any junkie with half a clue. Missing the first decent swell for months on the other hand, well he was pretty sure if he hadn't gone surfing, he may well have been arrested himself for taking out his gun and shooting every meth head in Redfern just for kicks.

"You look surprised Spidder," Smithy was on a roll now. "Perhaps next time you might want to think twice about dragging a photographer along to boost your ego. The very fact that you thought I might not find out makes me wonder if you're more stupid than you look. Are you stupid Spidder? Should I just forget this whole thing? Maybe I'm the one that's stupid for even considering this?" Smithy's complexion was now back to a nine. If Havoc looked closer, he felt sure he would see steam coming out of those bright red ears any second.

"I'm not stupid sir and neither are you. I'm still not sure how a couple of photos on the internet can get me undercover with the world's best surfers though?" Havoc was becoming a little flustered by Smithy's tirade.

"Steady Bruce, you will give yourself a heart attack," DS Patinsen jumped in before Smithy could continue his rant. Once again he was the voice of calm reason. He turned his attention to Havoc. "Dirth years ago you came bursting through my front door all excited because you had got your first sponsor. Do you remember that?"

"How could I forget?" Havoc replied. "That was a special day for me."

"And that sponsor was Homegrown Maniacs wasn't it?"

"Yes I'm still sponsored by them now. Although I don't bother asking them for too much these days. I don't need it, but they still chuck me some clothes and a bit of cash each year."

"Good I was hoping that would be the case. Then you must know the owner of Homegrown Maniacs?"

"Morpheus? Yeah I know him reasonably well. He seems a good guy. He's actually one of the few people who knows I went to the Police Academy. I'm not sure if he knows I'm undercover these days or thinks I just didn't make it. Why's that sir?"

"Morpheus? I thought his name was Kalgan Reid?"

"It is sir. His nickname is Morpheus. He's a bit of a conspiracy theorist. He's not big on governments and corporations controlling the whole world. Loves the Matrix movies so he gets called Morpheus."

"Sounds like a smart man," observed DS Patinsen.

"Sounds like a fucking idiot to me!" Smithy interrupted grumpily.

"In any case here's what we want you to do," DS Patinsen continued on smoothly. "First, get yourself on the next flight to the Gold Coast. We want you up there right now while the competition is still going and the killer is possibly still there. Now if I remember correctly you used to be friends and compete against Matt Wilson and that Bunker Haze character when you were younger. Were you still in contact with them?"

"Not really sir," replied Havoc impressed by his mentor's depth of memory. No wonder he was such a respected detective. "I've still got their phone numbers, and I've randomly surfed with them occasionally over the past few years. We've said hello and had a bit of a chat out in the water but that's about it. I mean our lives have gone down two different paths. They've been travelling all over the world living the party life and are almost never home. As far as they're aware I've been labouring on building sites around Sydney not doing much at all."

"We would like you to renew your friendship with Bunker Haze if possible," continued DS Patinsen. "Wilson's body was found at Haze's condo and while the police up there don't think he's involved they can't be sure. For all we know he could even be the next target. In any case he's still in the competition so he should be pretty easy to find for you. I'll be your handler for the time you are on this assignment, so you report to me directly and only to me. There will be no need for you to make contact with the local police at any stage unless you are in an emergency situation. Is that clear Dirth?"

"Yes sir!" Havoc replied incredibly grateful that he would be working with his mentor on what was easily the biggest assignment of his life so far.

"Good. Now I don't want you doing anything special. Certainly nothing risky. All I want you to do is get reacquainted with Haze and see if you can learn anything that the police investigation hasn't already turned up. Other than that, I just want you to wander around the contest area like any other interested spectator and listen to the gossip. You're a surfer. You can communicate with surfers far better than uniformed police can. See what you can uncover that way. But only to the end of the contest. After that the second part of the plan is more difficult."

"In what way sir?"

"You asked Senior Sergeant Smith before about why those photos of you were significant. Well, we would like you to use them and your friendship with this Morpheus fellow as leverage to convince him to give you a wildcard into the contest at Margaret River. I believe that Homegrown Maniacs are the naming rights sponsor for the event and have two wildcard spots available for anyone they choose."

"You want me to actually go in a surf contest?" Havoc couldn't quite believe what he was hearing.

"Now Spidder, this is not an excuse to go on a fucking surf holiday! Do you understand?" Smithy interjected. Suddenly he'd become Havoc's new hero, he had to have agreed to this for it to be happening. "I hope you see it for the opportunity it is and not fuck it up. You are on the thinnest of ice with this one and while normally I wouldn't give a flying fart if you blew it and became a security guard at a supermarket, my neck is on the line here too!"

"He's right Dirth," added DS Patinsen. "I know you well enough to know what you are thinking right now and I won't have it either. If there is a serial killer out there, then they have killed one victim at each of the past three events. There are two more events left in Australia for this person if he or she wants to keep going at the same pace. I don't think I need to tell you what a serious media and political shitstorm will occur if it happens again and we don't catch the killer."

"Yes sir!" replied Havoc but his mind was already elsewhere. This was a dream come true! He had always fantasized about competing on the GSA World Tour and now he had his chance so long as he could convince Morpheus to give him a wildcard. Not only that, there was always a chance the waves could get huge at Margaret River and that suited Havoc just fine thank you very much.

"If you have no more questions then you're dismissed," said Smithy disgustedly. "Oh and Spidder,"

"Yes Sir?"

"Wipe that fucking smile off your face before I change my mind!"

"Yes sir. Thank you sir!"

Chapter 9 GOOD TIMING

Bunker was crying again. He didn't know how long it had been since he'd last cried so much but it was probably when 'Buttons' the dog he'd grown up with, a blue heeler/kelpie cross, had to be put down. Bunker had really only had two good friends in his life thanks to his less than normal upbringing. Buttons had been one, Matt Wilson had been the other. Now he had lost both of them.

Childhood hadn't been easy on Bunker even though he never wanted for anything in his life. Being the only child of a billionaire and a model came with its own set of issues that few could understand. He was constantly in the spotlight and had to deal with cameras being shoved in his face from a very early age. He rarely saw his parents, his father was always too busy making his next big billion-dollar media deal and while his mum was there for him occasionally, she was nearly always off her head on drugs of some kind. So it was mostly left to a procession of carers to provide what little adult guidance and companionship Bunker received as he grew up.

School held little attraction for Bunker either. Naturally he had attended the most expensive private boarding schools in the region, but making friends was hard for the quietly spoken kid who cared only for the next time he could get to the beach. What his peers thought important, like playing team sports such as football, rugby or cricket and who's dad was making the most money, held no interest for him.

It was on a weekend at the beach that Bunker first met Matt Wilson. At ten years of age Bunker had already caught the surfing bug and he spent every possible second playing in the whitewash on the beach in front of his mansion on his brand-new Aloha surfboard. Somehow he became aware of Wilson in amidst the vast array of multi-cultural human weirdness that flocked to his beach every summer weekend. Wilson was just another little kid hidden amongst the local regular beach goers - the pasty white English tourists, large groups of Asians who couldn't swim, various local ethnic minorities like the Lebanese and Italians, a random collection of druggos and alcoholics recovering from last night's bender and his favourites- the slim, tanned European and South American goddesses.

Bunker immediately recognised a kindred spirit in Wilson. They could easily have been confused for brothers or even twins as they both were skinny little runts with freckled sunburned faces, short curly sun-bleached blonde hair and big white toothy smiles. The only difference was that while Bunker had all the latest clothing and surf accessories, Wilson wore a pair of old faded Quikbong board shorts passed down to him from his brothers and rode an ancient, sun-yellowed Hot Buttered surfboard that was covered in badly fixed dings.

Unlike Bunker, Wilson knew all about what it was like to go without something. He attended the public school with the worst reputation in the area and he lived with his single mother, two older brothers and a younger sister in a government welfare house several suburbs back from the beach. His dad had taken off when he was five and disappeared overseas never to be seen again, leaving his poor mum sole responsibility for the upbringing of four kids. Consequently she worked long hours, which left the kids to look after themselves and each other through much of their upbringing.

Despite the differences in their background, Bunker and Wilson both sort solace in the surf to wash away the problems associated with their lives. That shared love and connection with the ocean created a friendship that had been rock solid ever since. In no time they were swapping boards and marvelling at what each other had. Wilson could not believe what it was like to have such a light, shiny board under has feet and Bunker for his part was amazed at how much easier it was to stand up on the bigger, thicker and more practical surfboard that was Wilson's old pride and joy.

Bunker had been reluctant to mention his house was the huge mansion easily seen from where they were standing on the beach, perhaps fearing it would drive a wedge in their blossoming friendship. Instead, he was deliberately as vague as he could be about his life, casually saying he lived nearby and his dad worked away a lot. By the time he let on about where he lived and that he was heir to a media empire worth billions, they were already inseparable mates.

It wasn't long before Wilson spent most weekends staying at Bunker's home. Every daylight hour would see the two in the ocean on their surfboards and the nights were dedicated to talking about surfing and as they got older, girls.

With their improving surfing skills, Bunker began to use the perks of having an endless bank account to ensure that they were driven to wherever they thought the best waves would be on the coast that day. So long as he still went to school, Bunker's dad didn't care what he did on the weekends. Once Rupert Haze passed away his mum was happy to have him out of the house so she could bang the pool boy or whatever latest maintenance man took her fancy.

Wilson's mum was glad that her son had found a true friend and that some of the pressure of looking after four kids was relieved each weekend. She was understandably shocked and more than a little concerned the first time a limousine pulled up in her driveway one Friday after school to collect Wilson, but much of the fear was allayed when the beautiful, bright smile of a beaming Bunker Haze stepped out of the limo, introduced himself and yelled out to Wilson to 'hurry up coz the surf's pumping!'. She had to admit it was quite the comical site to see two scruffy surf grommets casually throw wax covered surfboards and salt encrusted wetsuits into the plush, very expensive interior of the limo and pile in next to them while still wearing their grass-stained school uniforms and mud-covered shoes.

Pretty soon they were entering local surf contests together and doing very well thanks to the advantages gained from travelling up and down the coast surfing a variety of waves. The contests were almost solely Wilson's idea. His impoverished upbringing had instilled a bit of competitive mongrel in him and a desire to do well. He dreamt of maybe one day become a professional surfer so he could buy a real house for his mum.

Bunker didn't care much for the contests and really only entered them because that's what Wilson wanted to do. The first time he had watched Wilson win a local contest, the look of wonder on his friend's face when he received his prizes of a legrope, a couple of pairs of shorts, some surf DVD's and a cheap trophy, was very confusing. Why did his friend care so much about winning a few cheap items that Bunker regularly gave to him anyway?

The answer came to Bunker when almost by accident he had won his first contest. It was a round of the New South Wales state titles held at a beautiful beach up the coast near Forster. He'd only entered because Wilson had asked him for help to get to the event as he had heard that some of the talent scouts from GoMerch, Quikbong, Ricool and Homegrown Maniacs might be there looking for the next up and coming surfer to sponsor. Bunker had reluctantly agreed and on a whim he entered the contest himself. He figured that at least he'd get to have a surf with only a couple of guys in the water while he stayed around to cheer his mate on.

What Bunker didn't count on was that the waves would be absolutely pumping for the contest. Right in front of the event scaffolding was the most perfect waves he had ever seen in his young life. It was a grommets dream with incredible glassy, barrelling beach break waves that seemed to peel for ever. The only trouble was that he could only surf them while in a heat and a 20-minute heat surfing those waves was nowhere near enough. The only way to surf such heaven longer was to keep winning heats, so that's what Bunker set out to do.

In the end Bunker went through the whole event undefeated. Wilson and Bunker were clearly the best two surfers in their age group and they met in the semifinal where Bunker just got the nod in a close heat. He then went on to smash his opponent in the final with the first ever perfect heat score of 20 out of 20 in a State Title.

When Bunker first stepped onto the podium to collect his prizes his initial feelings were more confused than anything. He'd felt a bit sad that he'd beaten his mate and although Wilson had said he'd been really happy for Bunker, he couldn't help but feeling some guilt for robbing Wilson of a chance to win in front of the potential sponsors he craved to impress. He'd also felt guilty because it had all been far too easy. Here were all these competitors that felt winning was everything. They trained, they analysed heats with their coaches, they talked strategy and when they paddled out they were 100% focused on winning any way they could. Bunker just caught waves and surfed them. His entire strategy had been to surf waves well so he could surf more of them.

But when the announcer excitedly talked about how amazing Bunker's waves had been in the final while handing him the trophy and the crowd cheered, Bunker felt something else. Something he hadn't really felt at all in his life up until then, pride. Pride in his achievements, pride in doing something for himself without the aid of his father's money (new surfboards and luxury travel aside of course) and pride in acceptance. He'd always been the weird kid at the rich school with no mates but now he was among people that understood him. They were surfers too and those surfers were now slapping him on the back and telling him how good he was. That part was a little uncomfortable for Bunker, but the tribal acceptance spoke to his core. This group of people liked Bunker for who he was and not how much money his dad was worth.

As the State Titles wore on, the sponsors had come snooping when it became obvious to everyone watching that Wilson and Bunker were the clear standouts. Wilson loved it and showed he had a shrewd head on his young shoulders as he played them off against each other seeking the best offer possible. His time spent growing up in government housing had taught him all he needed to know about getting the most out of any financial situation. Gordon Green at Quikbong won the right to add Wilson to his team and he rung his mum excitedly to get her to sign the contract on his behalf.

Bunker didn't really like Gordon Green, or most of the other industry reps that approached him that day, eager to get him to sign a piece of paper that he didn't understand. They reminded him too much of his father's slimy business associates. Besides which he had all the money in the world, and he didn't need any of the free stuff they were offering. The only person he did like was that guy with the weird name from Homegrown Maniacs, Morpheus.

Unlike the rest, Morpheus had done his homework before the event. A friend of his, who was a gun local surf coach- Drew Kling - had given Morpheus the heads up that Bunker was a potentially once in a generation natural talent. Morpheus trusted Kling implicitly and immediately did an internet search on Bunker. Understandably given who his father was, there were pages and pages of information on Bunker, and it was clear to Morpheus that he wouldn't be swayed by the usual promises of money and free product. In the end his sales pitch had been simple but incredibly effective.

Morpheus had observed Bunker from afar for most of the competition. Noting his closeness with Wilson and the way the two of them focussed solely on the surf and let nothing else distract them except the odd girl walking past. He'd left him alone and bided his time while all the other suit wearing industry reps had made their pitch, then sauntered up wearing nothing but boardshorts, a t-shirt and thongs.

"How ya going kid?" asked the tall, lanky Morpheus.

"Pretty good," Bunker replied shyly as he looked up suspiciously at Morpheus.

"Surf's pumping hey. Might even get better when the tide drops."

"You think so? Gee it's pretty amazing already. I can't even imagine it being better."

"Yeah, you might be right kid. These are the best waves I've seen at a competition for a long time. As soon as I saw them, I tried to enter the Open Division just so I could surf with only a couple of guys in the water. I was spewing there were no spots available."

"Do you surf too?" Bunker asked, feeling a little more comfortable talking with this stranger when it was about his favourite subject.

"Of course lad! Do you think I'd be here if I didn't surf?"

"But you're that guy from Homegrown Maniacs aren't you? None of those guys in suits from the other companies surf. I don't understand why they were talking to me if they didn't surf?"

"That's a good question kid and it proves you're a smart lad. My name is Kalgan Reid, but you can call me Morpheus." Morpheus offered his hand and Bunker shook it.

"I'm Bunker Haze. You can just call me Bunker."

"Well it's nice to meet you Bunker. You surf good kid. I like your style. Hopefully I will see you around in the surf sometime." Morpheus turned to wander off hoping that Bunker had taken the bait.

"Wait," called Bunker as Morpheus had taken his first couple of steps away. "Don't you want me to be on your team? Everyone else does."

"You're right lad. I'd love to have you on my team. But you don't need money or clothes. What do you want?"

"I don't know," said Bunker sheepishly. "I hadn't really thought about that."

"Okay well how about I take you surfing to a secret spot I know that might be perfect tomorrow? Guaranteed nobody out. Perfect lefthander. You can have a think on the way in the car and tell me what you want then."

"That sounds wicked! Can my friend Matt come too?" Bunker asked, his eyes lighting up in anticipation.

"Haha of course. I knew you wouldn't go anywhere without him."

Later on, back at the hotel room, the boys excitedly swapped stories about their new sponsors while each holding their trophies. That night was the first time ever that Bunker and Wilson had got drunk, and the next morning was the first of many times they would surf hungover together.

Morpheus was true to his word, and he drove them to a secret spot where they surfed perfect waves with not a soul around. He never did ask what Bunker wanted to be on his team, but over the next few years he regularly got on the phone to Bunker and took the boys surfing to remote hidden spots that few knew about. In many ways he was the father figure they both needed and he never begrudged Wilson surfing for an opposition company. As for Bunker, well the next time Morpheus picked him up to go surfing he was wearing a brand-new set of Homegrown Maniacs clothing that he had bought himself and his board was covered in HGM stickers. In the years since he was rarely seen wearing anything else, despite never having signed a contract to be on the team.

Morpheus had been the first to phone Bunker when the news leaked that Wilson had been found dead in his apartment. Bunker had been a blubbering mess when he took the call and four days later not much had changed. His phone was still ringing and the tears were never far away.

He'd been like a zombie on auto pilot. He was alive and breathing but not much else. Except for when he had a heat.

After the police had let him go his first thought had been to call up his drug suppliers and go on an absolute bender to completely numb himself to the pain of his loss. The first batch of drugs had arrived, and he was in the process of packing a cone when he got a call from Peter Hirt advising him that the contest would restart and its name had been changed in dedication to Matt Wilson.

For some reason that struck a chord with Bunker. He'd never won a GSA world surfing competition. He hadn't been competitive enough and didn't care enough to string a complete series of heat wins together all at once to win the whole thing. The fame, the groupies and watching Wilson do well had been enough for him. Now he wasn't sure if anything would be enough for him again, but what he did know was that if there was to be a contest dedicated to his best mate, then there was only one person who was going to win it.

After he hung up, Bunker flushed the recently purchased drugs down the toilet and then gone out and destroyed his opponents in the early heats on his way to a berth in the semifinals due to start tomorrow. He knew he could win but there was just one problem. It had now been the longest Bunker had gone without drugs or alcohol in his system since he was in his teens and his body was starting to let him know about it. Along with the crying he was shaking, scratching at himself and sleep was eluding him. Bunker had to admit that he was suffering some pretty nasty withdrawal symptoms.

"Fuck it," thought Bunker reaching for his phone to call in another supply of drugs. "I'll just have a little bit to take the edge off." But as he was about to dial his dealer's number the phone rang on its own accord. He looked to see who it was and was more than surprised to see the name staring back at him.

"Havoc dude! It's been a long time!" Bunker was startled by the depth of emotion he felt answering Havoc's call.

"Yeah hello Bunker, I know we haven't talked for ages but I just wanted to ring and say I'm really sorry about Matt. He was a good guy and I know you both loved each other dearly." Havoc said respectfully.

"Thanks Havoc. I've been struggling mate. I keep expecting to turn around and he will be there laughing at me, telling me it was all a big joke and everything is going to go back to normal," Bunker sighed choking back tears. "But I know it never will."

"Yeah mate I know how that feels. I was the same when my old man died. I wish I could say it gets better, but it doesn't really. Not with people you are that close to anyway. Over time you will eventually get used to it and the pain will dull, but it never fully goes away."

"Maybe that's a good thing though," said Bunker trying to be positive. "At least then I will always keep a part of him with me."

"That's a nice way to look at it Bunker. Hey listen mate, I just wanted to ring and let you know that I'm on the Gold Coast too. Came up for a bit of a break. So if I can do anything, or if you need someone to talk to don't hesitate to reach out. Sometimes it's not good to be alone in these situations. It can give space to let some pretty dark thoughts into your head."

"I'm okay Havoc but thanks for the offer," Bunker replied but then he remembered he had been about to call his drug dealer. "On second thoughts mate I think I might take you up on that. I've got a contest to win tomorrow so why don't you come around and we can talk tactics."

"Sounds like a good plan. Where abouts are you?"

"I'm staying at a hotel in Kirra. I couldn't face another second in that condo. I think that place will always have bad memories for me now. I'll probably sell it."

"Ok no worries. I'll bring a pizza and a couple of beers. See you soon."

"Yeah seeya mate. Thanks." Bunker hung up glad that Havoc had called. His timing had been spot on. A few minutes more and he probably would have been too wasted to even look at his phone and once he got started, he wasn't sure he would have been able to stop. Havoc had been right about the dark thoughts too. Bunker had felt the darkness creeping in, threatening to overwhelm him.

Now the darkness had receded a little and Bunker found that, for the moment at least, the tears had stopped.

Chapter 10 THE QUIKBONG PRO FINAL

Havoc had to pinch himself just to prove that he wasn't dreaming. Almost exactly 48 hours earlier he had been sitting in that office in Sydney watching little beads of spit fly out of Smithy's mouth while he was on his epic rant. Now, courtesy of Bunker Haze, Havoc sat up in the VIP area basking in the sun while overlooking the huge crowd waiting for the men's final of the Quikbong Pro to start.

Any second now Bunker would appear surrounded by security to paddle out and do battle against the Brazilian - Gabriel 'The Terminator' Andre - for the record million-dollar first place winners' cheque in perfect six foot Snapper Rocks. The crowd was massive! Surely the biggest ever to assemble for a surf contest anywhere in the world. It was a Saturday and the whole Gold Coast must have taken advantage of the day off to come down and be part of the action. While a large proportion of the crowd was naturally cheering for Bunker to complete the fairy tale and win his first ever GSA World Tour competition in the event dedicated to his best friend, there was still a huge number of manic, flag waving Brazilian fans who were loudly cheering for their hero as well.

The result was a wall of sound that reached fever pitch when the two athletes emerged from the competitor's area, boards under their arms, ready to make their way out into the surf zone. Havoc couldn't believe the depth of energy the crowd was creating. It gave him goose bumps! The only thing he'd experienced like it in his life before was when he had been lucky enough to attend an Australian Rules Football Grand Final at the MCG with his father where 100,000 spectators cheered for their team. That had been louder, but it was in a purpose built stadium. This was on a beach!

Havoc had stayed up with Bunker until about two in the morning. He didn't need to talk much or employ any subtle interrogation tactics to get Bunker to open up. Almost as soon as he had walked through the door and gave Bunker a hug, his friend had burst into tears, and everything had come pouring out like an infected wound that needed to be drained before it could heal.

Bunker retold the story of finding his friend dead in the spa and the horror of having to keep repeating what happened over and over to the police while they tried to find out if he was involved or not. The embarrassment he felt when they found his stash of drugs and of not being able to remember any of the girl's names that had been with him. Then the guilty relief when his driver had called to advise him that one of their ID's had been found in the limo. He talked of the pain he felt when talking to Matt Wilson's mother who would never see her little boy again and the different kind of pain he felt talking to his own mum, who was too high on drugs to really comprehend the loss he was feeling.

He told a dozen stories of adventures that he and Wilson had got up to over the years, the waves they had surfed around the world together, the girls they had been with and the drugs they had taken. He confessed he wanted to win the event badly for his friend and for reasons unknown to him, wanted to do it without the aid of drugs, but he was worried that his body would let him down as it was already rebelling against the lack of some sort of narcotic in his system. He had been getting periods where he shook uncontrollably and hadn't had any real sleep since the morning he walked out onto his balcony and his world had changed forever.

As he listened, Havoc could not help but feel a profound depth of sadness for Bunker. He'd known him for a long time as growing up the three of them often surfed together or occasionally competed against each other in local surf contests. They had been friends of a sort, but Wilson and Bunker were a dynamic duo who were so consumed by the depth of their own friendship that there was rarely room for a third person. Now that Wilson was gone, Bunker was the loneliest person on the planet and all the money and talent in the world couldn't change that.

As the night wore on, they shared a couple of beers and the stories kept flowing. Slowly Bunker seemed to relax and as he laid down on the couch Havoc could see that maybe precious sleep wasn't too far away.

"You got your alarm set for the morning bro?" Havoc asked. "Don't want you missing your heat."

"Yeah it's set," Bunker replied.

"We still haven't talked tactics about how you're going to win this thing."

"Don't need to. I'm going to smash the lot of them," Bunker yawned. Minutes later he was asleep. Havoc had got up and quietly let himself out.

And now, as the hooter sounded for the start of the final, Bunker had the chance to do exactly that. Both surfers paddled constantly against the sweep of the current which was trying to drag them out of position. At the start of any heat no surfer has priority to catch the first wave. So it can be a no holds barred, dog eat dog, paddle battle with arms, feet and elbows flying to see who is in the best position when the first set comes. After that the rotation begins and each surfer takes turns.

One of several reasons Gabriel Andre had earned the nickname 'The Terminator' was that he was ruthless in the opening paddle battle. He was supremely strong and incredibly fit and he loved to use that initial clash of tactics, ego, bravado and physical contact to fire himself up for the rest of the heat. It was a tactic that Andre was well known for. A lot of surfers would get sucked into the contest and try to beat The Terminator at his own game. It rarely worked but the problem was, if you sat back and let him have the first wave, it might be a good one and then he was off to a flying start and would be hard to overtake. It was a big reason why he was so hard to beat and, with the death of three of the world's best surfers, why he was odds on favourite to win his fourth world title at the end of the year.

Bunker let Andre have the inside position, so it appeared he wasn't interested in a paddle battle. A tactic that Havoc felt wasn't a bad one seeing as Bunker was a soul surfer who was at his best when he wasn't thinking about anything else and was just in a natural rhythm with the ocean. Bunker also had a slight advantage in that he was a 'Natural Foot' who surfed with his left foot forward. It meant he would be facing the wave as he took off which made it easier to negotiate the difficult backwash the rocks at Snapper created as he was jumping to his feet.

Andre on the other hand was a 'Goofy Foot' and surfed with his right foot forward which meant he had his back to the wave. What advantage Bunker may have had though, was negated by the fact that Andre was considered the best goofy foot surfer in the world in these types of conditions and had been in dozens of finals while this was Bunker's first.

The crowd could see the first set approaching and the noise level lifted dramatically. Andre was still on the inside and Bunker showed no signs that he wanted to fight for it. They both let the first wave go as the waves behind were clearly bigger. The second wave looked amazing but both surfers could see another even bigger wave behind it.

The Brazilians in the crowd began going mad. They were whistling and shouting and waving their flags furiously. Havoc felt he knew what Andre would do. With Bunker giving him first choice of the wave Andre wanted, he would have a half-hearted attempt at the second wave, just enough to make sure Bunker didn't catch it, before turning and sprinting out to catch the third. That way he would make sure he would be the only surfer to catch a wave in the first set.

As the second wave approached Bunker closed in a little and showed some interest in catching it, Andre saw him coming and moved to block him from paddling any further to the inside but still Bunker didn't appear to really care and was more just looking at Andre as if to say "Just pick one mate. Get it over with and I will get the next one." As the second wave lifted on the sand bank and prepared to break, Andre took a couple more half-hearted paddles to make sure Bunker wasn't going, then started to pull back to turn around to catch the next one.

It was that exact moment that Bunker had been waiting for and he struck like lightening. It was so sudden that almost nobody saw it coming, much less Gabriel Andre. Those couple of paddles Andre had taken and the extra momentum generated from the wave moving towards the beach had pushed him in a metre more than he would have liked. Bunker already had the nose of his surfboard pointed out to sea and he put his head down and sprint paddled as hard as he could trying to get behind Andre and out towards the third wave.

It took a second for Andre to realise what Bunker was doing. He'd been lulled into a false sense of security by all of Bunkers previous indifference and was caught off guard. Now both the Brazilians and Australians in the crowd roared as Andre took off after Bunker in a genuine, balls to the wall, paddle battle.

Bunker's trick had given him maybe a half board length lead on Andre, but the Brazilian was all over him clawing at his elbow and board as their arms clashed with each stroke. As the third and final wave in the set loomed largest of all on the bank both surfers were kicking and paddling furiously, sending up great plumes of white water that almost hid them from view.

Through all this Bunker maintained the slightest of leads over Andre, but it started to look to be all for nothing as the wave appeared as it would beat them both by breaking too far out. Andre seemed to think so too as he backed off slightly, perhaps conceding that Bunker had won but still paddling hard, forcing Bunker more and more into a position where it would be impossible to take off. Now the crowd was going berserk! Havoc couldn't help himself. He jumped to his feet and began screaming encouragement with the rest of them.

The wave stood high and began to pitch out. Bunker swung around impossibly late under the lip, took two quick paddles and jumped to his feet. Behind him Andre appeared to 'accidently' get caught in Bunker's surfboard leash. Suddenly Bunker was off balance and appeared to stumble as he tried to get his fins to engage while freefalling down the face of the wave. He lost all his speed and just before he was about to fall a huge section of wave tubed over the top off him and he disappeared from view.

The event commentator, Havoc and most of the rest of the crowd all groaned in disbelief as the wave continued to tube perfectly with Bunker nowhere to be seen. It had been a hell of a gutsy effort, but it was going to cost him a few minutes to get back into position and potentially a broken board. The wave spat air and water out of the tube as it compressed and continued to peel down the long sand bank. Anyone who had some hope Bunker might have survived gave up and cast their eyes back out to where Andre was sitting in anticipation of his first wave.

Suddenly there was a huge roar and Bunker came flying out of the tube and into a scintillating carve on the wave face before disappearing into another tube. This time there was no doubt about whether he would make it or not and when he emerged, he went straight into a series of blistering turns, each bigger and more radical than the last before finishing in the shore break with a huge aerial 360.

Everybody in the crowd went ballistic! Even the Brazilians. It was a moment that no one who watched it live, either at the beach, in a pub, or online would ever forget. There was only one place the judges could go with that kind of wave and within seconds the score was on the board.

All five judges gave it a perfect 10.

Chapter 11 THE KILLER

Like Havoc, The Killer was sitting in the VIP stands watching Bunker's amazing wave, rising with the packed beach and cheering as he had emerged from nowhere to instant glory and the adulation of the crowd. The Killer had seen enough to know who would win now. The momentum was with Bunker and nothing short of an act of God would save Gabriel Andre, but The Killer already knew that God didn't exist otherwise The Killer would already have been caught and put in jail.

The Killer wanted to leave and prepare for big future plans, but to leave now might arouse some suspicion. All around sat surf industry bigwigs chatting excitedly about what they were witnessing. This was set to be a momentous occasion and anyone leaving before it was over might attract unwanted attention and The Killer was learning to be nothing but careful.

The lessons learned from Kalani Johnson's demise spoke volumes. He should never have been able to paddle out and surf that day. Had he not hit his head on the reef, well who knows what secrets he might have been able to tell? Still the end result was all that mattered, wasn't it? And it seemed the Hawaiian police were no closer to an answer as the Indonesian police were in finding out what happened to Jimmy Slide. Even The Killer didn't know all the details there.

Matt Wilson was different. This time the planning was sound, but the Killer discovered the best plans in the world are worth nothing if the players in the game don't do what you expect. The Killer had needed to adapt and think on the fly. The result was a heightened adrenaline rush like nothing before. Unfortunately, it had faded all too quickly and already there was a yearning for more, a need to take it to another level.

The Killer wasn't doing it just for fun. No, that had been a more than pleasant bonus discovered along the way. There had always been a reason behind The Killer's actions, a goal worth striving to attain. Although, if that ultimate purpose hadn't been totally clear at first, it certainly was now.

The final ended and The Killer tried to slip away relatively unnoticed amongst the crowd. There was a lot to consider and so much delicious anticipation to savour. Did the result change anything? It was certainly unexpected.

Well, no doubt the cards would fall one way or another, but one thing was for certain, Margaret River was going to be a lot of fun…

Chapter 12 THE WILDCARD

Havoc had rewatched that wave online at least a dozen times since he'd left the beach. Now, while he waited for his flight back to Sydney, he logged on to watch it again. No matter how many times he viewed it, Havoc still found it hard to believe that Bunker had made that incredible tube.

Even the water angle, filmed from a jet ski and looking straight into the barrel, didn't give too many clues as to how he had done it. Bunker could be seen regaining his balance a half second after he had disappeared from the sight of the spectators on the beach, but he had no speed left and had been swallowed by the foam ball inside the tube. The tube had breathed then compressed spitting heavy mist out the exit and for a good couple of seconds Bunker couldn't even be seen from the jet ski. Yet somehow he'd pushed through that foam ball still standing on his board and had stayed in the tube, hidden from the beach for what seemed like ages, before emerging with another puff of mist, long blonde hair flowing behind him like some sort of God of the Seven Seas.

Havoc had heard stories about how the late, great Michael 'MP' Peterson used to get so deep in the tube on the Gold Coast point breaks that you couldn't see him and the only way you knew he was still in there was that he would whistle at you to keep off his wave. Havoc hadn't really believed that was possible until now. Bunker had done an MP.

Bunker later backed that wave up with a 9 point ride and in the end Gabriel Andre just couldn't touch him. Bunker had crushed The Terminator and won the event dedicated to his only real friend like he had sleepily promised he would do earlier that morning. He was chaired up the beach by Luke Perrot and Morpheus with tears in his eyes already overcome with the emotion of the moment.

Onstage he accepted his winner's cheque and giant trophy from Gordon Green then broke down again and started crying unashamedly while trying to deliver his acceptance speech in front of tens of thousands of new adoring fans. Everyone who witnessed Bunker's moment on the podium couldn't help but be affected as well. Everywhere Havoc had looked in the crowd he could see people crying too. Even Gabriel Andre, known for his lack of emotion, gave Bunker a genuine hug and perhaps quickly wiped a little moisture from his eyes when he thought the crowd couldn't see him. It had been a special moment that brought everybody together. A rare flash of true soul in the modern world of hedonistic, ego driven professional surfing.

Bunker would later announce that he would donate his entire million-dollar winner's prize towards setting up 'The Matt Wilson Foundation' to help kids from impoverished areas around the world learn to surf. When asked by a reporter why he didn't at least donate some of the money to the GoPayMe page set up to stop the last photos of Wilson's threesome being published he replied "Hell no! He would love that shit! Whoever started that page should donate it to his family or the new foundation. Willo' loved seeing his pecker in the magazines!" An hour later the page was taken down.

Havoc had thought about calling Bunker to congratulate him on his win but figured he would be too busy celebrating to answer his call, so he sent him a text instead. He was more than a little surprised when Bunker almost immediately called him back.

"Yo Havoc dude what's up? Thanks for the message man I really appreciate it," said a clearly much happier Bunker than when they last talked.

"No worries Bunker I'm stoked for you," Havoc replied. "I thought you'd already be off celebrating at a nightclub or something?"

"Haha yeah me too. I always thought if I won a comp Matt and I would chuck the biggest party ever and get really fucking loose, but I just don't feel like it man. I think I don't want to get fucked up anymore. Or maybe just a little bit instead." Bunker laughed self-consciously.

"That's cool Bunker. Good for you. I still can't believe you made that first wave."

"Me neither dude. I couldn't see a thing man. Just closed my eyes and kept going. Hey Havoc I just wanted to say thank you for the other night. You really helped me dude. Just to clear my head a bit. I appreciate it so thanks a lot. If there's anything I can do for you then just let me know. I owe you one."

"I'm glad I could help but I'm good mate, I don't need anything. You gave me that VIP ticket anyway, so it was worth it just to see that wave from a good view." Havoc was touched that Bunker had cared enough to call and say thanks.

"I mean it dude. Anything I can do to help just name it. I'll make it happen."

"Actually," said Havoc thinking. "There is something you might be able to help me with. Are you on good terms with Morpheus?"

"Yeah man, always. Especially after today haha. He and I go way back anyway. He's a good dude. Why do you want to know?"

"Do you think he would give me a wildcard into the Margaret River surf contest? It's kind of been a dream of mine." Havoc asked nervously. He hadn't really had any idea how to approach Morpheus to get a spot in the contest, but suddenly this opportunity seemed too good to miss.

"You want to go in the Margs contest? Fuck yeah dude that would be so sick! Fuck if the waves are big I'd hate to draw you in a heat. Morpheus loves you man. He was blown away by those photos at Cape Fear. They were fuckin' sick dude, you're a madman!"

"Thanks Bunker. Yeah that was a pretty special wave. I didn't think I was going to make that one either. So do you think he would go for it?" Havoc asked hopefully.

"Yeah man for sure. He's always asking me if there's anything I want but I've never needed anything. He owes me bigtime, but I don't think that will matter anyway. I reckon he's going to love the idea. I'll call him right now."

"Thanks Bunker I appreciate it. It would be a dream come true for me."

"No worries dude. Just don't smash me too hard if you draw me in the opening heat. I'm World Number One now haha."

"Fuck I didn't think about that. We could be in the first heat against each other. I suppose it would either be you or Gabriel." Havoc had forgotten that in most surf contests the top seeds go up against the wildcards in the opening round, meaning it will be a lottery of which of the top two surfers he would likely compete against.

"Who knows mate. Anyway don't worry about that now. I'll give Morpheus a buzz. Later dude." Bunker hung up.

It was only ten minutes later when Havoc's phone rang again. This time it was Morpheus.

"G'day Morpheus how are you?" asked Havoc struggling to contain the excitement in his voice.

"I'm good young fella. Are you still doing stupid shit on dirt bikes and the rest of your toys?" replied Morpheus. It was Havoc's love for all things adrenalin based that had first got Morpheus's attention. Homegrown Maniacs wasn't just a surf company. It was more of an extreme sport lifestyle brand dedicated to crazy people doing crazy things in their own backyard.

"You know me Morpheus. I can't help myself."

"Haha yes I do. So you want to be a pro surfer hey. Are you tired of working on building sites?"

"Who wouldn't be sick of that?" Havoc replied wondering whether Morpheus actually knew what he really was and was just being polite. He'd known that Havoc had gone to the Police Academy. Maybe he just thought Havoc hadn't passed or not wanted to continue? "I'm not sure I want to be a pro surfer but a few extra groupies never goes astray, oh and I've never surfed Margaret River."

"Oh it's for the groupies!" cried Morpheus laughing. "Well who am I to stand in the way of a good looking, virile young man and his groupies!"

"You mean…"

"Yep pack your bags lad, you're going to Margaret River."

"No way! Thank you so much Morpheus. You don't know how much it means to me." Havoc was beside himself.

"Not a problem Havoc. And you can thank Bunker too. He put a good word in for you. He told me what you did for him the night before the final. That's good work kid. I don't think you realise how much you helped. We both appreciate it."

"I didn't do much. Just sat up with him and let him talk. But I'm glad it helped." Havoc couldn't help but feeling a little proud at what Morpheus was saying.

"Yes, he doesn't have many real friends. The pitfall of being super rich I suppose. But he's a better lad than he knows and he certainly thinks a lot of you. To be honest I should have thought about you for the wild card myself. I've been meaning to contact you to congratulate you on those Cape Fear photos, but I've been too busy trying to organise the contest. Part of that was trying to think about who would be a great option for a wild card, but I just never put the two together. Still, if we are going to do this, we may as well do it right."

"What do you mean?"

"Well first things first get yourself into our warehouse in Sydney and grab anything you want from the latest range of merchandise. You're going to get plenty of media attention over there, so I don't want to see you in anything but HGM gear. How are you for surfboards?"

"I've got a couple of old faithfuls that will do the trick."

"No you don't. Those waves over there are thicker and meaner than here. Your boards won't cut it, trust me. I'll give the boys at Yahoo Surfboards in Dunsborough a call and tell them I'm buying and to get in touch with you. They know how to build boards for those conditions. Order at least five boards. You will snap a couple."

"Thanks Morpheus. I don't know what to say. Are you sure?" Havoc was bewildered with Morpheus's generosity.

"Absolutely. But I haven't finished yet. I want you to hook up with a local photographer down there if you can, Bill Broad. Broady is a gun behind the lens. I'll give him a call to see if he can do a surf shoot with you if the waves are good, but I also want you guys to do the whole extreme sport thing too. In the afternoons when it goes onshore go hit up the local skatepark. It's pretty sick, you'll like it. You can draw really fast lines there. Are you still riding two stroke dirt bikes?"

"Shit yeah, got a Yammy YZ250. Two bangers for life Morpheus. You should know that!" Havoc laughed.

"Good. Glad to hear you haven't sold your soul yet. There's a lad over there, Mud Dog his name is, kid's a fucking nutcase on a dirt bike. He can pull all sorts of backflip combos over 75 feet, he's got a foam pit, next gen ramps, the lot. I'll get him to organise a YZ250 for you and take you for a ride at his compound if the wind dies off. Broady will love that. He gets sick of photographing surfing sometimes."

"Wow! Thanks again Morpheus. This is all too much. I'm blown away. I really don't know what else to say." Havoc could scarcely believe how much his life had changed in the past few days.

"Just do the HGM brand proud Havoc and I will be happy. Oh and be careful over there kid. I hear there's a serial killer out there eradicating pro surfers for fun. Don't want to get mixed up with that guy do you? Although you extreme sports types would do anything for a rush I suppose. Anyway got to go. I'll be in touch." Morpheus hung up.

That last cryptic comment further raised suspicions Havoc had about how much Morpheus really knew about who he was. "No wonder his nickname is Morpheus," Havoc thought. "The guy seems to know a lot. Maybe I should just ask him outright who the killer is and save a bit of time?"

Part Two
THE HGM MARGARET RIVER MASTERS
South West Western Australia

Chapter 13 KEEP IT IN YOUR PANTS

Havoc got straight off the plane from the Gold Coast and caught a taxi back to his little two bedroom apartment near the beach in Cronulla. He unlocked the door, walked inside and gave a brief, contented sigh. The place wasn't much but it was his sanctuary from the outside dramas and once that door closed, he tried to leave the troubles of the world on the other side.

He'd lived there for a few years now and couldn't see himself moving anywhere else. It was a simple but practical setup with a small kitchen and space for a dining room table, couch and TV. There was a single bathroom and he'd converted the second bedroom into a weights and yoga room depending on his mood. Throughout the apartment the walls were adorned with pictures of Havoc riding dirt bikes, skating, free diving, snowboarding, wakeboarding and of course surfing. Pride of place was a huge, framed picture of his favourite shot from the sequence that old school Cronulla photographer Kris Strome had secretly taken that afternoon at Cape Fear.

Havoc loved living in Cronulla. Not far away was the train station that could take him straight into the city if he needed, but more importantly he was within walking distance of some quality local waves like Cronulla Point and his favourite, Shark Island. The beach breaks at Elouera were fun if he was desperate and there were some good reef breaks further to the north and east on the right day. All up it wasn't a bad place to call home for a keen surfer.

There wasn't much in the apartment that was of any real value to Havoc and he liked it that way. It was downstairs where he had his own separate, securely locked garage that the important stuff was kept.

His trusty old Toyota Land Cruiser 4WD Troop Carrier took up most of the room. He'd originally bought the beast while dreaming of travelling around Australia as it came with all the fruit for serious travel like long range tanks, spotlights, winch, heavy duty bull bar and roof rack. Inside there had been a bed, lots of storage and even a small kitchen. But that road trip never eventuated so he'd ended up stripping everything out to fit his YZ250 dirt bike in there, plus an old couch to sleep on when he wanted to go riding and stay the night with the boys.

All along one side of the garage was his board rack featuring lots of surfboards of various age, styles and sizes, a wakeboard, a snowboard, a bodyboard and several skateboards. Then there was the fishing rod rack with more rods than he'd use in a year, diving gear and another wall covered in the tools to keep everything in shape. It was a classic man cave.

Havoc chucked his travel bag on the bed and grabbed a Coopers Pale Ale out of the fridge. He sat on the couch, cracked his beer, turned the TV on, then muted the sound and grabbed his phone. It was time to check in with his handler and mentor, DS Patinsen. Since their meeting with Smithy, the only contact between Havoc and DS Patinsen had been a couple of texts just to let him know he was okay and would give a full report when he was back in town.

The phone rang once then was answered almost straight away.

"Dirth! I was wondering when you'd give me a call. How did it go up there, anything interesting to report?" DS Patinsen sounded happy to hear from him.

"Hi Patto, I mean sir!" Havoc had grown up with his dad calling his mentor 'Patto'. So that's what Havoc had called him since he was a little boy. It was a hard habit to break now that he had to address him formally when they were at work. "I haven't solved the case yet if that's what you mean."

"Why not? You young hotshots usually solve these sorts of cases before breakfast don't you? Then ride off into the sunset with the girl," DS Patinsen joked. "Well tell me what you can then I will fill you in on some new developments courtesy of the Queensland police."

"Well for starters sir I think they were right about Bunker. I don't think he's involved at all. I spent an evening talking to him as a friend and unless he's the world's best liar most of what he said sounded like the truth. His story is pretty much word for word what the police already have in the report. One thing though, he was adamant that Wilson wasn't taking any drugs other than maybe having a few beers and at worst a toke on a joint. Apparently although Wilson likes to party, he's usually pretty serious before a contest. He comes from a very poor family and didn't like taking handouts from Bunker, so he had plenty of incentive to do well."

"So he doesn't know how those drugs got in Wilson's system?"

"No sir. Not a clue. He admits that Wilson would have known where Bunker's stash was hidden and can't be sure if any was missing, especially seeing as it was found and taken away by the police, but he stands by his call that Wilson wouldn't have deliberately taken cocaine the night before a heat and would never have gone anywhere near Fentanyl at any time.

"But that's not all. Bunker claims that Wilson never uses Viagra. Reckons he was like the energizer bunny when he got with a girl. He could go all night and didn't need help. Apparently, it's something they were both proud of. Bunker claims that Wilson is the only person he had ever seen who could come close to matching him for endurance with the ladies and neither of them needed a blue pill. Not sure how true that is, could be a bit of locker room bragging but like I said before, I think mostly he was telling the truth. At least about the important stuff anyway." Havoc had burst out laughing when Bunker was telling some of the more extreme stories of his and Wilson's attempts to best each other at who could spend the longest time in the sack with the most willing participants.

"Okay that's good work Dirth and very interesting," said DS Patinsen thoughtfully. "I've got some information along those lines too but tell me what else you have to report first."

"There not a lot else sir. Bunker gave me a VIP pass, so I wandered around the competition site as you suggested. There were plenty of people talking about Wilson as you would expect, but it was all mostly just conjecture and wild theories. Nothing worth reporting. I'm sure you would know that Bunker won the event, which I have to admit was pretty bloody cool to see. What does worry me a bit is that if there is a serial killer, then he or she has basically killed the top two surfers in the world and Wilson was on his way up too. Now that Bunker has won the first completed event of the new year, he is the world number one. It could mean he really is a potential target in Margaret River."

"Hmm yes that's a good point. Best you keep a close eye on him when you are over there. I hear you managed to get that wild card. That's excellent Dirth."

"How did you know sir?" Havoc was impressed with DS Patinsen's knowledge once more. "I was going to tell you that next."

"No big secret there Dirth," replied DS Patinsen. "Homegrown Maniacs just issued a press release with the whole story. They made you sound like quite the hero. 'A real life XXX Xander Cage' it read if that means anything to you. It probably came out while you were on the plane. Senior Sergeant Smith won't be happy though. He bet me a hundred dollars that you wouldn't be able to get that wild card and we would have to pull some strings to make it happen. I know you better and had more faith in you."

"Did he really? The old bastard! So when do I get my cut?" Havoc was delighted that the lack of faith Smithy had in him had lost him a bet.

"Never you cheeky shit! You can call it a tiny repayment for all the times I bailed you out of trouble when you were younger. How about that?"

"Sounds fair," admitted Havoc. If DS Patinsen wanted to put a price on the help he'd given Havoc in the dark times, then he'd be paying him off for the rest of his life. "You said you had some information from the Queensland police?"

"Yes I do. You remember the girls that spent that night with Bunker? The ones that provided his alibi? Well at the time two of them remember seeing Wilson talk to a woman just before he disappeared. They were both pretty drunk at the time and the best description they could give of her was 'some blonde bitch' which as you know narrows it down to about half the Gold Coast."

"Yes not much to go on there," agreed Havoc.

"Indeed. But later one of them was scrolling through her Stalkbook news feed and came across some footage from the women's event. Claims she saw someone on there that looked a bit like the girl at the pub and called the police. Unfortunately, she didn't think to save the footage and thanks to one of the competitors basically surfing nude, there's about a million video grabs on Stalkbook to choose from, so the police may never find the exact one.

"What makes it worse," DS Patinsen continued. "Is that there were a lot of blonde girls surfing at the event and the witness is a long way from sure. Still the best the police can tell is that it might be one of the girls who made it to the semifinals, a woman named Dyanna Fream."

"Dyanna "The Dream" Fream," Havoc whistled. "That's interesting."

"Do you know her?"

"Not really sir. I know of her, that's about all. She's from down Wollongong way and likes the big waves so I'm surprised we haven't crossed paths, but she's been on the world tour for a while now so she's probably rarely home. She's got quite the reputation though. It's rumours only, but she's said to have a similar appetite for bedroom antics as Bunker and Wilson. It stands to reason that they've probably all slept together. Especially seeing as they would regularly be at the same events. I'm willing to bet she was in the area when all the murders happened too, but that could be said for most of the tour."

"Yes, that definitely all sounds feasible," said Patinsen pondering Havoc's information. "The Queensland police tried to get in touch with Fream, but she has already left her hotel and hasn't returned any messages so far."

"She's probably most likely on her way to Margaret River."

"That's what I thought too," agreed DS Patinsen. "No doubt that will be confirmed soon enough when we check the airlines. Dirth I want you to be extra careful over there. Remember this person has killed at least three times that we suspect. Whoever it is, will be unlikely to think twice about killing more and I don't want all the effort I spent bailing you out of trouble to be for nothing."

"Understood sir," Havoc knew that DS Patinsen cared a lot for him, but it was still comforting to hear. "How do you suggest I go about it?"

"As I said before, make sure you keep an eye on Bunker. I think you might be right that he could be the next target. You're going to be hanging at the same competition so make sure you bump into Fream and strike up a conversation with her, but for god's sake be careful. If she is the killer, we don't want you getting on her radar.

"But most importantly," DS Patinsen added. "I want you to keep an open mind. Fream could be our killer but it's just as likely she's innocent. There's plenty of blonde girls around the surf scene that fit the description. We need to be careful not to focus solely on females too. I know there was a sexual nature to how Slide's body was found, and Wilson had Viagra in his system, so it seems more likely our killer is female, but there's been plenty of red-blooded males who nobody knew had secret gay lovers.

"It could even be that our killer wants us to think it's sexual to throw us off the scent and it's about something else entirely," DS Patinsen continued. "So in your downtime have a good think about who might benefit from these people being dead. Maybe a competitor wants to get rid of his main rivals? There's a lot of money floating around the surfing industry now. More than enough to justify removing someone permanently for any number of reasons. Unfortunately, the possibilities are endless."

"I must admit I hadn't thought too much about money being potentially involved," conceded Havoc. "But you're right it could easily be the reason. A lot of money gets gambled on surfing events these days too, although I'm not sure what advantage you would get by killing the top guys. I'll make sure I'll always maintain an open mind sir."

"Now Dirth I don't want you to get too caught up in the surfing part of this. I know what you are like. Remember you are there to do a job, not go on a surfing holiday. And steer clear of your other outlandish pursuits while you are over there too. If you break your leg on a skateboard or motorbike you're no good to anyone. Senior Sergeant Smith is just waiting for an excuse to kick you out of the Undercover

Branch and back to walking the streets. Make sure you don't give it to him."

"Yes sir, I understand sir. I'll do my best. Will that be all?"

"Yes that's it. Good luck over there and say hello to your mum for me when you next talk to her. Oh and Dirth, one more thing."

"Yes sir?"

"Keep it in your pants when you deal with Fream. She could be a black widow spider just waiting to eat a young man like you for breakfast!"

"Yes sir. No crazy stuff and pants zipped sir." Havoc hung up and fetched himself another Coopers out of the fridge. He felt bad about lying to his mentor, but he had no intention of telling DS Patinsen that Morpheus had requested he do some photo sessions on both skateboards and dirt bikes.

As for keeping surfing to a minimum. Well, he was going undercover in the surfing industry as a competitive surfer, what did they expect him to do? Margaret River is one of the great surf destinations in the world and he'd never been there before. He was hardly going to sit on the beach, plus he owed it to Morpheus to put on a good show.

There was one thing he could do and that was to steer clear of Fream, except on a purely information gathering basis. That at least shouldn't be too hard. Although when Havoc thought of some of the photos he had seen of The Dream in a micro bikini he suddenly wasn't so sure.

Havoc shook his head and tried to erase the string of Dream Fream fantasies that swiftly appeared in his mind and picked the phone up again to call his mum.

Chapter 14 GOD BLESS FLIGHT ATTENDANTS

As always Havoc was enjoying his time sitting in the Sydney Airport lounge waiting for the boarding call for his flight to Perth. He wasn't one of those people who hated airports and travelling on airplanes. In fact, he was almost the total opposite. He loved every part of being in an airport and travelling to somewhere new and unique. It was the first step on a journey with infinite possibilities.

The adventure began the moment you stepped inside the airport. There was all sorts of food, little bars and coffee houses to choose from. Best of all was the smorgasbord of beautiful women from all over the world wearing a variety of sexy uniforms and travelling attire that sent an always active imagination into overdrive.

Havoc especially had a thing for stewardesses ever since he was a young traveller. He couldn't help himself. They were always so impeccably well dressed and presented a ready smile for a good-looking young surf adventurer.

The call to start boarding his flight sounded and Havoc got up and joined the queue. He glanced around, taking the chance to see who he'd be sharing the five-hour journey with. It's always a lottery as to who you end up sitting next to on a plane and like all lotteries, it's not easily won. No matter how many times you travel, you always seem to end up sitting next to the person with bad body odour that takes up half of your seat as well as their own.

For once Havoc was pleasantly surprised as he noticed several attractive young ladies in the line. More than what would be considered normal.

"Surely I'm going to get lucky this time and not get the fat dude," Havoc thought as he picked out his favourites from the group of passengers. "This is the best odds I've ever seen on a plane!"

Havoc scored a window seat on the very last row in the plane. He hoped that if he didn't get one of the good looking ladies sharing his row then at least he might get it to himself so he could stretch out and get some sleep. Moments later someone stopped and started to put their luggage in the overhead compartment. He looked up and discovered that for once the odds had been in his favour and he'd got a winning ticket.

She was in her early to mid-twenties, very attractive in a classy way with shoulder length straight blonde hair and an outfit that was conservative but sexy. She wore a tight black skirt that ended mid-thigh and a light coloured, button up top showing the barest bit of cleavage. A gentle waft of good perfume added to her appeal. She finished stowing the luggage away and looked down, appearing to notice Havoc for the first time. As soon as she did, she smiled warmly and introduced herself.

"Hi I'm Sofie," she said as she sat down and did up her seatbelt.

"Havoc," he replied holding out his hand and shaking hers gently.

"Havoc. That's an interesting name. I bet you were a handful for your parents when you were young!" Sofie said with a twinkle in her eye.

"Haha well it's my nickname actually, but yes I think you can say I kept them on their toes when I was growing up." Havoc liked her straight away. There was a flirty confidence in her demeanour, her smile was amazing, she had great legs and from what he could tell the rest of her was very appealing too. He was going to enjoy this flight immensely.

The two of them got talking straight away and the conversation flowed so easily that Havoc didn't even notice when the plane had taken off. He could tell that Sophie was at least a little interested in him too, but her friendliness was not just directed at him. She happily chatted with the air hostesses and once the plane was in the air and the seatbelt sign was off, she got up and walked around the plane, talking to some of the other attractive girls he'd noticed before. Curiosity got the better of him so when Sophie came back and resumed her seat, he had a question ready to go.

"So do you know all those girls Sophie?"

"Not really, but we are all stewardesses, so I've met most of them." she replied.

"Really? You mean they're all stewardesses?" Havoc nearly choked. Maybe he really had actually died and gone to heaven? Given he was being paid to fly to Margaret River to fulfill a lifelong dream to enter a professional surfing competition, it made sense. He whispered a quite prayer of thanks to 'Huey' the God of Surf for presenting him with the non-surfing equivalent of stumbling on the perfect wave.

"Well actually I'm not one yet, I'm in training. There's about twenty of us on this flight all heading to Perth for a couple of weeks for the same reason. Why are you smiling?" Sophie asked noting the smirk that had appeared on Havoc's lips.

"Ahh nothing really," Havoc replied. "I guess I'm maybe kind of laughing at my luck at ending up on a flight with twenty stewardesses."

"Well, I got lucky too," Sophie said eyeing him seductively. "I normally get the fat guy who smells like a cigar shop!"

The conversation continued to sparkle as they ordered a couple of bourbon and cokes from an older stewardess who knew that Sophie was part of the crew of trainees. The bourbons were downed quickly and replacements brought straight away. This time they requested double shots and although it was against airline policy, the stewardess poured them something closer to a triple. They were getting the VIP treatment.

As the drinks continued to disappear, Havoc delighted in being able to tell his story of being a rookie pro surfer who'd just been given his first big break. Sophie was suitably impressed and Havoc knew that within a date or two they would be getting busy. Unfortunately, he wasn't sure he had the luxury of that sort of time to work his magic. Chances were that the moment they both stepped off the plane would be the last they saw of each other.

Havoc was going to have to work fast. Normally he might aim to get a phone number and maybe a commitment to meet up later. Sofie had already commented that the girls were all catching a minibus from the airport to their accommodation, so he knew a rendezvous at his hotel was unlikely to happen. He considered his options and decided to go for broke. It was mission impossible, but what did he have to lose?

"So, Sophie, being a trainee air hostess and all, have you been to the Mile High Club yet?" he asked casually while surreptitiously observing her to see how she reacted to the question.

"No of course not!" she giggled nervously. "Besides I would get fired if I got caught."

"Well technically you haven't started work yet. Surely you've at least thought about it? You know, all those long hours in the sky, everyone's gone to sleep, a nod here, a wink there and wham, bam, thank you ma'am!"

"Well, I have thought about it. Who hasn't? But thinking about something and getting the nerve to do it are two completely different things," Sophie leaned in closer, providing a better look at her hidden cleavage, then whispered in his ear. "Why do you ask, are you getting horny?"

"What do you think?" Havoc replied, then throwing all caution out the window, he gently placed his hand on the bare skin of her leg. Sophie showed no sign of being upset by the move. Instead, she shifted a touch more towards him and ever so slightly opened her legs wider. He took that as a sign to continue and began lightly brushing her leg, feeling the electricity in that featherlike connection. He looked into her eyes and could see the hunger there.

"What do I think?" she asked, looking quickly up the aisle of the plane then turned back to him. "I think you should kiss me!"

Before Havoc could reply she leaned all the way in and kissed him fiercely.

She tasted of cherry lipstick, bourbon and just a hint of mint as her tongue darted in his mouth. Havoc was instantly hard as a rock. He hadn't been sure what to expect when he brought up the topic of the Mile High Club with Sophie, but not even in his wildest imagination would he have thought it would progress so quick.

They continued to kiss passionately, pausing every minute or so to look around and make sure they weren't being observed. They were lucky they were in the last row so nobody could sneak up on them. Havoc slid Sophie's skirt higher and traced his fingers up her leg until he found her panties. He could feel the heat radiating out of her core and began to rub gently, moisture already seeping through the thin material.

She moaned into his mouth as he pulled her panties aside. She stopped kissing him and put her head on his shoulder, breathing heavily in his ear as he started to work his fingers harder. She put her hand on the crotch of his shorts and gasped a little when she felt his hardness.

"Oh, is that for me?" she cooed in his ear as she began rubbing him. The restriction of the shorts was killing Havoc, his hardness threatening to tear a hole straight through the fabric. He wanted to rip their clothes off right there, but instead focussed on the work his fingers were doing, letting the sound and pace of her breathing guide him as to what felt best.

Her breathing quickened and so did his movements in response. He could tell she was nearing orgasm. Suddenly Sophie gasped and bit his earlobe hard. She grabbed his hand, holding it still as she convulsed violently, letting the delicious spasms rack her body while moaning softly. She gave one last little shudder then removed Havoc's hand from between her thighs.

"That was good Havoc, thank you," she whispered in his ear. "But I'm not going to fuck you."

She leaned back enjoying the look of disappointment on his face, pulled her skirt down, adjusted herself a little and then stood up.

Havoc looked up at her completely bewildered by what had just happened. His mouth was opening and closing without making a sound, like a goldfish gasping for air. Sophie looked at him and seeing his distress gave a little giggle. Reaching into the overhead locker she pulled out a blanket, smiled and put her finger to her lips beckoning him to silence. She sat back down and spread the blanket out over both their laps then reached underneath and unzipped Havoc's shorts.

Havoc had temporarily forgotten his hard-on, but it was still there in all its glory and he gave an involuntary groan of relief when it surged free of its restrictions. Sophie wasted no time and began expertly working his shaft with her hand. She leaned her head back on his shoulder and began whispering dirty talk in his ear, further enhancing the experience.

"That's a nice piece of wood you've got there Havoc. Too bad you can't stick it in me, and you know how wet I am right now don't you?"

she whispered huskily, her strokes picking up pace and intensity. "That's what you want isn't it? To shove that hard cock of yours in my dripping wet pussy. Or is it my arse you want?"

It was all too much for Havoc. The combination of Sophie's sex talk and her talented working of his member had him just seconds from exploding when abruptly she stopped. Havoc panicked for a second then saw Sophie looking straight at him with a mischievous gleam in her eye. She knew she was teasing him and was enjoying it immensely.

"Keep a look out!" she mouthed quietly as she pulled the blanket back, laid her head in his lap and pulled the blanket over.

Havoc groaned loudly as he felt those luscious cherry red lips envelope his hardness. He reached under the blanket with both hands, one hand sliding inside her top, feeling those firm breasts he'd had a sneaky peek at before. The fingers on his other hand combing through her hair as her mouth bobbed up and down on him. He closed his eyes as she started using her tongue as well. The feeling was exquisite, he could feel his orgasm building quickly, the hand previously caressing Sophie's hair now held her head in place as he started to thrust into her mouth ready to explode at any second…

"What on earth is going on here?"

Havoc's eyes flew open to see the stewardess looking furiously at him. Sophie leapt up, taking the blanket with her and exposing Havoc's swollen erection to the world. Havoc tried to hold his orgasm back, but it was too late. He begun spurting everywhere, all over the food table in front of him, all over the seats, all over the blanket, all over Sophie and all over himself!

"Sophie! I can't believe you would jeopardise your career like this! Grab your stuff! You're coming with me!" the stewardess said disgustedly, then she turned her attention to Havoc. "And as for you young man, clean up your mess and don't move from this seat until I decide whether or not to have the airport police waiting for you."

Sophie gave Havoc an unreadable look as she collected her luggage from the overhead locker and turned with her head bowed to follow the stewardess. Havoc surveyed the mess he had made and was about to go get some toilet paper to clean it up when he remembered the threat about staying in his seat. Airport police were usually Australian Federal Police, so he would have a hard time stopping this getting back to Smithy. Havoc's career would be in jeopardy, but even worse would be the disappointment on DS Patinsen's face.

He looked for something to use instead of toilet paper. The only thing that would do the job was the blanket lying on the floor that moments before was hiding one of the hottest moments in Havoc's life. He picked it up and commenced cleaning his seed off the food tray. As he did, he couldn't help but notice there was a lot of it and it was everywhere!

"Geez that was the mother of all loads!" he muttered to himself as he wiped a particularly large globule off the front of his shorts.

Chapter 15 MARGARET RIVER

Havoc opened the door of his little one-bedroom cabin, switched on the light and surveyed the room that would be his home for the next week or two. It was hardly the ultimate chick pulling den he had hoped for, but it did have one advantage, he was within walking distance of the town centre. Over the years he'd read plenty of stories from when the pro tour hit Margaret River and the town had a great reputation for its nightlife. All the pubs would be rocking with live music, or the latest DJ and every other venue would have something happening for the tourists driving down in their thousands from the city to enjoy.

Havoc had bought a carton of Coopers Pale Ale on the way through town, so he grabbed a beer out of the fridge and took a long scull of the nectar of the gods. He was looking forward to staying in one place for a while and focus on the job at hand, it had been a long week.

The stewardess that sprung Havoc and Sophie mid gravy stroke hadn't taken it any further. She probably realised that she would have been in just as much trouble for supplying the alcohol that had helped create the situation. Although after he'd cleaned up his mess, she did tell him off for corrupting a nice young lady and jeopardising her career. Havoc declined to point out that Sophie was a more than willing participant, instead thinking it wiser to keep his mouth shut.

When the stewardess went to leave Havoc sheepishly handed her the jizz covered blanket.

"I'm not going to get pregnant if I hold this for too long am I?" she had asked with mock disgust while making a show of grabbing it with just thumb and forefinger and holding it at arm's length out in front of her, so as to not be infected by the stiffening fabric.

Sophie had pretended not to notice Havoc when later he shuffled towards her to exit the plane, but just as he drew level, he felt her push something into his hand. He surreptitiously placed the item in his pocket and waited until he arrived at baggage retrieval before he looked to see what it was. He smiled when he saw it was her phone number. He liked Sophie for more than just her adventurous spirit and hot body. She seemed like a nice person too and he felt there was something unfinished there. Havoc found himself hoping their paths would cross again one day.

Once out of the airport Havoc picked up his Toyota 4WD hire car and checked into his hotel for the night. He wanted to get to Margaret River as soon as possible so he was up early the next day and on the road. With each mile he travelled south the road seemed to open up, the trees got thicker, the temperature cooled and the air tasted sweeter.

He had one stop which was the Yahoo Surfboards shop in Dunsborough where he was treated like royalty. They'd worked overtime to shape a quiver of boards for the powerful local waves plus they'd supplied him with Creatures Of Leisure deck grip and heavy-duty leg ropes. Lastly they chucked in some Dr Crack Wax and a couple of Shark Eyes wetsuits together with their crazy stickers of two huge eyeballs.

"Put these on the underneath of your board," the guy behind the counter said with a grin. "There's been some big sharks around lately and these might help."

Havoc turned onto Caves Road with local hip-hop legend Matty B blaring on the stereo. Half an hour later he got his first view of Margaret River Mainbreak and its surrounding waves. It was afternoon so the wind had gone onshore, but the swell looked solid, at least six to eight feet, maybe bigger.

Havoc pulled into the carpark and found himself a spot. It was busy with surfers coming and going, tourists having a gawk and the beginnings of the contest structure being set up at the far end. He got out of the car and stretched out some of the kinks from three hours spent behind the wheel. Out in the water there was about twenty surfers sharing the lineup and to his surprise, despite the onshore wind, the waves looked clean and inviting.

While he was here to do a job and hopefully catch a killer, Havoc's ego and desire to do the right thing by Morpheus meant he wanted to at least put on a half decent show in the competition. Unfortunately, he would be the only person in the whole event who had no experience surfing Mainbreak. That was a considerable disadvantage and the only way to overcome it was to get as much time in the water as he could before the event started.

So Havoc wasted no time grabbing one of his new Yahoo boards and getting it ready to go. He placed the deck grip on the tail, waxed the front section, then threw a couple of HGM stickers up near the nose and after a moment's thought, he flipped the board over and placed a big Shark Eyes sticker on the underneath. He didn't know if it would make a difference, but he'd had enough experience with sharks while spearfishing to know that they definitely behaved differently when they knew you could see them, as opposed to times when they thought you couldn't.

He ran down the stairs, did a couple of quick yoga stretches, then paddled out through the keyhole in the reef that allowed easy access to the surf further out to sea. The water was cool and wonderfully refreshing after a crazy week of airports, hire cars, taxis and crowded cities. It was a long paddle out to where the action happened, but it gave Havoc time to watch the waves and get a feel for the conditions. With each set that exploded on the reef he learnt a little more about where the best place to sit was and how the wave broke.

The crowd appeared to be a mix of local legends and pros getting some practice in. They were pretty easy to tell apart. Almost all the locals wore dark wetsuits while sitting furthest out to sea on much larger boards and when they took off, they drew long, confident lines honed from years of riding the same spot. The visiting professionals sat inside the locals, seeking waves they missed. They were all in bright wetsuits and rode much smaller boards that they could turn quickly on sharper, more aggressive angles.

Havoc initially sat inside everyone, waiting for the scraps of the scraps while he got used to the new board and new surf spot. Finding a wave to himself wasn't easy but slowly he picked up a couple as the afternoon wore on. With that his confidence built and his choice of waves got better. There was a beautiful crisp, rawness to the ocean that he immediately loved. The waves were bigger and more powerful than he expected with some of the sets pushing a solid ten foot. Morpheus had been right. He didn't have the boards for these conditions back home in Cronulla.

As darkness closed in and the crowd started to thin, Havoc took his chance to paddle right out the back to try and jag a proper set wave like what he would be looking for in a contest situation. He sat amongst the last few remaining locals, said a quick hello and waited his turn. While he sat there, he tried to get his bearings so he could find the spot again when needed. It was easy now because the surfers around him all knew exactly where to sit from experience, but when the contest started there would be nothing to guide him.

He noticed that most of the locals sat near a large bubble about five metres across that appeared in the water as a big set approached. It was no doubt caused by a lump of reef on the ocean floor and he decided that would be one of his marks when he was out there again. As the next set unloaded on the reef the locals took their turn and disappeared leaving Havoc alone to catch the last wave in near darkness and ride it all the way back to the keyhole a happy, contented man.

Now that he had checked into his cabin and had necked his first Coopers Pale Ale, Havoc pondered what his movements would be over the next few days so he logged into the Surfline swell report on his laptop computer. He was waiting for the page to load when his phone rang from a number he didn't recognise. He made a snap decision and answered it.

"Hello is that Havoc?" a male voice asked down the line.

"Yes it is."

"Hi Havoc it's Broady here. Morpheus gave me your number and said to give you a call. Are you in Margs yet?" Bill 'Broady' Broad was a full-time fireman, part time surf photographer and all-round fearless lunatic. He was one of the dying breed of genuine surf photographers left in the world that shunned the big money that could be found hiding in the bushes to catch a pro surfer in the act of something indecent.

Choosing instead to chase the pure soul of capturing the union of surfer and the ocean at its peak moment.

"Hi Broady, nice to hear from you. Yeah I got in earlier today. Just sat down with a beer to celebrate my first surf at Mainbreak actually."

"Perfect. I was hoping you were down. Morpheus was keen for us to hook up and do a couple of photo shoots. Have you seen the swell forecast?" Broady asked with a bit of excitement in his voice.

"No, I was just about to have a look when you called but to be honest, I've never been here before, so I'm not sure if it would make much sense to me anyway." Havoc replied.

"It's a bit of a mixed bag actually. Tomorrow looks good. Then the swell drops off for a few days. It stays small for the first couple of days of the contest waiting period then the swell picks up steadily until it gets huge and stormy about the middle of next week."

"So, what are your thoughts for tomorrow? Sounds like we better make the most of it."

"That depends. Mainbreak will be really good and I know you probably want to get as much practice as you can out there but how do you feel about surfing 'The Box'?"

"The Box! Mate I'd love to surf The Box! That's been on my wish list since I first saw pictures of it when I was a kid!" Havoc's day just got better. The Box was a short, shallow and very dangerous reef break situated just across the bay from Mainbreak. Every year around the time of the Margaret River contest, the tides and swell direction could usually be relied on to produce at least one really good day at The Box for the visiting professional surfers. Although it couldn't handle a huge swell, about eight foot was its maximum, it more than made up for it with the sheer dangerous brutality of the almost square tube it produced. Hence its name 'The Box'. The Box was a photographers dream and many a magazine cover shot had been taken out there over the years.

"I thought that might be the case," chuckled Broady. "I saw those crazy photos of you at Cape Fear. So what's your choice, Mainbreak or The Box? They will both be firing."

"The Box for sure," Havoc didn't even have to think about that one. "What's your plan?"

"Well I'm not going to lie to you. It's going to be a freaking circus that's for sure. Everyone is in town now and you can bet most of them are going to be out there. The tiny channel will be full of boats and jet skis loaded with cameras trying not to run each other over. I'll be swimming in the impact zone with a few other core guys and you will be sitting with twenty or more surfers in an area not much bigger than a car, all paddling over the top of each other to try and get a good one."

"Geez that sounds pretty full on, but I guessed it might be a bit like that," Havoc wasn't going to be put off. "All I need is one good wave and I will be happy anyway."

"Well I've got a plan that might get you a couple more but that depends if you are an early riser or not. I'm keen to swim out there before the sun comes up so I can photograph a couple of empty waves with the sunrise magic. It can be pretty cold and windy first thing so a lot of crew will wait an hour or more before they paddle out. We might get a few before anyone arrives or there might just be one or two guys. It will at least give you a chance to get a feel for it before the crowd descends."

"Wow you're a madman swimming all the way out there in the dark! What about the sharks?" Havoc was suddenly very grateful for the extra peace of mind those stickers on his boards represented.

"Yeah I've seen a few out there. You've just got to not think about them, or it will do your head in," Broady replied laughing. "It's the only way, but if it's you and me then it's a 50% chance you will get bitten. If there's a couple more out there, then it drops to 25% pretty quickly."

"Yeah right! Well you're the one swimming out there and at least I've got a surfboard for protection so you can count me in. What time are we meeting?"

"Well it gets light around sixish. So I'll meet you in The Box carpark at 5am. Sound good?"

"Yep. Thanks Broady. I'll see you in the morning. I'm looking forward to it!"

Chapter 16 THE BOX

"Fuck it's freezing fucking cold!" Havoc said with conviction through chattering teeth. It was still basically pitch dark but just the faintest brightening of the sky was starting to appear in the east. He had several sets of clothes on as he vigorously rubbed wax onto another of his new Yahoo boards while Broady had the back of his car open and was using the interior light to help him set up his underwater camera. Cold it may be, but Havoc knew it was about to get worse, at some stage he was going to have to put on a wetsuit still wet from the evening before.

They were parked in the carpark at the mouth of the Margaret River itself. Despite how cold and early it was they weren't alone, as further along the carpark a couple of other surfers were getting prepared in the darkness. The wind was a brisk offshore which was good news for the surf, but not so good for the temperature as it blew straight out of the cold inland forests.

"Fuck, fuck, jeezus fuck!" Havoc exclaimed as he pushed his way into his cold, wet wetsuit. It had been a rookie error leaving the wetsuit in a crumpled pile in the back of the hire car and forgetting all about it until the morning, so he had no one to blame but himself.

"You ready numb nuts?" Broady was standing there covered in rubber from head to toe with booties and a hood to go with his thick Shark Eyes wetsuit. "Let's go!"

They jogged about a kilometre around the beach through soft sand to where the paddle out point was. By then Havoc was feeling better as his body heat warmed up the water trapped in his wetsuit. As they waded out on the shallow reef to the main access point, Broady filled Havoc in on what to expect.

"Make sure you get the ones that don't have too much south in it. They will close out," he advised. "The secret is to take off as deep on the reef as possible and backdoor the whole thing and believe it or not the bigger ones can be a bit easier, there's more room in the tube."

The eastern sky had a nice pink hue to it as they jumped off the last bit of exposed reef then paddled out and around the back of the take-off zone. Broady showed Havoc where to sit, then moved in sixty metres or so to position himself to take photos. Havoc had to admire the photographer's bravery. The sun was still a while from rising, the water was dark, they were the only ones out there and the whole experience had the distinct feel of 'Feeding Time!'.

Havoc could see the other surfers that were in the carpark were only minutes away from joining them and more figures could be seen running along the beach too. He knew now was his best chance to get a couple of quick waves and get a bit of a feel for the place before the hassling began, so he made a pact with himself to go for a wave in the first set no matter what.

Fortunately he didn't have long to wait. A solid six foot set appeared out of the deep water off the back of the reef. He let the first one go but had a quick peak over his shoulder to see where it broke to help gauge if he was in the right spot, then he looked back out to sea at the next wave. He made a snap decision to go and swung his board towards shore and began paddling hard.

Unlike surfing the previous day when he had found he needed a bigger board, Broady had actually advised him to ride a smaller one to better fit the extreme curves of the wave. With less flotation under his chest and a strong offshore wind blowing up the face he knew he was going to have to paddle hard and even when he thought he had the wave, take two more paddles before he stood up.

He was almost blinded by the spray from the strong wind, but he stayed committed and continued paddling hard. He looked ahead and could see the water drawing hard off the shallow reef and his mind screamed at him that he was too deep, but Broady's earlier advice stayed clear in his head.

"Gooooo!!!" Broady screamed at him as he took those last two strokes, jumped to his feet and knifed straight under the pitching lip. For a couple of glorious seconds he stood there, slightly crouched with right hand lightly brushing the wall as the tube threw over the top of him. The sun still hadn't risen but there was enough golden light shining through to illuminate the inside of the dark blue cathedral. Broady was in the perfect spot and hooted at Havoc as he passed him in the tube before being spat into the channel a second later with a big grin on his face.

"Now that's a first wave at The Box!" Broady exclaimed gleefully as Havoc paddled past him. They gave each other a high five and Havoc sprinted back out to the take-off zone to get another one before the crowd hit.

The first two guys to join them were a couple of aspiring pros from America. They had seen his first wave and hearing his Australian accent, had mistaken him for a local. As a result, they were happy to share and take turns. Havoc got a couple more good ones, survived his first wipeout and was generally enjoying himself immensely as the crowd slowly grew. By the time the sun was fully up, there were three boats in the channel and about ten surfers in the water. A half hour later it was almost double that and by the time it was 9am the scene looked more like something out of the movie 'Water World' with Kevin Costner than it did a surfing location.

Havoc found himself surrounded by an absolute who's who of the surfing industry in the tight take-off zone. Bunker Haze had paddled straight up to him and given him a hug, Gabriel Andre was stony faced and ignoring everyone, local pro West Aussies Taj Long and young gun Jake Roberts were dominating the best sets while Claire Cooper and Stephanie Birch were having a fair crack at some solid ones too. There were Brazilians, South Africans, Hawaiians, Tahitians, French, Kiwi's and a bunch of underground local tube hounds all chasing a little piece of photographic glory.

Halfway towards the channel Broady sat in prime position with a bunch of water photographers lined up behind him. The channel itself bristled with cameras on a vartiety of small boats and jet skis, all somehow narrowly avoiding each other as they jostled for the best angle on the next set.

By mid morning The Box was about as good as it gets. The wind had backed off to a gentle offshore that was lightly grooming the clean six to eight foot swell into ruler edged perfection. The tide was high and the sun was shining brightly in a beautiful clear blue sky. All up it was a bloody good day to be alive. Havoc hadn't caught a wave for nearly an hour as the crowd was just too hungry, but he was enjoying being part of a lineup packed with the world's best. The energy from the couple of muesli bars he'd eaten earlier had long been used up, so he decided if he got another decent one, he'd go in.

Havoc slowly drifted out to sea until he was sitting amongst the furthest out pack of surfers. Amongst them were Taj Long and Jake Roberts, the rest Havoc had worked out weren't locals. A set came through and the two West Aussies took their pick. Havoc realised if a set came now, it would be his best chance.

On cue one of the bigger sets of the morning rose out of the deep water and the pack began jostling for position. Havoc completely ignored the first two waves, counting on them to take most of his direct competition out of the way and kept paddling out and to the right to try and maintain the best position for the third wave as it approached. At the last second he spun and paddled hard, leaving no room for anyone to sneak inside him. Out of the corner of his eye he could see the pack looking at him, eagerly awaiting the slightest hesitation on his part that might suggest he didn't really want the wave so they could pounce.

Havoc gave them no such hesitation and they backed off to let him go, a couple even hooted and called out encouragement. The wave surged, he jumped to his feet and was amazed at just how easy this one was compared to everything he'd caught before. He almost didn't have to try, instead he just stood tall, arms casually loose by his sides, like he was walking in the park and let the whole thing throw over his head. He relaxed and enjoyed the view from inside the tube. The shallow reef was clearly visible as it gurgled just below the surface and he could see the smile on Broady's face as he passed him and the rest of the water photographers happily clicking away. Then finally he could see nothing at all as the thick mist from the tube compression blew past him.

Havoc had his head down as the mist cleared while he pulled off the back of the wave and sat back down on his board. He could hear cheering from the boats and somewhere he recognized Broady's voice hollering too. He kept his head lowered, trying to hide his smile and act casual - as if it was just another normal, everyday tube, when close by he heard a female voice.

"That was a sick one!" the voice said and Havoc looked up to see the face of a goddess. He was speechless for a second while he tried to formulate some sort of reply that didn't make him look like a blithering idiot.

"Yeah I had to wait a while for that one but it was worth it," he spoke as nonchalantly as he could muster. The goddess had long blonde hair and striking green eyes, she wore a bright pink wetsuit with long sleeves, but unlike everyone else in the water the bottom half didn't go to her ankles, instead it ended right on the curve of her immaculate behind, exposing her long, tanned legs to the southwest sunshine. It took a few moments for Havoc to realise that the goddess was Dyanna Fream. No wonder they called her 'The Dream'!

Thoughts of hunger immediately disappeared and Havoc found himself drawn like a magnet into following Fream back out into the take-off zone. As they paddled together he tried to think of something to say to keep the conversation going. He looked at that perfect backside and legs, then blurted out.

"Geez your game wearing that wetsuit!" he said and Fream looked at him sharply, so he went on quickly. "I mean there's not much protection if you hit the reef."

Fream laughed and replied. "Yeah but you know how it is, got to keep the sponsors happy. I just better make sure I don't wipeout then I'll be fine. I'm Dyanna by the way," she said as she stopped paddling to offer her hand.

"Havoc, nice to meet you," he shook her hand and gave his best smile. God she was hot!

"Ahh so you're Havoc," she smiled back with a mischievous look in her eyes. "I'd wondered who this mysterious surfer was that got the wildcard and now I know. At least I can see you know how to surf and aren't just another pretty boy."

This time it was Havoc's turn to laugh as they continued to paddle back out. Once they got into position they sat up and the conversation continued. Havoc found himself immediately captivated by Fream. She was funny, cheeky, clearly highly intelligent and best of all, fearless in the surf.

Fream was obviously used to surfing with all the boys as when the next set came through, she simply called out "I'll have a go at this one!" and started paddling without concern for anyone else who might have been waiting longer and wanted it themselves. Instead, they all sat back and watched, perhaps interested to see if she had the courage to take off and the skill to make it. Those questions were answered emphatically when she casually threw herself over the ledge, then came flying out of the tube a few seconds later in a cloud of spray, pink wetsuit gleaming in the sun. She paddled back out and continued the conversation as if nothing much had happened. Havoc thought he might just have fallen in love!

They kept chatting and sharing waves almost oblivious to the crowd around them until the wind turned onshore and the surf quickly deteriorated. Havoc was the first back to the carpark. He took his time getting changed, planning to make sure he was still there when Fream arrived who was easily spotted in that pink wetsuit as she walked back with Claire Cooper and Stephanie Birch.

He had hoped to get a chance to ask for her phone number, but as he watched her with the others he suddenly felt way out of his league. They were three absolute Amazons in their prime. All super fit, extremely attractive athletes at the top of their sport and he was a green undercover cop pretending to be a pro surfer. The idea of approaching Fream while she was with the others and blatantly asking for her number intimidated him. He had to laugh at that, he wasn't frightened of heavy waves or big motocross jumps that might kill him, but the idea of asking a pretty girl for her number in front of her friends scared the shit out of him!

As the girls disappeared behind their cars to get changed, Havoc gave up on the idea and justified it by deciding that DS Patinsen probably wouldn't approve anyway. Instead, he cranked the stereo and climbed bare chested onto the bonnet of the car with a pair of binoculars to soak up some sun and watch the last desperate guys out at The Box see if they could milk one final tube out of the session.

Havoc was absorbed in watching a surfer through the binoculars fail to negotiate a difficult take-off and get pitched onto the reef when he heard someone approach. He lowered the binoculars and nearly choked when he saw it was Fream standing there unselfconsciously in a black bikini that left little to the imagination. He was suddenly very glad he was wearing his sunnies as she probably would have seen his eyes pop clear out of his head like sometimes happens in cartoons.

"So I was wondering when you were going to come and ask me for my number or are you gay?" Fream asked with that same mischievous smile he'd already seen a couple of times.

Havoc burst out laughing completely thrown off by her lack of subtlety. "Haha, no I'm not gay. To be honest I was trying to work up the courage, but I failed miserably."

"Ahh I see. They call him Havoc for he fears no wave, but the ladies terrify him! Kind of goes against your image doesn't it?"

"Well I don't really have an image but yes, I had similar thoughts myself. It's a bit sad really."

"Well are you going to ask me? You know what, just give me your fucking phone," she said holding out her hand. "The girls are waiting for me and if I have to wait for you to get your shit together, they'll be old and grey by the time I get back to the car!"

Havoc handed over his phone, she punched in her number and tossed it back to him. "I'll see you later hotshot and for fuck sakes don't take forever to use that thing will you!" she said gesturing to his phone then turned and walked off.

For the second time Havoc's eyes nearly popped out of his head. Now that she had her back to him, he could see that the black bikini was a G-string and he had never seen anything sexier in his life!

Chapter 17 WHERE HAVE ALL THE CAVEMEN GONE?

"So did he ask for your number?" Claire Cooper giggled as Fream returned to the car.

"No, can you believe that!" Fream replied bemused. "I had to practically shove it down his throat! What is it with these new age pretty boy metrosexuals today? Take me back to the Neanderthal times when they just clubbed you over the head and dragged you back to their cave."

"You're the one with the club these days aren't you Dy?" Stephanie Birch added a little testily.

"What do you mean by that Steph?" Fream asked looking at Birch and trying to work out whether she was joking or being a bitch.

"Oh nothing," Birch replied not giving anything away. She opened the door of her hire car and climbed in. "I'll see you ladies at the comp. Nice surfing with you today."

"Don't forget about what I said earlier Steph," Cooper called out. "It would be nice if the girls got together and forced Hirt into considering us a bit more when deciding when the women's heats ran."

"I'll think about it Claire," Birch closed the door and started up the car.

As the girls watched her drive off Cooper turned to Fream and asked, "Do you like her?"

"Not in the slightest," replied Fream with conviction. "Stuck up bitch that she is. Thinks she's too good for the rest of us!"

"I didn't care much one way or the other but lately I'm inclined to agree with you. I thought she would be all for my idea. Got to hand it to her though, she surfs good."

"That only makes it worse Claire. I'd expect that sort of indifference from that skank Totthil but not from the world champ." Fream could feel her temper rising.

"Does that mean you are on my side and will help me?" Cooper asked. She had changed out of her wetsuit and into a nice little denim skirt and midriff top. As always Fream thought she looked delicious.

"Of course girlfriend! I'm always on your side," on impulse Fream pushed Cooper up against the car and kissed her deeply. Cooper returned the kiss briefly but then seemed to come to her senses and lightly fended Fream away.

"Dreamy!" Cooper pretended to be scandalized. "Not here. You know there's cameras in every bush around here these days!"

"Oh rubbish!" replied Fream disappointed. "And besides it's only two adults kissing. Move along people, nothing to see here."

"C'mon let's go," Cooper climbed into her old Nissan Patrol. "I'll make you a cup of coffee at my house and then drop you off at your hotel."

Fream sighed and opened the passenger door and got in. She couldn't quite get a read on her friend. Maybe she really was in the friendzone?

Cooper put the car into reverse and backed out of the carpark. Both the girls were busy in their own thoughts so neither of them noticed that there was, in fact, a shadowed figure lurking in the bushes with a long lens.

"So, do you think that guy, what's his name, Havoc? Do you think he will call you?" Cooper asked once they were under way.

"He'd better if he knows what's good for him."

"Hmmm, are you hoping to get some action tonight?" Cooper gave Fream a quick glance and smile while she maintained her focus on the road. It was a strange comment for her to make. Maybe she was interested?

"Well, I was hoping to get some action tonight but from a different source." Fream replied pointedly, placing her hand on Cooper's thigh to illustrate her thoughts.

"Hey, you'll make me have a car accident," Cooper scolded her light heartedly, then further confused Fream with her mixed signals by moving her hand and changing the subject. "Did you see that final on the Gold Coast when Bunker beat Gabriel? How incredible was the crowd? The whole atmosphere on the beach was electric. God I would love to have a women's final in good waves with a crowd like that!"

"You were at the final? I thought you had flown back to see your sick mum?"

"Didn't I tell you? I missed my flight and when I called Mum to let her know she said she was feeling better and not to hurry back if I didn't want to."

"Oh I see. Well yes I was at the beach for the final. I was really happy for Bunker. He deserved it. How come I didn't see you?"

"I don't know. It was a huge crowd. I didn't hang around for long. Just watched the final and caught a plane home. Sorry, I should have called and let you know."

Fream chose not to reply to that and the rest of the short journey to Cooper's little house in nearby Prevally Park was made in silence. She decided that she was tired of the mixed signals she was getting from Cooper and it was time to be proactive and extricate herself from the situation.

They arrived at Coopers house and both got out of the car. There was a car behind them and Fream waited for it to pass before speaking.

"I think I might skip the coffee Claire, if it's alright with you," she said trying to hide her disappointment. "I'll just walk back to the hotel. It's not far."

"Okay Dreamy. You sure you don't want a lift? What about your boards?" Cooper asked brightly. If she was offput by Fream deciding to go home, she didn't show it.

"I'll pick them up later. It's not far anyway and it's a nice walk." Fream threw a skirt and top over her bikinis, they said their goodbyes and she started walking. She chose to take the long way and wandered down onto Gnarabup Beach to clear her head.

Her thoughts turned to Havoc. Against her better judgement she had liked him. She normally ruthlessly preyed on innocence and didn't think twice about it. 'Wam, Bam, Thank You Lamb' was her motto with the young boys. She suspected Havoc wasn't entirely innocent. He was too good looking and there was a self-confidence underlying his flirting that suggested he knew what he was doing more than he let on. He was a sexy bastard and Fream had liked what she saw when he casually sat bare chested on the bonnet of his car. He was taller and more muscled than most surfers, which she loved as she often found that she was as tall or taller than her lovers.

He could surf too. She knew that for a fact. Not many surfers would stand so casual in a big, mean tube like the first one she had seen him get at The Box. Especially considering he'd later told her it was his first surf out there. She didn't know why, but she always had a thing for surfers that were good in big waves. It wasn't like it guaranteed they were also good in bed, she'd long since disproved that theory, but she found herself hoping that Havoc didn't wait too long until he called her.

It was a day and a half later before Havoc finally got in touch. By then Fream had pretty much given up on him and decided that maybe he was gay after all. The surf had gone flat and if she wasn't so bored, she probably would have left his call unanswered to punish him for taking so long, but she couldn't help herself.

"Hi Dyanna it's Havoc."

"Havoc, who's Havoc? I don't know a Havoc. Sounds like nothing but trouble to me. Is this a prank call?" Fream wasn't going to let him off too easily.

"Yeah you know. Havoc, the guy that gets all the mad stand-up tubes at The Box."

"Nah still don't know. I saw a gumby get a head dip, is that who you mean?"

"Oh you're cruel Dyanna, you hurt my feelings!" Havoc laughed.

"What about my feelings? You waited two days to call me. Maybe you really are gay. Did you have a better offer or something? Were you down the gym comparing oiled up muscles with your bro's?" Fream was having a hard time pretending to be hurt and trying to hide the laughter from her voice.

"Nah I've just been hanging with Broady doing some photo shoots at the skate park and getting some practice in at Mainbreak. Gotta keep the sponsors happy. You know how it is," Havoc replied cheekily. "I was wondering if you had any plans over the next couple of nights, do you want to get together for a drink or something?"

"Maybe, what are you up to now?" the surf had gone flat and Fream was bored and desperately in need of a distraction.

"Actually Broady and I were about to drive up to Perth for the day. My sponsor wants me to do a motocross shoot. He likes the crossover extreme sports stuff."

"That sounds interesting. I didn't know you rode dirt bikes. What sort of photo shoot are you doing, freestyle or racing?" Fream was suddenly very interested.

"Freestyle motocross for sure. Racing is good for fitness and to get my bike skills up, but I love my FMX. There's a guy up there, Mud Dog his name is, he's got a compound with quite a few ramps and even a foam pit apparently. I haven't been there but Morpheus, the guy from Homegrown Maniacs reckons it's pretty sick."

"Sounds good. Have you got room for one more? I'd love to come up and watch."

"I don't see why not. Text me your address and we'll be around soon to pick you up."

Fream hung up and hopped straight into the shower to get ready. Her boring morning had suddenly got much more exciting. The combination of FMX and surf was an absolute leg opener as far as she was concerned. Havoc was already ticking some boxes for her but if he started tearing the compound up on a dirt bike then he'd better buckle up for a wild night!

Chapter 18 THE SHADOW IN THE BUSHES

Picker was in a foul mood as he crawled out of the undergrowth that was conveniently situated within photographic distance of Dirty Dy's hotel room. It had been a rough start to the week for the sleazebag photographer and it just hadn't gotten any better. He'd been skulking around in the bushes for days now and had nothing much more than lots of bites and scratches to show for it.

His run of bad luck had started not long after Bunker won the Quikbong Pro. Initially he was as ecstatic as anyone in the huge crowd that day with Bunker's win. Picker just couldn't see any downside to the most decadent surfer in all of pro surfing's history suddenly becoming the current world number one. Visions of hundreds of photos of Bunker in bedrooms, spas and back seats of limos doing the nasty with multiple groupies filled Picker's mind. He believed Bunker would help usher in a new age of complete hedonism after too many nice guy world champions.

Picker hadn't bothered to hang around to watch the presentations on the Gold Coast, he'd had much better things to do, like signing the contract for the purchase of the soon to be renamed 'Picker Kink Club'. With the confidence of knowing he had a payday coming in soon for an amount somewhere north of half a million dollars for the last photos of Matt Wilson, Picker had decided to fulfill his fantasy of purchasing his favourite sleaze club.

It hadn't been easy though, the owner was reluctant to sell and had asked an exorbitant price. Picker had tried to counter the offer by threatening to hide in the bushes outside the owner's house for the rest of his life and thereby discovering all his secrets. Unfortunately, that didn't get the reaction Picker was expecting. The owner had simply burst out laughing and reminded him that he owned the filthiest kink club on the Gold Coast, so everybody already knew he was a slimeball with dubious morals and sexual practices. There was nothing Picker could do, say, or photograph, that would do anything other than enhance the owner's reputation with the only public he cared about. They were the kind of people who liked to show up at his club wearing nothing but a skintight catsuit with a hole in the rear for easy access and carrying half a kilo of butter to enhance the experience. He had then further increased the price to punish Picker for his useless attempt at blackmail.

Picker knew he should have just walked away, let emotions calm down and not act desperate, but he couldn't help himself. He really wanted that club! In the end, against his better judgement, he had agreed to the ridiculous sum. He knew it would mean things would be tight financially for some time but believed that with the price still going up for the Wilson photos he would be fine. Even so he'd waited a day or two just to let the idea gel and make sure he didn't have any second thoughts.

Picker had taken Bunker's win as a sign from the universe that he was doing the right thing and had gone straight home, signed the contract to buy the club and emailed it off to the owner. He clicked send, got up and poured himself a vodka and Red Bull, racked up a couple of lines of cocaine and began to get organised to head down to his new club. He felt more content with his life than he had at any other time he could think of. Things had really fallen into place and the universe had been good to him for the past six months with the deaths of Slide and Wilson bringing in huge wads of cash, the promise of more to come with Bunker's win and now he had the sleaze club of his dreams.

That feeling of contentment lasted another ten minutes until Picker had done a quick check of his Stalkbook news feed before he left for the club. As he scrolled through a headline caught his eye, "Bunker Encourages Printing of Wilson Photos" it read. Intrigued Picker had clicked on the story and began reading. As he did, he began to feel sick. He got to the paragraph where Bunker had suggested that the GoPayMe page created to buy Wilson's last photos so they wouldn't be printed be taken down and the money given to his family, or a charity and he immediately stopped reading and grabbed his phone. He was relieved when Peter Hirt answered straight away.

"Hello Picker, what's up?"

"Hey Pete, I was just wondering if you'd checked what the price of those Wilson photos were at lately?" Picker asked dreading the answer he might get.

"Yes I did. They were up around the $650,000 mark last I checked and still going strong. I was just about to ring Gordon Green and call it in and get our money." Hirt replied.

Picker felt an immediate sense of relief then something occurred to him. "When did you last check the price?"

"Just before Bunker's final started. Why do you ask?"

Picker's heart dropped. "Did you hear Bunker's speech after he won?"

"No, I never hang around for that bullshit Picker. I've got better things to do with my time, you know that. I left as soon as the final finished."

"So, you don't know that he got up onstage and told those crew with the GoPayMe page to take it down because Wilson would have wanted his last photos to be printed."

The significance of Picker's news dawned on Hirt straight away. "Hang on Picker, I'll call you straight back."

The longer Picker waited for Hirt to call back, the worse that sick feeling in his stomach got. Deep down he knew that he was in trouble. He had over committed in buying the club and he was about to pay the price. It was a long hour before the phone finally rang.

"I've got bad news I'm afraid," Hirt said as soon as Picker answered. "The market for those photos has completely changed. That GoPayMe page is already gone and Gordon Green knows about it. With Bunker's little comment no one wants the photos anymore. Seems these sorts of things command a high price because the public get off on the idea that the celebrities don't want the photos published. The more they try and hide that stuff, the more the public wants to see it. With Bunker saying

Wilson wanted the world to see his junk, suddenly no one cares anymore. The price has fallen big time."

"Fuck!" Picker yelled into his mobile phone with feeling. "So what's the price now?"

"You're not going to like it. Ten grand."

"Fuck your kidding me! From $650,000 to $10,000 in what, a couple of hours! How the fuck did you let that happen Peter?"

"Hey don't blame me Picker. I told you days ago that I would wait until after the final and you gave me the thumbs up. You're lucky I got you ten grand. Green didn't even want to buy them anymore but offered the money because he felt sorry for us. Do you want me to take the deal or not?"

"Yeah whatever. Just get rid of them." Picker replied dejectedly. "I've got to go Pete, I will talk to you later.

Picker had immediately called the owner of the club to try and get out of the deal. When he realised Picker was in a predicament the owner laughed and advised he had a signed contract and was going to enforce it no matter what, but he could see his way to buy it back for half price. Picker then used some of the most obscene language he could think of to tell the owner where he could stick the offer and what he could do with it once it was there.

Picker could not believe how quickly and dramatically his world had changed in just a couple of hours. Sure, he now owned his dream club, and he still had the money from the photos of Jimmy Slide stashed away, but the near three quarter of a million dollar hit he'd taken on the Wilson photos and the radically high price he had agreed to for the club had crippled him. To make matters worse he really couldn't see a way out of the situation. He hadn't even properly read the financial statements of the club to see how much income it generated, but he suspected it was nowhere near enough. The only thing he could think of was to fly to Margaret River for the contest and hope his luck turned good again.

He'd been prowling the shadows of the Margaret River region ever since. Initially he'd gone straight to Taj Long's place hoping for a repeat of the photos that had kicked off the surge in his career. Just like those good old days, Picker had sneaked through the bush at the back of Long's house, only this time he was confronted with an eight foot high fence with some nasty spikes on top to prevent any chance of climbing over the top. Painted in large letters was a sign on the fence that read 'Fuck Off Picker You Sleazy Cunt!' removing any doubt as to why the fence was now there.

The rest of his usual haunts had proved equally fruitless. The worst had been when he had involuntarily sat on a bull ants' nest and didn't realise until a number of the vicious little bastards had invaded his clothing, then they all seemed to attack him at the same time. Picker had come charging out of the bushes howling in pain and removing clothing at a rapid rate. In his panic he'd tripped and gone headlong into a particularly thorny piece of undergrowth that found all the exposed parts of his body that the bull ants had missed!

In desperation for a lead, a very sore and itchy Picker had hidden up on the hill behind the toilets at The Box carpark when the surf was good. It wasn't a bad plan as it had the double bonus of being able to check out who was going in and out of the male toilets as well as keeping an eye on the pro surfers. Maybe if he was lucky, they would have their latest conquest with them and if she was famous enough, Picker could follow them back to wherever they were staying.

He thought his luck had changed when Dirty Dy and Claire Cooper had locked lips before stepping into Cooper's car. He'd squeezed off a couple of shots that the PG rated tabloids he supplied would love. Two of the world's best female surfers passionately kissing in public while clad only in bikinis should be worth quite a few dramatic headlines. But the real gold Picker was after would be the X rated stuff that he felt sure was soon to come.

He'd immediately run down and jumped in his car. He didn't bother to try and follow them as he felt sure there were only two places they could be going to. He hoped they were going to Cooper's house as he'd long since scoped that place and knew a good spot to hide. The other option would be Dirty Dy's hotel room. He had a place to hide there too, but being a hotel the bushes were more sparse and well manicured, making it far more difficult to stay concealed.

Picker had done a quick drive by Cooper's house with the tinted windows wound up to hide who was behind the wheel and had been delighted when he saw the two of them talking outside. However, as he parked nearby, he'd spotted Dirty Dy walking past with Cooper nowhere to be seen. He observed her for a while and decided there must have been some sort of lover's tiff and she was walking home alone.

With no more ideas left, Picker had been staking out Dirty Dy's hotel room ever since in the hope her renowned promiscuity would save him. But it had been a couple of days now and he was tired and hungry. He always carried a travel pack of food, alcohol and drugs in case he found himself in a situation like this where he needed to hide out for an extended period of time. Those supplies were now gone and the ant bites were itching like hell, so he made the call to give up and go back to his room for a shower and some sleep.

He'd just stood up and taken a step out of his hiding spot when he suddenly heard a noise.

"Oi, what the fuck are you doing?" a voice called harshly. He looked up and saw a big, dopey looking bloke with no neck and huge muscles angrily walking over towards him. He had the clothing and look of security, which was becoming common everywhere surfers frequented since someone started killing them.

"Are you hiding in the bushes like some kind of fucking rock spider?" No Neck continued. "Give me a look at what photos you've taken!" he demanded reaching out to take hold of Picker's camera.

"Don't you fucking touch me or my camera!" Picker roared at him and No Neck was so startled he stopped abruptly. Picker might be a fat little balding bloke, but no one touched his livelihood. "If you even so much as fucking think about it I will sue your arse so quickly and for so much money you won't even be able to afford another day in your fucking precious gym!" Picker knew the best way to deal with these brain-dead Neanderthals was to show no fear and go straight on the offense.

"Do you know what a Chuditch is?" Picker snarled and seeing the confusion on No Neck's face he continued on before he could say anything. "You don't! Well you fucking should. Especially if you live in these parts. It's a critically endangered species of marsupial and this area is one of the last locations in the world it can be found. That's what I'm trying to photograph you fucking moron. Search it next time you're on a computer instead of watching porn!"

Picker was actually mostly telling the truth. Of course he wasn't there to photograph furry little animals, unless they were involved in bizarre sexual practices, but the Chuditch was a real local marsupial that had been nearly wiped out by foxes and cats. It was always a good idea to have a ready made alibi on hand for just such an occasion. No Neck was confused now. His few brain cells struggling to comprehend what the angry little dwarf was saying. This wasn't how he'd seen this conversation going.

Picker was just starting to enjoy himself and was ready with his next verbal tirade when he noticed that Dirty Dy had emerged from her room and was getting into a 4WD hire car after a good-looking young man had opened the door for her. He realised this might be his chance, so he needed to get out of this situation as quickly as possible.

"I'll forgive you this time mate," he said in a much friendlier tone. "I know you are only doing your job. Make sure you look up the Chuditch, you might learn something. I'll see you around."

Before No Neck could say anything in reply Picker was on the move heading for his car. Luckily there was only one road out from where they were, so he was confident he would catch the mystery hire car soon enough. He threw his camera on the seat, fired up the motor and sprayed some gravel as he gunned his car onto the road in hot pursuit. He caught up with the hire car within a minute and drew close enough to make sure it was the one he was looking for, then he dropped as far back as he dared and settled in to see where the journey took them.

An hour later Picker was getting nervous. They had been heading north the whole time and he had a sneaking suspicion their destination was somewhere in Perth. Once they got near the city there was almost no chance he could continue to follow in all that traffic. He was wondering what to do when the car ahead pulled into a busy service station. Picker snuck in behind them and stopped at a petrol bowser pretending to get fuel.

It was then he saw three people get out of the car instead of the two he expected. He'd kept his distance so much and the car windows were tinted enough that he hadn't even realised there was a third person with them. He wasn't particularly concerned about that until he realised who the third person was. While he still had no idea who the good looking young man was who opened the car door, he immediately recognised surf photographer Bill Broad. If Broady was involved, then Picker knew that nothing untoward was going to happen. Whatever mission they were on, it wasn't one that Picker would be interested in.

With a sigh of disappointment Picker turned the car around and began the long drive back to his room for that shower and sleep he had craved hours earlier.

Chapter 19 BACKFLIPS WITH MUD DOG

The laughter was flowing and the stories got bigger in Havoc's hire car as the trio made their way north to Oakford, one of the outer suburbs of Perth where Mud Dog had his Freestyle Motocross compound. Broady entertained with some epic tales of shark encounters and other extreme situations he'd experienced while trying to photograph remote parts of the West Australian coastline. Fream had held nothing back when retelling some classic tales of debauchery from life on the pro surfing tour, but it was Havoc that really got the car rocking with laughter when he recounted how his attempt to join the Mile High Club had ended with him spraying semen like a fire hose all over the plane in front of an angry stewardess.

As the laughter subsided it had been Broady that brought up a subject that was also on Havoc's mind.

"So Dyanna what's your thoughts on the crew dying?" Broady asked, changing the mood in the car. "Do you think there is a serial killer out there working on eliminating the entire men's pro tour or is it something else?"

Fream took a long pause before answering, but if the question had made her uncomfortable, Havoc couldn't tell.

"I don't know," she replied. "I mean three sudden deaths of top male pro surfers in six months seems a little too much to be a coincidence. Whether it's the same person doing it, who knows? You have to remember these guys travel the world all year round. At every single stop there are masses of groupies wanting to fuck them, crew willing to supply them with any drug or kink they desire and others wanting to be friends so they can get a piece of what the groupies and drug suppliers are offering for free. The list goes on and any one of them in any country could be a whack-job.

"Also surfers are notoriously selfish hedonists and pro surfers are the worst," Fream continued. "It wouldn't take much for them to piss off the wrong person by taking more than was offered, sleeping with the wrong person's daughter or something as simple as not saying thanks in the appropriate way. So, is it just one person or a bunch of people? You tell me."

"Yeah I guess I had never thought about it that way," Havoc lied. He'd thought about little else except fantasizing about winning the Margaret River contest or getting lucky with Fream. "It must be pretty nerve wracking knowing that there could be a killer hanging out with you guys though. Have you had any weird experiences lately?"

"I have weird experiences every day of my life babe!" Fream laughed. "But anything weirder than normal, no. The cops actually called me about Matt's death. They thought I'd been with him the night he died. Some drunk skank at a pub reckoned she might have seen me there with him. It was pretty fucken laughable really. A drunk person saw a blonde in a pub on the Gold Coast. Quick let's arrest half the city!"

"So it wasn't you?" Havoc asked hoping he wasn't appearing too nosy.

"No, I was with someone the whole night. Once I gave them his number and he backed up my alibi they left me alone. I don't like cops much, so I was glad to get it over with. Some of them give me the creeps." Fream shivered. Havoc wished he wasn't driving so he could have watched Fream closer to pick up on any signs she might have been lying. Still if the police had confirmed her alibi, then it looked like she was in the clear for Wilson's death at least. Havoc was happy about that. Did that remove some of the ethics he was breaching if he slept with her? He wasn't sure.

"So what's your story hotshot?" Fream asked Havoc changing the subject. "You haven't told me where your nickname comes from. Are you a crazy man on a dirt bike or is it surf related?"

"Actually it's neither," replied Havoc. "You can't really be a crazy man on a dirt bike anyway, not like you can on a surfboard at least. On a surfboard you wipeout every day and there's plenty of times where you will catch a wave with almost certain knowledge you won't make it, but you go anyway. On a dirt bike you can't afford those mistakes. You need to be switched on and really think through what you're trying to achieve, what risks are involved and how can you go about mitigating those risks as much as possible. Sure, you still need to be brave and have good fear coping mechanisms in place, but there is no room for Havoc on a dirt bike. Not if you want to stay in one piece!"

"That's a long winded way of not answering my question Havoc," Fream eyed him suspiciously. "Is it something you don't want us to know."

"Yes and no. Let's just say that it's from a period in my life that I'm not particularly proud of and it has more to do with what happens if I get in a fight."

Few people knew the full story of how Havoc got his nickname and he liked it that way. Besides the energy in the car was positive and happy. He didn't want to spoil it.

"Fair enough. Well tell me this," Fream wasn't going to let him off so easily. "How does a city boy who lives on a metro beach become a FMX rider? Most FMX dudes I know are country boys that have grown up on a farm. Not much space in Cronulla."

"Actually there used to be some really good sand dunes just north of Cronulla when I was a kid," said Havoc thinking back. "Dad used to take me there all the time. Not sure how legal it was but most of the time there was no one there. I started to really like it and hassled him to take me to some local race meets. By local I mean the closest ones were probably a couple of hours away, but dad didn't seem to mind. I liked the racing enough, but some of the kids there introduced me to the old Crusty Demons and Homegrown Maniacs films. After that we were more interested in trying to do little tricks off the jumps than racing. I'm still friends with some of those guys now and they have their own compounds in different places. I go and visit and ride with them whenever I can. It's a good option when the surf's flat."

They reached the southern outskirts of Perth and the conversation slowed while the GPS guided them on a winding journey eastward.

Eventually it confirmed they'd reached their destination, but the trio weren't so sure as the compound wasn't easily spotted. Just then a bike and rider surged above the treetops, rotated upside down into a backflip, then while he was still upside down, the rider jumped off the seat and shifted right back so his legs were hanging fully extended off the back of the bike for a brief second. He then quickly repositioned himself back on the seat just as the bike was completing its rotation and disappeared back below the tree line. It was a manoeuvre known as a 'Super Flip' and only the best of the best could do it.

"Fuck that was sick!" exclaimed Broady and Fream at the same time. Havoc had to agree with them. His blood immediately started pumping. It was time to switch on!

They quickly parked and jumped out of the car. Broady grabbed his camera case and Havoc hefted his gear bag full of all his motocross riding equipment like specialised riding boots, body armour, gloves and helmet. They found the entrance to the compound and wandered in checking out everything the place had to offer.

Havoc loved what he saw. There were three standard competition jump ramps that had a roughly nine metre radius. Two looked like they were set at the normal competition distance of 75ft to the landing ramp. The third was in a bit closer at around 50ft. There was also a much steeper ramp that looked like it had a radius of around 6m, this was the kind of next generation ramp that was being built so riders could spend longer in the air to land double and even triple backflips.

Havoc's eyes lit up when he spied what was up the back corner of the compound. There was a large, rectangle, fenced off area with a height of around 8ft. Inside the fenced area were several layers of old tyres then the rest was filled right up to near the top of the fence with chunks of foam. Above the foam pit was a small electric crane used to winch the bike out of the pit. This allowed the rider to repeatedly practice really difficult tricks into the relative safety of the foam before he took the risk of trying to land them onto the hard, unforgiving dirt.

In the days when riders first started trying to land a backflip it was almost impossible to practice them. If they messed up, there was a good chance that bones were broken and it was six months before another attempt could be made. While it is a lot safer way to learn into a foam pit, plenty of riders have still got hurt from when the bike has landed on them or, in one or two instances, have nearly been cooked alive when the highly flammable foam has ignited. A good foam pit could cost fifteen or twenty thousand dollars to set up, so there aren't many in Australia and Havoc had always wanted to have a try. Today might be his chance.

As they walked further into the compound Havoc spied a familiar tall, long-haired figure holding a video camera and they walked over to say hello.

"Morpheus!" exclaimed Havoc. "I didn't know you were in West Oz."

Morpheus turned and spotted the group and smiled. "This is where the action is Havoc, I wouldn't miss it for the world," he said brightly. "Hello Broady, Hello Dy. Fancy seeing you here."

"Hello Morpheus. It's been a while." Fream replied.

"Do you two know each other? Why didn't you say?" Havoc said to Fream.

"Everybody knows Morpheus. Or should I say Morpheus knows everybody," Fream replied with a laugh. Havoc looked at them both suspiciously and was about to ask more when the FMX rider pulled up, hopped off his bike and took off his helmet.

"G'day I'm Mud Dog," he said extending his arm for a handshake. Mud Dog was a tallish, good looking young guy in his mid-twenties with sandy brown hair. His bare arms and hands were all completely covered in tattoos and Havoc guessed they probably extended to most of the rest of his body. Havoc shook his hand, introduced Broady and Fream and they all followed Mud Dog over to a nearby shed.

The shed was the man cave for the compound. An open roller door revealed a couple of old couches, a fridge, a big widescreen TV and an industrial size fan presumably to cool riders down after a hot riding session. There was a wall full of tools and all sorts of different motorbikes including a mean looking Harley Davidson, dirt bikes, minibikes and four wheelers, some in mint condition, others were in pieces.

"So Havoc what do you think of the compound?" Mud Dog asked. He took his riding jersey off revealing a muscular physique totally covered in mostly black and grey tattoos including a big, snarling tiger as his chest centrepiece and walked over to stand briefly in front of the fan. Havoc heard a little gasping sound from Fream and he turned to see her blatantly perving on Mud Dog. He knew exactly what she was thinking and had to hide a smile before he answered.

"It looks awesome Mud Dog. You've got it set up really well. I was stoked to see you have a foam pit. I've always wanted to learn to flip but have never had access to a pit."

"Yeah we can hit that later if you like. I'm guessing you're keen to have a ride, so this baby is yours for the day." Mud Dog gestured to a nearly new Yamaha YZ 250. "She's all fuelled up and ready to go. I borrowed it from a mate of mine. He looks after it really well, so whatever you do, don't crash it."

"Cheers Mud Dog. The bike's perfect. I'm stoked. Thanks!" Havoc got to work getting changed into his riding gear. While he was doing that Morpheus placed some Homegrown Maniacs stickers on strategic spots on the bike Havoc would be riding. Broady already had his camera out and was shooting a few lifestyle shots and Fream still hadn't taken her eyes off Mud Dog.

"I like your tattoos," she purred seductively.

"Yeah so does my girlfriend," Mud Dog had a grin on his face. He knew Fream's game.

"Oh does she have tattoos as well?" Fream cooed without missing a beat. "I'd like to meet her too!"

Morpheus burst out laughing. "Ahh Dy it's good to see you haven't changed one bit!"

"So Morpheus assures me you know your way around a dirt bike and I'm not going to have to call an ambulance," Mud Dog said to Havoc. "What's your plan out there?"

"I thought I'd maybe hit up that 50-footer you got there for a little while, just to get warmed up a bit." Havoc replied. "Then if I'm feeling comfortable, I might follow you for a couple of speed checks on the 75ft if that's okay. I'm pretty comfortable at 75ft but it's been a while and I'm bound to be a bit rusty. Hopefully I can squeeze off a couple of tricks for Broady. Won't be anything quite on your level though Mud Dog. We saw you do a super flip before. That was mental! After that I'd love to have a go in the pit."

Once Havoc was kitted up, he fired up his bike and did a couple of stretches while it warmed up. Mud Dog threw his gear back on and headed back out to continue his training session. The rest of the crew followed him and took up various vantage points around the compound to enjoy the free FMX show. Havoc could feel his adrenaline rising. The first couple of jumps were always the most nerve wracking. Once those were out of the way he usually settled down and got comfortable.

Havoc started off with a few speed runs up and down the compound, pulling wheelies and just generally giving the bike a bit of a run to make sure it was going to perform the way it was supposed to. Then without too much hesitation he lined up the 50ft ramp and jumped it. There was a brief rush of adrenaline while he was airborne when he realised he had hit the jump a little too fast, but he just caught the bottom of the landing ramp and rode out fine. He rode straight back around and hit the ramp a touch slower on the second pass, this time landing sweet. He was away.

After ten minutes on the 50ft ramp Havoc was feeling comfortable and even threw down a couple of basic FMX tricks for fun. It was time to step it up, so he rode over to where Mud Dog was playing on the 75ft ramp and started following him on a couple of speed checks. This allowed Havoc to gauge exactly what speed was required to jump the distance and land perfectly first go with minimal risk.

Three speed checks later Havoc felt comfortable enough and on the fourth pass he committed to the jump itself. He got it perfect first time and landed square in the middle of the downramp with a sigh of relief. The last thing he had wanted to do was look like an idiot and crash first jump. Now he could really get down to business.

The added distance and height gained from jumping the bigger ramp allowed Havoc extra time in the air to perform more complex tricks. He took turns with Mud Dog as they rode solidly for the next half hour. Slowly he built up confidence towards performing the toughest tricks he knew, but as he was doing so, he could feel the wind increasing too.

Any wind at all is the enemy of the FMX rider. If there's a slight breeze on the ground, then chances are it's a lot stronger ten metres above the ground. That's a recipe for disaster when it starts pushing the bike around in mid-air and you are only connected to it by one hand while performing a trick or perhaps not connected at all.

Havoc's favourite and most difficult trick was what is known as a 'Rock Solid'. A Rock Solid is where the rider let's go of the bike entirely while in mid-air, then spreads his arms and legs theatrically while sailing above his bike like superman himself, completely unconnected to it in any way, before reaching out and catching the bike in time to land safely. It's the kind of trick that can only be done in a no wind situation and Havoc knew if he didn't try one now it would be too late.

He played what he wanted to do in his mind as he swung around onto the start of the runup and kicked the bike into second gear. He hit the ramp and immediately jumped off the back of the bike and tried to spread his arms and extend his legs as much as possible. It all went well until just as he reached out to catch his bike it suddenly wasn't where he had left it! The wind had shifted the back end slightly in mid-air and Havoc was left madly trying to scramble back on with the landing ramp fast approaching.

Havoc's hands found the handlebars and he gripped tightly, but his feet were too late to find the foot pegs before he hit the downramp hard and slightly off angle. The bike bounced and bucked Havoc into the air still holding onto the handlebars but now with his legs trailing behind him level with the seat. The bike bounced again and fishtailed in the opposite direction and this time it bucked Havoc off, sending him flying through the air to crash heavily into the dirt in a cloud of dust.

Havoc lay there winded for a couple of seconds not moving while he forced air into his lungs and mentally checked his body for possible injuries. He was hurting bad in a couple of places, but nothing felt too off. He slowly got to his feet as everyone ran towards him in panic, but he waved that he was okay and hobbled over to check the bike. Fortunately for Havoc and the bike, he had held on just long enough to wash off some of the speed before he'd been tossed. They were both a little dirty and had a couple of scratches but were otherwise okay.

It drew a good round of applause and a few relieved backslaps from the crew watching. Luckily Broady had caught the trick at the peak moment before things had gone pear shaped and the photo looked insane. It was the best riding photo he had seen of himself and Havoc knew he wouldn't get a better one today. He decided to quit while he was ahead, although the big hug Fream had given him when she saw he was uninjured had him sorely tempted to try.

"Did you have a bit of a bingle rock star?" Mud Dog said as he pulled up next to Havoc. "You got good extension on that rock solid before the wind got you, it looked sick!. Are you okay? How's the bike?"

"The bikes fine, I'll have a few bruises tomorrow but all good," replied Havoc dusting himself off. "I think I might call it a day though. One crash is enough for me."

"No worries. If you're still keen though, that wind is from the right direction if you want to have a go at a flip. It won't affect you at all."

Havoc cast a wistful glance at the foam pit over in the corner and he knew he may never get a better chance. But if he was going to do it, he needed to do it right now while his body was still warm. He suspected as soon as he cooled down, he was going to be stiff and sore in a lot of places.

"Fuck it!" he said. "You should always get back on the horse shouldn't you? Okay Mud Dog what do I do? What's the secret to a backflip?"

"First just hit it once or twice and don't even try to flip," Mud Dog instructed. "Just so you know the right speed and what it's like to land in the pit. It's a bit harder landing than you might think but you'll be sweet. Once you are ready, just hit the ramp a bit slower than normal then at the last second throttle hard and lean back with it. Stay on the gas, it will help the bike come around and just keep pulling hard on the bars all the way.

"Whatever you do, try and to stay with your bike," Mud Dog continued. "Don't panic and throw the bike away if you can avoid it. I've seen crew throw the bike clean out of the pit or even throw it straight up in the air and have it land on them and the pit won't save you much if that happens."

Havoc digested Mud Dog's advice while everyone moved down to the foam pit to watch the action. As Havoc psyched himself up, Mud Dog gave a quick demo of riding the pit, only he performed a double backflip just to be a show off. Mud Dog had explained earlier that he had landed double backflips onto hard landing ramps previously, but it was such a dangerous trick he only did it when he needed to, such as during a big competition, or when he was being paid to do it in an extreme show. But he liked to do a few every day into the relative safety of the pit just to keep sharp.

They set the ramp at about 50ft from the foam pit and Havoc wasted no time doing a straight jump to get the feel. Once the bike had been winched out with the crane, he started it up again and rode to the top of the runup where he paused to think through what he was about to do.

"Remember stay on the gas, pull back hard and don't throw it!" Mud Dog yelled out from next to the crane. "Don't worry mate, you'll be sweet, you got this!"

Havoc took a couple more seconds to compose himself then kicked the bike into gear. He hit the ramp and tried to do what he was told but knew immediately he'd got the timing wrong. He suddenly found himself in mid-air with the front of the bike pointed straight up at the sky and rotating just enough that he felt he was going to land upside down with the bike on top of him.

Forgetting he had the safety of the foam pit he panicked and tried to push the bike away from him. Unfortunately, all his inertia was going in the wrong direction and all he managed to do was push the bike far away enough that he no longer had any control over it, but not far enough that he was at a safe distance. There was now a viciously spinning back wheel between his legs just millimetres from his wedding tackle as he fell into the pit and nothing he could do to avoid it. He hit the foam pit at the same time as his bike and closed his eyes waiting for that back wheel to tear through his riding pants and chew his manhood to bits!

He felt the wheel bite into the flesh of his thigh but mercifully it stopped just short of his pride and joy. He gave the thumbs up to the concerned onlookers on the crane platform and waited for Mud Dog to lower the cable.

"I told you not to throw the bike!" Mud Dog cried out with a big smile in his face before turning to the others. "Did I not say, 'Don't throw the bike'? You heard that right? I'm not imagining things? Fuck, no one ever listens to me!"

"I thought you'd have to become a priest there for a second." Fream called out. "Think of all those poor, broken hearted girls that nearly missed out on some action from the famous pro surfer Havoc!"

Havoc could only smile back. He knew he'd gone close to an unfortunate accident, but he also felt he knew what he'd done wrong. When the bike came out of the pit, he wasted no time getting back on it and riding back to the start of the runup for another go.

This time his timing and technique was a bit better and he got the bike most of the way around through the rotation. Back in the old days he would have landed straight on his front wheel and crashed heavily, almost certainly seriously hurting himself. But the foam pit took the landing perfectly and Havoc was amazed at how easy it had been.

On his third attempt Havoc got it right and had he been landing on a normal ramp, would have most likely ridden away clean. He backed that up with a couple more attempts and each had much the same result. He was beginning to feel comfortable with the technique required and being upside down on a motorbike. It was Mud Dog that asked him the question he had begun to ask himself.

"So do you want to step it up and try and land your first one to dirt? It looks like you've got it pretty dialled."

Havoc thought seriously about it for a minute before answering. "Nah I don't think so. You're right, I feel like I've got it worked out, but I'm probably better doing it another ten times or so first just to make sure. Besides I really don't want to hurt myself when I've always wanted an opportunity to compete in a big surf contest," he said nodding towards Morpheus. "But thanks so much Mud Dog. I won't forget this day for a long time. Maybe I might get some spare time to come here after the contest and finish the job."

They returned to the shed to change out of their riding gear and pack up. Havoc was just pulling off his boots when Mud Dog's girlfriend arrived and introduced herself as Tamala. She was a stunning brunette and did indeed have a large number of tattoos, albeit not as many as Mud Dog. She was chatting to Mud Dog and Fream wasted no time in wandering over to join the conversation. Havoc was discretely watching them when Morpheus took the chance to have a quiet word with him.

"You watch yourself with that one kid," he warned nodding towards Fream. "She's a nice enough girl but she will eat you alive. In many ways she reminds me a lot of you. You both like big waves and look for ways to fill that void when they aren't available. For you it's the bikes and skateboards and stuff, for her it's her nocturnal activities and with that comes a price paid in darkness. She's seen and done far too much not to have that blacken her soul at least a little. You're a pure soul Havoc, be careful she doesn't pass some of that darkness onto you."

"Yeah but look at her Morpheus," Havoc said as he admired Fream's curves from behind. "A night with that has got to be worth the risk surely."

Morpheus burst out laughing. "Said many a young man who later found himself cradling his balls in a sling and wondering what the fuck just happened. Well don't say I didn't warn you anyway young fella. You've got an interesting road to negotiate while you try to balance what's ahead of you with the life you already have."

"Just what do you know about the life I already have?" Havoc was tired of the cryptic comments that Morpheus kept giving him. It was time to get it out in the open.

"I know more than you might think," Morpheus once again burst into laughter. "But not as much as I would like."

It was another typically ambiguous answer, but Havoc wasn't going to let him get away with it this time. Unfortunately, before he could demand a proper answer, Fream and Broady wandered over and the chance was lost.

"Are you ready to go Havoc?" Broady asked. "It would be good to get a few miles under the belt before it got dark."

"Yeah let's go," Havoc replied. "It's been a good day, but I need to get some ice on these bruises soon. I can feel everything stiffening up already."

"Oh do tell!" Fream had that twinkle in her eye again.

"That was good riding today kid, I'm proud of you." Morpheus said patting Havoc on the back, perhaps sensing his frustration at not getting a straight answer. "Homegrown Maniacs will always have your back and don't forget I'm just a call away if you get in trouble. Good luck in the contest, if you draw Bunker in your first heat, I'm not going to know who to cheer for. Normally I always go for the underdog, but a world champion sponsored by HGM. Now that would be something!"

They said their goodbyes to Morpheus and Mud Dog and got on the road for the three-hour journey back to Margaret River. This time Havoc commandeered the backseat, so he had room to stretch out his bruised muscles while Broady drove and Fream rode shotgun in the front passenger seat.

"Oh man!" Havoc groaned as the soreness really started to kick in. "I wish I had a hot spa to soak in back at my room. I'm going to be hurting tomorrow."

"I have a spa in my room," Fream replied smiling brightly as she turned in her seat to look at him directly. "You're welcome to soak in that if you like."

"Oh that would be great Dyanna. If it's not too much trouble I might take you up on that for a while."

"No problem at all babe," she replied, then silently mouthed some words so Broady couldn't hear. It was getting dark, making it hard for Havoc to see her face clearly to properly lip read, but if he had to guess, it was "I'm going to fuck you tonight!"

Havoc smiled at the thought, he laid down across the back seat and tried to get himself comfortable enough to maybe pinch a bit of sleep on the way home. The way things were looking, there was a good chance he might need it!

Chapter 20 THE STING

Peter Hirt was in his element as he supervised the final details of the HGM Margaret River Masters due to start the following day. His phone had been ringing hot all afternoon while he conducted operations from the makeshift office he had set up in the luxury two story house the GSA had rented for him just minutes from the contest site.

It was perfect for his needs, with a big outdoor spa on the ground floor and a smaller version in the master bedroom upstairs along with a massive games room with pool table, arcade machine, giant tv screen and a banging stereo. Outside there was a fantastic outdoor bar, dining area and a pool surrounded by cushion covered sun lounges. It looked like the kind of house you would hire for a porn shoot and film ten different scenes without it ever looking the same. Hirt hoped he would at least be able to act out a few scenes himself over the next week.

The death of the three surfers had sparked phenomenal interest. It felt like just about every media outlet in the world had phoned or emailed requesting quotes and interviews. Much of the information they were chasing was around the murders and not the contest itself, but Hirt didn't care. The old adage of any publicity was good publicity rang true as far as he was concerned and the money kept pouring in.

The only minor problem was missing out on the payday for the Matt Wilson photos. Although his cut would have been close to $250,000 for less than a day's work, he'd got a perverse pleasure out of hearing the pain in Picker's voice when he realized he'd lost more than half a million dollars. That bald, seedy fucker could always do with being taken down a peg or two.

Hirt had laughed when it happened. What were the odds that Bunker would win the Quikbong Pro and use his time on stage to tell the world that Wilson wanted everybody to see his junk? At least the win had injected some interest in pro surfing outside of the three murders and it was the kind of interest Hirt could work with. Having a current world number one who is a billionaire playboy with a love for drugs and having sex with multiple women at the same time, made for a hell of a lot of content for every facet of the media from the lowest smut website to the most prestigious networks in the world. Especially seeing as Bunker technically owned some of those networks!

There was a knock at the door and if it was the person Hirt thought it was, then he knew he was in for a painful half hour. It was the unfortunate side effect of making the call to start the competition tomorrow. His suspicions were confirmed when he opened the door and Claire Cooper was standing there.

"Hi Claire. Come on in," Hirt said standing back to let Cooper in. She was unexpectedly dressed up a lot more than he was used to seeing and appeared a damn sight sexier for it. He'd seen her at the end of season celebration in Bali last year when she'd looked smoking hot, but then so did most of the girls who attended that night, so she hadn't exactly stood out from the crowd. Here and now with just the two of them, Hirt found himself very interested indeed.

Cooper wore a short white skirt that accentuated her nut brown skin and shapely legs. Her light blue top exposed a hint of her small but deliciously shaped cleavage. She even wore modest heels instead of the practical footwear he usually saw her in and had brought along a very expensive looking handbag. She'd clearly dressed specially for this meeting. Maybe this wouldn't be so painful after all?

"Thanks for taking the time out to see me Peter," Cooper said cheerfully, which was also a little unexpected. Initially Hirt had planned to show Cooper straight to his office and get the meeting over and done with as soon as possible. Now that he was seeing her looking so good and acting so friendly, he changed plan and opted to lead her out to the back courtyard bar with views of the pool and forest beyond.

"No problem Claire. I've always got time to see any of the surfers. It's a nice day so let's sit outside. This place is amazing, I think you will like it," Hirt opened the sliding door and gestured for Cooper to go first. While it appeared he was being the gentleman, it was really just so he could get a better look at her arse.

Cooper looked around appreciatively. "Wow you're right, it's spectacular! You can even see the river. Are you here on your own?"

"Yes, it gets hectic around contest time, so I like to have a quiet place to go to when I need to work with no distractions. It wouldn't normally be this expensive but there was nothing else available. The GSA paid for some and I had to cover the rest," Hirt lied. He didn't want her thinking the GSA was so cash rich he could have rented seven of these places if he wanted to. One for each night of the week. "Can I get you something to drink? I've got red and white wine, chardonnay, champagne, vodka, bourbon and beer."

"I'll have a chardonnay thanks Peter," Cooper replied.

Things really were getting interesting. Hirt had fully expected Cooper to decline his offer and ask for water or a soft drink instead, she was competing tomorrow.

While Cooper sat and placed her handbag on the table, Hirt wandered over to the outdoor bar, selected an unopened bottle of chardonnay and cracked the seal. He poured Cooper a healthy glass and a local Grove whiskey on the rocks for himself. He handed the glass to Cooper then raised his.

"Here's to you going well in the contest. Cheers!"

"Cheers to that," Cooper replied as they clinked glasses and took a drink. "Although you aren't making it easy for me…damn that's good! What chardonnay is that?"

"It's a local one from Leeuwin Estate. The 2020 Art Series Chardonnay. It would want to be good, it's $150 a bottle!"

"Are you trying to bribe me, so I won't give you a hard time about running the women's heats in small waves again?" Cooper asked him teasingly.

"Not at all. I merely thought nothing but the best for one of our most valuable athletes on tour. A lot of girls look up to you. That's very important to the GSA." Hirt had no idea if any of that was true, but it sounded reasonable, and he liked this version of Claire Cooper. Liked it very much.

"Good, because you're not going to get off that easy. Can you please give me one valid reason why you insist on sending us out to surf dribble all the time?"

"I can give you a few. First, it's a weekend and the crowds are always better on the weekend, so we are running heats no matter what unless it's dead flat. Let's not forget it's still going to be four foot the next couple of days, that's hardly flat."

"Yes, but later in the week is going to be perfect six to ten foot for several days," Cooper interrupted. "Why not then?"

"Then there's the sponsors. Homegrown Maniacs want the women's on the weekend for the glamour and publicity and then run the men's when it gets big."

"You're forgetting I'm sponsored by HGM. I've talked to Morpheus. He doesn't care when the girl's heats are on. In fact, he said he'd like to see what we could do in bigger surf."

Hirt chastised himself for that slip up. He had indeed forgotten that Cooper was on the HGM team. But he was an old hand at this and continued on.

"Well, he said something different to me. The GSA has a duty to the health of pro surfing in general and the bottom line is the men surf a lot better in those kinds of waves than the women. It's simple genetics. Girls can't surf! With the exception of you, Fream, Birch and one or two others, the rest of the girls on tour will be way out of their depth out there and make everybody look stupid," Hirt left off another big reason. Tiffany Tothill had promised him access to an area of her body that had been previously off limits, but only if the competition was held on the small days that suited her surfing. "You can stick it anywhere you want!" she had promised and that was an offer he had no intentions of turning down whatsoever.

"But if you don't give us the opportunity in those sorts of waves, how will we ever know what the rest of the girls are capable of?" Cooper was getting frustrated but then abruptly she changed tone. "Surely there is something I can do to convince you to give us a try?"

Hirt wasn't certain what was happening. Was she sending signals? Cooper had asked the question with a little smile and did he detect a subtle shifting forward as if to reveal a bit more of that petite cleavage he was having a hard time not staring at?

"Well, it's pretty close to set in stone for this competition. I could maybe see about moving the semifinals and final to a bigger day, but I can't promise anything. There's always Bells Beach I suppose. Why? What do you think you could do to help convince me?" Hirt had to be careful here. He wasn't sure what signals he was getting from Cooper, but if there was the slightest chance she was offering herself then he wanted in. He knew she was currently single so there was no boyfriend to get in the way of Cooper making the right 'business' decisions.

"That's why I'm asking you," her voice was lowered now, husky and sexy. "I don't know what you want, but maybe you can give me an idea of what I can do for you and the GSA. I'm very passionate about women's surfing. I'd do just about anything to further our sport, it means a lot to me."

Cooper had that little smile going again. Hirt was almost sure she was flirting with him. He had never considered Cooper to be a candidate for the casting couch, too aloof, hardnosed and too damn smart. Which made the possibility of what she might be offering even more appealing. Hirt became aware of the monumental hardness straining in his pants. He subtly adjusted himself to ease the tension and spoke on.

"Well maybe we can reach some kind of 'I'll scratch your back, you scratch mine deal'. What do you think?" he asked hopefully.

"I think that sounds like a great idea. What do you have in mind?" Cooper replied. Her smile widened and Hirt thought he caught a wink, but it was so fast he couldn't be sure if he had imagined it. His pulse was quickening and his hard-on got harder. Was that even possible? The thing was threatening to burst through the material like when Bruce Banner turns into The Hulk. Fuck he wanted her bad! It was time to bring this baby home.

"Stand up for me Claire," Hirt breathed.

She did as she was told and stood up out of her chair, smoothed her skirt down, adjusted her top a little, then walked around the side of the table so he had a full view of her immaculate figure.

"Now what?" Cooper asked softly as she leaned forward giving Hirt his best view yet of that cleavage.

"I think you know what. You're a big girl."

"No I don't Peter," she teased. "You're going to have to spell it out for me."

Hirt decided it was time to put it all on the line. It appeared Cooper did know the rules of the game after all. "I want you to take your clothes off and fuck me!"

Hirt watched Cooper closely to see her reaction. She didn't bat an eyelid, in fact he thought he detected a little smirk of triumph or satisfaction. It was on like donkey kong!

"So let me get this straight," she said seductively as she slightly lifted her skirt. "If I agree to fuck you right here and now, then you agree to make sure the women get to surf in good waves for the finals of Margaret River and during the Bells contest. Is that's what you are saying?"

"That sounds like a fair deal to me. What do you think?" Hirt was so horny he was in danger of blowing his load before he touched her.

"I don't know. Is that all?" Coopers serious voice defied the look she was giving him. Hirt now knew without doubt that he was going to be blowing the back out of the world number six rated women's surfer in a few minutes time.

"Well, you could chuck in a blowjob. That would be nice." Hirt was really enjoying himself now.

"I want to hear the deal from your mouth, so I know it's agreed. Spell it out for me."

"Okay. If you agree to slowly take those clothes off right now and get down on your knees and give me a blowjob before I bend you over this table and fuck you. I agree to hold the women's final later next week when the waves are good, and I will let you pick the days you want to run the women's heats at the Bells contest. That's the deal I'm offering you."

Cooper smiled at him and took a step closer and reached for a button on her top as if to comply then suddenly her whole demeanour changed.

"You slimy, seedy pile of dung!" she exploded. "I meant I would do anything for the GSA. You know like come in and work in the office or do promotional stuff to encourage more girls to take up surfing or maybe be a brand ambassador for the GSA. Not fucking give you a blowjob, you disgusting piece of filth!"

"Then get out Cooper! Go on, fuck off!" Hirt couldn't believe what had just happened and he felt an uncontrollable rage developing. "See where that gets you, you stuck up bitch! I run the show, hell I am the GSA. Enjoy a lifetime of one foot slop until you drop off the tour and go flip burgers for a living!"

Cooper saw the change come over Hirt and felt a surge of fear. His eyes blazed with a wrathful fury that she hadn't thought he was capable of, and he began opening and closing his hands like he wanted to physically assault her. Wisely she picked up her handbag and stormed out without saying another word, slamming the door behind her.

Hirt hurled the half-finished glass of $150 chardonnay at the closed door and it exploded in a satisfying shower of glass. He was beyond furious and it took all his self-restraint not to go after her. No one did that shit to him! She'd played him for a fool alright, but no harm done except a bruised ego and he would enjoy making Cooper's life a misery from now on, or maybe he should just go next level on her? He'd have to think further on that one.

Either way fuck that bitch! She'd got him horny and he hated a good hard-on going to waste! Angrily he reached for his phone. It was time to get a down payment from Tiffany Totthil for running those heats tomorrow.

Outside Claire Cooper hopped into her car, locked the doors and breathed a sigh of relief. A sixth sense had warned her that she might have been lucky to get that far unscathed. She opened her handbag, pulled out a little rectangular device and checked it was still recording. Satisfied that it had been, she switched it off, started up the engine and pulled out of the driveway singing a happy song.

Chapter 21 VAMPIRE NYMPHOMANIAC VOODOO MAGIC

Havoc was a mere shell of the human being he had been just a few days earlier. Back then he was a young, cocksure, pretend pro surfer and moto lord hoping he would get lucky. Now he was a zombie, no not a zombie, more like one of those ancient Egyptian mummies that had all their fluids removed so they would better last the centuries ahead.

He had spent the past 60 hours with The Dream and during that time she had methodically extracted more blood, sweat and semen from his body than he thought possible. The woman wasn't human, Havoc was positive of that. The only explanation that made any sense to him was that she had crash landed on Earth from a planet of vampire nymphomaniacs. Not that he was complaining!

They'd dropped Broady off at his home after the trip to Mud Dog's compound and Havoc had jumped in Fream's spa as soon as they walked in the door of her hotel room. While he lay there soaking his bruised body, Fream poured a couple of vodkas and changed into the little black bikini G-string combo he had briefly seen her wearing at the beach a few days before. He couldn't help but stare as she sashayed her way over carrying the drinks, taking her time as she did so he could fully appreciate what he was witnessing.

"Like what you see?" she asked seductively while performing a little spin allowing a glimpse of the G-string disappearing into that perfect backside.

"Not bad!" Havoc replied taking the offered glass of vodka. She splashed him for his lack of appreciation. He was trying to act cool, like this sort of thing happened to him every day, but it wasn't easy. Now that she was openly permitting him to admire her body instead of the quick glimpses he'd risked under the cover of sunglasses, he had to admit that she was absolutely drop dead stunning and he was batting way out of his league.

She looked different to most of the other girls Havoc had seen on the pro surfing tour. While her rivals generally sported a slim, athletic figure, Fream's was closer to an hourglass with delicious curvy hips and an impressive natural cleavage that Havoc imagined would be bloody annoying when laying on a surfboard and paddling all day. With the long blonde hair, green eyes that you could get lost in and those long legs she could easily be a lingerie model, porn star or married to a billionaire.

Havoc paused briefly before he took a sip of the vodka. Technically she was still a prime suspect as he hadn't yet had the chance to confirm with DS Patinsen that Fream did in fact have an alibi for the night of Wilson's murder. In the end he'd thrown caution to the wind and drunk the vodka instead of his much-preferred Coopers Pale Ale. He reasoned that he was already too far gone down this path to refuse a drink now and that the three previous murders were of top surfers while he was a mere wildcard.

"Not bad!" Fream repeated, faking disappointment as she joined him in the spa. She looked him straight in the eye then removed her top in one quick movement and threw it at him. "Well how about now?"

Havoc nearly choked as her bikini top hit him straight in the face. He let it sit there for a second while he regained his composure then casually removed it and placed it on the edge of the spa.

"Getting better," he replied with a cheeky smile. "What else have you got?"

The Dream didn't bother to answer. She pushed herself across the spa and climbed on Havoc's lap. She kissed him hungrily for a few seconds before sitting up and shoving an erect, cherry coloured nipple into his mouth. While Havoc went to work greedily sucking and grabbing at The Dream's weapons of mass distraction, she was busily tugging at the cord holding up his boardshorts. The knot came undone and his hard-on sprang free. The Dream made a little appreciative noise as she grabbed a firm hold and gave him a couple of quick strokes before pulling her bikini bottom aside and impaling herself in one smooth movement.

Havoc groaned loudly as he felt himself slide into the silky wetness of The Dream. She pulled her nipple out of his reach, grabbed him by the throat and forced her tongue in his mouth while she ground away on top of him sending waves crashing out of the spa.

She broke off the kiss then looked him straight in the eye and whispered. "What else have I got? Oh, you poor boy. You're going to regret those words!"

What followed was two full days and nights of sexual gymnastics that Havoc would have never thought possible. It seemed to him that they went through the entire book of the Kama Sutra then added a couple of chapters of their own. Pausing occasionally for food, a fresh drink or an hour or two of sleep, they bumped and ground their way through the spa, the bedroom, the sofa, the dining room table, on the floor, up against the walls, in the shower and even late at night on the veranda outside when no one was around. If there had of been a chandelier in the room, Havoc was pretty sure they would have found a way to swing from that too.

Havoc had lost count of the amount of times The Dream had made him crash the yoghurt truck and every time he did and thought he could go no further, she would work some of that vampire nymphomaniac voodoo magic and he would be hard again. He was scratched, bitten, slapped, choked, tied up and teased. On those few times he really did need a break, she would demand he use his mouth or hands to get the job done on her insatiable quest for her next orgasm.

Then the toys came out. Dildos and vibrators of all sorts of size, shape and colour were placed on the bed and Havoc was given a world class tutorial on how they could be best used.

It had finally ended when The Dream declared that she had a heat to surf in a few hours and needed to save a bit of energy for that. Havoc had forgotten the contest even existed or that there was a killer out there that he was supposed to catch! His whole world had shrunk to being a willing slave toy-boy to that amazing body that he was now very familiar with. He almost didn't know what to do with himself once his services were no longer required.

He'd chosen to go home, change out of the same clothes he had first put on nearly three days ago and have a shower. With the first day of competition about to start, he figured he would spend most of the day watching the women's action and meeting as many of the people involved in the tour as possible. Hopefully he could ferret out some information worth reporting back to DS Patinsen and he found himself secretly wishing Fream wouldn't want round two. He really needed a rest and maybe some time to let the skin grow back on his manhood!

A few hours later Havoc was hiding behind a pair of sunglasses in the competitor's area watching Fream's heat. The sun was shining and it was a glorious day in the southwest. The surf wasn't bad by a lot of places standards, but for Margaret River the three to five foot offerings were on the small side. Despite the smallish surf, Fream was doing a number on her opponent, a rookie to the tour named Belle Silva who'd made quite an impression at the previous event for wearing a bikini that literally left nothing to the imagination. It was far too cold for that here and both competitors were wearing wetsuits.

Fream had clearly set down the rules for their public interaction before he'd left her room earlier that morning. He could be friendly and say hello but anything other than that was off limits. It seemed that despite her in-your-face brand of flirting and willingness to wear very revealing clothing in public, actual matters of the bedroom were to be kept as private as possible. If she thought that Havoc would have been upset or offended by that after the time they had shared together, then she would have been pleasantly surprised when Havoc readily agreed to her terms. He of course had his own reasons for wanting to keep their affair well and truly out of the public eye.

The heat finished with an easy win for Fream and Havoc took the opportunity to get up and have a wander around. He marvelled at how just a few days earlier the entire contest structure hadn't existed, yet here it was complete with VIP viewing stands, giant replay screens, judges' box, media room and dining areas. The competitor's area had spas, massage tables, exercise bikes and all sorts of other items to aid making sure the athletes were warmed up and ready to surf when it was their turn. Havoc conceded that the whole operation appeared to be very professional and well run.

"Who are you?" Havoc's thoughts were interrupted by a female voice from behind him. He turned around to see another very attractive blonde looking at him with her hands on her hips. She was almost as good looking as Fream but where The Dream was all natural curves and raw sexiness, this new girl was definitely more of the new aged cosmetically enhanced variety. Her lips were unnaturally plump suggesting collagen or something similar, her nose looked too thin and sharp to not have been surgically adjusted and her boobs were far too large and upright for such a small frame. Her outfit would almost have put Fream to shame, with the tiniest bikini top barely covering her nipples and an impossibly tight pair of white shorts that accentuated a very pronounced camel toe.

"I'm Havoc," he replied offering his hand for a handshake. "Nice to meet you."

"I'm Tiffany. Tiffany Totthil," Totthil pouted her duck lips as she took his hand and shook it gently but didn't release it for a prolonged second or two. "I haven't seen you around before Havoc. What are you doing here?"

"Ah, I'm lucky enough to have a wild card for the men's event."

"Oh, I think I've heard of you. I didn't expect you to be so good looking though," she cooed unashamedly then grabbed his hand again and looked into his eyes. "We should hang out. It wasn't long ago I was new to the tour as well, so I could help you with any problems you might have. All you have to do is ask."

"Umm, yeah sure that sounds good," Havoc was a feeling a little uncomfortable with Totthil's approach. She was only a tiny little thing, but he felt a little like he was in the presence of an apex man predator. "I'm not sure I will be around for more than one event though," he said trying to think of a way to extract his hand without offending her. "I got lucky my sponsor saw some good photos of me online and in the magazines, so he rewarded me with the wildcard."

"Oh I'd love to see those photos!" Totthil let go of his hand on her own accord but then lightly grabbed him by the arm instead. "Are they on Instafamous? I love Instafamous. I've got nearly fifteen million followers and I'm on there all the time, so I'll have to look you up. We could hook up and do a collab, like a photo shoot or something. What's your Instafamous page name?"

"I don't have an Instafamous page," Havoc replied truthfully.

"What? You don't have an Instafamous page!" Tothill squeaked with confusion and let go of his arm. "But everybody has an Instafamous page. How do you plan on being famous?"

Before Havoc could answer another female voice interrupted.

"No Instafamous page. What good is he to you then Tiffany?" Fream strolled over to join them, hair still wet from her heat and with a faint hint of annoyance showing on her face. "How can you share likes and boost your profile if he doesn't exist in your world? Shame he's so good looking isn't it? I'm sure it would have made a nice change for you to fuck a guy that's not overweight and twice your age on your way to the top!"

Totthil pouted more duck lips and appeared lost for words as she looked first at Fream, then at Havoc. Then something appeared to click with her and she started giggling. "Are you already fucking him yourself Dirty Dy? I'm sorry I didn't mean to step on your toes. But isn't he a bit old for you? He's probably what, 22 maybe 23? Don't you like them younger and more virginal?"

"Hi I'm Havoc," Havoc said offering his hand to Fream before she had a chance to answer, he was hoping to diffuse the situation before it turned into a monster public catfight on his first day as a pro surfer. "You're Dyanna Fream aren't you? I watched your heat. That last wave was sick!"

"Thanks Havoc that's nice of you to say," Fream shook his hand with a slight twinkle in her eye. Then gestured towards Totthil "I'm sorry you had to meet the worst of the tour on your first day."

"Excuse me bitch!" Totthil's amusement turned to fury. "Take that back!"

"Why, what are you going to do about it?" Fream asked quietly but menacingly. "I eat little girls like you for breakfast. I'll make you an offer skank! Anytime you get sick of CEO's and judges I'll bring my strap on and show you what it's like to really get fucked! I promise I'll rock your world, turn you lesbian in five minutes. Or we could grab Havoc here and give you a good spit roast. What do you think?"

Totthil opened and closed her mouth trying to think of something smart to say back but no words came out. She was outclassed and outgunned on every level, and she knew it.

"Well it was nice to meet you Havoc," Totthil said attempting to regain her composure. "Don't forget to ask for help or advice if you need it. Despite what Dirty Dy here tells you, I'm happy to assist if I can and us young people need to stick together around the old bags!"

Totthil strutted off head held high, hips swaying, trying to maintain whatever dignity she had left.

Once she had gone and was out of earshot Havoc looked at Fream and it was all he could do not to burst out laughing.

"That was cruel," he said. "She was harmless."

"I know but I couldn't help myself," Fream conceded with a wry smile. "There's something about her that rubs me the wrong way. She represents everything that's wrong about this circus. She's not a real surfer, she dresses like a hooker and fucks her way through the tour."

Havoc raised an eyebrow at that last comment and this time it was Fream struggling to stop from bursting into laughter.

"Hey I like to bang cute young surfer boys, I happily admit it. But she uses those plastic tits of hers to cheat and get an advantage with the people that run this shitshow. I don't see any advantage for me humping your bone, do you? Except for the obvious of course," she said with that mischievous smile Havoc was beginning to realise meant trouble for him. "And besides what were you doing talking to her anyway? I leave you alone for an hour and you're already off tuning a fresh piece of arse. Didn't you get enough action? Have you still got a bit in the tank that I should know about?"

"Well she was pretty hot and a man's got to keep his options open…" Havoc teased, enjoying the fact that Fream may just be a little jealous.

"You can have her if you're not careful-"

"Haha please no," Havoc interjected. "Truth is she made me a little uncomfortable. I was trying to think of a way to get out of the conversation and you saved me."

"I've got to do some interviews and sign some autographs for an hour or two, you know, to keep the sponsors happy," she grinned. "After that I want to fuck. Do you think you can handle that pretty boy?"

Havoc would not have imagined it possible, but the stirring in his shorts suggested that at least one part of his body thought he could handle it.

"I thought you'd never ask."

Fream gave a quick laugh and walked over to where a camera team was setting up in front of the sponsor's billboard ready to do her post heat winners interview, so Havoc left to continue wandering the contest site. Mostly he just watched people and occasionally checked the action when a set came through. At the moment local girl Claire Cooper was struggling in a heat against a tiny little Japanese girl he had never heard of. Cooper looked out of sorts even though it was her home event and Havoc could sympathise, he was also feeling a bit lost with regards to what his next move might be too.

He'd ticked some personal boxes that he wanted to achieve while in Margs and had an amazing time in the process while being no closer to uncovering a killer. He'd stayed in touch with Bunker as best he could, but he was an enigma not easily tracked. Havoc had a feeling he was back on the drugs. Bunker wasn't taking calls and when he did, that steely focus from the Gold Coast was missing. Havoc tried to remind himself that he needed to be patient, but patience wasn't necessarily a good thing in this situation. The longer he took, the more likely someone walking around the competitor's tent had only a few days to live.

He spied someone casually observing the heat that he recognised from some of the publicity releases he'd read from the GSA and decided it was time to start being proactive.

"Excuse me," Havoc said approaching the figure. "Are you Peter Hirt?"

"Yes I am," Hirt replied looking a little annoyed at the intrusion. "Who are you?"

"I'm Havoc sir, I mean Dirth, Dirth Spidder," Havoc said offering his hand. "I'm the guy that Morpheus gave his wildcard to."

Hirt looked puzzled for a second then his expression changed and he shook Havoc's hand. "Dirth Spidder, yes I remember now. Although I've got to say Havoc is a much better name from my point of view and please call me Peter, not sir. Sorry my mind was elsewhere. Welcome to the GSA."

"Thanks Peter. I've got to say I'm really impressed by the professionalism of the whole event. It must take an incredible amount of work to make something this big run so smoothly."

"Thanks Havoc yes it does, although we've been doing it for so long now it's second nature to my team." Hirt's voice trailed off as he became distracted by Claire Cooper taking off on a wave. She surfed it really well and got herself back in the heat causing Hirt to swear quietly.

"You're not going for the local girl?" Havoc asked.

"What? Umm sorry you got me haha. No, I always cheer for the underdog and would love to see a Japanese surfer permanently on the tour, so I'm going for Kumiko. But don't tell anyone I told you. I'm supposed to be impartial."

"My lips are sealed Peter," Havoc said smiling. "You must have about the toughest job on the planet lately. Trying to keep all this together after losing three of your superstars."

"Yes it hasn't been easy. But an organisation has to be bigger than its heroes to survive. Stars come and go, but we will always be here putting on a show," Hirt leaned in a bit closer. "I'll let you in on a bit of a secret Havoc. Those guys had their time and it was fading anyway. The future for the GSA is guys like you and Bunker Haze and girls like Tiffany Totthil and Belle Silva. This place needed a cleanout and it's much better for it. Our media coverage is bigger than ever and we're rivalling the biggest sports in the world like golf, tennis and soccer. The money we are making…sorry I'm talking too much and probably boring you. Let's just say don't worry about the GSA Havoc, if you surf well and maintain the right image, there will be plenty of pay cheques and groupies for you to indulge in."

The conversation paused as a bigger than normal set approached the lineup. The Japanese surfer took off on the first wave and fell on her first turn. Cooper caught the bigger wave behind it and tore it to pieces. With less than a minute to go it would be enough to guarantee the win to the local surfer.

"Shit!" Hirt swore aloud before sheepishly looking around to see if anyone else had heard him. "It was nice to talk to you Havoc, but I've got to keep moving. Here let me introduce you to Picker then I will leave you to it."

As Havoc followed Hirt over towards a short, balding, weird looking dude he couldn't help but ask, "Why do you call him Picker?"

"You'll find out soon enough," Hirt replied with a short laugh. "Havoc this is Picker. Picker this is Havoc, the HGM wildcard. He's mates with Bunker so I'm sure you guys will probably get to know each other better at some stage haha. I will see you guys later."

Havoc reached out to shake Picker's hand, surprised that Hirt was aware that he knew Bunker. He thought he detected a hint of recognition in Picker's face, but he was sure he'd never met the photographer before. Picker's handshake was weak and sweaty and Havoc had to resist the urge to wipe his hand afterwards. He had heard of Picker before of course. Anyone who followed the world surf tour knew the name, although not always for good reasons.

"Havoc, is that your real name?" asked Picker. "I don't remember seeing it anywhere."

"Actually it's Dirth, Dirth Spidder, but almost everyone calls me Havoc."

"Oh I see," Picker excitedly pulled out a notebook and began writing furiously. "How do you spell that?"

Picker proceeded to ask a series of questions about Havoc and he was surprised that the photographer was so interested in him. Wildcards were usually just a bit of side entertainment for the local crowd and often considered cannon fodder for the more experienced surfers. They would have their brief moment of fame up until they were soundly beaten in their heat, then would disappear back into obscurity, never to be seen or heard of again.

"What do you think of the women's surfing?" Picker asked, changing the subject. "There's lots of hot girls on tour for a good looking young guy like you."

"They surf really well," Havoc replied suspiciously. "Claire Cooper just ripped that last wave she caught."

"Yeah, but what do you really think of them? What about Dyanna Fream? Surely you have seen Dirty Dy around? You can't miss her. Looks and acts like a porn star. Although most of them do."

"Umm I'm not sure," Havoc's radar had just been fully activated and he realised he needed to watch his words. "I think I might have seen her out at The Box a few days ago. There were a few girls out there charging."

"Really? I'm surprised," Picker said distractedly as his finger disappeared up his nose. "I thought you would have met her for sure. She usually makes a beeline for the new blood on the tour. Well nice to meet you Havoc. Like Peter said I'm sure we will see each other again. If there is anything I can help you with, and I mean anything, don't be afraid to ask. I always like to help out the new boys on tour."

Picker retrieved his finger from his nose, gave it a quick wipe on his shirt, then offered it for another handshake. Havoc had been taught long ago that if a man offers a handshake, then you always obliged and returned the favour. So, before he had a chance to stop himself, habit kicked in and he was again clasping Picker's clammy, sweaty, goober covered hand.

This time Havoc didn't resist the urge to wipe his hand afterwards.

Havoc used his free time to do some internet research. His conversation with Peter Hirt had got him thinking and he quickly learnt enough to confirm that he needed to call DS Patinsen. He found a quiet corner and dialled his mentor's number.

"Hello Dirth," said DS Patinsen in his typically calm voice. "I was beginning to think you might have already been the next victim!"

"Sorry sir," replied Havoc. "I didn't have much to report until now."

"Does that mean you have something for me?"

"I'm not sure sir," Havoc said cautiously. "First do you know if anything came of the lead on Dyanna Fream? She's at the contest and not arrested, so I'm assuming she's okay."

"Yes, she has an alibi. A young surfer confirmed he was with her all night in her hotel room. No one else saw them. Apparently she likes to keep things private, but the police who interviewed him did say he was quite smitten with her and probably would have said anything she asked him to. So, for what it's worth she is currently in the clear, but I'd still be careful around that one. I don't think we can completely rule her out yet."

"Understood sir. I had a brief but interesting conversation with the CEO of the Global Surf Association, Peter Hirt, earlier today and it got me thinking about something that you said to me the last time we talked."

"And what was that?"

"Just that I should think about who might stand to gain from those surfers being killed. The obvious being a rival or maybe someone gambling big money. But what about the GSA itself?"

"It's an interesting concept Dirth. What sent you down that road?"

"Well, when I was talking to Peter Hirt he was kind of distracted with watching the heat in the water at the time. Then he started rambling and kind of bragging about how the GSA was making lots of money. He said that they were bigger than the surfers and didn't need any heroes. He even said something along the lines of the dead surfers were past their prime and it was good they were gone."

"Did he really?" Patinsen sounded interested. "That's a pretty big call for a CEO to make. Jimmy Slide was one of the most famous sportsmen in the world. Hard to believe it would benefit the GSA for him to no longer be part of their tour."

"That's what I thought so too sir. So I did a quick search around the internet. I'm sure your financial wiz guys would be able to find more accurate information, but from what I can tell, since Slide's death the GSA and the surf industry in general has been making a killing. In fact, each death almost directly coincides with a stock price boost for most of the big companies in the weeks after. The GSA itself has made record half yearly profits and their memorial merchandise has been constantly selling out. Seems there is more money in these guys being dead than alive."

"That's really good work Dirth. I'll get our guys to look deeper into it. So, do you like this Peter Hirt for our killer or the GSA in general?

"I don't know sir. Maybe both? I didn't talk to him long enough. He kind of realised he was talking too much and took off before I could really get a handle on him, but it's got to be worth looking into. I don't have anything else at this stage anyway."

"Okay, well keep looking. When are you due to surf in the competition?"

"I'm not sure sir. I think there's a good chance it will be in two days, but it's a wake up and see scenario, so it could be any day."

"Well don't get too caught up in the hype Dirth. Remember first and foremost you are there to do a job. I'd be happy to see you lose so you can concentrate on finding the killer, but I suspect you have other ideas, so I will just say good luck and call me to let me know how you went. We can have a Patto and Havoc conversation instead of an official one."

"Thanks sir, that sounds great. Hopefully I've got a good story to tell!"

They said their goodbyes and Havoc hung up. A minute later his phone beeped alerting him that he had received a text. It simply read "Round 2 pretty boy!".

Chapter 22 PLANNING EXTORTION

"Then get out Cooper! Go on, fuck off! See where that gets you, you stuck up bitch! I run the show, hell I am the GSA. Enjoy a lifetime of one foot crap until you drop off the tour and go flip burgers for a living!"

"Oh my god Claire!" Fream exclaimed as Cooper turned off the tape recorder that had so beautifully caught Peter Hirt's epic blowup. "I can't believe you did that! You go girlfriend!"

Cooper couldn't help feeling proud at her friend's praise. Since losing unfairly to Tiffany Totthil on the Gold Coast she was determined to make sure the women's events were run with the same dedication to quality and prizemoney as the men's. With some guidance from her breathtakingly powerful benefactor, she'd become convinced that she needed some leverage to get anywhere. Unexpectedly she'd also enjoyed the shot of adrenalin from being proactive and going through with it. Even now, a few days later, as they sipped coffee around the dining room table of her little cottage in Prevally Park, she was pleasantly surprised at her success.

"Thanks Dreamy. I can't really believe I did it either. I thought for sure he'd see through me in the first 30 seconds, but I don't think his eyes ever went above my chest. If he'd looked up just for a moment, he might have seen the lie in my face, and it would've been all over."

"Oh I'm so proud of you," Fream gushed excitedly. "So, what happens next? What are you going to do with the tape?"

"I honestly don't know," Cooper replied while avoiding looking her friend in the eye, in case she too saw the lie. "I wasn't even sure I was going to bother, but then I got ripped by the judges against Tiffany again and Hirt made it clear that he told Parry to make sure I lost. I was just glad that Stephanie beat her in the final. If she had won the whole thing there's no telling what I would have done."

"Stephanie is just as bad," countered Fream. "She offered to do scissors, paper, rock for the first wave of our semifinal and I won. I should have known better, but I thought she sounded legit. So I stupidly paddled out with my guard down thinking she's going to let me have the first set. Then she sneaks inside me and gets the best wave of the heat!"

"Oh that cow! Now she's won two events in a row. She's going to be hard to beat for the world title!" Cooper was really starting to dislike Stephanie Birch. Although her benefactor had warned her not to bother, she'd tried again to get Birch's support and had been met with yet another wall of indifference. It was becoming clear that although Birch surfed well in bigger surf, she was happy to have the events run when it was small because it meant she maintained an advantage over her main competitors like Cooper, Fream and Hawaiian Karissa Kai.

"Yes, I'm going to make that bitch pays somehow, but you didn't answer my question," Fream persisted. "What's your plan with that tape?"

"I've been thinking about it, but I was hoping you might be able to help me," this time Cooper forced eye contact, hoping the lie wouldn't be revealed. "What do you think I should do?"

"Okay well let's think," Fream pondered. "First, what's your ultimate goal? Do you want Hirt gone or do you want to just level the playing field a little? You've got to be careful here Claire. He's a dangerous man with power and connections. You don't get to where he is without having played a hard game and have built up a lot of favours that he can call in if he needs them."

"Fuck that guy, let him try!" Cooper exclaimed passionately while trying to forget the fear that she had felt when she had confronted Hirt. Seeing the shocked look on Fream's face she realised that was an unusual outburst for her. "Sorry Dreamy. I never really thought of it that way. See, that's why I can't do this on my own. I just want everyone treated the same. Our prizemoney is half the men's and we always get forced to surf the worst conditions. We train just as hard as them and the crowd like to watch us just as much as the guys, even if it's not always for the right reasons."

"I agree with you Claire, but Hirt is a bigtime CEO with a colossal ego and lots of contacts who owe him favours. He's not going to like you blackmailing him and he could react in ways you don't even think of. There's also something else I think you should consider too…" Fream paused, thinking through what to say next.

"What's that?" Cooper asked after a couple of seconds.

"Have you seen how much money the GSA has been making ever since Slide was murdered? And it keeps going up with every death!"

"No, I had no idea, but how do you know?" Cooper lied. Her benefactor had patiently tutored her on it recently, but she was surprised that Fream was aware too.

"Look it's nothing really Claire. Just be careful around Peter Hirt. Trust me."

"I'm not scared of that asshole," Cooper replied passionately. She wasn't satisfied with her friends answer but decided not to push it. "And besides, with you on my side he will think twice about doing anything. Will you help me?"

"Against my better judgement, yes I will," Fream agreed reluctantly. "But let's not rush into things. The way I see it you have two choices. You can either blackmail Hirt himself and see where that gets you or release the tape to the media and hope that creates enough negative publicity to get him sacked. Both ideas come with their own set of pros and cons."

"Such as?" Cooper asked, although she suspected she knew the answers. Being brought up in a country town was hardly good practice for a career in extortion, but she was learning fast.

"Well, if you blackmail him, you tip your hand. He could threaten physical harm if you released the tape to the media or he could call your bluff and hope it goes away. There's enough misogynistic fuckers on the GSA Board of Directors that owe him favours that he could possibly ride out the publicity, especially if he knows it's coming.

"Same goes if you release it straight to the media. They are so used to the sordid shit that goes on with surfing these days that this just might only be worth a few headlines that will blow over with the next scandal. Then even if he does resign or is sacked, there's no guarantee the next person will be any better."

Cooper had different thoughts on the potential of Hirt's replacement but chose not to voice them. "That's good advice Dreamy thank you so much. I really don't think I could do this without you. I know I've been a bit strange lately and you've been really patient with me, even when you wanted more than I've been prepared to give." Cooper reached out tentatively and lightly clasped Fream's hand.

Fream gave her hand a little squeeze in return but surprised Cooper by pulling away. "That's okay Claire, but to be honest I don't think I'd have the energy anyway."

"Well I never! The famous libido of Dyanna 'The Dream' Fream does have limits after all," Cooper was surprised at Fream's reaction, then something occurred to her. "Wait a minute! It's that boy isn't it? Havoc?" she saw the look on Fream's face and knew it to be true and burst out laughing. "Has he worn you out? Have you finally met your match?"

"Well let's just say that he's better than most," Fream smiled conspiratorially. "I'm not complaining that's for sure, but I'm surprised you didn't notice when I walked in. I've been walking like a cowboy who's been too long in the saddle. God knows how I managed to stand on a surfboard!"

Cooper lost herself in another fresh burst of laughter. For a moment all her plans were forgotten and she was just another innocent girl talking to her best friend. "Now you are going to have to tell me the full story. I want to know everything and don't spare the details."

"How long have you got?" Fream replied. "You better make us another coffee."

Chapter 23 THE LAST SECOND HAIL MARY

Fream could see that Havoc was struggling badly and her heart went out to him. It was the final heat of the day at the HGM Margaret River Masters and whatever dreams he might have had of fame and fortune before paddling out certainly weren't coming true. He was all on his own against two relentless forces of nature and those forces were ruthlessly kicking his ass.

The first force of nature against him was the conditions. It was big, stormy and getting bigger. The waves had been continuously building from eight foot in the morning to a solid 12ft and Havoc had just copped a genuine 15ft set on the head, washing him hundreds of metres towards shore. It was a miracle his board and legrope were still in one piece.

The other force of nature was his opponent, Gabriel Andre. The Brazilian had luckily caught a wave just before the big set arrived and was safely cruising on the back of a jet ski while Havoc was getting mowed down by monsters that were almost peeling to the river mouth.

Fream was silently cheering for Havoc from the competitor's area along with a lot of other GSA people who appeared keenly interested in the events unfolding out to sea. It was almost split down the middle as to who they wanted to see win. In one corner there was a large and loud number of Brazilian surfers and their posse supporting their number one hero. In the other corner were the Aussies, including a very vocal Bunker Haze, Morpheus from HGM, Surfers Union rep Luke Perrot, as well as local boys Taj Long and Jake Roberts. Also on Havoc's side were the crew cheering because he was the underdog, or in some cases his easy going and talkative nature had already won him some friends, especially with the Hawaiian and South African boys who had been out at The Box a week earlier.

The score came through for Andre's wave and it was a 7. In these conditions that was a good score and he immediately caught another wave and got a 6. The heat was nearly half over, Havoc was behind 13 points to zero and hadn't even caught a wave.

"He's sitting in the wrong place," a frustrated Bunker lamented. "He needs to be further out and towards the right for sure. He's in no man's land."

"Yeah, you can tell he hasn't spent much time out there. He looks lost." observed Roberts.

Fream had to agree with them. It was the first time she had seen Havoc look anything but self-assured in the ocean. She didn't think it was the size that was putting him off his game. She knew enough about him now to know that not much scared him, in or out of the ocean. No, it was almost certainly a case of rookie nerves. It was a big occasion, and he wouldn't be human if he wasn't feeling the pressure of wanting to prove he deserved his shot against the world's best.

A set arrived and Havoc had priority. He was still out of position and was madly scrambling to get in a better spot. He let the first wave go and paddled hard for the second but missed it! The Aussie contingent groaned loudly. Havoc had lost priority and now Andre could pick any wave he wanted while already holding down a huge lead. It was just about all over.

Fream knew how Havoc probably felt right now. She had her own feelings of impending doom to deal with and she'd been grateful for the distraction that he'd provided her in the past week. Ever since the police had first contacted her about her whereabouts on the night Wilson was killed, she knew she could be in trouble. She'd been lucky she wasn't already in jail, but fortunately Bunker's groupie wasn't much of a witness, and she'd enough influence over the young surfer she had slept with earlier that day that he'd readily agreed to provide an alibi for the whole time. How long he continued to maintain his story was the disturbing question.

Then there was the issue of Cooper and her desire to blackmail Peter Hirt. Fream could have easily brought down Hirt over the years but as much as she didn't like the guy, he was very good at parts of his job and who knows what the next knob jockey who replaced him would be like? Sometimes it's better the devil you know, which she might have tried to explain to her friend except she could see Cooper was too far gone down the path to listen. She had opted for a temporary stall tactic while she tried to come up with a better solution.

Cooper's behaviour itself was a mystery. Ever since the presentation night in Bali she had noticed a change in her personality starting with that little black dress she wore. The shy, feminine tomboy that she used to be would never have worn such a revealing dress. Now Fream almost didn't know this sexier, more confidant woman, who had happily seduced a man while concealing a tape recorder.

The next set appeared and Andre found another diamond in the rough. It was a bit smoother than most of the other waves that had been coming through in what was increasingly becoming a giant washing machine and he surfed it well. With time running out Havoc had no choice but to catch the next wave which was shorter and partially ruined by the broken white water of Andre's wave. Still Havoc got in a couple of reasonable turns and at least would get some sort of score that might help quieten his nerves a little.

As they both raced back out to try and be first to the take-off zone and win priority the scores came through. Andre's wave netted him a 7.5 and Havoc a straight 5 point ride. Andre now had a 14.5 total score for his best two waves to Havoc's 5 points. It meant that with around two minutes to go Havoc needed a 9.5 out of 10 which was near impossible in the conditions and only one chance to get it. The only good news was that he won the paddle battle and had been awarded priority.

His supporters in the contest arena had all but given up on him. Roberts got up and turned to walk off proclaiming "It's all over" before Bunker assured him it was worth staying the last minute or so.

"Havoc's a gnarly dude man. I've seen him do some sick shit in his time. Trust me, he can do this!"

It appeared that Huey, the god of the ocean, had a flair for the dramatic as with a minute to go a big wave appeared on the horizon. The noise in the competitor's area rose dramatically as shouted words of encouragement and advice to both surfers came from all parties. Outside Fream could hear the onsite contest announcer getting excited too and the spectators began whistling and screaming along with him.

Havoc was too far out to sea to hear any of that, but it was clear he knew what was approaching because he was paddling out as hard as he could with Andre right on his heels trying to create extra pressure. He couldn't stop Havoc catching the wave, but he could still bend the rules and add a degree of difficulty to it. Fream had been trying to act disinterested in the outcome, but everyone was on their feet now cheering at the top of their lungs and she couldn't help but join them.

The wave was easily 12ft, maybe even bigger on the peak. At the last second Havoc swung his board late under the lip, took two paddles and jumped to his feet.

He free fell as thousands of tons of white water chased him down the face. He briefly disappeared in the maelstrom and the onlookers all groaned in unison before cheering again as he re-emerged and leaned into a strong bottom turn.

"Oh no it's going to close out!" Bunker cried and he was right. A huge wave was coming at him from the opposite direction and he was going to be caught in the middle, leaving Havoc with two choices - straighten out and go home embarrassed, or an all-out attack for death or glory. There was never a doubt what option he would choose.

Havoc maintained his bottom turn and threw himself and his board at the oncoming wave in a last second Hail Mary with no concern for his own safety whatsoever. It was the kind of thing you would do on a fun five-foot day, but not on a huge storm driven beast straight out of the Antarctic.

"No Fucken Way!!!" everyone screamed at once as he hit the lip of the oncoming monster and jammed hard on his inside rail sending a huge fan of spray into the air. He tried to ride out with the falling wave, but it was far too big and powerful. Havoc was simply evaporated into a 30ft high avalanche of white water.

Once again the crowd groaned, but then impossibly a little black figure appeared at the bottom of the avalanche still standing on his board and everyone went crazy. They were screaming and cheering, banging chairs into signs, thumping tables, stamping feet, anything that would make noise to help convince the judges to give Havoc the score.

"See! See! I told you!" Bunker was beyond excited as he slapped crew on the back and high fived everybody else. "My man Havoc is a gnarly dude man. Fuck that's got to be the score!"

The debate now raged throughout the area is to whether it was a 9.5 or not. The Brazilians, while admitting it was incredible, argued that it was only one manoeuvre and the judges rarely offered such high scores for a single turn. The rest believed that it was easily the most incredible thing seen all day and deserved to be rewarded accordingly. One thing they all agreed on was that it was going to be close.

Havoc and Andre had both reached the bottom of the stairs and still no scores had been locked in. It was clear that the judges were taking their time to make sure they got it right. They would be looking at the replays of Havoc's ride and also that of Andre's 7.5 to see whether it was a full two points higher or not. Both surfers shook hands before being swamped by the crowd and were busily signing autographs while they awaited the judges' decision.

Fream nearly had tears in her eyes she was so excited for Havoc and she knew he was going to get special treatment in the bedroom later on. Curiously there was also a few heart flutters which she ruthlessly attempted to stamp out. This was not the time to start having feelings for a pretty boy surfer!

She turned her attention back to the video screen that would announce the scores. There were five judges and the highest and lowest score would be discarded with the other three scores averaged out for the final score. If Havoc scored a 9.5 he would win, even though they would finish tied on total score he would win for having the highest single score.

Finally, the first score came through. It was a 9.7! Things looked good and the excitement level lifted. Could this be an incredible upset with a completely unknown wildcard taking out a world champion? The next score was a 9.6 and the impossible just became a little more possible. The next two scores came in straight after, a 9.4 and a 9.2. Now it was back to the exact same requirement. Anything below a 9.5 from the last judge wouldn't be enough.

The crowd went silent and held their breath. The surfers had stopped signing autographs and both were standing motionless waiting for the last score. The last judge was taking forever! Some of the crowd even started a slow hand clap trying to speed up the process but most stayed quiet and waited, praying for the score they wanted to hear. At last it came through, it was a 9.4! Havoc had fallen short by a tenth of a point from creating one of the biggest upsets in recent surf history.

Chapter 24 PARTY TIME

Havoc was devastated when he heard the last judge's score. He had missed out on defeating a former world champion and current favourite for this year's title by the barest of margins. That feeling only lasted until he walked into the competitors' area where he was instantly mobbed!

A wasted but happy looking Bunker was the first to get to him, completely surprising Havoc by crash tackling him with a big hug.

"Dude that was the sickest thing I've ever seen out there," he loudly proclaimed when he finally let Havoc go. "What were you even thinking trying that shit?"

"Not much!" Havoc conceded. Truth was he'd been incredibly frustrated at his poor performance and had thrown himself at the big closeout in the hope it would destroy him and provide something else to think about other than his impending embarrassment. He was just as surprised as everyone else that he had made it.

"I can't believe those judges didn't give you the score man," Bunker continued. "I thought you had him for sure!"

Others quickly followed Bunker's lead with back slaps and handshakes aplenty. They all had similar things to say about how the judges should have rewarded him with the win, but any bitterness Havoc might have had from the close loss quickly evaporated under the weight of acceptance from his peers. Even Gabriel Andre, The Terminator himself, who had not said a single word to him in the water and given him death stares the whole time, had put his arm around Havoc and given him a few words of respect and encouragement.

Once the surfers had all paid their respects a broadly smiling Morpheus approached. He bypassed Havoc's attempt at a handshake and went straight in for a hug.

"Sorry I couldn't get the win for you Morpheus," Havoc apologized as they broke contact.

"Nonsense kid," Morpheus smiled. "I'm impressed. You did the HGM team proud. That's no mean feat to score a 9.4 in your first ever GSA heat and against a former world champ no less. You've repaid my faith in you big time, now we just have to work out how to reward you."

"That's easy!" Bunker crashed the conversation before Havoc could answer. "Let's fucken party! Settlers Tavern tonight. The Southern River Band are playing. We can get our mosh on! It's going to be sick!"

"Shouldn't you be worried about your heat tomorrow?" Havoc didn't want his friend to jeopardise his shot at back-to-back wins and a big lead in the World Title race just to celebrate a loss.

"Nah didn't you hear?" Bunker replied happily. "They have put the event on hold. It's going to be 25 foot tomorrow and onshore. It will take a couple of days for the ocean to settle down after that. No excuses Havoc, we're tying one on tonight!"

Havoc looked at Morpheus for guidance and his sponsor merely smiled and shrugged his shoulders. "Sounds like a good plan to me Havoc. Bunker's right. The whole tour has the night off and The Southern River Band are a killer indie rock band, you will love them! Besides what else are you going to do?"

Havoc took a quick glance over to where he'd spied Fream earlier, but she wasn't there anymore and nowhere to be seen. He turned his attention back to the conversation and could tell from the sly grin on Morpheus's face that he knew exactly what Havoc had been thinking.

"Well what are we waiting for?"

Havoc felt right at home the moment he walked into The Settlers Tavern after stopping by his cabin for a shower, some food and a change of clothes. There was cool surf memorabilia on many of the walls, the place was packed with happy people and the sound of The Southern River Band playing the first couple of songs of their set put an instant smile on his face. Everywhere he looked he saw familiar faces from around the contest all taking advantage of the day off tomorrow. He went to the bar and ordered himself a Coopers Pale Ale and found himself a quiet little niche so he could relax, savour his incredible day and do a spot of people watching. After all there was a distinct possibility that somewhere in this pub was the killer he was looking for.

Bunker held court in one section of the bar surrounded by an entourage of beautiful women and other assorted hangers on. In front of him was a dozen bottles of champagne and a line of tequila shots that were instantly replaced the moment anyone necked one. In another section Gabriel Andre and a large Brazilian contingent were surrounded by another pack of incredible looking ladies. In a quieter corner Peter Hirt was in deep conversation with Morpheus, Surfers Union rep Luke Perrot and a few other industry types. Across from them there seemed to be almost the whole women's pro tour including Fream, Claire Cooper, Karissa Kai, Stephanie Birch, Tiffany Tothill, Sally Lord, Molly Perkins and Belle Silva, all happily getting drunk and occasionally busting some moves on the dance floor. Even Picker could be seen lurking in a dark section with some equally sordid dudes that looked like they would be more at home at a nightclub in Kings Cross at 2am than a surf pub in Margaret River.

Havoc hadn't been there long when a couple of young local surfers approached him carrying two jugs of beer. They refilled his glass and introduced themselves as Jarryd and DC. They'd seen his pictures from that wave at Cape Fear in the surfing mags and had watched his heat with interest earlier that day and wanted to say hello. Havoc took an instant liking to the two larrikans and it wasn't long before the beer and stories started flowing freely.

With tongues suitably lubricated and loosened, talk invariably turned to the subject of the heaviest waves on the planet and Black Rainbow was mentioned. Black Rainbow was a semi mythical death slab located somewhere deep on the south coast of Western Australia that had only been discovered in recent years and the photos that had emerged from it were like nothing Havoc had seen anywhere else in his life.

Jarryd and DC claimed that they not only knew where it was but had surfed it on a number of occasions. They insisted that despite the fact that conditions were horrible for Margaret River tomorrow, they would be good for Black Rainbow and they'd happily take him there if he was keen.

Havoc didn't believe them for one second and called it for piss talk. He'd watched the boys each buy several large jugs of beer and had happily helped drink them. He knew they were in the zone that kicks in at roughly the ten-beer stage where suddenly you are not only invincible, but the solutions to most of the world's problems simply open up in such a way that you wonder how nobody had ever thought of them before.

Unfortunately, in celebrating your new-found invincibility and world problem solver awareness, you have an eleventh beer and just as suddenly you become a mindless, slurring drongo that no one can understand. Then you wake up the next morning with a massive headache and no memory whatsoever of those incredible earth changing ideas.

The most likely scenario was that despite their assurances that they would pick him up very early to go on a mission to Black Rainbow, he would never hear from Jarryd and DC again. However, in the off chance there was some grain of truth in their stories, he gave them his cabin number and offered to buy the next round. He was very surprised when they refused, arguing that he was a guest in their town and they should pay.

The boys had just left Havoc to go to the bar when he felt someone grab his backside and he turned expecting to see Fream's impeccable rig standing behind him. Instead, it was the bald head and shiny, sweating face of Picker that he was greeted with.

"Hello Picker. How are you?" Havoc fought the urge to slap him. He was used to gay guys trying to pick him up and it didn't bother him in the slightest, but this was the first time one had blatantly copped a feel. Now he better understood why girls didn't like it. The man made his skin crawl!

"I'm fucken awesome Havoc. I heard you made quite the impression at the contest today. That's good. That's very good. I'm pleased to hear that!" Picker was clearly on drugs of some sort. His eyes were like saucers and he was grinding his teeth badly, not to mention the volumes of sweat that was pouring off him.

"Yes, well it would have been better if I won but never mind. Everyone seemed happy with what I did so that's good I guess." Havoc didn't really want to go into details too much in case Picker stayed to chat. He looked for Jarryd and DC to see if they could rescue him, but they were still stuck in the queue at the bar.

"Well from tomorrow things are going to change for Dirth 'Havoc' Spidder like you would never have thought," Picker said cryptically. "Of that I can promise you. You're going to be a star."

"I don't know about that. I lost maybe the only GSA heat I will ever go in. I can't see me achieving too much fame and fortune."

"Trust me Havoc. You'll see, you'll see. Just wait until tomorrow and it will all become clear. Picker knows these things," Picker said tapping his nose, but for once not shoving it up there and digging around. "I used to have a deal going with Matt Wilson back in the day and we could do the same. Like I said, I can help you Havoc, all you have to do is ask."

That sparked a bit of interest from Havoc. "A deal with Wilson. What kind of deal?"

"I'll say no more tonight Havoc. Tomorrow is soon enough. Here take this," Picker held out a business card and Havoc took it and put it in his pocket so as to not offend. Without another word Picker headed back to his seedy followers leaving Havoc feeling part confused and part violated. Fortunately, the boys turned up with a couple more jugs of beer.

"Who was that weirdo?" asked Jarryd as he topped up Havoc's glass.

"You really don't want to know," replied Havoc laughing. They clinked glasses and got back to having a good yarn.

Eventually Havoc left the boys chatting to some of their local mates and started moving around the pub striking up conversations here and there. He said hello and briefly chatted with Peter Hirt, did a couple of tequila shots with Bunker and Morpheus, then turned down an admittedly tempting offer from one of Bunker's groupies to give him a quick blowjob outside in the carpark. Gabriel Andre dragged Havoc into his group and introduced him around. Andre surprised him by being very friendly and his English was excellent, so they were soon trading stories and laughing like old mates. Andre even grabbed one of his super model entourage and introduced her to Havoc suggesting the two of them would get along very well.

The super model's name was Giselle and she seemed to like Havoc just fine. She was a typical classically tall, Latin beauty with long brown hair, dark eyes, tanned skin and endless legs made longer by the high heels she was wearing. The Southern River Band were late in their last set now and they were absolutely rocking the house. The mosh pit was a swarm of heaving, sweating bodies embracing the sick tunes and Giselle dragged him into the middle of it. Her style of mosh had a definite dirty dancing feel and before he knew it, she was rubbing herself all over him.

Giselle had all the right moves and Havoc's ego was getting a major boost from her very amorous attentions. She smoothly went from grinding her arse into his crotch, to throwing her arms around him, grabbing hold of his backside and pulling him in tight to gyrate in as close a simulation of sex as you could get with your clothes on. Despite the fact his body was responding accordingly and his erection pressed hard into her tight body, Havoc found his thoughts kept turning to another woman. After a couple of songs, he left Giselle on the dance floor telling her he was going to the toilet. He promised he would return, then went looking for Fream.

The whole pub was almost wall to wall bodies, so moving around quickly was near impossible. It took Havoc a good 15-20 minutes to do a proper scout of inside and outside and Fream was nowhere that he could find. Chastising himself for turning down the easy opportunity that had been on offer with such a stunning Latino, he returned to the dancefloor to rekindle the flame only to spy Giselle passionately kissing another guy. He'd blown his chance!

Havoc shook his head at his stupidity and went looking for Jarryd and DC to tell them about it. But they were nowhere to be seen either and as Havoc soon discovered, nor were most of the crew he knew. Within a few minutes last drinks was called, the Southern River Band finished their final encore and the bouncers started to shuffle people towards the door.

Havoc joined the people outside, took a quick look around, saw no one familiar except an inebriated Stephanie Birch crossing the street and decided he may as well do the walk of shame back to his cabin on his own, more than a little bemused at how he'd gone from 'King of The Dance Floor' to 'Larry No Mates' in such a short period of time.

Chapter 25 THE KILLER STRIKES

The Killer eyed the next target as she staggered up the dark street oblivious to her impending doom. It had actually been a fun night and The Killer had enjoyed mingling at the Settlers Tavern with all the crew involved with the surf contest. The Killer was aware that it was enjoyable not so much for the social interaction involved, but the sweetness of not knowing who the next victim was going to be. It was a such a delicious target rich environment and The Killer had taken time to talk to each of the potential next victims, waiting for a sign that would single out the unlucky prey from the ones who would sleep soundly tonight.

Most of the top men's and women's surfers were lurking somewhere in the pub, either on the dance floor, chatting at the bar or doing lines of whatever drugs they could get their hands on in the toilets. However only a few of them fitted the criteria to be on The Killer's list. People whose demise would contribute to the ultimate goal.

The Killer had chatted for a while with Bunker Haze. Bunker was typically off his face and would have been an easy target, but he didn't really meet the criteria, not yet anyway. The Killer actually liked Bunker, at least as much as it was possible for a murderer to like anyone. Beneath his super rich, playboy rock star exterior, The Killer recognised an equally troubled soul. Bunker would need to be eliminated one day, there was no doubt about that, but there were others higher on the list that warranted removing from the planet first.

Picker was lurking in a dark dingy corner of the pub with a typically sleazy bunch of society rejects. The Killer briefly considered ending Picker just for fun, as even though he wasn't on the list, it would be doing the world a public service.

That arrogant Brazilian world champion Gabriel Andre was high on the list and The Killer had spent some time studying him and those around him but decided it was too hard for tonight. He was never left alone and The Killer suspected at least a couple of Andre's group doubled as his bodyguards. He didn't appear to drink anything except drinks they purchased themselves then passed to Andre. It seemed that he at least, took his safety seriously and had been proactive in taking steps to make The Killer's job that much harder. That was a pleasing thought. It was about time such good work was treated with the respect it deserved.

The Killer had settled on a target and waited for the opportunity to spike her drink, but getting close enough to do the job was not easy.

Stephanie Birch, the multiple GSA world champion bitch that she was, didn't go out drinking much, but she'd just won the women's event to take a big lead in the World Title race and was celebrating. The Killer had never liked Birch and recent developments had put her near the top of the list, so the opportunity to take her out was simply too good to miss. Until now it must have seemed like only the men had to fear and respect The Killer's capabilities. After tonight they all would, just as it should be.

The Killer didn't have to wait long for the perfect opportunity and had slipped the Fentanyl into Birch's drink when her back was turned to talk to someone. It wasn't a huge dose, not enough to kill her or perhaps spark suspicion by changing the taste too much, but enough to get a non-drug taker sick and want to walk the few hundred metres to her accommodation. The simple act of a drug overdose was no longer enough for The Killer. More risk meant more reward.

Birch had taken the little laneway shortcut as The Killer knew she would. In other parts of the world people would avoid these kinds of shortcuts knowing it could hide all sorts of dubious characters, but here in a country town like Margaret River, a short cut was exactly that and no more. In the darkness there were several spots suitable for an ambush but tonight stealth wasn't really required, The Killer could see that Birch was having a hard time just staying on her feet.

Birch paused to vomit noisily into the bush and The Killer took the opportunity to draw closer, ready to strike. Some sort of sixth sense must have triggered a warning as Birch turned towards The Killer, eyes searching desperately for the source of the danger she felt. When she saw The Killer, she relaxed slightly.

"Oh, it's only you," Birch slurred. "God I feel so si..." she cut off when she saw the knife in The Killer's hand and reality began to dawn in her drug fogged mind. She opened her mouth as if to try and talk The Killer out of it, but no words came, she turned to run but her legs wouldn't work and she fell to her knees. The Killer struck…

Chapter 26 BLACK RAINBOW

The thumping and shouting seemed to come from a long way away, like being heard through a dense fog. Slowly that fog began to clear and Havoc groaned, realising that it wasn't just his head that felt like a hammer was bashing his skull into little pieces, someone was actually banging on his cabin door. But why on earth would anyone be waking him up at this hour? Surely he'd only been home from the pub for ten minutes?

A quick check on his phone revealed that it was 3.30am, so he turned it off, not wanting anything further to disturb his sleep. It was far too early to be awake while hungover in freezing cold Margaret River. Havoc tried to ignore the banging, but it only got louder and then he heard voices.

"C'mon Havoc get up! Black Rainbow will be on!"

Then it all started to come back to him. Havoc got up and opened the door to find Jarryd and DC on his doorstep in the pitch-black darkness, surprisingly bright eyed and raring to go.

"Were you still in bed ya soft cock?" Jarryd ribbed him light heartedly. "I thought you east coasters were hard core! C'mon let's go or do you want me to call your mum to come around and cook you breakfast?"

"Don't need to," replied Havoc sleepily. Then he grinned. "Your mum already did it for me. She's still back there if you want to say hello. She goes alright for an old bird!"

The boys all laughed and the cobwebs in Havoc's brain cleared remarkably fast when they informed him the swell buoys were reading seven metres and hadn't yet peaked. It took just minutes for Havoc to grab boards and wetsuits and head outside to where two old school

Toyota Land Cruiser troop carriers sat waiting with a couple of jet skis hitched behind them ready to go. The boys had clearly been up for a while getting things ready. It occurred to Havoc that he had seriously underestimated these two and his heart rate lifted a notch. Maybe he would get to surf Black Rainbow after all?

As he followed the boys out to the cars, he could make out that there was a fourth member of the team checking the straps holding down the jet skis by the red glow of the car's taillights. Something about this guy's profile was familiar to Havoc, but he couldn't put his finger on it until DC piped up.

"You know Broady don't ya?" he said and right then Havoc knew that this surf mission was 100% legit.

"G'day Havoc fancy seeing you here," Broady laughed as they shook hands.

"I thought these guys were full of shit!" Havoc replied laughing with him. "If I had of known the truth I would have held back on the beers a bit. I'm surprised Jarryd and DC are still walking. They were smashing them down last night!"

"We were buying two jugs at a time," DC informed him. "One full strength for a couple of boys there we thought might head down to Black Rainbow as well, so we wanted to slow them down a bit and gave them the hard stuff while we were on the Coopers mid strengths. We had them on the tequila shots later too, while we necked water! It's an expensive way to try and guarantee uncrowded surf but Black Rainbow is worth it. Hopefully they're still in bed and too hungover to follow us."

"It's an old trick," Jarryd said with a smile as he threw the last of Havoc's gear in the back of one of the cars. "Crew think you're a hard-core surf animal who parties all night and charges big surf by day. Gives you heaps of street cred and a few chicks as well. The way you were drinking we thought you were in on it, so we didn't say anything. Did you really not know the difference?"

"East Coasters are a different breed," Broady laughingly interrupted before Havoc could answer. "Too worried about their magazine profiles for anything else. C'mon Havoc you're with me."

Jarryd and DC piled into the other car and the boys got underway. It was still dark and the sun wasn't due to rise for a couple of hours yet but Havoc was too excited to sleep, instead he picked Broady's brain on everything from what to expect to what his fellow surfers were like.

"Mate those two are as core as it gets," Broady replied to Havoc's question about his future tow surfing partners. "And don't worry, they know their shit. Aside from the locals, Jarryd and DC have put in almost as much time at Black Rainbow as anyone. This is actually the first time I've been on a trip down there with them. Usually they would just turn up out of nowhere under their own steam and charge it. It's got to the point where it's like fuck it, let's go down together and save fuel."

"How come I haven't heard of them?" asked Havoc as the little convoy wound its way through consistent rain and a dense karri forest that reared just metres from either side of the road. Occasionally kangaroos bounced into vision or were caught seemingly paralysed into not moving by the approaching spotlights. It was a dangerous drive and Broady's eyes never left the road as he continued his story.

"It's because they aren't there for photos or fame. Just to surf the thing. It's the same with the locals down there. They don't care whether there's a photographer there or not. Guys like Shanna, Reefy, Krebs or Greggo- those guys just hunt waves like Black Rainbow all the time and couldn't give a stuff if someone took a picture or not. It's a beautiful thing. It's one of the reasons why I love it down there so much. The people and places are so far from the tabloid bullshit that is pro surfing these days it soothes the soul."

The conversation slowed and Havoc found himself thinking about what might be ahead of him. He'd seen photos of Black Rainbow and had always dreamed of surfing it. It was different to Cape Fear and despite Cape Fear's reputation as one of the deadliest waves in the world, in many ways Black Rainbow put it to shame. While Cape Fear broke just metres from the dry rock of the shore and not far from the biggest city in Australia, Black Rainbow was a much bigger wave that broke on an underwater pinnacle way out in the middle of the ocean, many kilometres from the nearest help if something went wrong.

The danger wasn't in hitting the rocks like you could at Cape Fear, instead it was the huge deep hole on the other side of the pinnacle that the sheer power of the wave could force you into. In a split second you could find yourself 20m below the surface while being cartwheeled in all directions with your eardrums blown, leaving no sense of equilibrium or where the surface and your next breath might be.

Serious injury and drowning were very real possibilities at Black Rainbow. Add to that it was a long way to the nearest hospital and huge great white sharks were regularly seen in the area and it's a miracle that no one had died there yet. Realistically it was only a matter of time.

As they continued to drive the rain died off and slowly it started to get light. They'd taken a number of turns on different forest roads in the dark and Havoc had to admit he was pretty lost. There hadn't been any mention of protecting the whereabouts of the location of the wave like there often is when surfers reveal secret spots to friends, but in this case there wasn't much point. Havoc couldn't have found his way here anyway.

Eventually they turned down an obscure dirt track and it led to a little boat ramp on the edge of a small river. With its tranquil setting of overhanging trees, tannin coloured water and the ocean nowhere to be seen, it hardly looked like somewhere near one of the most dangerous waves in the world.

The boys parked and started putting on their wetsuits, untying jet skis and preparing camera gear. The air was freezing cold and after dipping his foot in the icy river water, Havoc immediately wished he had brought a thicker wetsuit, a hood and some booties. He had them in his luggage when he flew over but given his foggy early morning brain, he'd completely forgot to grab them before they left the hotel room.

"Don't worry," said Jarryd seeing his obvious discomfort at the water temperature "The ocean is warmer than the river, by about one degree!" he laughed as he tossed a spare pair of booties and a wetsuit hood to Havoc. "Have these ya east coast fairy, they should help protect those delicate toes and pretty head of yours!"

Havoc smiled gratefully as he caught the extra warmth supplying items. It was the Aussie way to insult each other light heartedly and the friendly banter was making him feel part of the crew. Added to that he liked what he saw. The boys were going through an obviously well practised routine of checking every bit of equipment to make sure nothing was left to chance, all while scoffing as much energy providing food as they could consume.

With everything prepared, Jarryd and DC jumped on one jet ski complete with tow boards and a rescue sled while Havoc joined Broady and a case full of camera gear on the other. Together they roared along the river in the stunning misty, early morning golden light. There was something almost prehistoric about the environment they drove their modern machines through with huge trees overhanging the river and not a single house or sign of humanity in sight.

Broady drove while Havoc clung onto his waist still shivering from the cold despite wearing his wetsuit, borrowed booties and hood as well as a wool beanie on his head and several other heavy jumpers and jackets. All of them were similarly attired with as much clothing and rubber as they could find. Havoc realised it was no wonder so many surfers that lived on the south coast of Australia chose to grow beards. Any bit of extra warmth would have been gold.

"So where the fuck are we?" Havoc yelled over the roar of the jet ski. The question was asked not so much for the need to have an answer, but in an attempt to take his mind of the incredible cold that was rapidly finding its way to the depth of his soul.

"This river flows into a big estuary just around the next bend, which eventually meets the ocean," replied the tough West Oz waterman. "Then we have got to punch out through the waves at the estuary mouth and it's another forty minutes flat out along the coast dodging massive waves to get to Black Rainbow. It's a fucking mission but it will be worth it if it's on!"

At that moment the two skis emerged from the narrow confines of the river into the wide expanse of shallow water that was the estuary. Immediately the wind seemed to pick up and the water surface went from super calm to choppy, leaving no chance to talk further. It was just hang on and tuck in as close to Broady's back as possible to keep the wind chill down.

Twenty minutes later they were at the mouth of the estuary looking at the ocean and Havoc's heart sank. The waves were decent size, maybe six foot in surfer terms but by no means scary big. It looked like they had got skunked after all that effort. He looked over to the other ski expecting to see Jarryd and DC just as disappointed, instead they had huge smiles on their faces and were hooting.

"What are they so happy about?" he asked Broady.

"See that island out there," Broady called over the noise of the ski as he pointed to a large chunk of land out to sea. "Well that stops the swell getting in here. So if it's this big here then out in the open ocean it's going to be massive. Black Rainbow is going to be fucking pumping!!! Hold on mate, I'm going to give it some herbs!"

With that Broady and the other ski opened their throttles and raced across the water punching out through the waves and into the unknown.

As the jet skis sped their way along the rugged Southern Ocean coastline, it occurred to Havoc that this was as true a hardcore surfing adventure as he could get in today's modern era. A giant swell, a late-night gamble and a crazy journey to a random piece of ocean miles from anything. A bunch of newfound mates and some machinery that he hadn't checked himself were the only things between returning to civilization safely or disappearing in a part of the world that no one even knew he was in. It was raw, fucking dangerous and Havoc had never felt more alive and switched on. This was the shit he lived for!

The ocean was far from calm despite the light offshore winds. The storm that had created the rain they'd driven through had only just passed, leaving behind a very disturbed and lumpy surface making the ride far from comfortable. Eventually they pulled up at a spot that looked no different from anywhere else except they were a bit closer to the coast. They sat there idling for a couple of minutes while the ocean remained silent. For a moment Havoc thought it had all been for nothing, then without warning the horizon lifted.

Nothing in Havoc's life had prepared him for what he saw next. Words could not describe the sheer beauty and outright terrifying power he witnessed in that first ever set at Black Rainbow. The set was HUGE! Just a big, thick, dark lump of ocean that drew so much water off the reef underneath that it created an incredibly clean 20ft wave face that turned itself inside out and unloaded with a fury that was impossible to comprehend. The sun shone through the spray blown off the top of the black as death wave, creating an incredible rainbow and leaving no doubt in his mind as to how it got its name. Havoc had never seen anything more beautiful or frightening in his life!

Several waves followed the first, each equally as majestic and terrifying as the ones before it. Havoc was still trying to process what he'd seen when three more jet skis roared into the zone, each with two guys on them. It was hard to believe considering he felt like he was at the end of the earth. That was until Broady pointed out who they were as they arrived.

"Sick!" he yelled. "These are all the local crew. They're the best guys out here by miles and good lads to boot. "That's Greggo and Reefy," he said pointing to one ski. "And over there you've got Shanna and Crysso. Then you've got Krebs and Curts on that one, they're brothers," he said pointing to the other two. "They're all fucking fearless nutcases mate. They'll go anything. It's amazing they are all here actually. Usually one of them is in hospital or recovering with broken bones or something."

At that moment, the horizon began to lift and one of the jet skis fired into action. It was Greggo driving and Reefy holding onto the tow rope. At first the wave didn't look that big or like it would even break, but then Greggo turned the jet ski out to sea and accelerated flinging Reefy forward as he let go of the rope.

Without warning the whole ocean heaved and in a fraction of time the wave quadrupled in size to a 25ft behemoth with a lip three times thicker than Havoc thought possible. One slight mistake and it was all over as Reefy pulled into the biggest, thickest, scariest tube Havoc had ever seen. It didn't even appear real, Reefy looked like a stick figure on one of those crazy drawings he used to do in his schoolbooks.

The sound of Broady's camera motor drive accompanied their involuntarily screaming as he captured all the magic of the ride, but suddenly those screams of joy turned to horror as it all went incredibly pear shaped. One second Reefy looked on the road to glory, then a slight bit of chop caught the inside rail of his board and he stopped dead in his tracks. In milliseconds he was being sucked backwards up the face of the wave and moments later he became part of the 10ft thick lip as it hurled itself onto the reef with a sound like an earthquake.

"Faaarrrkkk!" yelled Broady. "Keep an eye out mate. That was fucking heavy! He could be under water for a while and there's no telling where and when he might come up!"

There was another wave approaching, but neither of them were looking at it. Instead they were searching for a head to pop up amongst all that churned up white water. Greggo was already in there on the ski looking for his mate, ready to pull him aboard at a moment's notice and get him out of the danger area before the next wave got him.

Havoc had a vague recollection of seeing someone get an amazing tube out of the corner of his eye on the next wave, but his whole focus was now on searching for Reefy. There was still no sign of him as the next wave passed over. One of the worst possible scenarios for a big wave surfer is a two wave hold down, where you are still under the water and getting thrashed around when the next one passes over, thereby repeating the dose before you even have a chance to get a single gasping lungful of air. That was the nightmare Reefy was now living.

Word quickly spread that Reefy was in trouble and all skis raced into the impact zone looking for their fallen comrade. Suddenly Reefy's head appeared above the water and the horrible, almost bestial sound that issued from his lips when he could finally breathe left no doubt that he was in a lot of pain. Suddenly something black breached the surface next to him and Havoc immediately thought he was being attacked by a shark, but before he could cry out he realised it was something else, something equally as horrible.

It was Reefy's leg. He'd broken his leg that badly that it was flapping in the water next to him, still attached thanks to skin, tendons and muscles but that was all. Both lower leg bones on one leg must have broken and it was only the thick wetsuit he had on that was holding everything together.

Within minutes they had Reefy strapped to the rescue sled on the back of one of the jet skis and after a quick conference all the local boys headed off to begin the long, slow haul back to civilisation to get their friend to medical care. Reefy was in huge amounts of pain, but he gave them a brave thumbs up as he disappeared up the coast clinging onto the sled as best he could. From here every jolt, bump and movement would be sheer agony until he was given the blessed relief of the pain killing green whistle several hours away at the nearest hospital.

Havoc was in shock as he and Broady sat on the jet ski in the safety of the deep channel. Jarryd and DC idled over on their ski and the four of them looked at each other in a kind of disbelief. One minute they had arrived to find huge, awe-inspiring waves and a bunch of crazy locals with smiling faces, the next they were on their own, worrying about how their friend would fare on the long journey to help. Those waves suddenly looked a lot less appealing than before. To make matters worse, the sun went behind a cloud, turning it gloomy and horrible. There was a bad feeling in the air.

"What do we do?" asked Jarryd "Fuck that was so heavy. I don't want to go through that but there's some sick ones and it's just us!"

"Yeah I know what you mean. It looks good but fuck!" agreed DC shaking his head "I'm a mess after seeing that shit. What about you Havoc?"

Havoc didn't know what to think. His mind was in overload as he tried to process everything that had happened in the hours since he'd been dragged hungover out of his hotel room. He didn't want to have come so far and not tried to at least catch one wave at Black Rainbow, but seeing a guy's leg snapped in half and flapping around like two sticks being held together by a piece of bark did nothing for his attitude. Not to mention he had a job to do and a murderer to catch. He was about to say that maybe they should cut their losses when there was movement on the horizon.

All four of them turned their heads as a huge wave approached the lineup. It lifted, pitched and unloaded into the most perfect 25ft tube Havoc knew he would ever see in his life. As the spray from the broken wave fell, creating another rainbow, the four adventurers looked at each other and laughed. Nothing really needed to be said, but it was Jarryd that voiced what they were all thinking anyway.

"Fuck that we're on!" he cried and they took off out the back to get into position for the next set that came through.

"Mate will you be alright driving the ski on your own?" Broady asked over his shoulder.

"Yeah, why what are you going to do?" replied Havoc wondering what the hell the photographer was up to.

"I'm going to go for a swim in there," he was pointing towards the white-water maelstrom that the previous wave had created. Havoc already knew that Broady was a nutcase photographer but to forsake the safety of the ski and swim into the impact zone where you are at the mercy of the great white sharks and the power of the ocean, just for a unique camera angle? Well, that was a whole new kind of stupidity right there.

A few minutes later he dropped Broady in a spot that no sane human would ever want to be, then drove back out into the channel to watch what transpired.

For the next hour or so Havoc was captivated as Jarryd and DC took turns riding tubes that defied description while Broady dodged death to capture it on film. It was clear that these three guys were in their element despite the remoteness of their situation and the sheer danger that every wave represented. It was the greatest show on Earth, and he was the sole witness.

Eventually the moment came that Havoc was part dreading and part craving when Jarryd and DC drove over to him.

'You're up mate!" DC called as he jumped off the rescue sled on the back of their ski and passed the board and tow rope to Havoc.

Havoc knew that from this point on he could not afford one moment's hesitation, or he might end up severely injured or worse. He settled his feet into the tow straps on the board, grabbed the rope and said the only two words he trusted himself to say.

"Let's go!"

Jarryd fired up the ski and started towing Havoc out to sea. Several times he looked over his shoulder to check on Havoc, perhaps gauging whether he was up for it or not. Cape Fear was one thing, Black Rainbow was on a level above almost any other wave on the planet.

"You got any pointers?" Havoc yelled over the noise of the engine.

"Yeah, when the wave breaks here," Jarryd replied pointing to the impact zone with a smile on his face. 'Don't be there!"

Havoc laughed in reply. He should have known he wouldn't get a straight answer.

"What sort of wave do you want?" Jarryd called out to him as they got into the tow zone. "You want a warmup, or go straight for glory?"

Havoc didn't know how to answer that one, so he left it to the gods. "Whatever comes through mate!" Jarryd gave him the thumbs up and killed the throttle. Now the waiting game begun. Havoc was floating several kilometres out to sea in the deepest, blackest water imaginable. Around him the ocean was alive. Further out he could see birds wheeling and diving where a school of tuna had driven baitfish to the surface, a pod of dolphins appeared on their way to share the bounty and Havoc begun feeling like shark food. He was just about to pull himself up the tow rope to get a bit closer to the false safety of the jet ski when Jarryd stood up and looked intently out to sea.

"We're on!" was all he said as he kicked the ski forward and Havoc's pulse rate went off the charts in response. He tried a few deep breaths to calm his mind as they picked up speed but to no avail. This was adrenalin overload and nothing was going to keep it under control, so Havoc went the other way. He shook his head, loosened his shoulders and fully let loose the chains that kept his true unbridled craziness under control. He reached into his core and embraced the madness that had earned him his nickname years ago.

"Fucken bring it on Jarryd! Fucken bring it!" he screamed psyching himself up.

At first it almost didn't look like a wave, or if it did it was a small one and he wondered why Jarryd was driving at it, but then he realised what his driver saw in it. The thing was so thick and had so much volume that it resembled what you might think a tsunami looked like, almost as if the entire ocean was behind this wave, forcing it onto the reef. His adrenalin red lined and needing a release Havoc let loose a primal howl from the very bottom of his lungs. Jarryd turned with a genuine look of concern on his face.

"Are you sure you want this one?" he yelled over the noise of the ski.

"Fuck yes! Put me in deep! I fucken want this thing!"

Jarryd nodded and returned focus to his job. The wave doubled, then tripled in size and Jarryd gave a quick squirt on the throttle and spun the ski ninety degrees, sling shotting Havoc into the wave.

Havoc let go of the rope and pointed the nose of the board almost directly towards shore. It was a good move as the wave jacked even further, leaving Havoc feeling like he was bombing incredibly fast down the steepest of hills on a skateboard. The wave was so vertical if he didn't have the aid of the foot straps, he would have separated from his board and become instant fish food.

The whole ocean threw out into a massive roaring tube you could have driven a truck through. Unlike his much smaller wave at The Box where he stood there all casual, this time he was in a full crouching survival stance despite being able to fit a basketball player on his shoulders and still not reached the roof.

Havoc was only partially aware of the size and magnitude of the tube he was in, nor did he notice Broady in the perfect spot for the photo, or DC standing on the ski in the channel with both arms above his head screaming at the top of his lungs. He had gone to another place where there was only room for one instinct, pure survival. No other thoughts entered his head except the subtle adjustments required to keep him in one piece for each millisecond he rode the wave.

There was a sound like a jet airplane breaking the sound barrier and a huge wall of mist came flying past Havoc turning the world white. He buckled and struggled to hold on and just when he though he couldn't stay on his feet any longer the mist cleared and he found himself in the safety of the channel. He threw his head back and let loose an emotional scream from the very depths of his soul. Right then was the peak of his life so far. Waves at Cape Fear and The Box, backflips on motorbikes or nights with The Dream had all been special, but they were nothing compared to what he had just experienced.

Jarryd appeared and he hopped on the back of his ski without saying a word. He was almost on auto pilot. He vaguely registered that DC had picked up Broady and they were driving over as well. They all had huge smiles on their faces, their mouths were moving and sounds were coming out, but Havoc's brain refused to process those sounds into words. He was still in that tube, still coming to grips with what he seen, what he'd felt and he wasn't sure if he'd ever be the same person again. At that moment he wasn't even sure if he ever wanted to surf again!

The boys were now eagerly looking at the photos through the back of Broady's water housing and were babbling to each other excitedly. When they showed Havoc, it took him a couple of seconds to realise it was actually him. The photos didn't even look real! Havoc knew the tube had been big, but from the inside looking out while in full survival mode he never comprehended just how big the wave was at its peak. The thing was enormous! And he was just a speck that had no place being where he was.

Broady quietly pronounced that it might be the best sequence he had ever shot and he was unlikely to get anything better. As if to emphasize the point, the sun went behind the clouds again and the wind started puffing onshore. It felt like there were still waves to be had but all three looked at Havoc to see what his thoughts were.

Havoc's emotions were conflicted. He'd just had the wave of his life, no doubt about that at all. Part of him wanted more. Why not? Another part recognised that anything after that might be an anticlimax and ruin the moment. He could end up like Reefy on his next wave. Did he want to risk that?

He looked out to sea, the wind was clearly picking up and they were a long way from home. He looked at his three new friends and experienced a profound sense of love for each of them. They had unselfishly given him a moment that would stay with him until the grave and asked nothing in return. He made his decision.

"Let's go home boys."

The long trip back to Margs was a blur to Havoc. He replayed every moment of that ride in his head over and over on countless occasions. He looked at the sequence on Broady's camera so many times that the photographer snatched it out of his hands and told him to leave it alone until he got home and could make copies, just in case something happened.

Too buzzed on leftover adrenalin he offered to drive and Broady took him up on the offer, curling up in the passenger seat and going to sleep. Nearing Margaret River, Havoc turned his mobile phone on and when it found a signal it lit up like a Christmas tree. It beeped over and over as it recognised each new voice mail and text. There was at least a dozen of them. Havoc picked up the phone and only needed to see the first text for his heart to sink.

"Fuck!" he said, and he put his foot to the floor…

Chapter 28 THE YIN TO EVERY YANG

The almost spiritual magic of a truly special day had been lost on Havoc in a way he would never have thought possible. His short time on the planet had taught him to believe in karma and that there was a yin to every yang. The universe had a unique way of balancing the good with the bad, even if you didn't see it at the time.

The yin had been probably the greatest moment of his life, a surreal monster tube at Black Rainbow that he would never forget and may never surpass. The yang was a text to say that at the same time, another pro surfer had been found dead. Multiple voicemails from DS Patinsen, each more frustrated than the last at not being able to reach Havoc, confirmed that the current world number one, Stephanie Birch, had been brutally murdered.

It had been incredibly difficult to say goodbye to a completely unaware Broady, Jarryd and DC when they arrived back at his cabin. He wished he'd waited to check those messages so he could have enjoyed just a few more moments basking in the afterglow of the day with them, especially considering he had probably made some friends for life. They had all been still on a high from their epic surf mission and wanted to swap stories while Havoc knew the moment they left, he had a phone call to make and it was going to get ugly.

Havoc delayed the inevitable by taking a quick shower and making himself something to eat. It was hardly a brave move, but he had wanted to take some time to mentally prepare for what he knew was ahead. All too soon his excuses ran out and he picked up his phone and called DS Patinsen.

"Oh, so you are still alive and remembered you work for the police department!" came a very unimpressed voice down the phone line. It had been a long time since Havoc had heard such disappointment from his mentor and rightly or wrongly, he immediately felt shame.

"I'm sorry sir. No excuses. The weather turned bad so the whole pro tour took the day off and so did I. I've been out of phone range all day and only just got back. I'm really embarrassed, I don't know what else to say!"

If DS Patinsen was mollified at all by Havoc's humility he didn't show it. "Dirth you know that's not an excuse. I warned you many times about staying professional and not getting caught up in the hype around your role. Senior Sergeant Smith is looking for any excuse to get rid of you and this is the best you can do! He's been screaming at me all day asking what progress you've been making and why you haven't found the killer. How do you think that went down when I couldn't even get in touch with you? I've had to lie to keep your head out of the noose yet again. I thought that rubbish ended years ago!"

"I know sir. I'm really sorry to have put you in that situation. There's not much you can say that will make me feel worse than I already do. I actually saw Stephanie Birch leave the Settlers Tavern last night. It's hard to comprehend that someone killed her not long after."

"Dirth I don't know whether that makes it better or worse," DS Patinsen's disappointment in Havoc wasn't going to be easily overcome. He sighed. "You'd better tell me all you know I guess."

"Well it's like I said sir," Havoc reported. "The contest was put on hold so just about everyone was at the Settlers Tavern. In fact, I can't think of anyone relevant to the case who wasn't. Peter Hirt was there, so was Dyanna Fream and everyone else. I remember seeing Stephanie Birch hanging with a lot of the girls from the pro tour. There was a big group of them that kind of occupied their own space in the pub and they occasionally hit the dance floor. Other than seeing Birch outside the pub at the end of the night looking a bit drunk I don't have much to add that might be relevant."

"So you didn't see anything suspicious? Nothing at all?"

"No sir. I wasn't exactly studying her at the time. I was on my way home when I saw her. I don't think she often drinks but she'd won the contest, so I thought she was just celebrating. Your message said she had been stabbed. Do you think it's related to the other murders?"

"At this stage there's no way to be certain. We are waiting on blood toxicology reports for any indication of drugs, but Birch was found in a little alley that is a well-used shortcut to her accommodation. She'd been stabbed multiple times with an ordinary kitchen knife. That's on a whole different level from the previous murders. Poisoning by drug overdose could be seen as less personal and doesn't involve the killer getting their hands dirty but stabbing someone comes with a much greater risk of being caught along with a significant increase in the level of intensity required to go through with it.

"It might suggest that it was someone else involved, or it could just be that our killer had something personal against Birch or is evolving and experimenting with different methods. Either way it's very worrying. Senior Sergeant Smith wants to pull you off the case. He feels you're out of your depth and I have to say I'm inclined to agree with him."

Havoc's heart sank. He knew there was no point pleading with his handler. DS Patinsen didn't respond to that sort of behaviour. He needed to be mature and logical, or he'd be on the next plane back to Sydney. He took a deep breath before he spoke.

"I understand your reasoning sir, but I'm here at ground zero and no one else is. I have been able to build a rapport with a lot of the crew involved and that was something you tasked me to do. You know that it takes time to build a level of trust when you go undercover so it would be a shame to waste it. Let me stay around until the end of the contest at least. Maybe I can find something that the uniforms and plain clothes miss."

"Luckily for you I said the same thing to the boss an hour ago," DS Patinsen said with a degree of resignation. "You're still in, but I want daily reports from now on. That thin ice you were on before is rapidly melting. Your career is on the line here Dirth."

"Thank you sir. I really appreciate your support. I won't let you down. If I may ask. Did anything come of looking into the GSA and Peter Hirt's finances?"

"Yes they did and it's one of the reasons I was able to push for you to stay. I've just had information on two fronts that puts him at the top of our list. As far as finances go you were right. Both the GSA and Hirt have made huge amounts of money out of the first three murders. It's a murky world of creative bookkeeping that our forensic accountants are wading through right now but the stock prices going through the roof alone is more than enough to justify murder. That's before you count the tribute merchandise sales and the huge increase in sponsorship and media revenue from the spike in publicity the GSA has enjoyed all around the world. All up I'd say it's probably been worth at least fifty million."

"Fifty million dollars!" Havoc whistled. "For that sort of money I might kill a couple myself."

"But the biggest thing we've uncovered is that Hirt is old friends with the president of The Cadaver Brothers, Trent 'Murder' Mercer," DS Patinsen's disappointment in Havoc seemed to have faded now and there was genuine excitement in his voice. "Officially Hirt uses a company Mercer owns to supply security for the contest. Unofficially Mercer also supplies drugs and girls for the VIP parties and members of The Cadaver Brothers are among the few who have been arrested in Australia for importing and supplying Fentanyl."

"Geez things just got real didn't they? So, what's the play with Hirt? Bring him in, throw a bit of mud at the walls and see if any of it sticks?" Havoc was glad to hear there was some good news in there somewhere.

"The local police should be bringing him in for an interview soon. I'm going to watch it online and ask a few questions if need be. Did you see him talking to Birch at all last night?"

"Not that I remember, but they were within ten metres of each other for most of the evening," Havoc recalled. He didn't want to admit to his handler that he'd spent the critical period in question on the dancefloor with a sexy Latino. "Stands to reason they would have at least said hi to each other at some stage."

"Okay well if you think of anything call me ASAP. I'll end the call now because I'm expecting to hear from the local police that they have Hirt any minute. Stay close to your phone and in range Dirth."

"Yes sir. Will do sir."

It was surprisingly less than an hour later when Havoc's phone buzzed revealing DS Patinsen with more news.

"That was quick sir," Havoc answered. "I thought it would take hours."

"Actually we're just on a break. We haven't finished with him yet as we had a bit of a delay getting his lawyer," DS Patinsen replied. "But I've got some different news for you and it's really thrown a spanner in the works. It's about Dyanna Fream. You saw her at the pub last night as well didn't you?"

"Yes sir, she was with a large group of girls all night that included Birch. They were drinking, talking and dancing together. Why's that?"

"That young lad that provided her alibi on the Gold Coast. Seems his guilty conscience got the better of him. When he heard that Birch had been killed, he got in touch with the Queensland Police and admitted that Fream had asked him to lie for her. Apparently, he was with her earlier that day, but then she left his hotel with plenty of time to dispatch Wilson. She's officially a suspect again. The local police are going to pick her up as well."

"Shit!" Havoc said with feeling. He had hoped she was free of any suspicion. If it ever got out that he had slept with a prime suspect in a murder case, he was going to be in a lot of trouble. "I did notice that she appeared to have left earlier that night. I think she might have gone before I saw Birch leaving anyway, so she might have had time to go and lie in wait for her."

"And why did you notice that Dirth?" DS Patinsen sounded suspicious.

"I'd talked to her a few times during the contest, same as I talked to everyone. Towards the end of the night I went looking for familiar faces. I was hoping that maybe with a few drinks under their belt I might learn something new, but everyone seemed to disappear at the same time. Birch was the only person I saw after that moment."

It was a good lie with enough truth in it that he hoped DS Patinsen's curiosity would be satisfied.

"Okay well I better go. The interview with Hirt should restart soon. Same deal Dirth. If you think of anything more about either of them then call me ASAP."

DS Patinsen hung up and left Havoc in a mix of emotions far too deep and complex for the average simple male surfer to properly deal with. He had really liked Fream. He knew he was probably just another stunt cock on her long list of conquests, but he'd secretly held a fantasy that he was a bit more than that to her and maybe there had been something meaningful between them. He'd been on the verge of calling her and telling the story of the trip to Black Rainbow. He felt sure she would have loved it and maybe even been a bit jealous that she wasn't invited.

Now that was all in the past. He knew he should come clean with DS Patinsen and tell him that he had slept with Fream. Even though it was after she had been initially ruled out as a suspect, he'd still be in a world of shit. It was a lame excuse and his mentor wouldn't buy it. No, it was better he didn't say anything and take the chance that no one would ever find out. At least he could be reasonably sure Fream would never mention it and seeing as they were the only two who knew anything had happened, then Havoc felt it was a risk worth taking,

If the yin was Havoc's decision to take the easy way out and not tell DS Patinsen, then the yang was that later he would come to regret that decision more than just about any he had made in his life so far.

Chapter 28 SOME UNCOMFORTABLE QUESTIONS

If Peter Hirt felt the same way as Havoc about the yin and yang of the universe it would have helped explain his past few days. It had all started going pear shaped around the time that bitch Claire Cooper showed up on his doorstep and he was annoyed at himself for dropping his guard and letting his dick make the decisions. Deep down he'd known that Cooper coming onto him was too good to be true. If he'd been thinking clearly with his actual brain and not the one between his legs, he would have spotted it easily. You don't get to be the CEO of the most influential company in a billion-dollar industry making rookie mistakes like that!

After their confrontation at his luxury Margaret River mansion, he'd taken a perverse enjoyment out of making sure Cooper lost her quarter final heat against Totthil. That also had the double bonus of putting him in Totthil's good books and she had shown her appreciation in her usual obedient style when she called around after lunch on a contest lay day. He was going to have to do some research on what sort of depraved acts he could get her to do next. He was fast running out of ideas.

Totthil had only just left and he had been feeling satisfyingly drained by her efforts when there was an unexpected knock at the door. His heart had skipped more than a couple of beats when he saw it was the boys in blue. He could tell immediately from their demeanour that it wasn't a police courtesy call and that he was in trouble. The only question remained was just how much trouble and what for? Typically, they weren't forthcoming with any information on those subjects until later when the answer would turn out to be lots and everything.

They'd allowed him no time to shower or change clothes. He hadn't been arrested but they made it clear they would if they had to. He'd been given enough leeway to grab his phone, wallet and keys then, still reeking of sex, he was escorted into the back of a paddy wagon. The 15 minute ride to the police station had been made in near total silence while Hirt pondered which of his many sins may be coming back to haunt him.

He'd wasted no time demanding his lawyer. Whatever it was they had on him, they weren't getting a word out of him until he had legal advice. His lawyer was based on the other side of Australia and he hoped that would throw them off their game enough to give him some time to mentally prepare for the interview to come, but they'd given him a choice, stay in custody and await his lawyer to fly out directly or do it now with his lawyer present online.

He'd chosen to get it over and done with so he could get back to making his plans come to fruition.

The police had come at him hard. Not just the local police but a Detective Sergeant Patinsen, who was also attending via the internet. They fired questions at him that showed a level of research into Hirt's life that had made him feel very uncomfortable, almost violated. Something or someone had tipped them off and Hirt didn't have a clue who or what it might have been.

At first he thought it could have been Picker. He wouldn't put it past that slimeball to rat him out to get some misguided revenge for the money falling through for Wilson's photos. He'd dropped that suspicion when the police began interrogating him about who took the Jimmy Slide death photos.

They'd then paid special attention to his financial activities and had shown an unnerving awareness of certain business dealings, but clearly they only knew part of the story there as well. That much at least had been a relief, but it was a strange line of questioning to be coming from local police and a Detective Sergeant from the other side of Australia. They would hardly be experts on complicated financial matters, so why were they doing the interrogation and not forensic accountants from the Australian Tax Office or something similar?

That was a question he had discussed with his high-priced lawyer when the police had called a coffee break about an hour into the interview. The trouble for Hirt was that there was so much illegal activity he was involved in and some of it was bad enough that he wouldn't even discuss it with his lawyer.

When they restarted again there had been a subtle shift in the police's demeanour. Hirt thought they were a touch less accusatory and a little friendlier. Eventually the real reason for the interview finally became clear when they mentioned that Stephanie Birch had been killed.

When he couldn't provide an alibi for where he was during the time she was killed the police got nasty. Then they moved onto trying to get his whereabouts for each of the other deaths at which point his lawyer demanded Hirt either be arrested and charged or let go. Fortunately, they chose to let him go and a few hours later he was back in his rented luxury house sipping a Grove Whiskey on the rocks to calm his nerves.

With a contest still to be finished there had been no time for Hirt to sit around and feel sorry for himself. The event restarted two days later and had been narrowly won by Gabriel Andre from local Jake Roberts in perfect 8-10 foot conditions. The Brazilian now led the world title race after a very publicly wasted Bunker Haze was knocked out in his first heat after Birch's murder. Despite that, or maybe because of it, the billionaire playboy was now getting unprecedented levels of media coverage all around the world.

Once again Hirt's workload went through the roof, not that he minded. After all it was partially of his own making. While overseeing the final moments of the HGM Margaret River Masters he also had to deal with the usual media shitstorm regarding Stephanie Birch's murder. He already had the blueprint for what to do nailed down perfectly by now, so the usual cut and paste press releases were supplied and the memorial merchandise was released in record time. The white bikinis and tube tops that looked like they had blood splashed all over them were particularly good sellers.

He had just felt like he was back on top of things when Claire Cooper phoned him and further messed with his yin and yang. Even now, a few hours after he had hung up on her in a fury, he was struggling to believe the nerve of that woman. Who would have thought she would have the balls to set him up and record the conversation? Surfers weren't meant to be that smart or that deceptive!

When she had told him about the recording and demanded a whole list of changes be made to the women's side of the tour, including holding their heats in better waves and with equal prizemoney to the men, he'd lost his shit. Maybe it was Cooper's unique ability to get under his skin? Whatever it was, the five-minute profanity and threat filled rant that he unleashed was of biblical proportions. In a way he hoped Cooper had taped that one. He would have liked to have it written down so he could repeat some of it the next time he needed to put one of his employees in line. They would never have made a mistake again that's for sure!

Cooper hadn't been fazed by the repeated and extremely creative ways that he had threatened to ruin her life. Instead, she had calmly let him rant and then informed him that she was a reasonable person and so long as the women weren't put out in small surf at Bells, she was prepared to give him time to get details prepared for the prizemoney increase. Otherwise, he could expect to hear his indecent proposal on every major news network in the world. Hirt had then unleashed another colourful outburst and hung up.

Now he was faced with the decision of what to actually do about it. He had no doubts that Cooper would call his bluff and release the tape if he didn't do what she asked. The first question he asked himself was did he really care? There's no doubt he wasn't particularly comfortable with his sexual advances going public, but would anyone who really mattered give a fuck?

He'd made a lot of money for some significant people and continued to do so. Plus, he knew too much so they'd ignore the bad press and let him keep his job. Or would they? Recently there was a vile woke movement becoming increasingly popular in the GSA that would just love to latch onto some good old fashioned workplace sexual harassment and bullying. They would certainly persecute him to further their cause and Hirt couldn't be sure his good work and willingness to do anything required to get the job done, both legally and illegally, would count for anything with the GSA Board of Directors if the publicity got really bad.

It's not like he needed the job or was short of money. Thanks to his hard work and investments he could live out the rest of his life in luxury without ever working another day, but Hirt got off on power. Power to make multi-million dollar deals on a daily basis, power to make women do his bidding no matter how much it disgusted them and power to do whatever the fuck he wanted with no concern for how illegal or immoral it was.

There was no way he was caving into Cooper's demands. He hated the thought he had been bested, but to let her win and get her way was a thousand times worse. Not to mention what other demands she may come up with later. Once a blackmailer has it over you there's nothing to stop it happening again and again. Cooper may say she will do the right thing, but she'd already shown an impressive ability to lie and deceive.

There was a third option to consider and that was removing Cooper from the equation altogether. Four top surfers had died recently, Cooper could easily be the fifth.

On a whim he did something he almost never did and went online to check the Surfline swell forecast for the upcoming Bells Beach contest. The first results he saw were a mistake, so he refreshed the page, only he got the same result again.

"Something's not right!" he said to himself and he triple checked everything to make sure that what he was looking at was indeed a forecast for the Bells region over the next week. Still not convinced he called up another wave prediction site and it too had the same thing to say. A quick check on the GSA Stalkbook page showed that thousands of people had seen the same thing- a huge angry purple blob indicating a massive swell, bigger than anything anyone had ever seen, was aimed squarely at Bells Beach in the early part of the contest waiting period.

The internet chat rooms were in a frenzy about the swell. "It will be biggest ever, bigger even than 1981!" called one troll. "At least 25ft, maybe bigger!" cried another and the best yet. "It's the 50 year storm straight out of 'Point Break'!"

Hirt couldn't control himself and he burst out laughing, the stress and tension of the past few days disappearing like clouds under hot sunshine. He continued to giggle like a little schoolboy as he typed out an email to send to his press team.

"Oh Claire," he said aloud to himself. "You wanted the girls in the big waves, well now you've got them!"

Chapter 29 A STAR IS BORN

Havoc unlocked the door to his cabin and went straight to the fridge for a Coopers Pale Ale. He slammed half of it down in one gulp and finished the rest moments later with a belch before opening another. It had been another day full of conflicting emotions, something that seemed all too common in his life lately.

Finals day had been hectic, but not in a good way. Bunker had turned up in the competitor's area for his morning heat still in party mode from the night before and clearly on drugs of some kind. His eyes were two red slits and walking straight was only possible thanks to the two giggling Instafamous bikini model/influencers holding him up from either side.

As soon as he saw Bunker, Havoc was immediately concerned that he might be The Killer's next victim and was suffering from the effects of taking Fentanyl. Oblivious to how it might look, he rushed over to Bunker and politely but forcibly took control of his friend from the girls.

"Havoc my main dude!" Bunker slurred as he suddenly recognized who was now supporting him. "Where's my locker? I need to get ready for my heat."

"Are you alright mate?" Havoc asked quietly as he escorted Bunker to the corner where his boards were stacked ready to go. Then he turned him around so he could look straight into those bloodshot eyes with conviction. "I mean like really alright, what are you on? Anything bad?"

Bunker swayed a little, then steadied, returned the gaze for a second, then stepped in and hugged Havoc.

"It's alright Havoc dude. I'm okay. I've got this," Bunker whispered as they embraced. "Stephanie's death opened some old wounds man, but

I want to go surf. I'm gunna lose man, I know that, but I'd rather be out there now than in here. I can talk to Willo out there."

Havoc stepped out of the hug and looked again at his friend. Yes, he looked wasted, but there was everybody else wasted and Bunker wasted. Bunker had been degrees of wasted most of his life.

"You sure you're okay?" Havoc needed to hear it one more time.

"Yes brother," smiled Bunker and Havoc relaxed a little.

"Then let's get you sorted mate."

Despite Bunker appearing to be only moderately wasted, Havoc was taking no chances with his friend and didn't leave his side while he was getting ready. A young local surfer arrived to act as caddy and paddle out Bunker's back up board in case he broke the one he was riding. Sensing an opportunity to stay closer for longer, Havoc pulled rank on the unlucky grommet and said he'd do the job himself. He felt a bit guilty at the look of devastation on the kid's face, but the risk to Bunker's safety quickly overruled that emotion.

Bunker was up against the super talented American goofy-foot rookie Cole Pinto and he threw Pinto off guard in the opening seconds of the heat by paddling up to him for a hug and a few words. Havoc thought it might be some kind of tactical ploy, but that proved to be wrong with Bunker showing no interest in winning the heat whatsoever.

He let Pinto have any wave he wanted and when Bunker finally got a great wave, he shared it with a pod of dolphins and spent the whole ride standing near motionless with his arms in the air in a salute to the dolphins who were surfing the wave better than he ever could. Even though he didn't do a single manoeuvre the judges still gave him a 4 point ride for the sheer beauty of the experience. It was his highest score of the heat.

Gabriel Andre beat Jake Roberts in a great final and moved to number one on the world rankings. As he watched Andre accept his million-dollar first prize cheque, Havoc conceded that perhaps he was a little jealous that it wasn't him on that winner's podium. He was surprised at that emotion as he didn't think the loss would have bothered him, but once he'd returned to the contest site the reality dawned that his little foray as a pro surfer was over and a form of depression had set in. The dream had been shattered all too quickly.

It didn't help that he was getting increasingly frustrated at his lack of progress on the case either. Once he was sure Bunker was okay and safely back at his nearby Gnarabup mansion, he'd spent every available moment at the event site, either wandering amongst the crowd, sitting in the VIP area or mooching around the competitor's zone. Mostly he eavesdropped in on random conversations, but occasionally he initiated banter, steering the discussion in directions he hoped might lead to something, but it had all been for nothing.

Earlier DS Patinsen had confirmed that a small level of fentanyl had been found in Birch's bloodstream. Not enough to kill her, but certainly enough for a non-drug taker to feel very sick and not function normally. That's why Havoc had reacted so quickly when he'd first seen Bunker. The drug had most likely been slipped into Birch's drink when Havoc was bumping uglies on the dance floor with Giselle. Unfortunately, that only added further suspicion to Fream being the prime suspect. He had seen her with Birch himself, not long before he'd begun talking to the Brazilian crew.

To make things worse, Fream had disappeared the next day. She'd hopped a plane to Melbourne, perhaps to get some early practice in at Bells, but had been uncontactable ever since. The Victorian police had been looking for her, but they weren't throwing too much manpower into the search. There wasn't a warrant out for her arrest yet and they believed she would turn up in a few days time at the Bells contest under her own steam.

Havoc had hoped that the interview with Peter Hirt might have uncovered some clues that would point the investigation back his way. Unfortunately, DS Patinsen had advised him that Hirt had been cool under pressure and revealed nothing of any value. There was still his connection to the Cadaver Brothers to research, but nothing much on the murder investigation. The only information they could cling to was that he didn't have decent alibis for any of the nights in question. He claimed to be either in his rented accommodation asleep, or in the case of Bali and the Gold Coast- doing the nasty with an unknown lady of the night.

Havoc would much prefer if it was Hirt or someone at the GSA involved. He didn't like Hirt, but he did find that he often thought fondly of his time with Fream and it was hard to believe that someone with such a passion for living could be a cold hearted killer. He felt like he had lived five lifetimes in those few glorious days he had spent with The Dream.

He finished his second beer and hesitated before shaking his head and cracking a third, promising himself it would be his last. He knew he shouldn't be drinking at all, but tonight was his last in Margaret River before he packed and made the drive back to Perth. Initially he'd planned to have a quiet night in his cabin and do some internet research, but then Bunker had rung to say that he was heading to Settlers Tavern with a bunch of models. He'd insisted that Havoc should join him and Havoc found little reason to decline. If Bunker was going out partying and someone had already been killed after a big night at Settlers, then Havoc was not about to risk the same thing happening to his friend.

He was six beers deep by the time he'd taken a shower and had something to eat. Deciding he was in the mood to bring some action home, he threw on his best HGM outfit and headed out the door for the 15 minute walk to the pub. This time if one of Bunker's groupies offered him a carpark blowjob, he had no intention of turning her down.

The walk helped clear his head a little and by the time he reached the inviting atmosphere of Settlers he was feeling better about his situation. He resolved to call DS Patinsen tomorrow and see if he could convince him to let Havoc fly to Victoria for the Bells contest. Seeing as there was still a killer at large and they didn't have anyone else as close as he was to the situation, he felt he had a decent argument.

It was already crowded and Havoc had to squeeze around people as he went on the search for Bunker and his entourage. It seemed that Havoc's one heat at Margaret River had made quite an impression as almost every second guy he shuffled past greeted him with enthusiasm.

"You're Havoc aren't you? Mate you're a fucken legend! Let me shake your hand, you're my hero!" said one particularly impressed punter as he tried to push past to get to the line for the bar.

It wasn't just the guys either. A surprising number of girls seemed to know who he was. One particularly well-endowed redhead in a short denim mini skirt and heels approached him with hunger in her eyes.

"Hello Havoc," she purred sexily as she thrust her cleavage into his eyeline "I've seen your work, you're very impressive. I want you to take me home and fuck me hard tonight!"

Havoc's jaw just about hit the ground. He'd been in the pub for less than ten minutes and this absolute fox was ready to go. He was trying to get his brain into gear to say something cool and charming when a big, burly looking dude came storming out of the crowd and grabbed the redhead forcibly by the arm.

"C'mon Michelle that's enough," he said dragging her away. As he did, he looked at Havoc and apologized. "Sorry mate, my wife gets a bit forward when she's had a few. Can't say I blame her though. You're a rock star haha!"

"Umm thanks," Havoc didn't know what else to say. He expected the dude to be angrier and maybe want to start a fight, not pay him a complement. It was very weird.

Havoc got in the cue at the bar behind two cute girls that looked barely old enough to be there. The taller of the two turned to talk to her friend and spied Havoc standing behind them. Recognition flared in her eyes, she giggled and whispered to her friend. "It's that Havoc guy!"

Her friend immediately turned around and her eyes lit up.

"Well hello," she said, barely stifling a giggle herself. "Aren't we lucky Roxy? Meeting a stud like Havoc as soon as we arrive. I'm Jane and this is Roxy."

"Hello ladies. Nice to meet you both. Are you from around here?" Havoc asked.

"No, we just got down from Perth," Roxy replied. "We're just here for a few days of fun."

They continued to make small talk while they waited for their turn to order drinks. When the bartender finally got to them Jane ordered for the girls and while she did, Roxy moved in close and whispered in his ear.

"You can have both of us if you want sexy man. We don't mind sharing," she followed it up with a little bite on his earlobe.

For the second time in a few minutes Havoc had to pick his jaw up off the floor. He had heard plenty of stories about how easy it was for pro surfers to pick up girls but until now he never fully understood. And he wasn't even a pro surfer! All he had done was lose his first heat and girls were practically throwing themselves at him! What would it be like if he won?

While they looked a bit young, he was at a pub, so they had to be at least 18 years old and they were both attractive in a too much makeup, skinny, night club groupie kind of way. Threesomes don't exactly get offered on a daily basis, so Havoc made up his mind that he would take the girls up on their offer. He was just about to reply when someone gave him a big bear hug from behind and lifted him off his feet.

"Havoc you fucken stallion!" Bunker cried happily as he let Havoc back down. "Dude you are 'The Man'. I swear we must be brothers from another mother. Get over here. You don't need to be standing in line for drinks, I've got shitloads. Anything you want my man, especially for a stud like you."

Bunker dragged Havoc away from a disappointed Roxy and Jane. He gave them an apologetic look and shrug of the shoulders and let Bunker lead him off. He couldn't believe he was letting his mate drag him away from a potential threesome, but the night was still young, and he hoped the girls weren't going anywhere soon. Seconds later he had almost forgotten they existed as Bunker introduced him to an entourage of groupies that was nothing short of staggering.

"Girls this is Havoc," he announced to a group of at least a dozen ladies, none of which were any less than an 8 out of 10. "He's the fucken porn star dude I was telling you about. This guy's got a fucken wang on him and he knows how to use it!"

It was a strange thing for Bunker to say and Havoc didn't know how to reply, but the girls all smiled and looked at him appreciatively, so he just smiled back and mumbled a hello.

"Here ya go legend!" Bunker said thrusting a Coopers and a tequila shot in Havoc's hands. He then passed shots to all the other girls surrounding him along with a slice of lemon and a dash of salt. As one they all licked the salt off their hands, downed the tequila shot, then sucked on the slice of lemon. Bunker immediately poured everyone another and they repeated the dose. Havoc felt his senses fire up. Now this was rock star living! High quality tequila with a good mate and an absurd amount of incredibly sexy women! It didn't get much better than this!

"So you got to ride the Dream Train," Bunker slapped Havoc on the back. "I'm so proud of you dude."

"What do you mean?" Havoc asked suspiciously, the makings of a sick feeling in his stomach stirred uneasily.

"The Dream dude! You tapped Dyanna Fream! Well maybe tapped isn't the right word. Looks like you laid down some serious porn star moves my man. I thought my game was pretty good, but I might need to take some lessons from you!"

That was not what Havoc wanted to hear. "But how did you know? We didn't tell anyone."

"Dude don't you know? It's all over the internet so it's probably going to be in the magazines soon too. The pictures are awesome man. I haven't seen the movies yet, but word is you put in one hell of a performance."

"Fuck are you serious?" Havoc was horrified. "How the fuck is it on the internet? Neither of us took any photos."

Bunker laughed. "Welcome to pro surfing dude. Someone must have been hiding outside with a camera, probably Picker. That's the sort of shit he likes to pull."

Havoc thought back to when Picker had made cryptic comments about how he was soon going to be famous and that they could help each other. Those comments now made a lot more sense. The dirty scumbag must have been hiding somewhere outside. That would also go a long way to explain why those random girls had hit on him so quickly earlier, they had most likely seen the footage. Probably half the pub had.

Havoc pulled out his phone and searched his name and Fream's. Sure enough dozens of websites and Stalkbook pages displayed photos and videos of the two of them in the full throes of intense, adventurous sex.

The photographer had clearly spent a long time capturing the action from a variety of angles in both photos and video. Most pages featured a few teasing images with the rest hidden behind a paywall. It seems someone was making a lot of money out of their private lives. Havoc was fucking furious and had never felt so sick in his life. It was just as well Picker was nowhere to be seen, as he would almost certainly be needing a trip to the hospital.

His next thought was that he should call DS Patinsen and give him the heads up. He knew that he was now in a whole new bucket of shit that probably meant his time as an undercover cop was over and maybe the police force for good. He owed it to his mentor to let him know before he found out another way. The thought of Senior Sergeant Smith finding out first was horrific!

Havoc glanced at his watch. It would be two hours later in Sydney so DS Patinsen would be in bed asleep. Havoc chickened out from calling and waking him and instead sent a text saying, "Call me as soon as you get this message". With luck he wouldn't get a call until the morning. He had one last night to enjoy himself before a world of hurt was coming his way.

He put his phone back in his pocket and looked around the group of girls. A short, curvy brunette with remarkably large breasts for her tiny waist was giving him a look that was not hard to interpret. She'd seen the photos and wanted her turn. Havoc didn't even bother with any small talk, he was pissed off and didn't care what happened, so he put his arm around her waist and dragged her close, then whispered in her ear.

"Which one of these girls do you want to come home with us?"

She smiled and pointed to a tall, skinny, waif like blonde that looked like she was straight off the catwalk. She was almost the complete opposite in looks in every way to the brunette except they were both smoking hot.

"Perfect," Havoc said then he turned to Bunker. "Pour me another fucken' tequila brother! Havoc is on the loose tonight!"

The sound of his phone ringing dragged Havoc out of an all too short sleep. He groaned and reached over and grabbed the phone off the bedside table, checking the time before he answered. It was 6am and DS Patinsen was on the line. He decided to let the call go through to message bank to give himself a couple of minutes to get his extremely foggy brain into gear. It was not a call he should be taking hungover, but that ship had sailed and he had no one to blame but himself. He got up and took a huge drink of water and quickly jumped in the shower.

The girls were still asleep in bed when he got out. He took a second to admire the various bits of nakedness that poked out from under the covers before opening the sliding door and stepping outside to make the call that would probably have a big impact on his future.

It went about exactly as expected. DS Patinsen was livid that Havoc had slept with Fream and even more livid that he had failed to mention it until it had become public knowledge.

"You're a fucking idiot Dirth!" DS Patinsen swore for the first time Havoc could ever recall. "Why on earth would you jeopardise your entire career, hell your entire LIFE, for a roll in the hay?"

"Sir, you told me she had an alibi for the time of Wilson's murder, so I no longer thought she was involved in the case. Once I found out she might be still a suspect I never contacted her again," Havoc pleaded his pathetic excuse. "And besides, how was I to know some dirty scumbag was hiding in the bushes?"

"I'm not even going to dignify that rubbish with a reply Dirth. You know that for what it is, complete and utter bullshit! I'm so angry right now I don't even know what to say anymore. Your father would be so disappointed in you."

Those last words were a knife in the guts for Havoc and DS Patinsen probably knew it. The regard of his father had meant everything to Havoc when he was alive and it hadn't dimmed since his death. But Philip Spidder was well known for having a ratbag streak and didn't always follow the rules. His mother had told him that was part of the reason why he was loved so much, it was a character trait that Havoc had inherited and taken to the next level.

"So what happens now sir?" Havoc asked, not willing to listen to any more talk regarding his father.

"I don't know Dirth," DS Patinsen sighed sounding defeated. Havoc thought that was worse than him being angry. "I have to call Senior Sergeant Smith and advise him of the situation. He's going to have a field day and no doubt recommend that you be removed from the case immediately. My guess is that won't be enough though, he will want you gone from undercover work and maybe the police force altogether. That might be hard for him to achieve without a lot of effort, but you know he doesn't like you, so anything is possible."

With that depressing advice they said their goodbyes with DS Patinsen advising Havoc that he would call back after he had spoken with Senior Sergeant Smith. Havoc pocketed his phone and walked back to his cabin wondering what the fuck he was going to do with his life if he lost his job. Like a lot of young people, he'd never really known what he had wanted to do with his life. There had been a stability in joining the police force that was something he could rely on without the rock to cling to that had been his father.

He gently slid open the door, stepped back into his cabin and pondered what was ahead for him. Despite the shit he was in he couldn't help but smile as he watched the girls sleeping peacefully. They had barely moved while he'd been on the phone. Hardly surprising seeing as they'd only been asleep for a few hours after downing a lot of tequila at the pub, then staggering back to the cabin to get it on.

If Havoc did end up losing his job, then one thing he knew for sure was that the past few weeks had been an adventure that he would never forget. He'd met amazing people, almost learnt to backflip a dirt bike, surfed incredible waves and had some peak sexual experiences thrown in for good measure. His time with Dyanna Fream had been mind blowing but the memory of those few days was now darkened by the fact that it had all been captured on film and she could be a ruthless killer.

Last night hadn't been tainted though. It shone bright in his memory despite the amount of alcohol involved. The girls had been as much into each other as they were into him, making for a truly unforgettable experience. It had been like being on the set of a porn movie where you could join in any time you wanted. Havoc would sit back and watch the girls enjoy themselves, then insert himself into the action whenever he got super horny and couldn't contain himself any longer. They would enthusiastically double team him before turning their attention back to each other when he needed a break.

Havoc had even bust out a few new moves that Fream had shown him just a week earlier that were very well received by both blonde and brunette. Each girl seemingly striving for a bigger and louder orgasm than the last. He was surprised that they didn't wake the whole caravan park, but he drew the line when they suggested they get out their phones and start filming the session.

The brunette turned over in her sleep revealing a big, fake breast and large chocolate nipple. She must have disturbed her friend as she too moved and a long, slender leg emerged from the covers. Havoc felt a familiar stirring in his loins and decided any further thoughts about his future could wait awhile. He drew back the covers and shimmied in between the two.

"Good morning ladies!"

A few hours later Havoc was again wakened by the ringing of his mobile phone. He answered it absentmindedly thinking it would be DS Patinsen. Instead, it was someone completely unexpected.

"Hello Havoc this is Peter Hirt here. How are you?"

Caught unawares Havoc managed to stumble out some sort of reply. "Um I'm good Peter. How about yourself?"

"Oh, just the usual Havoc," Hirt replied. "Trying to keep the GSA afloat, putting out spot fires, dealing with the issues of dead surfers and organising the Bells contest. It's a never-ending shit fight but I can't complain."

"You must have a tough job that's for sure," he was a little bewildered to be talking to Hirt. Did he somehow know Havoc was undercover? "I must say I'm a bit surprised that you have called me."

"That's because I've got some good news Havoc. How would you like another wildcard?"

Havoc was stunned. Did he hear right? Did he just get offered another chance at the pro surfing dream? "Another wildcard, what do you mean?"

"It's pretty simple Havoc. Every contest the main sponsor gets to pick one wildcard and the GSA gets to pick the other. You got your wildcard at Margaret River thanks to your sponsor, Homegrown Maniacs. This time the GSA is offering you our wildcard if you want it."

Havoc was completely caught off guard. "But why would you give me the wildcard? I'm a nobody and I didn't exactly kill it in my heat."

"Well that's where you're wrong Havoc," Hirt replied. "You may not have won your heat, but you won a lot of hearts with that last wave. You were within a bee's dick of defeating a former world champion and current world number one, but more importantly thanks to your little romp with Dirty Dy, you are the hottest thing in surfing right now. Nice going by the way. I've been there myself, she's a firecracker!"

Havoc had to stop himself from reacting to that. During one of their relaxed cuddling moments in between sex sessions, Fream had told him the story of when she was a young rookie Hirt had made it clear that if she wanted to be on the world tour, she would have to sleep with him. She had agreed and had regretted it ever since. Havoc had been disgusted with Hirt then and nothing had changed since. It was part of the reason he didn't like him and hoped he got arrested.

"I don't know what to say Peter. I'm shocked. This is totally unexpected," Havoc managed to blurt out.

"Ha! Then just say 'Thank you' and 'I will see you at Bells."

"Thank you Peter. I will see you Bells."

Chapter 30 A CAMEL'S ARMPIT

Dyanna Fream's world was closing in around her. The police had been chasing her, as she knew they would. That young surfer toyboy who had provided her with the alibi for Wilson's death at least had the decency to let her know that he was phoning the police to change his story before he had done so.

Fream had tried to talk him out of it of course but couldn't even remember his name, which didn't help. She'd even promised him all sorts of sexual favours next time she was on the Gold Coast if he stayed silent. That had almost done the trick. He'd wavered for a second but then held firm. Who would have thought a guilty conscience could outweigh another night with her? Maybe she was losing her mojo?

That was the second time in recent history that she'd had that thought. The first was when she had watched Havoc bump and grind with some Brazilian skank on the dancefloor in Margaret River. She'd patiently waited for him to come up to her that night and suggest they revisit the action of earlier in the week, but it never happened. It didn't matter that she would have rejected him anyway, she'd had things to do and besides, it didn't pay to have some love-struck wannabe pro surfer following her around like a lost puppy.

So, when he all but ignored her and worse, had hooked up with someone else, she'd been more than pissed off. She must have been watching him too much because Stephanie Birch had picked up on it and taken great delight in making Havoc's rejection one of the themes of the evening.

She didn't know why it should bother her. Havoc moving on only made things easier, but even now she found herself thinking of him and she never did that. Normally once she had fucked a guy, he may as well not exist anymore, but somehow Havoc had been different and she didn't know why. True, he had been better than most in bed and he had a good rig, but that shouldn't have mattered. Surely she wasn't having feelings for someone? That really was a complication she didn't need.

Their affair had suddenly become tabloid fodder which really pissed her off. She'd been careful to maintain her privacy for a significant reason and now it had unravelled in a big way. She rarely brought guys back to her place! That was one of the rules that she had always abided by because she had seen photographers hiding in the bushes outside her hotel room hoping to catch her out far too often. So why did she drop the ball with Havoc?

The only positive that had come out of the whole unpleasant situation was that her social media profile had grown massively. She had got at least a million new Instafamous fans in just a few days. It was quite possible she had become the most popular female surfer alive and perhaps only Gabriel Andre rivalled her in the men's. Gordon Green at Quikbong had phoned to say that he was very happy and that she would soon be getting a bonus due to the strong sales of her merchandise.

It was just a shame that the police had her on their radar. Fream had good reason to hate the police and to steer well clear of them, but that was becoming increasingly hard to do. As soon as she knew they were looking for her, she had moved hotels in Torquay and paid for the new room in cash. It was a short-term solution that would last only as long as her first heat at Bells. She still had every intention of competing, after all they had nothing on her other than a fake alibi and the hazy memories of a drunk groupie.

In the meantime, she planned on surfing Bells as much as possible. She had two reasonably good results in the first two contests of the year. With Birch gone, a good result at Bells might just see her leading the GSA world title contest rankings. From there who knows what might happen. Every surfer on the tour dreams of being a World Champion!

Fream's thoughts were interrupted by her phone ringing, it was Claire Cooper.

"Hey sexy what's up?"

"Hello Dreamy," Cooper replied. "Are you all set for Bells?"

"Of course. I've been surfing there or Winkipop twice a day. How about you?"

"I've just got into town so I will probably see you out there soon. I wanted to give you a heads up though. I think we may finally surf some real waves in a contest."

"What do you mean? Have you seen the forecast?"

"No but I rang Peter Hirt and told him I had the recording. I said if he doesn't put us out in good waves at Bells and arrange equal pay with the men by the next contest, I would release the tape to the media. I think he's going to do it."

"Oh Claire I thought we'd talked about being careful and holding off. Hirt's dangerous. You know that."

"I know Dreamy but I couldn't wait any longer. I'm tired of letting that bastard dictate to us. I thought you would be happy. It will suit you if the contest is held in big waves."

"Of course I'm happy Claire but I'm also worried about you. What happens if he decides not to do what you tell him and instead comes after you?"

"Oh he won't Dreamy, you worry too much. I'm not scared of him anyway."

Cooper's fearlessness surprised Fream. She certainly wasn't afraid of much when she was in the water, but she'd always seemed a bit timid and unsure on the land. Lately that was changing and a new, much more self-confidant Claire Cooper had been emerging. Fream wasn't sure if she liked it or not.

"Well you sound like you know what you are doing Claire so that's good," Fream decided to change the subject. "I can't believe Stephanie was killed. We were only talking to her just a few hours before it happened."

"I know right!" Cooper replied. "I mean neither of us liked her, but she was stabbed to death! That's so heavy!"

They continued sharing small talk about Birch. They discussed what it meant to not have her on tour anymore and when the upcoming funeral might be. Fream was surprised at just how insincere Cooper sounded throughout the whole chat. Almost like she didn't really care one way or another. It wasn't that different from how Fream herself often felt. There was a strange, almost businesslike coldness that Cooper had begun showing in recent times. Not for the first time in recent months she wondered just how much she really knew about the real Claire Cooper.

They promised to catch up in the surf soon and hung up. Fream poured herself a vodka on the rocks and held it up to the light in her hotel room, looking at it as she swished it around in the glass. She contemplated whether she should add some orange juice to dilute it a bit and give it some flavour. With a shrug of her shoulders, she tossed the whole drink down in one go, then poured another as she savoured the burn of the strong alcohol content of the first one. This time she did add some orange juice.

She threw herself down on her bed and once again her thoughts went straight back to Havoc. She was angry at herself now. He kept taking up space in her head no matter how hard she tried to stop thinking about him. It was like that old trick where someone tells you that you aren't allowed to think of a camel's armpit for at least ten seconds. As a result, no matter how bizarre the notion of a camel's armpit is, it's all you can think of.

She really didn't have time for this shit but then there he was, standing tall and oh so casual in a barrel at the Box, then later sitting shirtless on his car, toned body gleaming in the sun with a cheeky smile on his face. She had been super impressed as she watched him overcome his fears on the dirt bike and she shuddered at the many memories she had of him naked and rock hard as he gazed at her body in wonder.

There was a mystery to Havoc as well. Maybe that's why she couldn't get him out of her head? Unlike so many others she had been with who wanted to tell her his life story in a worthless attempt to impress her, Havoc talked little of his past but asked a lot of questions about her instead. She had been uncomfortable with some of that probing and had tried to deflect the conversation back to stories of a younger Havoc.

He in turn had given up only morsels of information, such as his father passing away tragically, but had then skilfully steered the subject back to her. It had almost been like a battle of wills as each tried to probe the other to find out more about what made the other tick, while giving away as little about themselves as possible. Neither acknowledging they were in a contest, but expertly sparring nevertheless.

She had bumped into Morpheus out in the surf at Bells and he had informed her that Havoc had been offered another wildcard. This time by Peter Hirt and the GSA itself. He suspected it was due to the unfortunate pile of photos and videos of the two of them that were currently one of the most searched items on the internet in the world.

She was happy that something good had come out of those photos for Havoc as well. While Fream had gained a massive boost to her profile and most likely a few extra zeros on her next pay cheque, she'd been a public figure for a long time, so the crazy attention she got was an expected part of the life she had chosen. Havoc on the other hand was clearly a private person who'd been suddenly thrust into the public spotlight through no real fault of his own. He didn't stand to gain anything from his pecker being displayed to every corner of the world.

Fream smiled at that thought. She fired up her computer and checked out some of the images online. There was no doubt the two of them looked good together. Two bodies in their prime putting on a hell of a show even though they didn't know it at the time. Perhaps it was more impressive to the internet trolls for that reason alone. Unlike many of the millions of porn films out there, this was consensual sex on par with the best porn scenes ever created, only neither knew they were being filmed.

There was no doubt in Fream's mind that Havoc deserved another crack at a wildcard. Plenty of pro surfers and media types whose opinions counted for something agreed that Havoc's final attack on that huge closeout was the most impressive single moment of the whole Margaret River contest. It may not have got him the win, but he won a lot of hearts. She had seen the instant respect that even Gabriel Andre had bestowed on Havoc later that night at the Settlers Tavern. The Terminator almost never let people into his inner circle, yet there he was with his arm around Havoc and a beaming smile on his face.

Now Havoc would be somewhere nearby in Torquay. Or if he wasn't, he would be on a plane on his way over soon. Fream decided she liked that idea and she realised that looking at the footage of their performance online had made her extremely horny. She shook her head at herself for thinking what she was thinking but then decided "What the fuck! Who cares?".

Picking up her phone she searched Havoc's number.

Chapter 31 HIGH STAKES POKER

It took all of Havoc's powers of self-control not to answer the call from Fream. He wanted to hear her voice again, he wanted to be part scandalized, part mystified and very aroused by her rampant sexuality. He wanted to tell her all about Black Rainbow and that he'd been offered a wildcard into the Bells competition so they would see each other again. That he looked forward to seeing her, laughing with her, cuddling with her and yes, fucking each other's brains out.

Instead, he watched the phone ring out and go to voicemail, then continued packing for the drive back up to Perth. He had tried to call DS Patinsen to tell him about the wildcard, but he was either out of range or on another call. Havoc was excited about the opportunity that this wildcard presented and was adamant that this time he would not only win at least one heat but also uncover the killer or damn well die trying. He would not be distracted by a six foot blonde nymphomaniac Amazon or overawed by the situation in the surf. He'd surfed Bells quite a bit since he was a kid and hopefully would not suffer from getting lost at sea like his Margaret River experience.

His phone rang again and Havoc was happy to see that this time it was DS Patinsen.

"Hello sir how are you?" Havoc asked cheerfully.

"Not so well Dirth," DS Patinsen replied sounding very serious. "I've got bad news I'm afraid."

Havoc's heart sunk. He had an idea what the news might be. "Why sir, what's happened?"

"You have been suspended and ordered to come home while an investigation is conducted into your affair with Dyanna Fream."

"But sir I've just been offered another wildcard to the Bells contest. I will still be right in the middle of the whole organisation. It might take weeks or months to get someone into a situation of trust like I am at the moment, if that's even possible. In the meantime, how many more people might get killed?"

"Well, you probably should have thought about that before you slept with Fream," DS Patinsen sighed resignedly. "I'm sorry Dirth, I tried to fight it but there was nothing I could do. I warned you repeatedly this might happen if you weren't careful, but like always you went ahead and did it anyway."

"That makes no sense sir!" Havoc couldn't believe this was happening. "We've worked hard to get me undercover. If you want to fit in with the surf crowd, then you're not going to do it by following the rules. The only reason I've been offered the wildcard is because I slept with Fream. I didn't want or ask for the publicity but that's what got me through the door. Peter Hirt said as much when he called me. Surely that's got to count for something?"

"Dirth I don't think you understand the gravity of the situation you have got yourself into. You're supposed to be undercover but from what I can tell, you will soon be featuring on the front cover of international magazines having sex with the prime suspect in a murder investigation! That's not something easily explained to the people higher up the food chain. If the press ever gets hold of the fact you are law enforcement, we will be crucified. You're just going to have to man up, take it on the chin and try and work your way back into Senior Sergeant Smith's good books."

Havoc didn't like the sound of that. It was more like mission impossible than he cared to admit. He very much doubted that Smithy would ever take his foot off his throat now that he had Havoc right where he wanted him.

"So that's it then? And when somebody else is killed Smithy will shrug his shoulders and say, 'We tried hard but no one will miss another dead surfer'. That's not what I signed up for sir!"

"I understand how you feel Dirth but as I said my hands are tied on this. Come home and we will see what we can do to resurrect the situation."

Havoc decided he didn't want to continue the conversation anymore. He was over it.

"Okay sir I will call you when I'm back in Sydney."

He hung up, grabbed the last Coopers Pale Ale from the fridge and sat down on the bed to contemplate his next move. The girls had thanked him for a good night, kissed him on the cheek and left an hour or so earlier. They had not asked for a phone number, nor did they offer theirs. Evidently, they knew the rules of the game better than he did, as he had felt obliged to do both in a misguided attempt to pretend the night meant something other than just cheap sex.

Havoc suspected he was at one of those forks in the road where a decision one way or another would majorly impact his life. The way he saw it he had two options. The first was to do as ordered and fly home to face the music. If he did that at least he would still have DS Patinsen's respect and maybe keep his job, even if it probably meant he would have to eat the large pile of dung that Smithy would happily force feed him over the next few months or even years.

Option two was to say 'You know what? I don't really give a fuck!' and fly to Victoria and take up his wildcard. It would most likely mean he no longer had a job, but did that really matter? After all he was young and was no stranger to labouring on a building site. He wouldn't starve, but he might have to give up his apartment.

Then there was the other thought that he kept trying to keep under control but just wouldn't go away. Could he become a pro surfer? Was he good enough to do this full time? He felt sure Morpheus would back him and clearly the GSA saw something in him, even if it was just looks and who he'd slept with. Every kid who surfed dreamt of being a pro surfer and Havoc was no different. Like most, he had recognised that thought for just what it was, a dream, but now there was a slight chance it could become reality.

Also there was still a killer to be caught. Havoc certainly wasn't going to be involved in the capture if he was stuck in Sydney and unless the killer made a mistake, he or she might never be caught at all.

Havoc thought about what that meant. Matt Wilson wasn't a close friend by any means, but he'd still shared a few surfs with him and Wilson was a loveable character who never did the wrong thing by anyone. He'd died trying to provide for his family. Havoc had surfed with Stephanie Birch at The Box and been impressed by her bravado. The others that had been killed had all been surfers in the prime of their lives just like he was. In another world they could have been friends. They most certainly had family who were still hurting right now, knowing that no one had been caught and held responsible. To walk away would be akin to saying that all of that meant nothing.

The more he thought about it the more Havoc realised it wasn't unlike the situation he faced when the waves at Cape Fear or Black Rainbow first approached him. The smart play would have been to take the safe option and live to fight another day, but at what cost to his heart, his soul and everything that he stood for?

With his decision made Havoc went online and booked his flight to Victoria and a hire car. This time he was paying for it himself so there was no flash 4WD, just the cheapest little shitbox he could find. He checked out of his cabin in Margaret River and got on the road for the three hour drive to Perth Airport.

The music blaring on the stereo in the car did nothing to quieten the myriads of thoughts going through Havoc's brain and no matter how hard he tried to make it otherwise, almost all of them involved one person. Finally it was all too much and he decided there was only one thing to do, it was time to double down and risk it all in a game of poker with the highest stakes possible on the line - people's lives. He put his phone on speaker and dialled Dyanna 'The Dream' Fream.

The phone rang a few times then was picked up.

"Well if it isn't the long lost Havoc," Fream said, clearly not particularly happy. "Didn't I fuck you good enough for a complimentary phone call or some sort of communication?"

"Hello Dy," replied Havoc sheepishly." I'm sorry. I've had a lot on my plate lately but that's no excuse. I should have called."

"Yeah I saw you dancing with that plate. She looked pretty hot. Where was my invite? We could have shared her!"

Havoc couldn't help himself, he burst out laughing. "Oh Dy you never cease to surprise me. To be honest I ditched her and went looking for you, but you'd disappeared. Where did you get to?"

"Oh the girls were giving me the shits and you looked pretty happy so I went home."

"Which girls?"

"What do you care hotshot?" Fream sounded annoyed. "Just the usual pro surf bitchiness. Nothing for you to worry your pretty head about."

"Except one of those girls got killed a bit later," Havoc felt it was time to get on the front foot about all this and confront Fream and see where it went. "You don't sound too upset that one of your own was murdered."

"Yeah, well it seems that's just par for the course these days now doesn't it?" Fream said agitated. "It's just another thing we have to deal with. You know how it is, photographers hiding in bushes, CEO's demanding sex so we can go on tour, the girls getting to surf shitty waves for shitty pay and now someone is trying to kill us. Just another day for a female pro surfer really."

It was a passionate outburst from Fream and Havoc immediately felt like a bit of a dick for bringing it up, but he had to know how she felt. His gut feeling was Fream wasn't the killer but how well did he really know her? And let's face it, human history is littered with people who had no idea that the person closest to them was a monster.

"I'm sorry Dy," Havoc said, trying to smooth things over. "I guess it shook me up that I was there that night and saw Stephanie leave the pub and next thing I hear she's dead."

"Well how do you think it feels for me?" Fream was really fired up now. "The fucken police are chasing me! They think I might have done it!"

"Well, have you talked to them about it?" It was an uncomfortable line of questioning for Havoc, but one he knew he needed to pursue regardless. At the very least he wanted to try and allay any doubts he might have about Fream before he saw her again. The last thing he wanted to do was wake up with a knife in his guts, or even not wake up at all!

"No fuck them! I've got good reason not to trust those cunts! I'm sorry I don't normally use that word, but all coppers are cunts in my book! If someone blew up every cop station in Australia, I'd give them a fucken medal!"

It was an outburst that hurt Havoc. After all he was one of those people that Fream so passionately hated. He knew there would be a reason, and probably a legitimate one, but his intuition told him it wasn't something he should probe further right now. Clearly it was a touchy subject with Fream and she might just clam up altogether and tell him to go fuck himself.

"So what's your plan then?" Havoc asked in a gentle, more relaxed tone. "Just go out there and win Bells and tell the coppers and the rest of the world to go fuck themselves?"

"Got it in one," Fream replied in a little less hostile manner. "You're smarter than you look hotshot!"

"Yeah well I have my moments," Havoc paused for a second, thinking about what his next move should be. "So why did you call me Dy? You made it clear that what we shared was a short-term thing, but now you are acting all upset that I didn't contact you and that I danced with some other random chick. That's hardly straight out of your playbook from what I can tell."

Fream was slow in replying and Havoc could tell his comments had struck home.

"I don't know Havoc. Maybe I wanted to see you again? Maybe I was just pissed off that you did what I asked and left me alone when I actually wanted more? Maybe my life is just that fucked up that I don't know what I want? Where the fuck are you anyway?"

"Halfway back to Perth Airport. I'll be in Melbourne late tonight."

"Do you want me to pick you up?" Fream said in an apologetic tone.

"I would love you to, but I've got to pick up a hire car anyway. Maybe we can meet when I get there. Are you in Torquay?"

"Yes, I will text you the address when you get here."

"Does this mean we are OK?"

"I don't know hotshot. I guess you will just have to wait and see," Fream sounded herself for the first time in their conversation. "I hear you got the wildcard. I guess fucking me does have its advantages after all. I had to sleep my way onto the tour. It looks like you've managed to do the same thing!"

"Yes but I think I got a better deal out of it than you did," Havoc replied cheekily. "Although I did have to do it a lot more often than you, so I guess that evens it out a bit."

"Careful hotshot," Fream said trying to hide her amusement. "Don't go getting too cocky. You're still on thin ice with me."

"I've got a feeling that's the safest place to be with you Dy."

"Then you really are smarter than you look. There's a surprise! Okay then text me when you get to Melbourne and make sure you get some sleep on the plane. You won't be getting much when you get here."

Part Three
THE RICOOL BELLS BEACH CLASSIC
Torquay Victoria

Chapter 32 AN INDECENT PROPOSAL

"We'd be really good together, you know that don't you?" cooed the perfect silicone enhanced breasts that currently occupied most of Havoc's vision and mental space. "Your ah, considerable talents and mine combined would make us both a lot of money. Think about it. Right now you are the hottest new thing in surfing, but what happens when this contest is over? What will you do then? Do you think that dickless fuck Peter Hirt will keep giving you wildcards? No, by the end of Bells you will suddenly find yourself short of friends and the pro tour will go on as if you never even existed. We can change that."

Tiffany Totthil had wasted no time pulling Havoc into a quiet backstage corner of the Ricool Bells Beach Classic pre-event media night. She was in full blown barbie doll sex strumpet mode. Despite the typically freezing cold Torquay evening she'd chosen to wear as little as possible. Her already long blonde hair was made longer with extensions that cascaded all the way down to her tiny pert backside, perfectly framed by a pair of tight little blue denim shorts with frayed edges. A pair of ridiculously high heels somehow supported immaculately tanned and toned legs, and her top was nothing but a tiny little piece of white fabric that seemed to accentuate rather than hide the large pink nipples prominently on display thanks to the icy temperature.

Havoc had been the subject of Totthil's advances a few times now and had been proud of himself for not weakening, but this time while his common sense screamed at him to run away, her sheer wanton sexuality was triggering a whole different reaction from another part of his body. Thanks to a renewing of his acquaintance with Dyanna Fream, who's bed he'd left just a few hours earlier, he was hardly begging for action, yet here he was caught like a deer in the headlights of that plastic, yet fantastic body being so obviously offered for him to enjoy.

Like his previous encounters with Totthil, Havoc felt a bit like the male praying mantis or black widow spider waiting to be consumed by his mate after sex, but still unable to resist her charms. Desperately he looked about for Fream, hoping to find an escape before he completely succumbed, but she was nowhere to be seen.

"She's not here," Totthil whispered reading his mind. She leaned in closer, allowing Havoc to breathe in her intoxicating perfume and get an even better view of everything that was on offer to him. "I haven't seen her all night. If she is here then the media will have her and they won't let her go without asking lots of questions, thanks to you."

"What do you mean?" Havoc asked nervously.

"Oh, you know what I mean Havoc," Totthil pouted sexily as she lightly kissed his neck, plump collagen infused lips promising pleasures unlimited. She undid the button on her shorts, then the zip. Reaching out she grabbed Havoc's hand, forcing it down inside the space she had created and holding it there while she gyrated against his fingers. She was warm, wet and very aroused. "Everybody wants to know what it's like to fuck the hottest guy on tour."

Havoc groaned as Totthil pushed his fingers deeper inside her, he felt powerless to stop her now, just a sex toy for her amusement. With her other hand she grasped the hardness in his pants and he knew with a certainty that this was going to happen. No red-blooded male could resist this kind of temptation. Besides what did he owe Fream? She certainly wasn't promising to be anything other than a friends with benefits situation, so why shouldn't he do this?

Abruptly she pulled his hand out of her pants, for a split-second Havoc thought it might have all been some kind of tease, but then she greedily sucked on his fingers, tasting her own juices all while maintaining eye contact. That was it for Havoc, the last vestiges of self-control crumbled, he spun Totthil around so he could tear those shorts all the way off and take her from behind right then and there, regardless of the media gathering next door.

At that exact moment a camera flash went off. Someone had been watching them, but he didn't wait around to find out who it was. Instead, he took advantage of the distraction and bolted for the door that opened back out into the media room. As he reached for the handle, he heard an exasperated Totthil exclaim. "What's with the flash you fucking amateur?"

"So you're telling me Tiffany had a photographer waiting to try and get photos of the two of you together?" Fream asked incredulously. When Havoc nodded his agreement, she burst out laughing. "Oh man that's a whole new level on the twisted fucked up skankometer. That woman would sell her soul for another Instafamous like!"

They were back lying in bed at Fream's hotel room in a relaxed post sex state after the media night had wrapped up. Fream hadn't turned up to the event stating that she hated doing them. Havoc suspected it was more to do with the police still looking for her, but he didn't push the matter. Instead, he used the opportunity to fuck the encounter with Totthil out of his system and in moments they had been tearing at each other's clothing in a sexual frenzy.

Once the passion had subsided Havoc had told Fream the full story, albeit conveniently leaving out the bit where he had finally lost control and was about to give Totthil exactly what she wanted. He decided now was the time for some questions that needed to be asked.

"Have you talked to the police yet?" Havoc tried to ask the question lightly, like it was just relaxed pillow talk, but he knew it wouldn't go down too well. Fream's immediate reaction confirmed that. She stiffened a little and moved slightly away from him.

"Wow, way to ruin the mood hotshot!" she replied firmly.

"Well I worry about you," Havoc said trying to smooth it over as best he could. "And sometimes I wonder if they are going to come storming through that door any second. The media would have a lot of fun with that one."

Fream sighed. She was quiet for a moment, thinking through what she wanted to say before she started to speak. "No I haven't," Havoc wanted to say something more but Fream cut him off. "And before you say anything, I know I should. It's just that I've got some issues with the police and it's hard to get past them. Yet I know that the longer I hide the worse it looks."

"Why do they want to speak to you anyway?"

Once again Fream took her time before answering. "Because I was with Matt the night he died, and I got someone to lie for me to cover it up. He's gone back to the police to admit that it was just a story. Since then, I've been lying low trying to work out my next move."

"But if you didn't do anything wrong, why didn't you just go to them straight away and just tell the truth?"

Fream looked uncomfortable. Havoc more than ever wanted to believe she wasn't the killer but nothing she was saying was convincing him otherwise.

"In hindsight yes I should have," she continued. "But I wanted to have sex with him and he just wanted to go to bed. He loved to party but not before a heat. I didn't want to take no for an answer, so I spiked his drink with cocaine and Viagra. I know what that sounds like, but we were mates and had done that shit together plenty of times. It was no big deal. Except a few hours after I left, he winds up dead in the spa I fucked him in."

"Mmm I can see how that would look," Havoc said, his mind racing through the implications of what he was hearing while also trying to ignore the pangs of jealousy those words aroused. "But if you got a taxi out of there, wouldn't that clear you if you left before Matt died."

"I don't know, maybe. I thought of that, figured that the cops would check the records of anyone picked up from there. I got an Uber not a taxi but still, I would think all that stuff would have been checked. But when they first talked to me, they didn't seem to know anything, and I'd been with that other guy earlier that night. It just seemed easier to get him to say we'd fucked for a few extra hours and be done with it. And besides like I said, I've got other reasons to not trust the cops."

"Do you want to tell me?" Havoc knew it was a sore spot, but he had to ask.

"There's not much to tell really. I made the mistake of fucking a cop back in my hometown when I was younger. Had a bit of a thing for the uniform you know," Fream smiled ruefully. "But he was shit in bed and didn't like the idea of it being a one night only deal. He started stalking me, like turning up at my place at all hours of the day and night, or down the beach, at the pub, wherever I was really. It was easy for him to do and get away with when he's in a patrol car and wears a badge.

"When I didn't let him back in my pants, he promised he would ruin me and my career. I complained but his cop pals took his side. It was pretty fucking scary there for a while, to the point I haven't been home for a few years now. I've heard he's got a woman now, but I still don't trust him. I figured if he found out I was caught up in Matt's murder he might do something to cause me more problems."

Fream fell silent and not knowing what else to say, Havoc reached out and gently squeezed her hand. She responded by moving closer to Havoc and cuddling up to him. By some unspoken agreement neither said anything further. Tomorrow was a big day for both of them with the event due to start and a huge swell on its way. Within minutes Fream was asleep, but it took much longer for Havoc to drift off. Their conversation had given him much to think about.

First and foremost, tomorrow he at least owed DS Patinsen the courtesy of a call to advise he had gone against orders. He knew just how disappointed his mentor would be and that hurt more than the likelihood of losing his job. Would the new information he had uncovered help his situation? Somehow he doubted it.

Chapter 33: AN UNNERVING REVELATION

Bunker had never felt so out of control and lost in his whole life as he did right now. For a man who was basically a walking drug experimentation lab, that might not sound particularly strange. However, the last time Bunker's thoughts weren't clouded by some kind of mind-altering substance for any period longer than a day or two was when he was in a school uniform.

He'd managed to stay away from hard drugs since the night of the Quikbong Pro final on the Gold Coast. A diet of weed and alcohol had still been a daily feature up until the news about Birch's murder sent him on a proper bender that only started to slow down when Havoc suddenly appeared by his side on finals day at Margaret River. They'd gone out and partied that night, but the next day Bunker made a decision to go cold turkey and so far he'd stayed strong.

It was something Havoc had said that night that had helped trigger his sobriety. The two of them had been standing by the bar, surrounded by alcohol and hot chicks. It was a moment when he should have felt on top of the world, but instead he had felt a profound sense of loneliness. The one person he wanted to party with would never be there again.

Havoc must have sensed the moment because he pulled Bunker into a hug and talked quietly in his ear.

"All this," Havoc said pointing at the drinks lined up on the bar and the girls surrounding him. "All this will always be here mate. You've got the money and the looks, this shit is yours until the day you die. But right now you've got a chance to do something only a few people will ever do. You can be a world champion! All you've done lately in the memory of

Matt, imagine how proud he'd be if you won a world title?" Havoc again gestured to the drinks and the girls. "Don't let this shallow bullshit distract you from that brother," Havoc tapped Bunker on his chest where his heart beat strongly. "You're a better man than you realise, and this is your moment to show that to the world!"

Havoc gave him another hug and Bunker was close enough to tears that he couldn't manage a reply. Instead, he just hugged his friend back while he composed himself. Finally, he was able to mumble "I love you brother!" and they broke off the hug, Bunker wiped away the tears that were threatening and they went back to partying like nothing had happened.

Bunker had woken up the next morning with that conversation still in his head and made the decision to remove as many distractions in his life as he could and focus solely on the world title. All drugs, alcohol, social media and girls went out the window, (although he still wasn't sure about the no sex thing).

It was the second time in as many weeks that Havoc had been a positive influence on his life. Given what he now knew about him, he was in an uncomfortable position about what to do next.

Despite being a high functioning alcoholic and drug addict, Bunker had to admit a new form of clarity was beginning to manifest itself. A fog he hadn't even realised existed was lifting and the sun seemed to shine a little brighter for it, but it came at a price. Going cold turkey on hard drugs after the Gold Coast had been brutal enough with the shakes, the sweats and the itches that never stopped, but he had self-medicated that by still indulging in plenty of drinking and a steady intake of marijuana. Now that he was trying to be completely sober, things were tougher still. The worst was when he tried to go to bed. Sleep was now foreign to him and on the rare occasions it came, it was accompanied by the most vivid and out of control dreams he had ever experienced.

Many of those dreams featured Matt Wilson. He missed his friend dearly when he was awake but at night he was visited by him constantly. In the rare, good dreams, Wilson would be there smiling and joking like nothing had happened. More often though, he would have his back to Bunker, either paddling or walking away and no amount of calling out would get him to turn and say hello. Bunker would wake from these with an overwhelming sadness that he felt may never go away.

He took some small solace in knowing he was at least being proactive about Wilson's death. He'd made sure Wilson's mum would never have to work again and set up the Matt Wilson Foundation, which in a short time was already on its way towards making a difference in places like Indonesia, the Philippines and Sri Lanka where kids couldn't afford the basics to live, let alone surfboards. That was the public side of his activity, it was the private side that was now concerning him the most.

Not trusting the police to do their job, Bunker had hired one of the most prestigious and respected private investigation companies in the country. With money being no object, he gave them the single task of looking into everyone who had anything to do with the GSA, starting with all the surfers and the big-name industry players, to see if they could find any information about Wilson's killer.

Despite the investigation only going for a few short weeks Bunker was unprepared for the colossal amount of dirt they'd uncovered. There were dodgy business ventures everywhere, underground narcotics dealers, secret drug addictions and illicit affairs of every kind imaginable. Some of those affairs were so sordid and twisted even Bunker had trouble looking the people involved in the eye when he saw them in public.

Unfortunately, they had uncovered nothing obvious in the search for the killer that their inside sources at the police didn't already know about. Despite all the various misdeeds that had been revealed, it was the news about Havoc that troubled him the most.

When Bunker had first talked to the owner of Galese Private Investigations- Les Galese- a big red headed dude who looked like he'd seen more than a few fights in his life, he hadn't even thought of Havoc. In fact, if he had of, he would have said "Don't bother looking into him, he's not the guy…" but he'd instructed them to look at everybody involved in the tour, and they had done just that.

It was during Galese's most recent report when he'd asked a simple question that rocked Bunker's world.

"How well do you know Dirth Spidder?" Galese asked.

"Who's that?" Bunker replied, then it dawned on him. "Oh, you mean Havoc? Pretty well man. We've been surfing together since we were kids. He's a good dude."

"Do you know what he does for a living?" Galese asked tentatively.

"Yeah, he's a labourer or something. Works on building sites, that sort of stuff," Bunker was suddenly worried. "Why, what do you know?"

"Well, did you know that he went to the police academy?"

"Havoc? Nah dude you've got the wrong guy. No way he'd be trying out to be a copper!"

"Well, that's where you're wrong. I'm 100% sure he went to the police academy. The best I can tell is that he graduated too. After that it gets a bit hazy. My guess is he's either working on building sites like you said, or that he is still a cop and is undercover."

"Havoc an undercover cop? No chance!"

"It took a lot of work and a few favours to uncover what we know so it isn't as strange as it may sound to you. For an organisation to go into that much effort to hide a person's background suggests it was done for an important reason. My guess is that if he is who I think he is, then his goal is the same as yours, to find whoever killed your friend."

The news rocked Bunker to the core. He had been through his fair share of conflicts with law enforcement, including undercover police and as a result, they weren't his favourite human beings. Now he was being told that the one person that had been going some way towards filling the void created by Wilson's death was an undercover cop!

Everything that had gone on between them felt lessened to Bunker. The lies that had suddenly been uncovered now sat like acid in his stomach. That late night call up on the Gold Coast took on a whole new meaning. It wasn't a friend looking out for him, but a cop using their relationship to sneakily interrogate him to find out what he knew. That favour to get him the wildcard into the Margaret River competition was purely so he could continue to infiltrate the tight surfing brotherhood.

"So, what do you think I should do?" Bunker finally said to Galese.

"About Spidder?" Galese asked as he stroked his impressive red moustache. These days he rarely got out in the field, but Bunker had basically hired his entire firm and paid top dollar in doing so. He figured it was the least he could do to travel from his base in Kings Cross, Sydney, down to Torquay and run the operation personally. He also had to admit that despite his initial misconception that he was working for just another spoiled rich boy, he actually liked his employer.

When he saw Bunker's nod of agreement he continued on. "Well it's up to you. If, like you said, your whole purpose is to find your friend's murderer then my advice is to hold off. It can't hurt to have other people with the same goals as you, especially the police. And if we do find out something significant, you haven't said what you want us to do with that information? Maybe you might want to pass it onto him?"

Bunker was confused. He hadn't really thought that far ahead. He'd had fantasies of inflicting all sorts of pain and retribution on his friend's killer but when he really thought about it, he knew that anything like that was beyond him. Hiring Galese had been about as far as his thoughts had gone down the revenge path.

Galese could see that Bunker was a bit lost and didn't know what to do, so he didn't push him any further. He promised to be in contact soon and turned to leave, but just as he walked out the door of Bunker's luxury Torquay mansion, he turned back to him with a thoughtful expression on his face.

"I can see you are upset about your friend being an undercover policeman," Galese said quietly. "But think about it from his point of view. Someone is killing the world's best surfers. One of which was a friend to both of you. Right now, you are number two in the world and he's put himself as close to you as he can without making it obvious. Perhaps he's trying to protect you as well?"

With that comment Galese left. Bunker immediately felt the need to reach for a bong or a bottle of tequila to try and make sense of what was going on. Luckily, he had the foresight to clear all of that stuff out of the mansion before he moved in. After a few minutes of fighting the demons whispering in his ear that all he needed to do was make one phone call and his problems would be solved, he was able to reach for his phone and dial a different number altogether.

"Hello kid," Morpheus's smooth voice came down the line. For some reason Bunker loved that Morpheus still called him 'kid', despite knowing each other for nearly 10 years. "How goes the preparations for Bells. You know there's a monster swell coming?"

"Yeah man. Tuesday could be huge!" Bunker replied excitedly, forgetting his troubles for a moment. "I mean like really huge dude! Like Point Break 50 year storm kind of thing! I've been surfing all week testing out some big boards."

"Nah Tuesday will just be the lemon next to the pie. Wednesday is going to be the biggest day for sure," replied Morpheus, then he paused thoughtfully. "But I sense there's another reason for you to call me. What's up kid?"

Bunker paused for a second. "It's about Havoc," he said. "I've found out something about him and I'm not sure what to do."

"I'd suggest doing nothing," said Morpheus sternly. "Friends like him don't come around too often. Especially for someone in your position. Who he is and what he does shouldn't be important to you."

"Wait, what?" Bunker tried to process Morpheus's strange reply. "Do you mean you know what he is?"

Morpheus laughed. "Of course I do. I know what he is, but more importantly, I know who he is. There's not much I don't know kid, especially about the people I care about. I think you should be careful about saying too much more out of respect to a good mate who cares about you for who you are and not for your money."

Bunker was a little lost for words. This was not how he was expecting the conversation to go but Morpheus's advice, along with the last comment from Les Galese, went a long way to lifting the weight from his shoulders.

"Yeah you're right Morpheus," Bunker replied thoughtfully as he felt a ray of sunshine in his troubled mind. 'I guess I've been a little lost lately and that came as a bit of a shock. But I love Havoc. I don't know where I'd be without him right now."

"Don't worry about it kid and I know he loves you too," said Morpheus. "Now onto more important things. Let's talk about what we need to do to get you a win at Bells."

Chapter 34 THE NEW LOVER

Just like Morpheus predicted the peak of the swell arrived at Bells later than expected. A very anxious Claire Cooper had to admit to herself she was extremely thankful for that as she watched the male surfers prepare for their first heats in what could only be described as ridiculously giant conditions.

For the twentieth time in the past half hour or so Cooper checked her phone. She was expecting a call and it was overdue. Not that the caller ever seemed to care whether it messed with Cooper's schedule or not. Sometimes she wondered whether the caller even cared about her at all, but she was too far gone now. Despite the pain Cooper reluctantly believed would come one day, she was committed to seeing this through.

Peter Hirt had been true to his word and sent the girls out in the big surf. Leading up to that day, he had gleefully trumpeted in all his media interviews about how the GSA fully supported women's surfing and that they had complete faith the ladies would do themselves proud in waves of real consequence.

Cooper knew better, but she had to admit that Hirt had done exactly what she had asked him to do. Who could have predicted that the biggest swell ever to hit Bells Beach during a competition would coincide with her underhanded push for equality in men's and women's surfing?

Hirt had not been able to control his delight when he advised her that he had done just as she had blackmailed him to do. The first rounds of the women's heats had been scheduled to be held straight up when the swell was due to peak. When she'd argued that he had gone too far the other way, he'd blown his top.

"Cooper I've fucking done exactly what you asked me to do!" Hirt snarled down the phone. "Just so you know, your little blackmail scenario is nothing more than a flea bite on my arse. I don't like it, but I sure as hell can live with it. If you continue to try and use it against me then I'm going to call your fucking bluff and put the girls out in the worst conditions I can find at every competition for the rest of your short-lived career. If you decide to release that tape, then I can promise that you will live to regret it, if you live at all. Do I make myself clear?"

Cooper felt her anger rising. It took a lot of self-control not to call his double bluff and immediately go public with the tape, but she knew she couldn't. The person who dominated most of her thoughts had big plans for Peter Hirt and the GSA. So, Cooper did what she was told and against all her natural instincts, she'd let Hirt win this little verbal battle and pretended to be suitably chastised and hung up. At least her cool, calm head would be rewarded later with the thing she craved most - approval. She looked forward to that like someone lost in the desert looks forward to their first drink of water.

There had been a few sleepless nights leading up to the first day of competition but when Cooper got her first glimpse of the ocean as she drove into Bells on the opening morning she was relieved to see that while it was clearly big, maybe in the 6-10ft range, it was a far cry from what her most vivid nightmares had suggested it might be.

In fact, the waves had been amazing. Everybody had stepped up and broke new ground for women's surfing, just like she knew they would. In an event dedicated to Stephanie Birch, all the usual suspects stood out and ripped. Cooper herself had surfed some of the waves of her life and had won all her heats easily. Dyanna Fream, Karissa Kai, Molly Perkins and Sally Lord were all standouts, but across the board everyone could be proud of their efforts.

Despite what she knew about Tiffany Totthil, Cooper even had to admit a grudging respect for her after she surprised everybody by surfing well in her win over Belle Silva. Although somehow the heat had been mysteriously rescheduled from being held late in the day to much earlier before the swell had really started to build.

Cooper wasn't sure whether the reschedule was to suit the girl's lesser ability in big surf or to take full advantage of media coverage for the ludicrous 'Sea Thru' wetsuits they were both wearing. She shuddered at the thought of how they had both looked running through the crowd appearing to be almost naked, not sure whether the development was a necessary evil, or had set women's surfing back ten years.

At least Cooper could relax from worrying about her own progress in the competition for a couple of days while the men got their heats underway. Instead, she could focus on the rest of the goals she shared with the person she was expecting the call from.

The past 6-8 months or so hadn't been easy for Cooper. This time last year she was engaged to be married to her high school sweetheart. They were both country kids living a nice, well planned, comfortable existence. Everything had been simple and easy. While Cooper focussed on her quest for a world title, her fiancée acted as her manager, taking care of sponsorship negotiations and all the bookings and minor details required when travelling almost nonstop around the globe.

It should have been the time of their lives yet looking back Cooper realised it had also been boring. Or perhaps uninspiring was the right word? With each competition that Cooper had failed to meet her expectations, she had lost a little of the magic of the journey and she had even begun to resent her fiancée for his unflappable belief that she would be a world champion.

Then just weeks before the big world title showdown at Keramas in Bali she'd met someone else and everything had changed. Excitement and passion had come roaring into her life in a way she had never experienced before. Suddenly the colours of Cooper's world were so much more vivid and enticing, but with it had come much sadness and turmoil. Jimmy Slide had been murdered and the pro tour would never be as fun and innocent to her as it once was.

Sometimes she missed the simplicity of her previous relationship. Her fiancée had supported her 100% and always backed down and let her make the final decision in any conflicts they had about what best to do next. Perhaps that's why she left him? Maybe she had needed to be told what to do more? Certainly, whenever she was around her new lover she tended to lose all sense of herself and surrendered to the desire to please. Recently she often wondered where her own goals finished and the new ones that had been instilled in her commenced.

Finally the call she had been so desperately waiting for came.

"It's all happening," said the voice on the other end, not even waiting for Cooper to say hello. "My guess is it will be sometime in the next two days."

"So what are we going to do to stop-" replied Cooper.

"We will do nothing," interrupted the caller, leaving no room for discussion. "You will do nothing! Do I make myself clear?"

"But she's my fr-"

There was a click as the person on the other end hung up before Cooper could finish her sentence.

Chapter 35 SATANIC THUNDER

Picker strutted through the Bells contest arena liked a jumped-up peacock with his feathers on full display. The lord of sleaze was back in full flight and nothing could fuck with his mojo. In his mind he was the new age John Travolta grooving down the street in Saturday Night Fever, dancing to a tune nobody else could hear and owning every second of it.

His outfit had to be seen to be believed. It was a purple velvet suit with leopard print trim and matching top hat that looked like it belonged more in a Hollywood pimp comedy movie than at the longest running surfing contest on the planet. It was the gaudiest, ugliest thing anyone had ever seen, and Picker loved it!

With the cool half million dollars and counting he'd pocketed for the Havoc and Dirty Dy photos, Picker had gone a long way towards bailing himself out of the financial hole that he had been in thanks to his dubious decision to buy the renamed Picker Kink Club. He'd also decided to treat himself to a bit of a makeover and the first thing on his list was to do something about that sweaty, shiny, half bald head that always looked back at him whenever he'd walked past a mirror.

Picker had lashed out on the latest and greatest hair replacement treatment and had undergone the surgery just a few days ago. As a result, his head looked like a lumpy red sausage, hence his decision to wear the worst hat ever seen at a pro surfing event. He'd also booked himself in for some bicep and pectoral muscle implants to make his pasty, pudgy body look like it had muscle tone and was planning to top it off with some butt surgery to shape his flabby arse into a more aesthetically pleasing firm and protruding version.

He initially thought about missing the Bells contest altogether and getting everything done at once but the party scene around Torquay during the contest period had been good to him over the years. His favourite had been a few years back when he'd snuck into a famous surfboard shaper's end of competition party. It had been a nerve-wracking experience as he jumped fences and sneaked through backyards in the dark, all while fearing he would disturb a neighbourhood dog and be eaten alive.

It had proven to be well worth it though when he captured a former women's world champ on her hands and knees while a well known surf journalist hammered her from behind in a raw display of animal passion. That in itself was only mildly newsworthy, but given they were both married to other people at the time and had previously treated Picker with disdain, he'd taken great delight in ending one marriage and most likely doing some serious damage to the other.

Picker also wanted to remind everyone that he was still a photographer who got the job done. His reputation had been slipping recently with the Matt Wilson footage being useless and not being able to claim responsibility for the Jimmy Slide photos, despite the rearranging of Slide's body being some of his best work.

This time the Havoc and Dirty Dy fuckfest proudly carried his name wherever it was published. The arse kissing sycophants that he liked to keep around him had all told him how amazing his work was and how much they admired him. He'd got some dirty looks too, but he was used to that and didn't give a fuck about them. He was Picker and he was a player once again.

As he pranced into the VIP area Picker hoped he would spot Havoc. He'd heard Havoc had got the wildcard into Bells and knew for sure that it was his fine work hiding in the bushes that had made that happen. Peter Hirt had told him as much the last time they had talked when they'd discussed Hirt's brokerage fee for marketing the photos.

So Picker felt sure that Havoc would be happy to see him. Maybe they could discuss working together in the future? They could definitely help each other's career, that's for sure. In fact, the more Picker thought about it, the more he felt Havoc owed him big time. Without Picker,

Havoc would already have been a forgotten name. No one remembers a random wildcard who loses his first heat and then fades into obscurity, but right now according to the internet, Havoc was almost as famous as any surf star on the planet, even though he didn't have social media.

Yes, Havoc owed him alright and Picker couldn't wait to see that look of adulation on his face when he thanked him for his supreme photography skills. Of course, he would play it cool when Havoc started to fawn over him and ask when they could do more. Maybe imply he was busy, and his services didn't come cheap? He'd wait for Havoc to plead poverty and to start begging, then suggest there were other ways that payment could be made. Picker had seen Havoc's impressive rig in full flight pounding away at Dirty Dy and he wanted some of that!

Picker's luck was in and he spied Havoc walking away from the cafeteria with some food. He walked up behind Havoc with a smile on his face and announced loudly. "Well, if it isn't surfing's new rock star, or should I say cock star!"

Havoc turned around amiably but as soon as he saw it was Picker his whole body tensed, and his normally friendly eyes went cold as ice with pure fury. Picker had never seen a person's demeanour change so quickly and drastically. His cockiness was replaced by dread and he suddenly realised he might have made a major mistake and completely misread the situation.

Dropping his food to the floor, Havoc grabbed Picker by the throat with one hand, lifted him easily into the air and began squeezing tightly. He then marched him a few steps across the cafeteria and pinned him against the wall, feet still dangling above the ground. Struggling to breathe, Picker's eyes searched frantically for someone to rush to his rescue and pull this maniac off him, but help wasn't coming despite lots of people watching on intently.

Havoc leaned in close, muscles bulging as the rage he felt aided strength to the single arm holding Picker's considerable weight aloft. He squeezed tighter, Picker's face began to redden, and his mouth opened and closed like a fish gasping for air that wasn't coming.

"Did you ever wonder how I got my nickname?" Havoc snarled menacingly. Picker felt his bladder lose control and he began to piss himself. "If you ever take another picture of me or Dyanna Fream again you will find out. If you so much as point a camera at either of us even just signing an autograph, I will fucking end you! You got that?" Havoc's face was now so close that Picker feared he was going to bite his nose clean off his head, such was the wrath emanating from those terrifying eyes.

"Do you understand me?" Havoc roared and Picker felt that grip tighten further around his throat. Would he just rip it out altogether, Roadhouse style? Picker certainly thought it was a possibility. Despite his fear and desperate need to breathe, his primal survival instinct kicked in allowing his brain to work just enough to nod his head vigorously a few times.

With that Picker saw some of that frightening satanic thunder drain from Havoc's face, then just as quickly it came back again and Havoc slapped him incredibly hard across the face with an open hand sending his hat flying. He shaped to do it again, then thought better of it and instead threw Picker to the ground and stormed off leaving his uneaten food sitting next to the dishevelled photographer.

Lying in a crumpled heap and trying frantically to work some oxygen into his lungs, Picker tasted blood and felt sure that at least one tooth had been loosened. He looked up expecting to see people rushing to help him up and provide some sympathy, but no one appeared to be willing to help. In fact, he thought he heard some light applause. It was then he noticed his hat sitting a few feet away and he realised that his red sausage head was now visible to everyone.

Embarrassment fed him strength, allowing Picker to struggle to his feet and retrieve the hat. Without looking at anyone he turned and hurried out of the VIP area straight to where his car was parked some distance away. Along the route he became aware of people pointing and laughing at him, further increasing his embarrassment.

Picker lifted his pace and eventually got to his car. It was only when he hurriedly sat in his seat that he felt the wetness and realised he had pissed himself expansively and the large wet stain on his purple pants was highly visible. No wonder everyone had been laughing at him!

Angry now, Picker started the car and roared out of the carpark on his way back to his hotel room in Torquay. Once he put some distance between him and that petrifying human being, Picker's strange brand of courage begun to return.

It wasn't like he hadn't been threatened before, that happened on an almost weekly basis. It took some nerve to do the kind of stalking he did considering the risks associated with the long list of dangerous and potentially lethal creatures he might come across crawling through the undergrowth along with the furious people who had caught him in the act. Not even someone as skilful as Picker at hiding in the bushes can go undetected every time.

But this was different. Picker had never been so terrified in his life. He'd looked into Havoc's eyes and seen his own mortality. There had been a few moments when he genuinely thought he might be killed by the unhinged behaviour of the demon who had so easily pinned him against the wall with one hand. Then there was the humiliation he had experienced in front of his peers which in the long run might hurt more. Picker had thought his little display would remind everyone of who he was. Instead, he had been sent packing in a way that his reputation might never recover from.

As he neared Torquay, Picker took advantage of the moment to shove a finger up his nose to engage in one of his favourite pastimes. While he scratched around looking for a little nugget of goodness, he failed to notice the traffic lights ahead turn red. The traffic slowed to a standstill, but Picker was distracted trying to dislodge a particularly stubborn booger. Before he had the chance to register the need to stop, he slammed into the car in front of him. There was a sharp stab of pain and then everything went black...

Chapter 36 DON'T POKE THE BEAR

Havoc was a nest of conflicting emotions as he thundered out of the VIP area following his altercation with Picker. The worst part was that he was an hour from paddling out in his heat and the surf was massive! He definitely did not need this kind of distraction!

He was ashamed that he had unleashed the beast that was the real 'Havoc' after being so careful to keep him chained away for a long period of time. He took no pride or satisfaction in the fear he saw in the pudgy little man's eyes, nor the applause that followed him after he had slapped a basically helpless man and left him lying on the floor in a pile of his own piss (and what the fuck was with Picker's weird, red, splotchy head anyway?).

On the other hand, Havoc knew the slimy little turd had deserved every bit of it and more. Those couple of days and nights with Fream stood out as golden memories in Havoc's life and to know that Picker was hiding outside with a camera was hard to process. Somehow it had cheapened the experience. It was made worse by being splashed over countless websites and tabloid magazines with all sorts of attention seeking headlines that ranged from sordid to disgusting such as:

'Dirty Dy Does The Dirty'

'Dirty Dy Rides The Havoc Train'

'Female Pro Surfer in Marathon Smut Session'

'When Pro Surfing Meets Porn'

The stories that accompanied the photos were equally outrageous and rarely contained a single element of truth other than the obvious - that they had engaged in a very impressive sexual marathon.

Despite that, Havoc had thought he'd got past his hatred for Picker. During the past few days he'd spent with Fream, they'd talked a lot about the invasion of privacy they'd experienced. They'd been angry, they'd laughed, they'd cried and they'd cringed at the life changing embarrassment of their situation and how their families might feel.

One of Havoc's first phone calls had been to his mum. It wasn't a difficult call to make as she had always been open minded, but he didn't want her to hear it from another source before he'd told her the full story. It went about the way he thought it would. She'd laughed at him, then gone online while they were still talking to check the action and commented that "At least you put on a good show Dirth". She had seen her son get himself in worse situations than this one. This time at least she had a great story to tell her friends at their next coffee catch up. That is, of course, if Fream didn't turn out to be a psychotic serial killer.

In the end Havoc and Fream had agreed the best thing to do was let it go. While both strongly wished it had never gone public, there was nothing that could change that now. So, they resolved to focus on the positives that had come out of it - Havoc had gotten another crack at the big show and Fream had suddenly become the most popular female surfer in the world.

Unfortunately, all that 'Forgive and Forget' bullshit had gone out the window the moment that smarmy prick had said "Or should I say cock star!"

Havoc had immediately gone white hot. The darkness inside him smashed its way to the surface and Havoc had known from past experience that there was no way he could fight it. The best he could do was ride the monster in a hope he could somehow keep the damage to a minimum. He believed he'd done well to keep it to just merely choking the terrified photographer half to death, but just as he had dropped his guard and thought it was all over, the beast surged back into control and had slapped Picker hard.

Havoc had been scared to see the damage he'd done. The slap wasn't at full power, but he was a strong man and Picker wasn't. He'd seen that Picker was still moving and took that as a sign he hadn't accidently killed him and gotten out of there quickly in case the beast had another trick up his sleeve.

With no other idea what to do, Havoc went and sat next to his locker in the competitor's section and tried to get his head straight. The last thing he needed was his mind messed up when he was about to paddle out into a seriously dangerous ocean. He'd hoped to eat something before his heat to get a bit of extra energy, but that was now accompanying Picker on the cafeteria floor. Probably just as well, his nerves were red lining so keeping food in his stomach might have been impossible.

Outside he could hear the roar of the crowd, the sound of the booming waves and the event commentators going crazy. There was an incredible vitality in the ocean that was feeding the people on land. Everyone knew they were witnessing something special. Suddenly it was all too much. He felt overwhelmed, like he didn't belong here. He wanted to vomit and run far away to a quiet beach with no one around.

At that moment Gabriel Andre came into the room accompanied by some of his entourage. Havoc glanced up and for a second they locked eyes. Gone was the friendly demeanour that Andre had displayed back at the Settlers Tavern and instead The Terminator looked back at him and sneered. He then made a gesture as if cutting his throat and pointed at Havoc. The message was clear- 'I'm going to kill you!'

This time Havoc didn't have the willpower to fight the beast and instead he embraced it. He surged to his feet with a roar of fury and charged at Andre with hands in fighting position ready to unleash his full mixed martial arts training. World champ or not, he was going to rip his fucking head off!

Andre clearly knew his way around a fight as he immediately took up a defensive posture preparing to absorb the attack. Just as Havoc was about to launch, a wall of muscle from Andre's crew stepped between them. Havoc's arms were pinned by a guy on either side while another stood in front, pushing him in the chest and effectively blocking all access to their man.

There was loud shouting and lots of words in Brazilian and English flying around everywhere but none of it registered with Havoc as he strained to get to Andre. He gave another push against the wall and suddenly he felt intense pain in his left arm and shoulder as it was wrenched behind his back and a Latin voice spoke softly in his ear.

"Don't make me break your arm bro!"

It was one of the guys Havoc had shared a few drinks with only a week or two before when he'd partied at the Settlers Tavern with the Brazilian contingent. That quiet, confident, yet pleading voice reached Havoc in a way none of the shouting could have. He felt some of the red mist evaporate and relaxed slightly. He allowed the wall to push him back a couple of steps and as he did he caught a glimpse of Andre over the shoulder of one of his bodyguards. This time he took enormous satisfaction in the brief flicker of fear he saw in those eyes.

The bodyguards pushed him back onto the chair he'd been sitting on and stood at close range, ready to spring back into action if Havoc lit up again. The thud of the pounding of his heart in his ears slowly dissipated, only to be replaced by the myriad of sounds of the chaos he had created. It had been a long time since two surfers had to be separated from going at each other and no one appeared to know what to do about it.

Havoc blinked, awareness slowly coming back to him as the beast subsided and he tried to make sense of the noise, but the shouting in English and Portuguese continued. For a moment his anger rose again and he felt a sudden need to test Andre's muscle boys, then a familiar face appeared in front of him.

"Come on kid, let's get you out of here," Morpheus said as he pulled Havoc out from amongst the bodyguards and led him outside to a quieter spot overlooking the Bells lineup. As they sat down another huge set of waves poured through, catching the competitors out of position, much to the delight and awe of the thousands scattered all around the headland.

"Well kid," Morpheus laughed while clapping him on his now sore shoulder. "One thing's for sure. Everyone around here is going to think twice before they fuck with you again!"

The jest did little to lighten Havoc's mood, but he was grateful for it anyway. He looked at his sponsor and recognised the concern of a friend. He'd seen it before when DS Patinsen had been there to rescue a younger

Havoc out of whatever trouble he had got himself into. Suddenly a thought occurred to him.

"How the fuck were you there at just the right time to pull me out of that?" he asked. "Are you some kind of psychic or something? Is that why they call you Morpheus?"

"Maybe," laughed Morpheus. "But in this case it was nothing like that. I just heard you had a little confrontation with Picker and came looking for you to make sure your head was in the right space for your heat."

"It wasn't," admitted Havoc. "But Gabriel fucked up."

"How did he do that?" asked Morpheus with a knowing look.

"Because he poked the bear," Havoc stared at Morpheus, eyes shining intently. "He gave a stupid motion, as if he was going to cut my throat. Probably thought it would psych me out or something. He's going to regret that because out there," Havoc gestured to another monster wave. "Out there, that's me, that's my shit. World titles don't mean jack when you're out in that. I was confused before, but now I'm just fucking angry!"

With that Havoc stood up and reached down to clasp Morpheus's hand and pulled him up into an embrace. "Thanks my friend," he said. "I'm going to go beat up a world champion now."

"Good work kid," Morpheus said smiling as Havoc walked away. "Just make sure you do it in the ocean, not on land. In case you didn't notice, that didn't work out so well for you!"

Feeling much better Havoc walked back to his locker. He got plenty of stares as he did, whether it was for his run in with Picker or Andre he didn't know and didn't care. Not bothering to watch the surf he threw on his wetsuit and contest rash shirt and started to do some stretches. He'd seen enough of the waves and felt if he watched anymore, he was in danger of his adrenalin redlining again. That would come soon enough when he got out there.

"What boards do you want me to take?" asked a familiar voice. It was his friend Harry Brand, a Torquay local and former Bells wildcard himself. As an experienced surfer in huge Bells, Brand was doubling both as an advisor to Havoc and his board caddy in case he broke a board and needed a replacement while still in his heat.

"Those two," Havoc said pointing at the second and third biggest Yahoo surfboards he had in his quiver. Then he grabbed the biggest he had. "This one is coming with me."

Havoc took a deep breath and jogged past all the competitors and VIP's watching the event. It was time and he was ready.

Chapter 37 A TOSS OF THE COIN

The Killer watched Havoc jog past on his way out of the VIP area and down the stairs to compete in his heat. There were not many surfers on The Killer's radar that were relatively safe but Havoc was one of them. Due to unexpected recent events, so was Bunker Haze, who would never know how close he had become to being the next victim. Of course, if either of them got in The Killer's way, then they were fair game.

"Poor misguided Havoc," The Killer thought. "He really can't see what's right in front of his face!"

With every surfer that had been happily disposed of, the ultimate goal should have felt closer, but The Killer was discovering that the next primary target was fluid and ever changing. Recently The Killer had thought that three more people were required to be removed from the living, now it was just two, plus a bonus one that was purely for the enjoyment of it.

There was one real question that hadn't been addressed though - Once The Killer had reached that beautiful ambition, what would happen next? Nothing had even come close to the adrenalin rush of getting away with the ultimate crime. The unexpected thrill that occurred when Stephanie Birch had recognised what was happening and who was responsible, then unsuccessfully tried to run away, had been intoxicating!

Perhaps there was no need to stop? It was clear the hedonistic surfing fraternity and its wonderfully dystopian world ruled by social media and the GSA didn't really want to see The Killer caught, so why stop? Wouldn't it be something to just kill for fun? Now there was a dream!

In the meantime, there was still a job to finish. Two targets remained. One would be infinitely more enjoyable and far easier than the other, then there was the bonus kill to savour. The Killer sat and thought out the possibilities. Was it possible to step up the game and kill two at once? Logistics were considered and scenarios contemplated, but no matter which way the problem was approached, a solution remained evasive.

The makings of a plan slowly started to evolve. It was delicious, but there still remained the decision of what to do first, or rather, who to do first? It was either the incredibly difficult single kill, or the equally difficult, but much more pleasurable double kill. It made sense to leave the best to last and concentrate on the single target but why deny a pleasure now on the assumption that it will be just as appealing later?

It really was a toss of the coin situation, so there was only one thing for it. The Killer fished a $1 coin out of a pocket and threw it in the air, all while laughing inwardly at the thought that somewhere out there, three people had no idea their lives depended on how it landed.

Chapter 38 HAVOC VS THE TERMINATOR

Havoc felt oddly calm as he jogged down the iconic Bells Beach staircase. In his previous heat against Gabriel Andre, he had been a jumble of nerves and his mind had been racing in a million different directions. He'd wanted to prove that he deserved his wildcard at Margaret River but had felt guilty that he was doing something he had always dreamed of, while he should have been trying to catch a serial killer.

Once again those thoughts and feelings had threatened to derail him, but there was a freedom in knowing he had nothing to lose and in this moment that really was the case. His career as an undercover cop was probably over and it was highly unlikely he had what it took to be a professional surfer.

So, there was a big chance that he would soon be on the tools at a building site for real instead of just as a cover. There was an appealing simplicity to that. He would no longer have to pretend to be someone he wasn't and constantly lie to the people around him, he could just be Havoc.

Halfway down the stairs he took another deep breath and paused to take it all in. He wanted to remember this moment as it would never come again. He looked at the crowd and they mostly seemed to be cheering and supporting him. That surprised him, but then he remembered that he was the underground Aussie wildcard up against the former Brazilian world champ in an Australian surf competition. These were his people.

He spotted a gorgeous brunette waving a banner that said, 'Hey Havoc, Do Me Next!' and any residual tension left him as he laughed at just how much his life had changed in such a few short weeks. On a whim he walked over to her, bowed and kissed her hand theatrically. The already noisy crowd erupted with delight. As he continued down the stairs, he reflected that if everything else went pear-shaped then maybe he could set up his own Lonely Fans page and make a living with that instead.

The massive swell meant the Bells shore break was intense, so Havoc waited patiently for the right moment to take it on. He said a quiet prayer to Huey the god of surf as he dug his feet into the yellow and black sand to try and scratch off any oily residue that may cause him to slip at a crucial moment. If this had been back in 1981 when it was last this big for a competition, he would have already been paddling out at least fifteen minutes earlier, but just beyond the shore break sat a jet ski waiting to whisk him all the way out into prime position for the start of the heat. They would also be there to rescue him if things went bad and give him a lift back out after he caught a wave. A far cry from what surfers in the old days had to deal with.

He was just about to paddle out when his senses picked up that someone was approaching. He turned in time to be engulfed in a bear hug from Bunker.

"I love you brother," his friend said emotionally. "Good luck out there."

For a moment Havoc was lost for words. Then they flowed.

"I love you too mate," he replied. "And don't worry, I got this. Gabriel got me once but it's not happening again. You'll be back to world number one when this is all done."

"I know brother, I know. But that's not what is important to me right now," Bunker replied. "When this is all over, we need to talk. There's some stuff you need to hear. Important shit about things that mean a lot to both of us. You know what I mean?"

Havoc was too caught up in the moment to think too deeply about Bunker's words, so he nodded, then hugged his mate again and turned and charged the shore break without hesitation.

The ride out on the jet ski would be forever stitched into Havoc's brain. The waves were truly ginormous! It was so big it looked like they were breaking in slow motion, such was the time it took for the lip of the pitching wave to reach the surface of the ocean and break, sending plumes of white water 50ft high. The noise when that explosion occurred could be clearly heard over the sound of the jet ski's engine.

It was the biggest surf Havoc had ever been out in. Just how big was difficult to gauge until a competitor took off on a wave. Then it looked like some kind of silly cartoon that people drew for fun. But it wasn't just the size of the waves, it was the fact that the perfect light offshore conditions had groomed these monsters into something so special and amazing it was hard to comprehend.

The jet ski driver stopped at the drop off point about 100 metres from the main take off zone, wished him good luck and slowly drove away. Harry Brand was already there on the first of his back up boards, he would go in and get another if one was broken. Havoc was going to cruise over to him for a chat about the conditions but at that moment Gabriel Andre arrived.

Without hesitating Havoc paddled straight over to Andre and got in his face. The Terminator had long been known for destroying his opponents, both in paddle battles and tactically, only this was different. He'd never come up against an opponent who 100% really didn't give a shit about the outcome but was hell bent on playing the game anyway.

As the last seconds ticked by in the current heat, the two surfers paddled into the lineup and Havoc made sure he was never more than a few centimetres from Andre at all times. They regularly bumped arms and boards, each striving for an advantage and neither giving an inch.

"Your hired goons can't protect you now!" Havoc growled at Andre as he tried to further intimidate the world champ. Unexpectedly Andre turned and laughed at him.

"Do you think you scared me?" he said in his thick Brazilian accent with a big smile on his face. "No my friend, I was scared one of my guys would break you before I got the chance to defeat you again. I like you Havoc, I will enjoy beating you once more. Then maybe we get in the ring and we can fight there too huh?"

It was such an unexpected response that for a moment Havoc was stunned, then he burst out laughing. "I like you too Gabe," he said unable to control his smile. "Let's do this!" and with that he increased his efforts to paddle over the top of his opponent.

The siren blasted for the end of the previous heat and moments later sounded again to signal the start of the new one. For the moment there were no obvious sets on the horizon, so they stopped paddling. The waves were breaking over an area almost the size of a football field, yet the two surfers sat within touching distance of each other.

Havoc was determined to see if he could rattle his opponent at his own game. If Andre paddled a few feet, then Havoc did the same. The only trouble was that Andre kept smiling at him. Rather than being rattled, he looked like he was thoroughly enjoying himself. The waves were massive for fuck sakes! Surely he should be at least a little bit worried?

The minutes ticked by and the ocean went quiet. Nearly every day's competitive surfing went like this. In some heats the waves poured through, while others felt like a wave was never going to come. Havoc begun to suspect they were going to get one of those dud heats.

A few waves passed through that on another day might have been huge scores, but they were half the size of what had been on offer in previous heats. Neither surfer looked at them. Ten minutes elapsed and no waves had been caught. Both surfers had now given up on paddling on top of each other and were quietly sitting there waiting for the ocean to wake up again.

Havoc stole a quick glance at Andre. That smile had gone and if anything, he finally looked a little worried, but why? Havoc tried to think it through and slowly the answer came to him. The longer the heat played out with no waves caught, the more luck became a factor. In a heat where they both caught a lot of waves it stood to reason that a former world champ's sheer natural talent and experience would win out most of the time. But in a heat where the best two waves wins and each surfer might only catch two waves, Havoc just might luck into the best ones.

Encouraged by that thought, Havoc stole a quick glance back at the coast trying to work out if he was in the right spot should a set come through. He had discussed lineup markers with Harry Brand and they had come up with a few ideas, but with the swell bigger than almost any other day in history, one man's guess as to the best spot to sit was as good as the next.

Havoc decided to paddle out a bit further as he suddenly got a gut feeling that something was about to happen. He hoped that Andre might let him go so he could put a bit of space between them, but Andre followed straight away and then picked up the pace. It seemed he was getting the same message from his senses too. A set was coming.

The horizon darkened as gigantic swell lines started appearing out to sea. Now the race was on with both surfers paddling nearly as hard as they could. It was a race on two fronts. They were fighting to be the surfer closest to the breaking part of the wave, but that came with the risk that they would paddle too close and instead of catching a wave the size of an apartment building, it could land on their head!

Havoc thought his extra size and longer arms might give him the edge in the paddle battle, but he soon realized that Andre had him covered due to being a full-time pro surfer rather than a dreamer more accustomed to chasing drug dealers around the streets. With no other option, Havoc decided to try and recreate the move that Bunker had successfully pulled on Andre back on the Gold Coast to get the best wave.

Havoc slowed and tried to appear to give up. The first wave of the set was in the 12ft range but both surfers ignored it, oblivious to the incredible level of noise coming from the crowd so far away on the shore. Behind it was the most perfect wave Havoc had seen in his life and his adrenalin overloaded. It was at least a solid 15ft, maybe bigger, just a big clean wall that oozed possibilities.

Andre increased his paddling speed and Havoc was content to match it and go no faster. He was keeping a bit in reserve hoping he could surprise Andre with a last second sprint paddle to sneak inside him for best position.

The wave approached getting bigger by the second, Havoc waited until the last moment, then with his head down he pulled the trigger and pounced. It was like the old 'The Fast and The Furious' movies where the racers would go head-to-head at full speed, but then each would have a nitrous oxide boost they could unleash in the final seconds for that extra kick at the finish line. Havoc opened his own personal internal NOS canister to full, trying to tap into that special reserve of power and energy that every person has, but not necessarily knows how to access.

Once he got on the inside of Andre, Havoc didn't stop. He gave it everything he had and more, furiously stroking into a position where he felt only he could catch the wave. Andre chased him hard and matched him for a second but then suddenly he was gone. Havoc felt a little surge of elation, he knew he had him!

He risked a glance over his right shoulder, expecting to see Andre right there still pushing, but he couldn't see him at all. He panicked for a second thinking somehow Andre had pulled a miracle move and was coming up the other side. Instead, Havoc caught a glimpse of him paddling hard in the opposite direction, heading wide and out to sea as fast as he could go.

Havoc had been so absorbed in trying to win the opening paddle battle that it was only then that he realised there was an even bigger wave behind the one he was trying to catch. Too late he realized he had fallen for the classic rookie mistake where the more experienced opponent pretends he wants a wave and sells the rotten lemon to the inexperienced newbie, then scores the diamond behind it.

Havoc didn't have time to ponder his mistake. There was still a 15-20ft wave he had to deal with that was hardly a rotten lemon, in fact it was the most beautiful looking thing he'd seen in his life. With Andre no longer on his tail he paused for a second, double checked he was happy with his position, took one deep breath, spun his board around and started paddling.

A wave this big is not easily caught. So much wind and water moves up the face that it's really difficult to get enough downward momentum to catch it, but the sheer perfection of the conditions worked in Havoc's favour. For a moment he was held weightless at the top of the monster, he panicked thinking he'd made a mistake and was about to cop the beating of a lifetime, then suddenly he was dropping down a magical wall of glass at a speed beyond anything he'd experienced before in the ocean.

Havoc surfed that wave better than any he had in his entire life. It felt like he was snowboarding in perfect powder as he drew out long bottom turns followed by big arcing hooks in the pocket, sending huge plumes of spray high into the sky. In a way it was easy surfing. When the waves are bad, you have to do something special to make the wave special. When the wave literally could not be any more perfect, then all that's needed is to synchronise your surfing to match its rhythm.

Havoc pulled off the back of the wave feeling an incredible surge of elation. The waves at Cape Fear and Black Rainbow had probably both been scarier due to their life-threatening demeanour, but the drama of this being in a competition against The Terminator added a new level of intensity.

He signalled to the jet ski to come and pick him up then looked back out to sea in time to be treated to a front row seat for the last part of Andre's wave. It was bigger than Havoc's and Andre simply destroyed it. Everything he did was more critical and on point than what Havoc felt he had done. Havoc's heart sank, he knew his wave was as good as any that had been ridden all morning, the only trouble was that Andre's could be even better.

Moments later the ski dropped Havoc back in the lineup in time to hear the scores called out. The judges had awarded Havoc with an above excellent score of 8.5, but moments later announced Andre's as a 9.5. There was only one way to win now, his next wave had to produce a near perfect score because Andre was sure to get another good one in the last half of the heat.

Havoc had priority so he sat waiting for something special. A couple of reasonable sets came through and Andre took advantage of Havoc's patience by catching them. He got a 7, then a 7.8 and then an 8.7 on a wave that Havoc had tried to catch but found himself out of position.

Now Havoc needed a near impossible 9.7 to win the heat with less than two minutes to go. It was all over and he could sense the onset of the recently familiar feeling of being overwhelmed by a situation he didn't belong in. Before it had a chance to really take hold, he took a moment to step away from being too absorbed in the outcome of the competition. He looked over his shoulder at the Bells headland packed with spectators, then back out to sea and thanked the universe for giving him this incredibly spiritual moment amongst the chaos of the past couple of months.

Andre paddled up super close to him to try and add some extra pressure in the last couple of minutes, but Havoc was having none of it. Instead, he smiled at his opponent and reached over to shake his hand.

"Well done my friend," he said emotionally. "That first wave was fucking amazing!"

That threw Andre for a second and he wasn't sure how to react. He half shook Havoc's hand back but then pushed him away mumbling something like "It's not over yet."

Deciding he wanted to be alone for the last 90 seconds, Havoc ignored Andre as he paddled away to get some personal space and further reflect on the experience while it lasted. He turned his thoughts inwards as he looked into the deep blue-black water. The chances of him ever getting another wildcard were incredibly slim and seeing as he was no closer to finding the serial killer after going against orders, it was also highly unlikely he still had a job. When he paddled in from this heat he would have to face some serious life changing decisions. He decided this new challenge didn't scare him, rather he relished the idea of the freedom it might bring.

Havoc suddenly became aware of a lot of noise coming from shore. He'd drifted off into his own little existence and when he looked up, he was stunned to see a next-level massive set approaching that completely filled his range of vision from one corner of the horizon to the other.

Fear surged as he paddled frantically out to sea in pure survival mode. It looked like he was about to suffer a shitload of 25-30ft waves on the head and no jet ski was coming to his rescue until the ocean was done with him. Unless of course he was able to catch one and get himself out of the danger zone.

Havoc wasn't aware of Andre's position, but it didn't really matter, he had priority so whatever wave he wanted was his and there was nothing the Brazilian could do about it. If it was possible to catch one, then his dilemma was that if he went an early wave like previously, would he then turn to see Andre on a bigger one behind it? Or if he let one go, would there be enough time in the heat for him to even catch the next one and maybe still win this thing?

The decision was made for him by the ocean. Despite paddling as hard as he could, Havoc couldn't get into a position to catch the first wave. A brief glance towards shore revealed that Andre was in a worse position. That little handshake that Havoc had offered before paddling away had the unexpected bonus in causing Andre to drop his guard and not move until it was too late, meaning he was almost certainly going to be obliterated by the whole set.

Havoc scratched over the top of the first wave and the next stood up like a massive closeout stretching from Bells way down past Winkipop. Was it too big? Was that even possible? This really was true homage to the mythical Point Break 50-year storm!

The seconds counted down towards the end of the heat and Havoc continued paddling desperately while the biggest wave ever seen in GSA competitive surfing for decades did its best to mow him down. The wave lifted, threatening to break, but the offshore wind was having an effect, holding the lip from pitching for precious moments as he paddled up the face.

Havoc made an impulsive decision and recklessly spun towards shore, took two or three frantic paddles then jumped to his feet. It didn't matter whether the heat had finished or not, this was the biggest wave Havoc had ever seen. He was not going to let it go unridden.

The huge crowd on the shore were treated to a truly epic sequence of events. They'd been touched by the handshake, then they'd seen what lurked on the horizon and knew for long moments what was coming before the surfers themselves realised. It was like watching a horror movie where they recognised the bad guy was coming and wanted to shout out and warn the innocent but couldn't. Then they witnessed both surfers paddling for their lives, Havoc just escaping the first one and Andre throwing his board and diving as deep as he could under a monster with the surety of more pain to come.

It was hard to know what they were saying after that. It was either "Go or "No" but the sheer volume of their collective voices drowned out all understanding while the commentator tried to count down the seconds - five, four, Havoc spun and paddled, three, two, one - then sometime just before, during, or after the siren, he'd taken off.

They'd groaned as one as it appeared to be straight up suicide. Havoc had none of the forward momentum usually required to catch a wave so big and he'd simply vanished into an avalanche of white water so colossal that drowning or serious injury could be the only outcomes.

But unbeknown to the crowd, Havoc had got a surprisingly good roll in and even though he felt himself being buckled by the white water and he'd disappeared to anyone watching, he had just enough speed to outrun being totally swallowed. He grimly hung on and suddenly he was free and leaning into a bottom turn with a massive wall ahead of him. The wave stood up beyond vertical and then started to heave violently.

Bells isn't normally known as a tube, but to Havoc that's what the wave looked like it was going to do and if he didn't pull up under that pitching lip, then it was going to destroy him anyway. Instinct kicked in and he crouched low into a strong, survival tube stance. He braced for it to all collapse and engulf him, but instead suddenly found himself in the middle of a vortex of ocean beyond comprehension.

The crowd roared as Havoc emerged from the white-water maelstrom, but when he disappeared into an impossibly big tube they groaned once more. For a few precious seconds the wave peeled off and he was nowhere to be seen. They gave up on him. Unlike Bunker's wave back at Snapper Rocks where the wave was a genuine tube so the impossible was always possible, this was Bells and people rarely got tubed, let alone made ridiculous ones on waves the size of the Titanic!

Havoc felt the same way as the crowd. Despite how big the wave was, the tube itself wasn't anywhere near as open and navigable as the ones at Cape Fear and Black Rainbow. Instead, there was just a small hole in the madness that represented his only chance of avoiding Armageddon.

Havoc drove for that opening and suddenly he punched through, emerging into clear air and sending the crowd into unprecedented levels of frenzy. This time there was no perfect snowboard style carves. The wave was so much bigger than any before that it required every adjustment to be done carefully to avoid the board skipping out. It didn't matter, Havoc surfed the wave way down the coast through to Winkipop and beyond, drawing huge lines as the wave peeled further than any wave ridden in a heat at Bells in history.

In the crowd's view there was little doubt Havoc had got the score he needed but still you never know what the judges might be thinking. Then there was the worry about if he had even got to his feet in time before the hooter had sounded.

Fortunately, it took just seconds for those questions to be answered and a riot to be avoided. The score came in as a perfect 10 across the board and the wildcard known almost solely for his bedroom manoeuvres had knocked out a three-time world champion and the current world number one.

For one final time in the heat, the entire headland went absolutely fucking ballistic!

Chapter 39 THE 50 YEAR STORM

As finals day for both the men's and women's event commenced, Peter Hirt had to grudgingly admit that he'd got caught up in the hype of the '50 year storm'. Normally he really didn't give a shit about the surf. Instead, he focussed on the logistics of trying to run the event in a way that made him and the GSA the most money, while also manoeuvring himself into the underwear of whatever strumpet currently tickled his fancy the most.

But in the week leading up to the contest it seemed every single media platform across the world only wanted to know about the giant swell coming. Surprisingly they were far less interested in what was normally red-hot tabloid fodder, such as the wildcard being awarded to the latest internet sex sensation, or the current war between Quikbong, GoMerch and Ricool in the race to develop the next generation 'Sea Thru' ladies wetsuits. This new technology allowed surfers to enjoy the warmth of a wetsuit, but still appear to wear nothing more than the skimpiest of thong bikinis, or if you preferred, nothing at all.

It was a beautiful concept that the GSA had covertly helped fund through their secret partial ownership of those companies. Hirt hated that some of the contests had to be held in water that was simply far too cold to wear just a G-string. The worldwide media had gone berserk over Belle Silva's Sea Thru bikini at The Quikbong Pro on the Gold Coast, but until now that wouldn't have been a possibility in the frigid Bells Beach conditions.

Both Tiffany Totthil and Belle Silva had worn their sponsors versions of the Sea Thru wetsuit in their heat a few days previously. Totthil had gone with the more conservative approach and worn a couple of small pieces of cotton underneath her wetsuit that just barely covered her nipples and mound, while Silva opted to go for the Sea Thru bikini under the Sea Thru wetsuit look.

Hirt had never been prouder of his work than when the two girls, looking virtually completely naked, ran through a crowd dressed almost solely in warm hoodies, beanies and tracksuit pants. Their delightfully tanned skin a stark contrast to the heavy, dark clothing that surrounded them. It reminded him of when a streaker would run onto the field of a big Australian Rules Football game.

Remarkably, despite how slutty the girls looked, the recent murder of Stephanie Birch and the deliciousness of the Havoc/Dirty Dy affair, Hirt had found himself consistently being asked for a quote about the surf's potential to mirror the 50 year storm from Point Break. Somehow the surfing itself had become the focus of the media and for a short while he had found himself lost for what to say.

Ever the professional though, Hirt quickly read the room and began delivering the sound bites that the media wanted to hear:

"The GSA has decided to run the women's heats in the biggest surf in their competitive history!" he trumpeted. "We have full faith they will exceed all expectations and do themselves and the GSA proud.

"Brazilian Gabriel Andre is the current world number one with Aussie's Bunker Haze and Jake Roberts hot on his heels. Whoever best handles the extreme surf predicted will take a commanding lead into the back half of the season."

Fearing the media would then want follow up quotes, Hirt forced himself to watch some heats and somehow found himself enthralled in the spectacle. He almost felt guilty about it, like he was going against everything he stood for.

The Havoc vs Andre heat had been a ball tearer. No one would have believed that a relatively unknown wildcard given a spot due solely to his prowess in the bedroom could take out the current world number one. When Havoc had got that last wave Hirt had wanted to jump up and punch the air along with the rest of the crowd, but he knew it wouldn't be a good look for the CEO to be seen cheering for any surfer, much less than one that had just beaten someone as popular as Andre with such a huge chunk of the GSA's revenue coming from Brazil.

Just as extraordinary was that Havoc had kept winning and there was no reason why he couldn't go all the way to the final. On the other side of the heat draw his mate Bunker Haze seemed to be past whatever had caused his hiccup at Margaret River and had been winning his heats easily. There was a very real possibility those two would meet in the final. The previously unknown but current new age sexual phenomenon, competing against one of the most debauched human beings on the planet, in some of the biggest surf ever seen for a contest! Now that really was a final that Hirt could get excited about!

The ladies had also surprised him. Putting them out in big surf had been a win/win situation for Hirt. If they had performed badly then he forever had good ammunition to throw at Claire Cooper or the next feminist do-gooder that came along complaining about when the women's heats were held. If they went well, then he looked like a genius that knew all along that the women were more than capable of stepping up. That alone should help him remove the underwear of a couple of the next generation's hottest young female surfers!

In the end they had blown minds. As the surf had continued to build over the course of that first day none of the girls had showed signs of being overwhelmed and their sheer bravado had sent the world media into a frenzy.

The usual suspects in big waves had made it through to the quarter finals scheduled to start soon. They included Dirty Dy, Claire Cooper, Sally Lord, Molly Perkins and Karissa Kai, but the real shock for many was that Tiffany Totthil was still in the event. Although unlike a lot of others, Hirt wasn't surprised that beneath that tiny frame and fluffy barbie doll demeanour lurked some real balls. He knew what drove Totthil better than anyone.

To be fair he'd pulled some strings to give her the best of conditions and opponents. It was always hard to say no to her when he knew what she was capable of in the bedroom and how good she'd looked in that Sea Thru wetsuit. It had made him extra horny for her little arse, so he'd made his usual request for Totthil to come to his rented mansion in order to defile her in some new and inappropriate ways.

Then had come possibly the biggest shock of the lot. Totthil had denied him! That had rarely happened before and never when he'd done exactly as she'd asked. While he'd had other plans for Totthil long term, this had changed everything. He was majorly pissed off and the only thing that stopped him from acting immediately was that he was also focused on reacquainting himself with Dirty Dy.

Like most of the world, Hirt had a thing for Dirty Dy. He still vividly remembered that one glorious night he'd had her at his disposal when she was new to the tour. Despite making a lot of money from his cut of Picker's photos, the recent footage of her with Havoc had done nothing but fan the flames of desire into a raging inferno. Not only that, but her Instafamous profile had gone ballistic. She was now the most popular surfer in the world. The thought of having his way with someone so famous and with such an amazing body was intoxicating!

Dirty Dy believed she was untouchable, but the recent lessons learnt with Claire Cooper had taught him that allowing these skanks to think they had any power over him was akin to career suicide. He was all powerful with far too many connections. He knew too much about too many important people and had made such huge sums of money for the GSA that he felt untouchable. Let them tell the world their stories. He was confident that he would come out on top in the end.

So, he would have Dirty Dy again or she would live to regret it. It was time to step up his game and show these bitches who's boss. Dirty Dy and Totthil were both going to regret messing with Hirt before too long and Claire Cooper was not going to get away with her blackmail bullshit either. Murder Mercer had once again come through and supplied him with the goods to help make it happen.

Hirt's phone beeped. He checked the message and smiled. The plans he was putting into place were coming into fruition. He could already feel his cock harden in his pants.

Chapter 40 HAVOC MAKES A BREAKTHROUGH

Havoc arrived early for finals day feeling ten foot tall and bullet proof. Somehow, he had backed up his win over Gabriel Andre with several more and was still in the event. His quarter final wasn't due to start until a bit later in the morning, but he'd wanted to soak in every moment of the day.

He found himself a little vantage point where he could watch the sets and settled down to relax. The swell was smaller now, but still a solid 8-10ft and about as good as Bells gets. Moments later he felt a tap on his shoulder and turned to see Bunker standing there smiling at him.

"G'day Bunker, how are you mate?" asked Havoc as he stood to offer a handshake.

Bunker took one look at Havoc's offered hand then laughed at him. "Get here Havoc dude," he said pulling Havoc into a bearhug. "I've been trying to get you alone for days man."

Bunker had been the first person to congratulate Havoc when he'd left the water after his astonishing last wave victory over Andre. Since then, it had been a whirlwind of countless media interviews whenever Havoc was available. They'd mostly been fun except at least half of them had also wanted to take the opportunity to ask about his newfound porn stardom.

His talk with DS Patinsen had been less fun. He'd initially been surprisingly jovial and had congratulated Havoc on his win, but he soon made it obvious he was extremely disappointed with Havoc's choice to disobey orders. According to his mentor, Senior Sergeant Smith wasn't anywhere near as upset. Apparently the many creative and horrible repercussions he had in mind for Havoc's disobedience meant that the old bastard had actually been happy for a change.

Despite the awkwardness of the situation the conversation had naturally got around to the hunt for the killer. There was genuine frustration in DS Patinsen's voice when Havoc reluctantly admitted that he had still been seeing Fream, but that was tempered slightly when he revealed the new information she'd provided. Later DS Patinsen confirmed that the Queensland Police had mistakenly checked only taxis and not Uber drivers. Fream's movements had since been confirmed by a check with Uber, but that still didn't clear her for Wilson's murder. His body had spent so much time in the spa before Bunker found him that a time of death was difficult to determine.

The call had ended with Patinsen saying "While you are over there Dirth you may as well catch that killer," and although Havoc had promised he would try, the reality was he felt no closer now than when he was back in Margaret River. He was always thinking about it, he'd run countless scenarios through his mind and spent every available moment researching on the net or through police resources, but nothing significant had turned up. Either the killer was very good or very lucky. Maybe a bit of both?

Havoc sat back down and Bunker joined him. They both stared at the sets in comfortable silence. Eventually Havoc's curiosity got the better of him.

"So, you said you've been trying to get me alone?"

Bunker paused before replying, trying to put into words what his brain wanted to say.

"You know Willo meant everything to me?" he eventually blurted out. It was more of a statement than a question. Havoc nodded in reply. "Well once I sat down and thought about it, I decided that there were three things I wanted to do for him. The first was to make sure his family didn't have to worry about money and to set up that charity in his name to help underprivileged kids like he was. I also wanted to win a world title for him because that's all he ever talked about and lastly catch the fucker that killed him."

Bunkers eyes blazed fiercely with those last words. Sometimes it was easy to forget that behind that surf stoner persona lurked a very caring, passionate human being.

"I decided to hire a private investigator," Bunker continued. "Or rather an entire firm. No point having all the money in the world and not using it hey?" he smiled at Havoc, then paused again and took a deep breath. "I'm telling you this because one of the things they found out was that you're doing the same." Bunker looked directly at Havoc, and he felt the strength of that gaze. He suspected he knew what Bunker was talking about, but still decided it was best to play dumb.

"What do you mean mate?" Havoc asked.

"I know who you really are and what you really do," Bunker replied quietly. "You know, in the past I haven't particularly liked your kind, but I wanted you to know that I appreciate what you are trying to do for Willo. I'm guessing that you've also been keeping an eye on me as well, so I would like to thank you for that too dude and that your secret is safe with me."

For a few moments Havoc was silent as he tried to think through the ramifications of what Bunker had just said. It was always the greatest fear when going undercover that someone would find out who you were, and Havoc was lucky it had been a friend and not an enemy who had uncovered the truth. But where did this leave him? Should he deny it and hope he could convince Bunker otherwise? He looked at his friend and could see the weight of the world on those shoulders. This hadn't been an easy conversation for him. Havoc decided Bunker deserved the truth.

"Who else knows?" he asked.

"As far as I know just the main guy at the private investigation firm, Les Galese... and Morpheus," replied Bunker. Then seeing the look on Havoc's face, he quickly added. "I didn't tell him dude. I went to him when I found out because I didn't know what to do, but he already knew."

Havoc gave a quick laugh. "Fucking Morpheus. Is there anything that guy doesn't know? Any idea how he found out?"

Bunker shrugged his shoulders. "Dunno' man. I kind of got the impression he's known for a long time. He seems to like to know everything about the crew on his team."

"What about this Galese character? What's his story?"

"I think you can trust him. It was him that suggested I talk to you and share any information we dig up. For what it's worth it sounded like it wasn't easy to uncover who you were, so I think you're okay," Bunker shook his head and quietly chuckled. "So you really are an undercover cop? Fuck I would never have guessed man. You sure fooled me, and I've known you half my life!"

"Probably why I did," Havoc conceded. "You weren't looking any deeper, so it would have been easy to miss. I'm sorry I had to lie to you Bunker, but that's the fucked-up rules of the game."

"Must be hard man. Having to live that lie all the time."

"Yeah it's been harder this time because I've been around friends and people I care about and respect. Normally it's not so bad, well the lying part at least, because I'm just there to do a job and catch some lowlife drug dealer or something. But it wears you down. Sometimes I just want to pack everything up and go camp in the bush away from everyone. Probably get that chance soon anyway, might have lost my job." Havoc said ruefully.

"Really!" Bunker said surprised. "Why what happened?"

"I wasn't getting anywhere with finding the killer and I was at Black Rainbow when they found Birch's body. Then there's the photos of me on every media website in the world balls deep in a potential suspect!" Havoc couldn't help laugh at the absurdity of how that sounded.

"You think Dy is a suspect? Really?" Bunker asked. "I can't see her doing that man. Her and Willo were pretty good mates."

"Yeah, me too," admitted Havoc. "Initially there was some evidence that pointed towards her. Then we found out later she had lied to the police, but I just couldn't believe she was capable of it. I was worried I was thinking with my dick and not seeing the obvious with her."

"You know she was with Willo on that last night?" Bunker asked and Havoc nodded in reply. "I was pretty drugged fucked at the time and didn't remember seeing her, but later when I sobered up thanks to you dude, some of that shit came back to me and I was pissed man. Called her up looking for someone to get angry at. Accused her of killing him, then blamed her for not protecting him. She was fucken lost too man. Crying and shit. She tried to give it to me too, said I was living with Willo so why didn't I protect him?

"I kept at her man," Bunker continued emotionally. "Just to give me that release from all the anger and shit I had. She finally told me she'd slipped him some cocaine and Viagra in his vodka," he smiled sheepishly. "I wanted to fucken go her for that, but then I remembered how much shit I'd dropped in his drinks in the past. Anyway, she swears they fucked for a few hours then she caught an Uber home so he could get some sleep before his heat. She sounded pretty upset dude. I believed her but I still got Galese to look into it."

Havoc shook his head. Once again Fream had not told him the full story. Why didn't she mention the phone call between her and Bunker? Was there a reason or just her private nature? Havoc reminded himself he was still probably just a short term toyboy for Fream, so she wasn't obliged to tell him, but it still hurt that she hadn't.

"Fuck if only we had this conversation sooner it could have saved a lot of shit," said Havoc ruefully. "Dy finally admitted as much to me the other day. I knew she'd been avoiding the police but couldn't confront her about it for obvious reasons. She'd been acting weird anyway, so when I pushed her on it, she finally told me the full story."

"So why was she running from the cops if she didn't do anything?" Bunker asked confused.

"That was the question I wanted answered," Havoc replied. "And a reason why she stayed a suspect. Turns out she's had some issues with one guy in particular. Some local detective down in her old hometown wouldn't take no for an answer and had been stalking her. He'd pulled some dodgy shit and got a few of his boys to hassle her as well, so she has a pretty low view of the police."

"Yeah I get that man!" Bunker said, then looked at Havoc apologetically, realising who he was talking to. "So why the fuck are you still doing this if you've lost your job?"

"Same reason as you I guess," said Havoc shrugging his shoulders. "I haven't technically lost my job yet because I was supposed to go home and face the music, but I came here instead. Didn't want to give them the chance.

"And besides, I don't like the idea of Matt's killer getting away with it either and I can't help but feel that there's far too many cops who don't seem to care if someone is knocking off a few surfers. Maybe they figure the killer will mess up sooner or later? And if he takes a few more with him then it's no great loss. I mean there's hardly a national manhunt going on is there? They don't even want me on the case!"

"No dude. It's like nobody cares but us," said Bunker sorrowfully. "And I'm not even sure we care enough."

Havoc looked at his friend for a second then realised an obvious question hadn't been asked yet. "So why talk to me now?"

"It's like I said, Galese suggested I share any information we dig up," Bunker replied. "At first I just wanted to know who the killer was so I could kill him myself, but then I realised that shit's not for me man. So the next best thing was to talk to you."

"Do you mean you know who the killer is?" Havoc asked hopefully.

"Nah man. If I did we wouldn't be still sitting here, I would have told you straight up. But I wanted to let you know we were looking too and tell you everything we've found. In case it helps."

"It might, what have you got?"

"I dunno man. I got Galese to look into everyone I could think of. And believe me there's some pretty fucken twisted shit going on out there that would blow your mind man," Bunker shook his head dumbfounded. "But most of it's just kinky shit, or drugs, or cheating shit ya know? Just the usual fucked up pro tour stuff!"

Bunker took a look around to make sure no one was within earshot and then continued on a bit quieter but more intense than before.

"But it's that Peter Hirt guy man. He's one bad ass dude," he looked pointedly at Havoc. "He's making a lot of money out of crew dying right now."

"I looked into that," Havoc nodded. "All that memorial merchandise is making a killing."

"Yeah man, but did you know that Hirt and the GSA secretly own big chunks of the major surf brands as well?"

"Really?" Havoc whistled blown away. "So Hirt and the GSA are double dipping with all of this merchandise stuff. Then there's the crazy media attention around the comps these days. Fuck they must be making some serious coin!"

"Enough millions to give me a run for my money," Bunker agreed with a wry smile. "Did you also know that Hirt markets Picker's photos and takes a cut? And that it was Picker who shot those photos of Slide on the beach?"

'Fuck no I didn't!" Havoc's brain went into meltdown. "So Hirt has been triple dipping! He's making money off the photos of Slide, Willo and even me! He's also making money with whatever deal he has going with the GSA and they own significant shares in the major surf brands! So he's raking it in there too?"

"Then there's the drugs and hookers," Bunker nodded. "Do you know that Hirt is best mates with the head of that bikie gang- The Cadaver Brothers?"

"Trent 'Murder' Mercer," Havoc nodded. "I knew they occasionally did business. Didn't realise they were best mates though."

"Yeah, they grew up in the same neighbourhood. Didn't go to the same school or anything, but they've been doing shady shit together since they were kids man. Fuck knows how Hirt even got the job at the GSA. Galese is looking into it, but he thinks it's dodgy as fuck. Like maybe he's got some dirt on some of the GSA board members. Probably got footage of them shooting up or rooting hookers or something."

Havoc tried to process what this all meant. Hirt was now clearly suspect number one. His alibis for the killings were dodgy at best and he's best mates with the head of a major bikie gang that was one of the few illegal organisations in Australia known to deal in Fentanyl, a drug found in the blood of at least three of the four murders. The companies he represented or partly owned was also making a biblical amount of money out of the fallout from the murders.

"With everything you say, Hirt could be our man. There's something I don't understand though," Havoc pondered. "If it is him, why kill who he's killed? I mean surely if it's publicity he's after, it's better to kill a few of the lesser known surfers and keep your number one guys alive. Or if your goal is to kill the best of them for extra impact, then why kill Matt? He was pretty high on the rankings, but he wasn't gunning for a world title like Jimmy Slide, Kalani Johnson or Birch. If his goal is to knock off the best then why not kill you, Gabriel or Karissa Kai instead?"

"I dunno man, maybe we're next?" Bunker replied with a rueful smile. "I mean Willo was pretty out there with his fan base. He had a following dude. I remember him telling me his Instafamous page had more likes than any other surfer. He was proud of that. Said he was already a world champ!"

Their conversation fell silent for a moment as they watched Dyanna Fream and Sally Lord jog down the Bells staircase for their quarter final. Havoc had planned to watch Fream's heat, but there was a lot of new information to unpick and a call to DS Patinsen needed to be done before Hirt killed again. It was time to get some police resources onto this. Surely with some renewed points of focus they could come up with something to pin on him?

A few ideas started occurring to Havoc. He needed to get on the internet to do some research. He stood up and offered his hand to Bunker, when Bunker reached out to shake it Havoc gripped it firmly and pulled his friend to his feet and into another bear hug.

"Thank you so much mate," he said incredibly grateful that his friend had taken time out from preparing for finals day to talk to him. "Please let me know if you hear any more. I promise I won't kick your arse too hard if we meet in the final."

Bunker laughed long and hard.

Chapter 41 SOMETHING IS VERY WRONG

Something was very wrong with Dyanna Fream. She'd chosen to return to her hotel room after winning her quarter final heat but now she was regretting it. Whatever was going on, she was pretty sure that she might need a doctor or ambulance soon and both had been readily on hand at the contest site.

She retraced her steps, trying to work out why she was suddenly so sick. The day had started eventfully when she'd crossed paths with a surprisingly aggressive Tiffany Totthil. No one had expected Totthil to do well in these conditions and Fream had to admit a grudging respect for her courage to have got so far. In a way she was happy to acknowledge Totthil as a genuine rival now, someone to be respected and not just seen as window dressing for the women's world tour.

She'd even gone so far as to approach Totthil while she was retrieving something from her locker next to Fream's. She'd offered a hug to her potential semifinal opponent in a gesture of that goodwill, but the normally meek Totthil had not been ready or willing to accept the olive branch.

"Fuck off bitch!" she had snarled angrily. "You've been calling me a skank and a slut for how long? Well look at you, you fucking whore! Nice and convenient that Picker just happened to be outside your window hey? Fucking hypocritical cunt!"

It was quite the tirade, made almost humorous coming from a tiny blonde with her oversize fake boobs and shaved vagina barely covered in her Sea Thru wetsuit, but there was some real venom in it.

If the rant was meant to throw Fream off her game, it had the opposite effect. Fream narrowly defeated Sally Lord in the most perfect conditions that she'd ever surfed in a competition. Then sometime on the drive back to Torquay she began feeling sick and it had got worse by the minute.

It was almost like she was on drugs. Fream was never one to shy away from a good night on the party drugs, but ever since she'd slipped Matt Wilson that cocktail of cocaine and Viagra and he'd wound up dead, she'd steered clear of anything but alcohol. Havoc had been a good influence, she'd dropped her guard roughly around her 10th orgasm on their first night together and offered to take some coke with him so they could keep on rolling, but he'd refused, adamant that it wasn't his thing. She was surprised at the relief she'd felt with that answer and hadn't even bothered to bring it with her when she left Margaret River.

The world started spinning violently as she staggered towards her bed to try and lay down and compose herself. She took several steps then collapsed in a heap on the floor, unable to find the strength to move any further.

She lay there completely disorientated for a minute or two. Her brain registered that she needed to call for help but couldn't think straight enough to remember where her phone was. Even if she could find it, she wasn't sure she was capable of making the call, but she knew she had to at least try. Some basic primal intuition was screaming that her life was in danger.

She was relieved to hear the front door open and someone step inside. It was probably Havoc calling in to see how she went in her heat. She was grateful that she must have forgotten to lock the door in her disorientation. Footsteps approached, but Fream couldn't even lift her head to say anything.

"Well, well, well, what do we have here?" said a familiar voice. "What's the matter skank? Can't move? Having trouble speaking? You look like shit, you fucking slut!"

For the first time in her entire life, Dyanna Fream felt pure, unadulterated fear.

Chapter 42 THE PERILS OF BEING INSTAFAMOUS

Havoc's conversation with Bunker had stirred a few ideas so he grabbed his laptop, found a relatively quiet spot where he could still watch the surf and disappeared down the internet rabbit hole.

It took him a while to find the information he was looking for. Something Bunker had said about popularity and Instafamous likes had resonated with Havoc. The trouble was that it's simple enough to find out who the most popular surfer is right now, but finding out who was the most popular surfer at a previous moment in time wasn't so easy.

Fortunately, there was enough internet chat rooms, Stalkbook pages and websites out there dedicated to every single aspect of pro surfing that Havoc was able to begin to create a picture of who was the most popular and when. He was only getting half the picture though, so he bit the bullet and finally created his own Instafamous profile. He wasn't happy about it, but now he could properly start searching through the millions of Instafamous posts and comments.

They were all there of course. Every pro surfer had an Instafamous page and regularly posted about their lives, some more so than others. Havoc was surprised to see how often Fream uploaded photos and thoughts from her life despite her assurances to him that she hated it. She hadn't posted much about the photos of the two of them except to mention the difficulties of having your privacy so easily abused when you're a public figure.

The comments were long and varied on this one. Many sympathised with her and plenty more suggested they could do a better job than

Havoc in the bedroom if given the chance. After reading a few of these Havoc had to move on quickly, there were some extremely disturbing ones amongst them that certainly cast a shadow over the benefits of being Instafamous. Already he was beginning to regret creating his own profile.

Unsurprisingly Tiffany Totthil didn't let too many hours go by without some sort of update on what she was thinking/feeling/eating. Her latest ponderings were about whether she should start a Lonely Fans page or not. Based on the reaction, Havoc decided she'd be mad if she didn't. There were tens of thousands of comments from admirers saying they would subscribe in a heartbeat. For a moment Havoc entertained the idea that he should take Totthil up on her previous offer of sex on tap. She was a long way from ugly and if he played his cards right, he might never have to work again! He quickly discarded the notion as sheer stupidity, but not without a moment's regret at the idea of being a toyboy to a slightly deranged millionaire sexpot.

All the murdered surfers still had their profiles online, it seemed the owners of Instafamous were reluctant to take them down as they still got huge amounts of web traffic. Havoc spent a bit of time looking through the comments made since each had passed away. Theories on who the killer might be were many and varied but nothing stood out as possibly coming from someone who actually knew something about the killings.

Slowly a pattern began to emerge in the information he was looking for. Havoc double checked the data to make sure he was right and with that confirmation came a sickening feeling. He did a quick search of the competitor's area for Fream, but no one had seen her since she had finished her post heat winners' interview, nor had they seen Peter Hirt. He grabbed his phone and tried to call Fream. He was relieved to hear the phone ring, but concern blossomed when she failed answer. That wasn't unusual, she could be in the shower or something, but his gut instinct told him something was wrong. He tried Hirt's phone and got the same result.

He checked his watch and saw that his quarter final heat was due to start soon. Did he have enough time to race back to her hotel room and see if she's okay? If he got there and she was fine, then he'd look like an idiot arriving late to the biggest heat of his career. If undercover police work was his past and pro surfing his future, then he should be doing his stretches and heat preparation right now. But Fream was his friend, and he'd never forgive himself if he chose to go surfing when someone he cared about was in trouble.

He made his decision, grabbed his keys, wallet and phone, then hurried off to where his hire car was parked. As he did he dialled DS Patinsen.

There was no answer but Havoc left a message.

"Patto it's Havoc!" he yelled into the phone. "I think I know who the killer is and it's not Fream, but she might be the next victim! I just tried to call her but there's no answer so I'm on my way to her hotel room now. If you get this message send a squad car there just in case. If she's okay tell them to say they are there to take her in for questioning and get her out of there!"

He hung up as he reached his car and wasted no time roaring out of the carpark and straight into finals day gridlock at The Riccool Bells Beach Classic.

Chapter 43 BLACK WIDOW SPIDER

Peter Hirt was horny as fuck at the prospect of what was to come. The whole way over to Fream's hotel room he had been rubbing at the bulge in his pants as visions filled his head of having that spectacular Amazonian body at his mercy once again. This time things would be different. He would take his time and savour every moment. He would wallow in his pleasure and take great delight in Fream's displeasure.

Her hotel room door was unlocked as he knew it would be. He stepped inside, still fondling his raging hard on. Fream was there where he expected and like she had promised, she was already laying on her stomach, half naked and tied to the bedframe, ready and waiting for him.

He took several steps towards her and began undoing his pants, knowing if he didn't free his cock from its confines soon, he would explode. He changed his plan, fuck taking his time, he was going to pound the shit out of her right now and leave the savouring of the moment until later.

She must have sensed his approach because she turned her head to look at him. It was only then that he realized she had a ball gag strapped to her mouth so she couldn't speak. He was about to complement her on being so accommodating when his brain finally saw past that incredible tanned body in the BDSM outfit to the dazed look in her eyes and the real fear there. He immediately knew something was very wrong.

There was a noise behind him, he felt a sudden pain in the back of his head, and he passed out...

When Hirt woke up groggy from the blow to his head he was laying on the floor with his hands and feet zip tied together and something had been jammed in his mouth so he couldn't talk. "Ahh the scum bucket awakes. I bet you weren't expecting this when I texted you from bitch face's phone!" said The Killer. For it could be no doubt that this was the deranged person responsible for murdering professional surfers. The fact that it was Tiffany Totthil seemed absurd, but he knew it to be the truth. It was at that moment he realised that he had truly fucked up!

"You fucken arsehole!" snarled Totthil as she aimed a swift kick into Hirt's stomach sending the air whooshing from his lungs. He tried desperately to suck oxygen through the cloth in his mouth while Totthil continued her tirade. "Did you imagine I was going to let you do all that depraved shit to me and not make you pay for it ten times over? When you jammed your cock up my arse and laughed at the pain it caused me, did you really think it was something you could do without fear of retribution?"

Fortunately for Hirt he couldn't say anything due to whatever was stuffed in his mouth, otherwise he might have been forced to admit that yes, he had thought he had free reign to abuse Totthil's body. He should have known better and now the tables had turned.

She kicked him again, this time in the groin, sending a bolt of agony through his body like Hirt had never experienced before. Then she took a couple of steps over to a comatose looking Fream and rapidly slapped her a couple of times.

"Wakey wakey skank!" Totthil hissed. "Don't want you to miss the show because you're next. But don't worry, I won't be long. Got a semifinal to win after all. It's a pity you won't be there to try and stop me!"

She reached into a bag and pulled out a large rubber object. It took a few seconds for Hirt to realise it was a huge black strap-on dildo at least a foot long and nearly as round as his fist. Hirt had a horrifying feeling he knew what was coming next.

"Do you remember when I asked you to use lube and you refused? You said you liked to feel the resistance, but I think you just enjoyed the pain it caused me." Totthil stepped into the straps and began securing the dildo around her waist. The huge rubber penis looked almost comical protruding from such a tiny female frame, but Hirt found nothing funny about the situation whatsoever.

"Well don't worry sweetie, I won't be so inconsiderate to you. My toy is so much bigger than your tiny dick. It's going to need some help if I'm going to fit the whole thing in your arse. I wonder if you have ever been sodomised before? Probably not. Which means you're in for a treat, well rather I am. I don't think you will enjoy it so much. And as for you slut," Totthil growled slapping Fream again. "Remember when you threatened to do me with a strap-on in front of Havoc? Well I wonder how your boyfriend is going to feel when you are both discovered dead from accidental drug overdoses after yet another sordid sex session? This time butt fucking the head of the GSA with a strap-on!"

Totthil went back into her bag and fished out a tube of what was most likely lubricant. She squeezed the tube onto the monstrous fake extremity and began coating it thoroughly.

"Think of all the possibilities!" she cooed delightedly. "Which one of you was The Killer? Or was it both of you in a deal cooked up to make this skanky whore the most popular surfer on Instafamous and a world champion? How many heat wins did you get from fucking the guy running every contest? Oh the internet is going to love this! You'll both be dead in such an embarrassing way that even your closest friends and families will be ashamed to admit they knew you. I'll be the most Instafamous surfer in the world and your legacy will be nothing but a sordid fucked up postal note in the history of pro surfing!"

With that Totthil flipped Hirt onto his stomach and pulled his pants down. The rampaging erection that he had possessed just minutes before was long gone, replaced by a tiny, bruised wiener attached to a terrified human being. All his plans, all his money and all his achievements were for nothing now. He was about to be arse raped by a five foot nothing blonde with a huge chip on her shoulder and a massive fake black cock!

Hirt felt the pressure on his arse as Totthil wasted no time pushing herself into his no-go zone. The pain was immediate and intense, he began screaming wordlessly into his gag when suddenly there was a loud knock on the door and a pleading voice.

"Dy are you there?"

"Fucking Havoc!" whispered Totthil as she immediately withdrew from Hirt and reached for the baseball bat that she had used to knock him out. "Stay there my toys, I won't be long!"

Chapter 44 PSYCHOTIC BARBIE DOLL

Every fibre of Havoc's existence screamed at him that something was wrong with Fream, but no matter how many times he smashed the horn of his car to try and get the traffic in front to let him through faster, there was no respite. At one stage he even contemplated ditching the car and running, but as he got closer to Torquay the traffic eased and he started to make some ground.

While he was stuck in gridlock he retried calling Fream, then Peter Hirt and then DS Patinsen. No one answered sending his panic through the roof!

Finally Havoc was relieved to see DS Patinsen returning his call.

"Are you okay Dirth?" asked his mentor worriedly. "You never call me Patto. Something must be wrong! Who's The Killer? What on earth is going on?"

"Yes sir I'm fine but I think something is going down and Fream is in grave danger!" Havoc yelled as he roared up the inside of the traffic stopped at the lights. Without hesitation he ran the red light, narrowly missing a car coming from his right, then continued on.

"The police are on their way there now," replied DS Patinsen hurriedly. "I called them before I called you. Tell me what you know."

"I think Tiffany Totthil might be the serial killer and Fream her next target," Havoc shouted over the horns of other furious drivers as he accelerated through another intersection. "They both should be at the contest site right now preparing for their heat against each other but are nowhere to be seen. If I'm right, and I hope to fuck I'm not, Totthil plans to get rid of her opponent before they even get in the water!"

"Have you tried ringing Peter Hirt? He might have them doing some media commitments that you don't know about."

"Yes sir I thought of that but no luck so far. I'm just getting to Fream's hotel room now. I'll call you back as soon as I can!"

Havoc hung up as he roared into the hotel carpark and slammed on the brakes sending gravel flying everywhere. He jumped out of the car without even bothering to turn off the ignition. He knew he'd look like an idiot if nothing was wrong, but he was prepared to suffer that humiliation.

He ran as fast as he could to her door and tried to open it without bothering to knock. It was locked, so he immediately started banging on the door.

"Dy are you there?" he called out loudly. Not bothering to wait for an answer he tried the door handle again and then knocked even louder. "Hey Dy you're late for your heat, is everything okay?"

There was no answer. He checked the windows but couldn't see through the curtains. He'd noticed Fream's hire car in the parking lot, so unless she had got a lift with someone back to the contest site she should be inside. He knocked again. Still no answer.

He stood back and gave the door a hard kick. It was built solid and stayed closed but moved enough to give Havoc some hope. He kicked it again, then used some of his Muay Thai practice and commenced a relentless, calculated assault on the door but it refused to give way. Havoc was committed, he was going to be up for the cost of a door on top of his embarrassment but that wasn't going to stop him.

He kept on kicking until finally the lock gave way. Havoc wasted no time and charged straight into the room. He immediately recognised Fream tied to the bed lying motionless in some kind of sex outfit. Was she dead? And who was that on the floor with his pants around his ankles and his naked arse in the air for everyone to see. What the fuck was going on?

He had a millisecond to take the whole scene in, then he heard a sound behind him and realized that there was a fourth person in the room.

His reflexes kicked in and he ducked instinctively. There was a whoosh and something hard smacked a glancing blow to the top of his head. Havoc went down but he was still conscious. That split second reaction had probably been enough to save his life. He tumbled to the floor and turned to confront his assailant in time to see a furious Tiffany Totthil raising a baseball bat ready to take a second big swing at his head. A blow aimed to kill.

"Oh Havoc you poor fuck," she said as she swung hard. "Your timing sucks!"

Havoc raised both hands and tried to roll to protect himself and get out of the swing zone. The bat struck another brutal strike to his skull, but his forearms took enough of the impact to keep him in the game at a cost of a fractured bone or two.

Pain roared through Havoc's body. Totthil wasted no time preparing for another swing while Havoc desperately tried to regain his composure. He wasn't about to be bested by a psychotic barbie doll with a baseball bat and what was that fucking thing she was wearing around her waist anyway?

Havoc swept out his leg trying to knock Totthil off her feet before she connected but was only partially successful. She stumbled meaning the blow failed to land as intended but still hit with enough force to send another flood of agony through Havoc's body. His adrenalin surged as he knew this was a life or death struggle.

Totthil gave up trying smash Havoc's brain out of his skull and instead commenced raining random blows wherever there was exposed flesh. She might not have looked intimidating, but years of surfing had made her strong and each connection leached a little more resistance from Havoc. She was relentless and all he could do was struggle to protect himself while she gave him no leeway to find a way back into the fight. Totthil was winning.

At that moment police sirens could be heard in the distance.

"Those sirens are for you," Havoc mumbled through blood-soaked lips, hoping that he was telling the truth. "Called the cops on the way here."

"Fuck!" yelled Totthil furiously. "Fuck, fuck, fuck!"

She continued to rain blows on Havoc, but they'd lost some of their sting. It was just as well. By now he was just curled up in a ball hoping that the assault would end.

Then suddenly Totthil was gone out the door and from what Havoc could tell, straight into the car he'd conveniently left still running outside. He laid there almost motionless for a moment trying to gather his thoughts. There would be no chasing after her, for she had delivered a beating that would take some time to recover from, both physically and emotionally.

The sirens continued to get closer, a sound came from his left and he glanced over to see a half-naked Peter Hirt all zip tied up and looking at him pleadingly. So that's who the other person in the room was! How did he get here?

Then he remembered Fream and ignoring Hirt for the moment, he pushed himself to his knees and dragged himself over to her unmoving figure, praying she wasn't dead. He ripped the ball gag off her head, untied her and immediately checked her pulse and breathing. She was bleeding slightly through her nose and mouth, but he was relieved to discover that she was alive, although her pulse was weak and erratic. She opened her eyes slightly in panic then recognised Havoc.

"Hello hotshot," she whispered groggily. "You took your time getting here."

Havoc gave a brief laugh then kissed her gently on the forehead. He heard another noise coming from Hirt and reluctantly left Fream to attend to him. He grabbed a knife from the kitchen and cut the zip ties. Hirt wasted no time pulling up his pants and composing himself, the sirens were very close now. It would be just a minute or two before they came through the door.

"Well I must say Havoc your timing is impeccable," Hirt muttered sheepishly, then he rubbed at his tender arse. "Well maybe not entirely impeccable. 30 seconds earlier would have been appreciated but I'm not complaining."

"What the fuck happened here Peter?" Havoc asked looking around the room and surveying the carnage. He hobbled over to the bag Tothill had left behind and kicked it open. Inside were several knives, a hammer, more zip ties, strong tape, sex toys and syringes full of what was probably drugs. She had certainly come prepared.

"We don't have time for the full story right now," replied Hirt. "But just promise me you won't mention how you found me. It's bad enough that bitch got the best of me but if word got out she…well you know…"

"Your secret's safe with me," Havoc said with conviction, suddenly embarrassed by the battering that he had copped from the same source. How did such a small person get the better of three much bigger opponents?

Havoc went back to check on Fream. She was still barely conscious, so he sat next to her and lifted her head onto his lap.

"Stay awake Dy," he whispered gently stroking her hair. "The police will be here any second and we will call an ambulance."

Moments later the police burst into the room. Havoc wasn't sure if they had been advised that there was an undercover officer on the scene and to protect his identity, but it didn't matter. Hirt took over the situation immediately and unveiled a polished description of what went down that was straight out of the CEO guidebook for damage control and positive spin. Havoc wasn't required to say much so he remained mostly silent while maintaining his vigil over Fream.

"So where do you think this Tiffany Totthil might be now?" asked one of the uniformed policemen.

Havoc and Hirt both looked at each other. They were thinking the same thing. There was only one place Totthil would be, where all her fans were.

"Let me make a call," said Hirt as he pulled out his phone, dialled Luke Perrot and put it on speaker so everyone could hear. "Hey Luke, have you seen Tiffany recently?"

"Yes Pete she just arrived a few minutes ago and is paddling out for her heat right now," Perrot replied sounding frantic. "But there's no sign of Fream at all and Havoc didn't show up for his heat either. I've been trying to ring both their phones for a while, but they just ring out. I don't know what to do!"

The policemen in the room immediately got on their radio to send squad cars to the event to arrest Totthil.

"Now listen to me carefully," Hirt said seriously. "I don't want you to tell this to anyone if you don't have to. Fream and Havoc are with me and they are okay, but the police are on the way to arrest Totthil right now for murder so whatever you do, don't let her out of your sight!"

"Really! Do you mean Totthil is the killer? Fuck me!" Perrot was understandably bewildered.

"Yeah, but like I said for fuck sakes don't tell anyone unless you have to," Hirt yelled to get the point across. "She is fucking dangerous!"

"It's alright Pete, we'll get her when she comes back in!" assured Perrot.

"She's not coming back," said Havoc to nobody in particular.

Chapter 44 Aftermath

Havoc was right. While he and Fream were both being loaded into ambulances, Tiffany Totthil, the five-foot nothing psycho soon to be known as the Barbie Doll Killer, stayed out in the water and surfed perfect Bells Beach on her own. Not only that, but she surfed better than she ever had in her life, drawing huge praise from event announcers and rapturous applause from the massive crowd on the hill.

All the commentators on the live media broadcast agreed it was her greatest moment while discussing theories as to why Fream had not showed up. With Havoc also missing his heat, there was plenty of cryptic suggestions that maybe they had overdone things in their private lives and had failed to leave the bedroom.

As dozens of police arrived at the event site and several helicopters appeared in the sky, the rumour mill went into overdrive. But it wasn't until a bunch of armed elite Victorian Special Operations Group (SOG) officers in wetsuits boarded some of the contest jet skis, that the full impact of the seriousness of what was going on began to register with everybody.

Most were still unaware of the reason for all the fuss when Totthil was marched through the crowd surrounded by a dozen burly SOG officers. In fact, they were downright angry that one of their favourites was being removed from the contest arena in such a spectacular way.

Rather than hide amidst her captors, Totthil stood proud with tits and vagina barely covered underneath her Sea Thru wetsuit and began waving to the crowd, further fuelling their anger. They began pushing back at the police as they tried to force their way through to her while chanting 'Free Tiffany!' and 'Let Tiffany Go!'.

For a moment it looked like there would be a full-scale riot but fortunately it was still early in the day and not enough beer had been drunk for anyone to do anything stupid in front of some of the most hardcore coppers in Australia. Totthil was eventually safely bundled into the back of a paddy wagon and taken out of there with a police escort that the Prime Minister of Australia would have been happy with.

Havoc awoke in hospital the next day feeling like someone had bashed him within an inch of his life, which of course they had.

"You are lucky," the doctor said brightly as he gave Havoc a large dose of pain medication to swallow. "If you weren't so strong and fit, you might well be dead. As it is, aside from a few minor broken bones and a lot of bruises, you're in remarkably good shape."

Havoc tried to smile but that small movement of his facial muscles triggered a groan instead. Totthil had connected with his head often enough that his swollen lips looked even bigger than hers without the help of a collagen injection. The rest of him felt worse. He hurt in places he didn't even know existed.

"There's a visitor to see you if you feel up to it?"

Havoc brightened. He had hoped that Fream would come to see him. He'd asked about her and been told that apart from a few nasty side effects from the Fentanyl, she was fine. But it was DS Patinsen who came through the door.

"Dirth my boy, congratulations on solving your first big case!" his mentor beamed happily while Havoc tried to hide his disappointment that it wasn't Fream.

"Thanks sir. Although I don't feel much like celebrating."

"Yes, the doctor informed me you took quite a beating, but you saved at least two lives and who knows how many more Totthil would have killed if you hadn't caught her. You've done a fantastic job. How did you work out it was her?"

"I guess it was a cross between some research and a gut feeling," Havoc grimaced at the pain the effort of speaking was causing him, but he continued. "Bunker said something to me about Willo being the most popular surfer on Instafamous at the time of his murder and when I researched the other deaths, I discovered that they had all been in the same position. The only person I'd met who had been completely obsessed with her Instafamous following was Totthil. It didn't seem much to go on, but I had nothing else. Turns out I was right."

"Well, I'm proud of you Dirth. I might not have agreed with your methods to get there, but sometimes with undercover work that's what needs to be done. I know it must be hard feeling the way you do now, lying in hospital all beaten up while others take credit for your good work, but remember some of your friends are alive because of you. If what you are telling me is true, then not only did you save Fream, but Bunker and Andre might have been next.

"And if that doesn't cheer you up, this should. Senior Sergeant Smith has agreed to end your suspension and return you to full duties. I'll be recommending you be promoted as soon as possible. When you heal up of course."

Havoc didn't know how to answer that. He still liked the idea of finding a new career. Maybe finally using that Toyota Landcruiser for the reason he bought it in the first place. Just pack his boards, get on the road and live the dream. Was now the time to quit? He decided it was and began thinking about how he could break the news to his mentor. As he tried to form the words he needed, he felt the effects of the strong pain medication kicking in and he passed out.

Elsewhere in the same hospital Picker sat in his intensive care unit bed feeling like dog shit. The doctors had advised him that he had rear ended the car so hard while picking his nose that his finger had been driven up into his skull. His brain had been bruised and there was no telling what long term damage might have occurred.

They were already asking him questions about his moods, or people he missed and might want to see. They were worried that Picker might have damaged the area of the brain that is related to emotions like happiness, sympathy, empathy and general human interaction. He told them everything was fine but deep down he knew it wasn't. Something was missing and try as he might, he felt nothing anymore. Except pain and anger. Those feelings were still there, running deep and intense every second he was awake.

Picker picked up a mirror. The thing that stared back at him was barely recognisable as a human being. His nose had been split in half by the impact and was heavily bandaged, both his eyes were black like a raccoon and his already lumpy skull from the hair surgery prior to the accident was twice as bad. He looked like something out of a horror movie.

There was only one person responsible for this fucked up situation and he was going to sorely regret ever messing with Picker. That anger became white hot as the agony increased while he waited for the latest dose of pain medication to take effect. To help ease the suffering he began planning how he was going to make Havoc, and everyone who was close to him, pay in ways that not even their worst nightmares could imagine.

Tiffany Totthil relaxedly performed some yoga stretches in her jail cell having successfully achieved her lifetime goals. Her second place finish at Bells Beach was enough to make her the number one female surfer in the world and the publicity she received from her arrest had sent her Instafamous following rocketing past Gabriel Andre and Dyanna Fream into the stratosphere. Her newly created Lonely Fans page had been live for just a few days and she already had over a million subscribers at $50 each per month.

She would be an extremely wealthy woman when she got out of jail and that wasn't as unlikely as it sounded. Because Tiffany Totthil knew important stuff about important people and that information was going to be worth a lot more than her Lonely Fans account very soon.

Bunker was in a dark place, yet officially he was on top of the world. Not only had he won the iconic Bells trophy meaning he was the current world number one, but his childhood friend's killer had been caught and according to private investigator Les Galese, that was thanks to Havoc.

Unfortunately, rather than make him feel better, he felt much worse. He'd fucked Totthil in the very same spa the night before she had murdered Matt Wilson. From the moment she'd joined the GSA world tour, Bunker and Wilson had made a bet with each other as to who would be the first to get in her pants. They'd both had several attempts, but for some reason Totthil had been playing hard to get before that night. So, when Bunker had 'won' the bet he had taken great delight in announcing himself as the premier stud of the two.

Now he could only think that she'd relented purely to gain information to help murder Wilson the following night. It was a bitter pill to swallow and as soon as he realised he had contributed to his best mate's death, he had made the call to his drug dealer.

The doorbell rang and Bunker knew who it would be. For the size of the bender he felt coming, he needed to go straight to the source.

The door opened and Trent "Murder" Mercer stepped inside.

A few days later Peter Hirt sat back on the couch in his luxury Burleigh Heads pad sipping a Grove Whiskey on the rocks and shaking his head at how he had managed to land on his feet once again. The controversy surrounding Tiffany Totthil's arrest on finals day was the number one news item worldwide and the jaw dropping sales of the "Free Tiffany" and "Tiffany is Innocent" merchandise was sending the GSA's bank accounts to unprecedented levels.

He'd almost pushed his luck too far this time but hell, that's what made life worth living! The rush he had got banging Totthil while secretly knowing she was the serial killer and would probably one day seek revenge had exceeded everything else in his life by a very long way.

He was amazed no one had guessed his involvement. Not only did nothing go on within the GSA that he didn't know about, but Totthil had purchased Fentanyl from Murder Mercer's own dealers!

All it had cost him was a brief, but extremely painful invasion of his previously virginal rear end. It was a small price to pay for the millions it had made for him and a select group of very powerful people. Meanwhile the shady deals he had been working on with Murder Mercer were almost ready to bear fruit. Pretty soon he would be so rich and untouchable that he could pull some serious porn star shit with anyone he wanted, every night for the rest of his life.

Now the only question was what to do with those bitches Claire Cooper and Dyanna Fream?

Once again Claire Cooper found herself sitting by her phone, impatiently waiting for an overdue call from her benefactor. She didn't like to think too deeply about how that made her feel

"Hello my sexy pet," purred the female voice down the line and Cooper immediately felt herself get flustered. "Well done on winning your first big GSA contest."

"Thanks, I couldn't have done it without you," replied Cooper eager to please. That voice was like sexual chocolate, it took away her control.

"Now that Totthil and Birch are out of the way, you and Fream are leading the race for the world title and who knows what sort of damage that little cluster fuck might do to her mental state. If she's okay, well there's plenty we can do to make sure she's no longer a threat."

"If you say so," Cooper always felt helpless when talking to this powerful woman. "But she's my friend, so I'm glad she's okay."

"Yet you were happy to let Tiffany kill her if she could. What a curious woman you are," her benefactor chuckled huskily. "The Barbie Doll Killer! What an appropriate name for that vicious little minx. I told you to leave her doing her thing and look what almost happened. If only Havoc hadn't come to the rescue we would have been rid of our other major problems too. I wonder if Hirt knew she was the killer and went there anyway, or was just too stupid to see what was right in front of him? I think he probably knew. Twisted son of a bitch that he is, he probably got off on the whole thing."

"So, what do we do now?" Cooper was keen to change the subject. She didn't like that she had submitted and agreed to let Totthil try and kill Fream.

"We stay smart and be patient. If all goes well by the end of the year, I will be running the GSA and you will be world champion."

"I'd like that, thank you."

"You're welcome my pet. Now let's talk about what I expect you to wear when I next see you."

Dyanna Fream was still not completely over the effects of the overdose of Fentanyl that Totthil had given her. She'd been released by the hospital a few days earlier and without even talking to Havoc, she'd immediately jumped on a plane to Portugal for the next competition to try and avoid the media circus around Totthil's attempt to murder both her and Peter Hirt.

She wasn't sure why she had run from Havoc so quickly. Despite being out of it on drugs, she vividly remembered him affectionately holding her head in his lap while they waited for an ambulance. At that moment she'd probably never felt so safe and loved. There was no doubt she owed him her life now, but that made her feel strangely uncomfortable.

Her phone rang. She didn't recognise the number but from the first few digits she realised it came from her hometown. Without thinking it through, she answered.

"Hello whore!" came the male voice down the line. She immediately recognised who it was and her heart dropped. "You've been prostituting yourself around again I see."

Fream knew she should just hang up and not engage but she couldn't help herself.

"What do you want you fucken arsehole?" she yelled angrily into the phone. "You've got a girlfriend so why don't you fucken leave me alone?"

"Well, that would be no fun, would it?" laughed Detective Steve Haren of the Wollongong Police Department. "In fact, I think you've been getting off a little too easily lately. So much so that I've been thinking of taking some overdue holidays. I've heard Portugal is good this time of year, or maybe I'll go to Brazil or South Africa. I don't know, so many decisions to make and you know how I love my surf competitions!"

With that the phone went dead and Fream burst into tears.

EPILOUGE

Havoc had only known the prison guard for a few minutes but already he didn't like him. It had quickly become clear that he was an unintelligent oaf who got drunk on the power that his job allowed him. This was his realm and in here he might as well be God.

"You're a lucky man," the guard said with a wink of one of his little piggy eyes and a sneer revealing yellow teeth as he unlocked the door to the interview room in the maximum security section of the Victorian Metro Correction Centre. "I'd like me to have some of that snatch. Maybe I will later."

Havoc resisted the urge to punch the neanderthal into next week and instead turned to look at the sole occupant of the room. Even though she was a third of the size of both of them, he knew what she was capable of. He decided he'd like to see the guard try.

With one last slimy yellowed smile the guard shut the door behind Havoc and left the two alone. Despite wearing unflattering high-vis prison inmate clothing, Tiffany Totthil still somehow managed to look smoking hot. The hair extensions were gone, but her remaining long blonde hair was tied back in a ponytail, accentuating high cheekbones and the finely sculptured nose job. Several buttons were left undone on her undersized top to keep those glorious fake breasts on prominent display. Havoc couldn't quite believe that she was getting away with the look in prison, but he supposed being a multi-millionaire serial killer must have its perks.

When he'd first been asked by DS Patinsen to talk to Totthil he had immediately refused. He didn't want anything to do with this deranged psychopath who had come so close to killing him. That was when Senior

Sergent Smith had stepped in. "That's an order, not a request Spidder," the bloated monster had said with evident glee. "Although I can totally understand you being scared. She did kick your arse after all."

"Havoc it's good to see you," Totthil purred sexily. "I'd get up and give you a big hug but, you know…" she gestured to the set of handcuffs linking her right hand to the heavy metal table separating them. "Sit down, let's have a chat."

Havoc remained standing. "Why am I here?" he responded angrily. "You tried to kill me!" He cursed himself for the arousal he felt at that moment. It shouldn't exist after what she had done to him, but instead he felt it stronger than ever. Why was that? Was it the bad girl thing? He'd heard plenty of stories of beautiful, perfectly sane women falling in love with serial killers. Or was it simply because she oozed pure sex appeal while being handcuffed to a table, unable to get away?

Totthil smiled knowingly at him, as if she was aware of exactly what was going through his mind. "Oh come on Havoc, that was just a little lovers tiff. No harm no foul. Now please, sit. We've got a lot to discuss and I'm sure your superiors wouldn't have sent you all the way down here to come home empty handed, would they?"

Havoc was caught off guard. How could she possibly know he was undercover? During his briefing with Smithy and DS Patinsen they had discussed theories as to why Totthil would only talk to him and no one else. She had refused point blank through her lawyer to say one word to the police, only that she had important information to tell them and wouldn't do so until after seeing Havoc first. One uncomfortable possibility was that somehow she knew who Havoc was, but no one really thought that would be the reason.

"What do you mean my superiors?" he said trying to keep his composure. "I'm not sure what my boss on the building site has to do with-"

"Oh come on Havoc let's not waste time with that bullshit! You're a rookie cop who went undercover on the GSA tour to try and find a killer blah blah blah," she said waving her hand towards the seat, gesturing for him to sit once more. When she saw his obvious discomfort she added, "Relax. I won't tell anyone and besides, I think we've reached a certain level of trust in our relationship. You lied to me about who you are and what you do, and I hit you a couple of times with a baseball bat. I think that makes us even, don't you?"

Havoc's shoulders slumped a little, he sighed and took the seat. "How did you guess?"

"I didn't," Totthil admitted. "But nearly a million dollars a day on Lonely Fans can buy you a lot of information if you know where to spend it."

She smiled and leaned forward, deliberately giving Havoc a clear view of that silicone enhanced cleavage. He was pretty sure that at least one nipple was now on full display, but he refused to look, not wanting to give her the satisfaction of knowing the effect she was having on him. "You know we really should do that collab," she whispered huskily. "You and me on Lonely Fans, wow! You could quit this rubbish you do right now and never have to work another day in your life. Just chase perfect waves wherever and whenever you want. Think about the girls you could have Havoc!"

Havoc didn't want to spend too much time pondering how good that sounded, the temptation was real. "There's only one problem with that," he replied. "You're in here and unlikely to get out for a long time."

"Oh pfft, you don't really think I'm going to be stuck in here the rest of my life, do you? With what I'm worth and what I know?" Totthil shook her head with disappointment. "Haven't you learnt anything from watching how people like Hirt operate?"

A chill went through Havoc then as it dawned on him that he wasn't just dealing with a deadly Black Widow Spider, but a highly intelligent one. This was a ruthless woman who had easily convinced everyone around her that she was nothing but a vacuous blonde bimbo all while making tens of millions of dollars, successfully killing at least four people in multiple countries, and going within a whisker of adding three more to that list.

Havoc was trying to think of something to say when Totthil's attitude changed from disappointment to delight in a heartbeat. "I see you have an Instafamous page now and already over a million followers! Although you really need to post more if we are going to work together," she said smiling broadly as she reached out to touch his arm with her unchained left hand. "But you better be careful, I hear that being a popular surfer online can be dangerous to your health."

Havoc realised that while Tiffany Totthil may be intellectual, like most serial killers, she also wasn't completely sane. He was playing a dangerous game here and he didn't know the rules. Angrily he removed his arm from her touch. "Okay so I'll ask you again. Why am I here?"

Totthil wasn't put off by his reaction, instead she leaned even further forward. Both nipples were visible now. It was all too much for a young red-blooded male and Havoc lost the battle, despite his anger his eyes lowered, and he stared involuntarily at what Totthil was flaunting.

It was at that moment she chose to say the four words that would forever change his life.

"I didn't kill Slide."

To be continued…

Acknowledgements

This book is the work of pure fiction and while I have obviously taken certain characteristics of real individuals to help give life to the many varied fun characters in this book, it's simply a tounge in cheek dig at the world of pro surfing and its unique individuals that I love so much. It was a hell of a lot of fun to write and I hope it took you the reader on an enjoyable journey.

Big thanks first and foremost of course to my mum and to Gill for being a legend through many fishing adventurers and fun life experiences in general.

To beautiful Sonya for her love, positivity and advice throughout the final stages of this book. Kalgan for picking me up in Bali when my world had gone to shit and being part of many epic surf sessions since.

John Borgiono for the rundown on police hierarchy and procedure. All my various editorial friends who helped contribute to the final copy you read here including Sarah, Karlina, Anthea, Morpheus and my good mate Devo who is the most inspirational human being I know.

Darren and Amelia from Peppermint Grove Beach Holiday Park for letting me set up the Tent Hilton and giving me a job to get me through the final stage of the book. Claire and Matt whose donations of camping equipment helped turn the Tent Hilton into a cool writing studio.

The beautiful family at Warung Dewa at Cucukan in Bali, the best place I've found to overcome writer's block. Bronia for the journey to the Kimberley's that allowed me to take the time off to finally write this book and provide inspiration for the next.

Russell Ord for the epic cover photo. The guys at Aint That Swell Podcast, Lipped Podcast and especially to Adz and Namu at Barrelled

Surf Podcast for keeping me sane in the many years of downtime I had in between surf sessions.

To some of the original great surf satirists who's work I loved growing up - Tony Edwards for Captain Goodvibes, Mark Sutherland for Gonad Man and almost everything DC Green wrote.

And finally thanks to all the weird and wonderful people I have met or followed over the years that provided inspiration for the epic characters in this book. Fact really is stranger than fiction.

About The Author

Leith 'Holtzy' Holtzman has been an extreme sports photographer, film maker and journalist for more than 30 years. His work has been published all around the world in respected magazines such as Tracks, Surfing World, Freerider MX, Waves, Australian Surfing Life, Carve, Riptide and many more.

Holtzy's film credits include three surf films, a bodyboard film and the first ever Australian FMX film 'Homegrown Maniacs' which was a huge success and spawned three more HGM films plus the stand alone FMX road trip documentary 'The Warpt Big Gap Challenge'.

Holtzy also wrote, produced, directed, filmed, edited and occasionally starred in his own successful TV series 'Homegrown Maniacs TV' which aired for a number of years on Foxtel.

He currently lives off grid in a tent in the wilds of Western Australia while he writes his next literary masterpiece.

www.ingramcontent.com/pod-product-compliance
Lightning Source LLC
Chambersburg PA
CBHW030542190726
48283CB00006B/1981